Praise for

Conversations
with the Fat Girl

"Filled with deliciousness, but its calories are far from empty. Liza Palmer has created, to borrow her own heroine Maggie's phrase, a pink pastry box o'magic."

—Gayle Brandeis, author of *Fruitflesh: Seeds of Inspiration for Women Who Write* and *The Book of Dead Birds: A Novel*

"In this touching story from Liza Palmer, Maggie learns to let go, move on, and—finally—trust herself. This is a from-the-heart debut you won't soon forget!"

—Megan Crane, author of *English as a Second Language* and *Everyone Else's Girl*

"This is the story about two best friends, boundary issues, and the unraveling of a shared history. Liza Palmer puts her finger delicately, yet forcefully, on the crucial moment in every failing freindship, the one where we must choose either to untangle and extricate ourselves or become erased by our own compliance.

—Amanda Stern, author of *The Long Haul*

"*Conversations with the Fat Girl* is a wry, dry, and ultimately winning novel featuring a saucy heroine to whom all girls (fat and thin) will relate: Maggie starts out looking for excuses, but ends up finding herself."

—Wendy Shanker, *The Fat Girls' Guide to Life*

Conversations
with the Fat Girl

Liza Palmer

NEW YORK   BOSTON

5 Spot

Warner Books
Time Warner Book Group
1271 Avenue of the Americas, New York, NY 10020
Visit our Web site at www.twbookmark.com.

5 Spot and the 5 Spot logo are trademarks of Time Warner Book Group Inc.

Printed in the United States of America

First Edition: September 2005
10 9 8 7 6 5 4 3 2 1

Library of Congress Cataloging-in-Publication Data

Palmer, Liza.
  Conversations with the fat girl / Liza Palmer—1st ed.
    p. cm.
  Summary: "An overweight waitress ponders her relationship with her best friend, who had once been overweight herself, as her friend prepares for a wedding"—Provided by publisher.
    ISBN 0-446-69395-2
  1. Overweight women—Fiction. 2. Female friendship—Fiction. 3. Waitresses—Fiction. 4. Weddings—Fiction. I. Title.
    PS3616.A343C66 2005
    813'.6—dc22   2005010562

Text design by Meryl Sussman Levavi
Cover design by Brigid Pearson
Cover photo: Comstock Images

For my mom

*The risk it takes to remain tight inside the bud
is more painful than the risk it takes to blossom.*

—ANAÏS NIN

CHAPTER ONE

Depends on the Size of the House

Why is a bulldozer in front of my house? There is a handwritten note pierced on the nail where my summer wreath once hung. The summer wreath now lies on the ground next to my front door. I coax my dog, Solo, back inside and pull the door closed.

> *Dear Tenant:*
> *I hope this note finds you well. I have decided to turn the back house into a lap pool. Please vacate by the end of the week.*

It is already Thursday. I keep reading.

> *It has been a pleasure being your landlord for the past three years and I wish you the very best of luck. Please let me know if you need a reference, as I would be honored to let everyone know what a great tenant you were. Thank you.*
> *Sincerely,*
> *Faye Mabb, landlord* ☺

I hold the lime-green scalloped note in my hand and look to the front house. My landlady is notorious for stunts like this. I thought painting my house at 4 a.m. was bad, but nothing remotely compares with this. The bulldozer's a nice touch.

I always thought I got lucky finding Faye Mabb's back house: decent rent and a safe location. Over the last three years, I've learned to keep my head down and stay out of her way.

I squeeze past the dusty bulldozer and walk the fifty or so feet to Faye's front door. Note in hand, I ring her doorbell. Faye opens the door quickly. I know she has been watching the events of the morning unfold through a crack in her yellowing curtains.

"I'm tearing down that back house," Faye burbles through the metal screen door.

"*My* house? How can you tear down my house?" The note is now wet with my perspiration. The tips of my fingers are starting to turn a grainy lime-green color.

"In forty-eight hours," Faye says. Even through the metal screen door I can see she is decked out in full regalia. Her white-rimmed sunglasses are perched atop her ratted bottle-blond hair. She is wearing her usual floral, skirted bathing suit, folds of tanned, leathery flesh cascading out top and bottom.

"You can't kick me out in forty-eight hours. I've got nowhere to go." I have my hand on the cold, metal screen door.

"Maybe you and your little dog can live in that Fancy New Car of yours." Faye gestures out toward the street with her mass of teased hair.

"At least give me a week. I can find a place in a week." Faye is swirling the ice in her ever-present highball, poking at the cubes with her bejeweled fingers.

"Fine. A week." Faye cocks her head back and takes a long look at me.

"Thank you." I oblige. The ice cubes flutter around the glass excitedly as her hands shake with glee . . . glee or the first stages of liver failure. Fingers crossed for liver failure.

"But the bulldozer stays." And *then* she slams the door.

I back away slowly and continue to the street, where my Fancy New Car awaits.

For now, the best way to deal with this is not to deal with it at all. I get in my Fancy New Car, leave my soon-to-be-demolished life, and head toward my mom's house, which rests in the hills overlooking the Rose Bowl.

◆

Pasadena, a suburb just outside Los Angeles, bursts with scenes straight from the California postcards off the spinning rack. Children playing outside, blond beauties in convertibles, and incredibly fit people running for fun, a pastime I never quite bought into. Rumor has it that each year thousands of people move to Pasadena after watching the Rose Parade. But I grew up here and could never imagine living anywhere else.

Even though Pasadena is several freeways away from LA proper, the religion of perfection is still widely practiced here. Walking into local malls or filling my car with gas, I have often felt like I've stumbled into a casting call for the newest sitcom: "Pretty Girl 4" or "Hunk 2." If you've ever been told you're beautiful or "should go into acting," you end up here. This means the top 1 percent of the beautiful people in the nation are just walking around the city, willy-nilly. Then there are people like me, who anywhere else would be categorized as "normal." But in LA, if you're over a size 0 you're just shy of a circus sideshow.

It's the beginning of summer and I have the air-conditioning on in my Fancy New Car, a Volkswagen Beetle. A car that is neither Fancy, nor New. It's just newer, and apparently fancier, than my last car. Somehow it has made Faye Mabb nervous that there may be some type of revolution a-brewin'.

Even in the confines of my air-conditioned car, I feel hot already. My long brown hair is up in its usual ponytail. I check myself out in the rearview mirror at a stoplight. I try to focus on the good. The brown eyes seem inviting, but are they almond-shaped because I am "exotic" or is it just my cheeks pushing them up so fiercely? My lips are full, which is a plus considering they are the gatekeepers to the gapped front teeth lurking behind them.

The V-neck T-shirt and Adidas workout pants are already sticking to my body. I swore I wouldn't be here again. Hot and uncomfortable. I have made New Year's resolution after New Year's resolution swearing to lose weight once and for all by summer. Summer, with its tank tops and bathing suits dangling in front of me as the constant brass ring just out of reach. I want to be able to dress appropriately for the climate and not feel the need to hide under layers of clothes that are far too hot and way too confining. It is approximately two hundred degrees outside but I actually considered putting on my long black sweater over the shirt due to paranoia regarding back fat. What if I couldn't control it by tugging and/or strategic lunch-table placement?

There is an implicit understanding that Mom is driven everywhere. She has her light brown hair done every four weeks, nails manicured every week, and is presented with new, shiny baubles on every calendarable holiday by her beloved new husband. My mom has looked exactly the same for as long as I can remember. She stands a mere five foot two, and as I grew taller it became apparent that I got no genes from her side of the family. Like my sister, who's possibly even shorter, Mom is physically tiny. Once again, it became apparent that I got no genes from her side of the family. Insulated in winter clothing, which in LA means a flirty sweater, my mom probably doesn't tip the scales at a hundred pounds. But her presence cannot be missed. One raised eyebrow, one purse of the lips, and whole civilizations topple. I question my dependence on her. She has always been the family sounding board, and my sister and I have tried to be hers. I don't trust this quake-ridden California earth, but I would walk sure-footed on my mother's word.

She sits in the passenger seat fiddling with the seat belt as we drive to lunch at EuroPane. We discuss the cost of fighting Faye Mabb and her "eviction." My mom is a divorce lawyer in town and begins the conversation by educating me on just how illegal Faye's little eviction is. The question then becomes whether or not I want to stay.

"She was laughing and joking about me and the dog living in the back of my car," I tell my mother as we order at the counter.

Wooden tables and chairs dot the bakery's cement floor. It's the wafting smells of fresh bread and pastries rather than flourishes of decor that make this bakery a great destination.

"Joking about you having to live in the back of the car? She said that? Asshole." Mom takes a bite of her strawberry yogurt parfait as I make an apologetic face at the server. When my two nieces were learning to speak, the family feared their first word would be *asshole*, based on its ample usage by their dear, doting Grammy.

"I've been meaning to get out of there anyway. This is just a way of nudging me out earlier. I'm okay with it. I really am." My voice cracks as I pull two diet sodas out of the self-serve refrigerator and rig my chair so my back will face the wall.

"Everything is going to be okay—better than okay." Mom stirs in her granola.

"I know . . . I know."

I think about languid Sundays with coffee brewing and Solo at the foot of my bed. The Household Chore Chart I made. I begin to cry. When Mom looks at me, I valiantly brush the tears away. I feel eight years old again.

"Change is hard," Mom says.

"But it's the only home Solo has ever really known. I mean she . . . she . . ."

"Solo is a dog. She'll be fine. However hard this is, it will be so much better than what you've got now."

"I can't conceive of moving right now. Olivia's wedding is coming up in less than two months. She's my best friend, for chrissakes, and I can't even get it together in time for her wedding? I am totally uprooting and . . . and when am I going to be able to start my new exercise and diet regimen? I've got a fucking bridesmaid's dress to get into, for the love of God. I had my life a certain way, and now it's totally . . . totally . . . this sucks." Can a twenty-seven-year-old woman stomp her foot in public?

Frustrated and ready to move on, Mom changes the subject and we begin discussing possible outfits for Olivia's wedding. This brings up a sore subject. I am going to be nowhere near where I want to be for that wedding. Another date that comes and goes as I fail miserably. I can see the red circle around the wedding date now. Mom assures me we'll find a dress. I stopped looking in mirrors a long time ago because I never liked what I saw. I want to look nice and be comfortable. I can't do that if I'm still where I am now. I start having flashbacks of my freshman year in high school when Mom said those same words: "We'll find a dress." Sometimes a sow's ear is just a sow's ear.

His name was John Sheridan. (Yes, The John Sheridan. Every high school has one, different name perhaps, but they all have one.) His blue eyes were only accentuated by dark hair, a body with broad shoulders that tapered into a perfect V at the waist. He was at the top of the junior class, played water polo, and actively dated the mythical Caroline Pond. (Yes, The Caroline Pond. Every high school has one.) John began tutoring me in French class. Tutoring, speaking, dating, kissing, you've got to start somewhere. All I knew how to say was *"Je ne comprends pas,"* which means "I don't understand." I argued this was the only sentence I needed to survive. I liked the class for two reasons: The John Sheridan and the crêpes our teacher, Madame Hart, made every Thursday.

During one of our tutorials, John mentioned that Caroline Pond couldn't go to the homecoming dance. Her parents were receiving some volunteer award the same night as homecoming. Caroline had to go to the Volunteer Gala Ball Fund-Raiser, and John was left out in the cold.

John Sheridan must have seen me as a project of sorts. I was so asexual, no one would think his relationship with Caroline Pond was on the rocks if he took me to the dance. On top of this, he was known for his charity work. Going to the dance with me would be just another day at the soup kitchen. Pushing this ugly truth aside, I paraded around like I had landed the date of a lifetime. I was going to homecoming with The John Sheridan, the only man alive to look good in a Speedo. Now, what was I going to wear?

At first, Mom, my older sister, Kate, and I naively looked in the Young Women's department. I was not looking forward to a day of taking off my clothes, trying on dresses, and enduring my mom and random salesladies asking "how everything is." To keep the shopping experience from becoming a complete fiasco, I pointed out some problem with each dress. I looked fat. And each dress only accentuated that. But I couldn't say that to my Mom. It would break her heart. She couldn't fix that I saw myself as fat. I felt horrible every time she tossed another possibility over the slatted door of the dressing room. I'd always feared that hell was really some type of Orwellian reality in which I would be damned forever to the harsh lights, 360-degree mirrors, and those damn slatted doors of department store changing rooms. So I only told her about things she could fix. That way at least my mom stayed unbroken. "My boobs don't fit" was always a popular reason. Who could argue with that? "It's tight in the arms" was also safe. For some reason, "tight in the arms" was not as hard hitting as, "I'm a fat fuck, Mom. Just wrap me up in a tarp, put some lipstick on me, and roll me in the direction of The John Sheridan."

We finally found what we were looking for in the Mother of the Bride department: a tight pink crêpe dress with a dropped waist and Peter Pan collar. Pleats fell down the front of the dress. Mom said they drew the eye away from my Area, a term I used when referring to my ever-burgeoning belly. Of course pleats drew the eye away; that would tend to be the case when one's eyes had so many other places on which to feast. It was not my first choice, but first-choice outfits didn't come in my size. We bought the dress.

John drove us to a local Italian restaurant that Caroline had recommended. Apparently, Caroline Pond "recommended" a lot. Throughout our dinner, almost every one of John's sentences started with "Caroline says," as he parroted some Pond Bit o'Wisdom. When he wasn't repeating something verbatim that Caroline said, he stared at the breadbasket in the center of the table, tapping his fingers on the large diving watch that dwarfed his left arm. I sat before him like a child before a magician—waiting for him to perform as I had always dreamed. But I was disappointed. It was like catching that same magician smoking a cigarette and bouncing a buxom trapeze artist on his knee out behind the big top.

By the time the waitress asked if we'd like to see the dessert menu, I was actively mourning The John Sheridan I had come to love: The John Sheridan who had the personality I put together out of various S. E. Hinton characters with sprinkles from the Knights of the Round Table. The John Sheridan who sat before me now at this tiny Italian restaurant somewhere in the San Gabriel Valley was nothing like my creation. He didn't smoke cigarettes he rolled himself, and I doubt he even knew the first thing about swordplay to defend my honor.

The night ended with us driving by Caroline Pond's house to see if she was home from her Volunteer Gala Ball Fund-Raiser. She was. I waited in the car for thirty minutes while Caroline told John about her evening, so John could recount every detail back to me on the long ride home. John yelled to Caroline that he would be back in "twenty" and hopped in the car. As we pulled into the driveway of my house, I remember thinking how awkward these last moments were going to be. What was the end of a date like? Is this where he would finally unveil the real John Sheridan? I tried to remember every detail so I could retell the story of my first kiss to Olivia. Olivia who had set her sights on Ben Dunn, the senior starting quarterback who made The John Sheridan look like The Hunchback of Notre Dame and was famous for referring to girls he had been with as "They've Been Done by Ben Dunn." Classy.

I sat still in the passenger seat trying to put what I thought was my best *kiss-me* face on. I remember pouting my lips a little and slightly glazing over my eyes. In retrospect, it must have looked like I was having a small stroke.

John quickly announced that he had fun but it was getting late, so . . . Had he learned nothing from his days at the Round Table? John leaned over and wrapped one single arm around my shoulder as his car idled loudly. He then proceeded to pat at my back like an impatient mom burping her full-to-bursting new baby. I kept both arms at my side and just sat there, floating above what was happening. Did he not want to give me the wrong idea? I floated back down just in time for one last pat. I pressed a smile out and stepped from the car. Did he think he just gave me some big, beautiful moment I would cherish and retell at family dinners? Could he have possibly thought it was anything but awkward and embarrassing for both of us? No, John Sheridan believed he had given me the thrill of a lifetime. I just felt robbed.

"Why don't you give yourself a fucking break?" Mom snaps me out of my walk down Memory Lane.

At this point, a small blond family turns around.

"Could you hold it down?" I beg.

"You never give yourself a break. You're going to drive yourself crazy if you live like this for the next couple of months. The wedding is not about you. It's about Olivia and Adam. I know this is completely foreign to you, but a lot of people think you're pretty amazing looking." Mom sips her diet soda and glares at the small blond family, a Pasadena fixture.

"What about my house?" I whimper.

"What about it? You've outgrown it, Maggie. Faye Mabb did you a favor. The only favor she'll ever do anyone, I'm sure."

On the way home from dropping Mom off, I allow myself to imagine my new home: an airy summer cottage with hardwood floors and tons of windows. I begin switching radio stations, desperate to find the correct soundtrack for my vision. The chiffon draperies dance in the wind as classical music lilts through thick Craftsman-style walls. (Do all of the radio stations play advertisements at the same time?) In the fantasy, I walk out on the porch with my mug of steaming coffee, put my hand on the aged gray banister, and look out at the lush flora and fauna as the sun slowly rises in the dewy morning hours. A song finally comes on that I enjoy. I tap along on the steering wheel, quietly humming to myself.

Who needs that shithole of a house I'm living in now, anyway? Truth is, it really isn't all that great. The water pressure feels like a slow piss. I have to share my residence with thousands of spiders. I have visions of myself sleeping at night with them, not Solo, at the foot of my bed. Solo was miserable in that backyard being tortured by the legions of cats and their devil offspring.

Faye's back house was the first place I ever lived by myself. I paid the rent, the water, and the phone bill by myself. I have to believe I've got more of that in me. Somehow losing this house has become the queen of all my other unaccomplished goals and red-circled failures. Surely I can find a new place to live.

I pull into an office supply store. Once inside, I ask the man behind the counter if he thinks I can pack a whole house with just thirty-six boxes.

"Depends on the size of the house," he says. His vest is hanging on his body as if management throws them on their employees in some warped party game gone horribly awry.

"I'm not packing the actual house, you know," I say, noticing his name is Dennis, who according to the enlarged mug shot on the wall behind him is the newly crowned Employee of the Month.

"Yeah, I . . . I'm saying that if you got a big house, you pro'ly have a lotta stuff. Little house . . ." He trails off, as any Employee of the Month would.

"Little stuff. I get it."

I buy all thirty-six boxes, thank the Employee of the Month, and cart the boxes out to my car. I stop at the local health food store and pick up the only unhealthful things inside: ginger cookies, chocolate stars, and the closest thing to a soda I can find. I grab a couple of apples on the way to the counter and some cans of tuna. That way the guy at the checkout might not notice the bad stuff. Then I throw in a different type of soda—a mandarin orange soda. Now he'll think I'm shopping for a roommate: a roommate who enjoys mandarin orange soda, ginger cookies, and chocolate stars. I'll tell him I'd like these items bagged separately.

I pull down my street feeling newly empowered. For three long years, I begged Faye Mabb to treat me civilly. For three long years, I had to park my car on the street, even though Faye Mabb's long, sacred driveway sat unused after she stopped driving altogether.

Today I will pull into The Sacred Driveway right behind the bulldozer. Faye stands in all of her bathing-suited finery at the edge of the driveway, trowel in one hand, the other held akimbo at her withering, pachyderm hips.

"Can I help you?" I ask, opening the trunk of my Fancy New Car.

"You're supposed to park out front," Faye says, her tongue pushing at the corners of her tight-lipped mouth in search of loose bits of saliva.

I straighten my back and breathe deeply.

"Yeah, well, about that. Since I'm going to be moving out, I figure I should have full access to The Driveway. I can't start moving my stuff out if I'm parked all the way out on the street, now can I?" I realize my arms are frozen in a game-show hostess manner and The Driveway is now behind Door Number Two.

"You just pulled in," Faye manages to say as she digs out the loose saliva from the corners of her mouth and proceeds to investigate.

"I bought these boxes and I have to take them all the way

into the house," I say, pointing to my destination one foot away from where I am standing. Suddenly *all the way* seems exaggerated.

"So take them in and then move the car." Faye flicks the saliva from her fingers, then bends down to weed her bed of tulips, giving me enough visual material to populate every nightmare I will ever have.

I think about it for one second. What is she going to do? I've already been evicted and I know I can take her if it comes down to that.

"I'm going to keep my car parked here," I say.

The wind blows my hair over my shoulder, and I imagine the slow-motion shot of a girl victorious walking into her house. One foot falls in front of the other, hips locking into place. Faye Mabb standing there, throwing her fist to the sky, arms flapping like the bat she is, and saying, "That girl. Who can control that girl?" My Fancy New Car will stay there as a reminder to Faye of the dawning of a new age.

It's all fun and games until a few hours later when Faye's son, Stan, stops by and blocks my Fancy New Car in The Sacred Driveway. I now have to knock on Faye's door and beg Stan to move his car, promising never to raise my voice to his harpy of a mother ever again.

I decide to put a call into Olivia on my cell phone as I get in my car to leave for work. The battery is low, so this will be a short call. I am already ten minutes late, and I'll hear about my tardiness throughout my entire five-hour shift at the coffeehouse. My manager, Cole, will see to that.

CHAPTER TWO

Thar She Blows

Olivia Morten and I met when we were twelve years old. We found each other in physical education class. Olivia and I would stand against the chain-link fence and watch as the team captains chose every other student, until it got down to the two "fat girls." At that age, this just meant I was developing earlier than all the other girls. Olivia, on the other hand, was officially overweight—even at the age of twelve. As the agonizing minutes passed, we were eventually chosen and promptly benched.

At first I hated Olivia. People began to lump us together as one single Fat Entity—moving about the playground in an amoeba-like fashion, glomming onto groups of people at will. Before Olivia came along, the cliques of girls at my school tolerated me. I convinced myself I was on the outside because I was a little chunkier than most. I never once took into consideration that they just might not like me. With Olivia, I was now part of a new club I didn't want to belong to. I imagined there was this constant deliberation about the "fat girls." Olivia couldn't run, but she could catch and throw. I could never catch and throw, but I could run. Who was the better athlete? Who was more agreeable? Who was more desperate? I never questioned whether these scenarios were based on actual facts. Once you're labeled in school, no amount of factual information can unstick it from your psyche.

When it was just me, I was never under such a microscope. Before Olivia, I would position myself just outside a group of popular girls, craning to hear the latest gossip and noteworthy fashion tips. I laughed when they laughed and sputtered nonsense when they spoke to me. But it worked. It worked for me and my twelve-year-old fantasy of what friendship was supposed to be. As the months passed, I found myself forever on the outside of the group at the end of that picnic table, craning my neck and never getting any closer. I wanted to be popular. I wanted the life they led. The valentines. The designer clothes. The pack of friends.

Olivia was cocky for a twelve-year-old. Hers was always the first hand to go up after any question. I heard she beat up Reed Anderson in fifth grade for calling her out in kickball. I found myself drawn to that. Day after day, after spending my obligatory time at the end of the popular table, I would walk up to Olivia with her tinfoil-wrapped soda. She was consistently flippant and never once asked me to sit down. One day, I motioned for her to scoot over, and she begrudgingly obliged. I tried complimenting her lunch. I tried gossiping about the other girls. Nothing. Then one day I cracked a joke about squirrels and our math teacher and for the first time I made Olivia Morten laugh. I held this position in her life for the next fifteen years.

By the time we reached our high school years, we had developed a rich fantasy life. One of our favorites took place in an upscale, imaginary bar in Old Town Pasadena. Olivia and I, both pounds lighter and under the tutelage of a well-respected stylist, toast with our flutes of bubbling champagne and scan the room. Mary Benicci, Gretchen Bliss, and Shannon Shimasaki enter the imaginary establishment. Our hatred of Mary Benicci, Gretchen Bliss, and Shannon Shimasaki bridged both the imaginary and real worlds. They were on the high school swim team, had dates to every dance, shopped at the mall, and had pictures mounted on their dressers of all the events they attended with their endless ranks of smiling, tanned-faced friends.

The fantasy would inevitably turn to revenge. The threesome of she-devils enter the bar to our raised flutes of champagne. We turn around slowly. The record screeches to a halt (it appears there is now a circa-1970 record player in this establishment). The years have not been kind to the threesome. Mary is "intimately corresponding" with prison inmates. Gretchen refuses to admit that her high school sweetheart has been seen canoodling with an as-yet-unnamed man and Shannon has gained approximately three hundred pounds, causing her friends to worry she's "eating herself to death." Our equally fit lovers— The John Sheridan, now a veterinarian, and Ben Dunn, a movie star—join us. John and Ben chime in as we point at Shannon Shimasaki's stomach, squealing, "Looks like you've found what we lost," at the top of our lungs, gales of our laughter filling the restaurant. We then ooh and ahh at Mary Benicci's proclivity for prison inmates and shudder at the thought of turning a straight man gay. This all takes place as "our men" both break down in tears as they propose marriage in tandem on bended knee.

Back in our sweaty, pimple-ridden real world, Olivia and I ordered up our usuals at a local fast-food eatery and tried to forget a future both of us knew would never happen.

By the time Olivia and I went off to college, she could be officially classified as "morbidly obese." I was gaining ten to fifteen pounds a year pretty steadily, but I had to go some to catch up to Olivia. We spent four years at University of California at Berkeley hiding in the library and driving across the Golden Gate Bridge late at night—she told me it made her feel weightless.

One night during our senior year, Olivia drove me to the entrance of the Golden Gate Bridge. She parked the brand-new car her parents gave her for getting whatever it was she did to have her parents lavish gifts on her. We got out of the car and headed to the walkway of the big orange bridge. It was a freezing night in San Francisco, but the wind felt good and the city smelled wonderful. I looked down at the water and saw the lights of the city twinkling back at me. Olivia was leaning over the fence and down at the water below. A passing car of young males with nothing better to do honked and yelled out, "Thar she blows." Olivia straightened herself and turned to me. Her blond hair was now dyed a more sunflower color with beautiful highlights. Her skin had cleared up nicely, and she was dressed in the height of plus-size fashion. But at that angle, on that night, on that bridge, she was still just another fat girl. I was good at giving advice and picking Olivia up after these kinds of comments, but I could never follow these prescriptions myself. Had someone yelled that at me, I would have been deciding whether to just go right over the side of the bridge. While Olivia dressed to get attention, I made a promise to myself to blend in to the background as much as possible.

My life is about never putting myself into that situation. I *never* call attention to myself. That is the code I live by. I don't go into movie theaters late. I don't buy tank tops. I don't sing along with the car radio. I try never to walk in front of anyone. I constantly pull at my clothes. I walk with my eyes to the ground. I constantly apologize for myself. I don't like hugs. I don't look in mirrors. I don't smile in pictures because of a possible double-chin incident. It boils down to this: If I am invisible, no one can make fun of me.

Olivia didn't have the ability to become invisible. Her sheer size made her the epitome of visible. But it was visibility at a distance. You couldn't avoid looking at her and how big she had gotten. But you also couldn't touch her or get close to her because of how big she'd gotten.

That night, I remember smiling at her and coming toward her. I had my whole speech planned; I was even working on a joke about how at least they were well read enough to make an obscure whaling reference here in San Francisco. She tilted her head back so that I could see her take a slow swallow. I could see her breath in the cold night air as she finally exhaled. Olivia was never one to talk about the pain we shared or the shame we carried with us. I never said a word.

The next day, she made the calls to set up her gastric bypass surgery.

◆

"Hey Olivia, it's me," I trail off on her answering machine, thinking that maybe she'll pick up after hearing who it is.

She does. "Wait!" Olivia picks up huffing and puffing.

"What are you doing?" I squeal.

"I was bringing groceries in. What's going on?" I can hear the crinkles of a bag in the background.

I imagine my best friend now. It's been five years since the surgery. After the first round, going under the knife became second nature to Olivia. She went in for two more plastic surgeries to "correct" certain problems and side effects of the surgery. Her goal: the elusive size 2.

Her hair is perfect. A blond, messy shag that takes forty-five minutes to look like it's right out of the shower and windblown to perfection. She has dark brown eyes that until recently went unnoticed because they were hidden by bangs, excess flesh, or her habit of never looking anyone in the eye. She is probably wearing full eye makeup and just a swipe of pink lip gloss. I can see her pressed white peacoat and camel shift dress now. Olivia swore she would never wear black once she started losing weight. I've never seen so much as a black barrette in her perfect blond hair.

But she's still my Olivia. The tinfoil-wrapped colas are still her history, just as they are mine. Her life is now eerily mirroring our high school fantasies. I just thought it would involve me more.

"I have to move in one week," I say, turning down Colorado Boulevard.

"Girl, you should have moved a long time ago." I can hear cans being put on tile counters and cabinets being open and closed. The contents of those cans will be eaten one tablespoon at a time.

"Yeah, I know. I just feel a little guilty because this is happening right now. With the wedding and everything," I say.

"Oh, don't worry; it won't affect me. Come on, now, that's crazy talk," Olivia says.

"Right . . . right. How's Adam?" I stop at a red light and watch the minutes pass. I'm sure Cole is doing the exact same thing right now.

"Fabulous. He's in India for some Doctors Without Borders thing." Olivia sighs.

Olivia met Dr. Adam Farrell when he was the featured speaker at a PR event she put on for his hospital. It was almost a full year and half after she graduated from Berkeley and nearly two years after the surgery that changed her life forever. Dr. Farrell flew in from Washington, DC, and when Olivia met him at the airport she knew then that he was the man she would marry.

She still has the sign she held at the airport with the words
DR. FARRELL. I hear it will be on display at the wedding. She will
probably have armed guards surrounding it. They were engaged
a few years later, and not too long after, Olivia packed up her
West Coast life and moved three thousand miles away.

"I'm coming out to Pasadena this weekend. We're looking at
the wedding site and meeting with the event planner one more
time. She keeps saying she can't do Italian café lights, but I
know she can. Remember that wedding we saw the summer before college? They had Italian café lights, so she can go fuck herself. I'll hang them myself if I have to." Olivia has been studying
the Pasadena City Hall gardens since she was fifteen years old,
and she has always counted on the fabled Italian café lights.
Usually upscale Pasadena brides choose the venerable Ritz-
Carlton for their wedding festivities, but for some reason Olivia
has always set her sights on the Pasadena City Hall gardens. It's
as if she wants some kind of public exhibition of her success.
Everyone in town can witness a wedding at the gardens. Everyone in town can see Olivia in her tiny dress, with her perfect
man and the fucking Italian café lights.

"You're flying?" I ask, remembering the last time she flew
here from her new home in Washington, DC, she needed a
cocktail of Valium and anti-anxiety pills, chased with two shots
of straight vodka, just to get on the plane.

"Yes, I'm flying."

"We won't dwell on it. I'm sure you'll be fine," I say, knowing she will crash and die in a fiery explosion and that she'll
have several long minutes to think while plummeting to her
death. I, too, am a little shaky about the whole flying thing.
Olivia and I finalize the details of her weekend visit as I park behind the coffeehouse and ready myself for the explanation of a
lifetime.

CHAPTER THREE

"Choose a Man from Among You to Come Fight Me"

Joe's Joe for the Average Joe is in the newly gentrified Playhouse District of Pasadena. The coffeehouse was refurbished about eight years ago. Most of the architecture and decor were kept the same as in the early 1960s, when it was a local greasy spoon. The vinyl booths exhale as the clientele slide themselves across, and the smell of fifty-year-old grease is an accepted part of the ambience. The counter area was redone so people could order then seat themselves. Better for them, better for us. I started working here the summer after I got my master's in museum studies from San Francisco State University. This was supposed to be a summer job. After two years, I still begin every shift by questioning what I really want to do when I grow up. Instead I just keep asking whether that four-dollar coffee will be for here or to go.

"I'm sorry. I'm sorry," I say, walking past the counter not making eye contact with anyone.

"That's three nights in a row you've been late. I don't want to give you The Talk. But The Talk is what you shall have if it happens again." Cole has his hands on the counter, a washrag pinned underneath as though I have caught him midclean. His voice raises every hair on the back of my neck. As I turn to begin my excuses, Cole is ready. His arms are now across his wide chest, washrag dangling, eyebrows raised, mouth slightly open. Cole in a nutshell.

Cole Trosclair seemingly had it all in high school. Now he is just an ex-football-jock with old jerseys dotting his daily wardrobe. But I still feel I'm intruding on him in some sexless, work-colleague kind of way after two long years. If I were skinnier, he'd be nicer. If I were quicker with the jokes, he'd be my friend. I have visions of him defending me in the glow of his television late at night at one of his sports parties, a bunch of guys sitting around talking about titties. Cole defending me, saying, "If you just got to know her," and the other guys nodding.

Do I have to wait until I am officially in the right to toss yet another rock at this Goliath? At some point, isn't that rock supposed to catch him between the eyes and I am free? Is there some other version of the story where Goliath is champion?

"Wasn't that technically The Talk?" I say, my tiny pebble hurtling through the air.

"Yes, it was. Now, let's never have it happen again, young lady." Cole picks up his espresso and leans back on the counter, my tiny pebble landing at his feet.

"I got kicked out of my house," I say, emerging from the back room as I tie my apron around my waist.

"You're still fifteen minutes late." Cole yawns.

"Can you lay off for one second? Huh? I . . . got . . . kicked . . . out. And I have one week to find a new place." I pause but Cole says nothing. I continue. "Anything?"

"Fine. Why did you get kicked out?" Cole acquiesces.

"She says she's putting in a lap pool," I say, pushing my chest out in some desperate knee-jerk reaction.

"Do you believe her?"

"What's not to believe? There's a bulldozer in front of my door," I say, diving chest-first into a pot of fresh coffee.

"Poor, stupid, little Maggie . . ."

He called me *little.*

"She's trying to get you out with no argument," Cole continues.

I look over the coffeepot in time to see Domĕnic Brown amble into the empty coffeehouse, his black hair flipping just right. Little flips right by the ears. Little flips I just want to bite off, they're so perfect. His pale skin only accentuates those dark features. His pants are low-slung, and I can see that brown leather belt just peeking out where his thrift store, secondhand T-shirt is hitched up in the back.

I cock my head a little to the right. I've found, through hours of practice in the privacy of my own bathroom, this makes me look skinnier. The mirror on the back wall—that's what makes me look fat. No practice necessary for that little revelation.

I try to smile as offhandedly as I can. No big deal, just saying hi. Just being breezy, brother.

"Could I get a hot lemon toddy, please?" A tiny blond woman stands before me. Did I miss Domenic's smile back? Did he even smile back?

"For here or to go?" I stammer to this blond saboteur as I get my last glimpse of Domenic walking through the swinging back door.

"Here, please."

I move away from the counter and stare at Domenic doing his usual routine before he comes on shift. His real name is Domenico. I was in the office late one night and caught a glance at (okay, ransacked) his file, and found his W-2 form. Later, I

offhandedly asked him where his name came from. He explained that his grandmother is a sculptor and suggested they
name him Domenico, after Michelangelo's teacher. I remember
sighing and maybe fainting. It's all such a blur.

I would love to call him Domenico. To be the only one who
could. For *now* I'll call him Domenic. He grabs an apron as he
eyes the radio and judges the previous busboy's taste in music,
usually ending with an eye roll. He finishes tying his apron
while flipping through his own CDs. He puts one in and presses
PLAY while grabbing the plastic bin for dirty dishes. He opens
the door and . . .

Cole trains his deep-set blue-green eyes on a foursome at
the counter who are obviously on their way to the Pasadena
Playhouse down the block. I pass the blond her hot toddy, and
she tips us a nice fat quarter. We'll all eat like kings tonight.
Domenic Brown floats by and shoots me that crooked grin of
his. Damn, that boy has mastered breezy.

"What can I get you?" Cole is speaking to no one in particular. Everyone in the coffeehouse infers he is speaking to the
foursome, as they are first in line.

"Just one second, please." The leader of the foursome
speaks to Cole in a way that you shouldn't speak to Cole.

Cole leans back on the counter and slowly picks up his
espresso mug.

"She's not tearing it down," Cole says through sips.

"What?" I am imagining biting off flips of perfect dark hair
and whispering *Domenico*.

"She's not really tearing it down." Cole raises his voice and
turns his body so that he is squaring me off. I almost look to the
uptight foursome for help. Do I digress and agree that Cole is
now an expert in landlady pathology?

"And where is this coming from?" I ask.

"I just know. She's just batty enough to make up some crazy shit like that."

"And you know this because . . ."

"I'm just saying," Cole interrupts.

"Sir? I'd like . . ." The leader of the foursome starts in when there is a perceived lull.

"Why do you care anyway?" I ask. Knowing when to stop talking about something has never been one of my strengths.

"Sir?" the leader of the stylish foursome interjects.

Cole picks up his espresso mug, which looks like a child's tea set piece in his mitt of a hand, makes eye contact with the man, and turns his back on my question and me.

"I think we're ready over here," the man stutters.

Cole has won. The man is now half the man he was when he walked in. Cole sets down his espresso mug and once again lifts his eyebrows, opens his mouth just enough, and crosses his arms across his wide chest, washrag dangling. I count five "sorrys," three "if you don't minds" and a whopping six "when you get the chances."

The foursome tips Cole an extra five dollars. All I can think about is my question hanging in the air. Unanswered and deafening.

"D. Brown, get your scrawny ass out here." Cole acts like we're all in the locker room right before the big game and we've all got fancy nicknames.

Domenic walks out of the back room with a plastic bin under one arm, head tilted up, questioning. There is nothing extraordinary about him. He is not someone people would label as beautiful. But as Cole sets down his espresso teacup, Domenic Brown never picks up his pace or apologizes for being ten minutes later than I was. I am smitten.

"Did you see that album I left for you?" Cole asks.

Cole is one of these guys who still calls CDs *albums*. On a good day, when feeling particularly hip, he'll call them *LPs*. Those are days of wonder.

"I liked the hit in song five, the obscure Won-G the Haiti Boy song was unexpected, and I really liked the bridge on the hidden track," Domenic says, busying himself refilling the many sugars that a California coffeehouse offers: Raw, Bagged, Fake, Cubed Raw, Cubed White . . . the mind reels.

"Hidden track?" I ask. I know damn well what a hidden track is, but I have to get in on this conversation. Now, Haiti Boy, I have no idea.

"Sometimes bands will put a song at the end of their CD and won't tell anyone, or let it be programmed in. It's actually nice if you don't know about it." Domenic's pants are pooching out in the back as he bends over to grab the larger sugar boxes from underneath the condiment stand. I am not breathing. This is my favorite time of day. I call it my Guess Which Boxers Domenic Brown, My Future Husband, Is Wearing game. I'm working on shortening the name, but for right now let's just stick with that. The audience is quiet. The drumroll . . . the suspense is killing me. The bend. The squat. Light blue with a Scottish plaid waist. Nice. Very nice. Worth the wait.

"I live by that shit," Cole says into his mug, hitting the *t* in *shit* with particular vigor.

"It's equivalent to the B sides of the twentieth century, you know," Domenic says. It is difficult to keep my head cocked at just the right angle and still be mindful of my reflection in the mirror behind me as Domenic talks.

I tend to wear shirts that fall over my apron, even though I secretly know this makes me look bigger than I am. That way there is no illegal tucking involved. Not only is my Area the problem, but also now a whole extra piece of thick fabric is added to the mix. The logic is that maybe people will think it's *all* apron. Of course, there are no Ass Aprons on the market, and therefore this is left to the eye of the beholder.

"Give me an example." I am going to draw this conversation out until the very bones of it lie decomposing at my feet.

"Okay, I'll tailor one for you." Cole thwarts my plan by interrupting.

"I hate to intrude, but is there someone here who can clean off one of those tables out front?" A much-too-old man stands before us in a full, tight . . . oh so tight . . . bicycle outfit.

"Hey, Domenic, you're the busboy, go bus." Cole lifts his eyebrow.

"Yeah, I guess I am." Domenic puts the canisters of sugars back under the condiment stand, slams the small door, picks up his bin, and follows the man out front, not turning around once.

"Why do you have to talk to him like that?" I say.

"Like what?"

"You're the busboy. Go bus?" I mimic his voice in the most patronizing, bossy way possible.

"Jesus, Maggie. This is a business. And when you're in a business you have to talk fancy business talk . . . not puppies and kittens."

"At no point did I want you to refer to a goddamn puppy or a kitten." I am set on protecting my man.

"Why don't we try not to have a sailor mouth in this family establishment, young lady," Cole says.

"Oh, and Scrawny Ass is sweeping kindergarten classrooms across the nation? Remember? Scrawny Ass? Ass?"

"We're not doin' this." Cole bangs the espresso out of the coffee handle and turns his back on me a second time.

I stand there one second too long with my mouth open, anticipating Cole's next move. There isn't one. His next move turns out to be ignoring me.

I storm into the back room in search of chocolate syrup and to get away from Cole and my hanging, belligerent questioning.

"Did you get my invite for Movie Night next week? I left it in your cubbie," Peregrine says as she sits in the employee smoking section, which consists of three plastic white chairs and an upturned milk crate just outside the door to the back room. She extinguishes her cigarette on her boot and flicks it as far into the night as it can go. The word *cubbie* sounds ridiculous coming out of her mouth. Her dyed blue-black hair is twirled around in twenty buns all over her head. She is wearing a small, Japanese-style silk shirt with a black leather skirt.

Peregrine was born Leila Williams in a penthouse in Manhattan. She grew up among the fashion elite, her mother being a celebrated designer. When it was her turn to take her place next to her mother's fur-clad throne, Leila moved to LA and renamed herself Peregrine, like the falcon. Peregrine says she transplanted herself here from New York to pursue a fashion career. No one ever questions this move, even though moving away from New York and her mother's connections to pursue a fashion career seems a bit backward. After ten years, all she has to show for her dream is a mannequin in her living room sporting the same pinned Eisenhower jacket she's had on display since she took it out of the moving van. She never talks about her deferred dream in a negative way, and no one dares to ask her what's taking so long.

Over the years, Peregrine and I have become friends. Her Movie Nights, Poker Nights, Trivia Parties, and holiday get-togethers are legendary. She designs her own invitations and makes all of us feel like the party wouldn't be the same without us. Peregrine is that person who brings everyone together. But after the cards are dealt and the beers are cracked open, you've got to be willing to listen. Peregrine will spin yarn after yarn about herself and never once look up and notice that you've slit your wrists and scrawled I AM NOT HAPPY in your own blood on the wall behind you. Still, within minutes you're back to laughing and having a great time. After the night is through, you walk away remembering the night as the most fun you've had in a long time. I guess a night with Peregrine is what I've been told childbirth is like—you forget the pain and just remember the beauty of it all.

"Yeah, thanks. Can I let you know later if I can make it? What are you still doing here?" I ask, trying to change the subject. The memory of the last event still has some remnants of pain. The splendor of selective memory hasn't kicked in yet.

"Getting a smoke in before the drive home. What was going on out there?"

"Nothing," I say, searching for the chocolate syrup. The last thing I want to do is tell Peregrine about Cole being an asshole to Domenic and have him walk through the back door.

"Talked about nothing for a good long while."

"I just don't like how Cole talks to people sometimes," I say on tippy-toes, reaching for the chocolate syrup.

"That's just Cole. He's a cranky son of a bitch. You can't keep taking it personally, lamb. You know, when I first met Cole he was just coming off his big knee injury that cost him his scholarship. It's talks like that where I know he's just an embittered little old man who is pissed off about everything. It's not just you." I know Peregrine is right. This isn't about who's right or wrong. And I know this conversation will continue until I agree with her.

"I think *he* thinks he means it." I pull down the syrup and begin to wipe the dust from the top of the can. I try to make my comment sound as offhanded as possible.

"Once again, he's an asshole. You just can't take it person-ally," Peregrine says, taking her apron off and going into the back room, where the smoking employees leave the mouthwash.

"I'm not taking it personally. I just don't like it," I say over Peregrine's gargles. She spits.

Peregrine stares at me from the bathroom. Silent. I know this look and I usually don't like the sermon that inevitably follows.

"What?" I blurt, clutching my chocolate syrup to my bosom. The sooner we start this lesson, the sooner it'll be over.

"You've always been so sensitive. I think it's getting to the point where you've got to grow up a little. I mean Cole is Cole. I think you're being a little self-centered." I can't fathom how I'm being called self-centered while the person telling me about this character flaw is staring at herself in the bathroom mirror. Pere-grine tears herself away for one second to shoot me that ma-tronly smirk of hers.

"For shit's sake, Maggie, get back behind the counter." Cole's voice oozes into the back room.

I stare at Peregrine, not even turning around to see Cole. I can feel the back door swinging wildly from his entrance and exit. My eyebrows are so high they are now touching my hairline. I wait.

Peregrine steps out of the bathroom and straightens her shirt. I am holding on to that can of chocolate syrup like it is my firstborn. And yet I'm a little cocky. How could I not take that personally? I await her epiphany. She purses her lips and looks off into the distance.

"I'd better get back," I say, turning.

"Ahhhh, sweet pea, he's an asshole—you're just so sensitive. Just think about what I said." Peregrine sighs.

Unbelievable.

CHAPTER FOUR

Me and Marcus Aurelius

After Cal, I was accepted at San Francisco State University's museum studies program. I'd majored in art history at Cal and was so dedicated to the restoration and preservation of great art that I decided to make that my career. I was good at it. My obsessive attention to detail and ability to work long hours, without interruption, put me at the top of my class. I went back to Pasadena after those years excited and ready to take my place in the working world. I found the job at Joe's a few weeks after my return from the Bay Area. I told myself I would apply to jobs in my field throughout that summer and be out of there by fall. I applied over and over again and was rejected. I kept going to interviews and sending résumés, but I was still working at Joe's as I celebrated Thanksgiving with my family. I gave up easily and far too soon. Joe's was just easier.

The coffeemaker begins brewing as I wake up the next morning. I feel relieved that it's my day off, but dread that it will be spent sifting, cleaning, and readying for the big move. I start in the kitchen, the room with the most things I can live without

for the next few weeks. I decide to pick up a paper this afternoon and start the phone calls to prospective landlords.

I pack various cabinets of pots, pans, cookie sheets, and
most of the dishes. I am beginning to get into the deeper recesses of the cabinets. I find old tape recorders, videotapes, and
other knickknacks I can't remember having. After finding
enough stuff I haven't seen in forever, I go outside, drag in a
plastic trash can, and begin to maniacally toss everything I
haven't used in the past year. I feel lighter but sad for a bygone
era that is now being dragged out trash can by trash can. In another cabinet, I find shoe boxes of pictures that tumble out at
my feet. I have apparently been stuffing them in the cabinet and
not in the shoe boxes for some time now.

To open or not to open? That is the question. A shoe box
filled to the rim with old pictures and memorabilia is an invitation to open Pandora's box. I pull off my head the old baby hat
that I've been wearing since I packed the "hat drawer" earlier
this morning and settle in.

Old school pictures and candid photographs take me back
to a time I don't want to relive, just as I knew they would. Flipping through them, I feel teleported to that world: Olivia and I
the day she got her first car, our college graduation from Cal,
and the day Olivia, my sister, and I went up to the mountains
when we saw it snowing on the news—we just packed up and
started driving.

Pictures of Olivia and I in our early twenties in San Francisco and Washington, DC, take up most of this shoe box:
Olivia and I at one of our many outings at the Golden Gate
Bridge. Olivia and I lunching in Tiburon. Olivia and I toasting
with Blue Hawaiians at a Georgetown bar. I remember that
night—the Blue Hawaiian night—the first time I stayed with
Olivia and Adam in their apartment.

I was deep into my third year of the master's program at San Francisco State and trying to get used to a San Francisco without Olivia. I met Olivia and Adam at a Spanish tapas bar in DC for dinner after flying in that afternoon. As I walked into the restaurant, I couldn't miss the two of them. She was stunning in her white pantsuit with bright yellow pointy heels, but she paled in comparison to how impossibly beautiful Adam was. That night, he was wearing a black suit with a brilliant blue buttondown shirt, which opened to reveal his perfect chest. His golden hair was cut short and moussed to perfection. Upon my arrival, Adam stood to greet me. I remember my breath catching. I'd forgotten how tall he was. When I gathered my wits again, I ordered a sautéed mushroom appetizer. I remember thinking that if I just ate the mushrooms, I would not officially be going off whatever diet I was on that night. The mushrooms tasted great, and I felt even better for sticking to this new mysterious mushroom diet I'd discovered.

After dinner, Olivia, Adam, and I moved to a bar in the Foggy Bottom district. I bought drinks we heard other people ordering and then we saw *them*. Two girls, who looked like they were having the best time, had beautiful neon-blue drinks in huge, oversize hurricane glasses in front of them. Olivia and I got the bartender's attention, pointed to the girls, and babbled something like, "Gimme, gimme, them blue drinkies." He presented us with two of our very own Blue Hawaiians. We toasted, giggled like schoolgirls again, and I drank. And drank. They tasted like candy, so I ordered more. And more. The only thing I really remember is getting up early the next morning to the undeniable gurglings of a hangover. I was in Olivia and Adam's tiny apartment sleeping in the living room on a camping mattress Adam had loaned me. Olivia and Adam slept in the only bedroom, which I had to quietly pass through to get to the only bathroom. As the hangover found its legs, I found I was losing any control over holding anything down. In a panic, I decided to take a shower, figuring I could throw up all I wanted and they wouldn't hear.

I creaked open the bedroom door to find Olivia sleeping in a queen-size bed all by herself and her brand-new fiancé, Dr. Adam Farrell, sleeping in another queen-size bed right next to it. There was a large sleeping bag clipped to the window blocking all natural light. Adam lay there with blankets pulled to his perfectly chiseled chin, bright orange earplugs tucked tight, and a black sleeping mask. I was paralyzed, but I feared that throwing up while staring at the sleeping couple might be a little unnerving for all of us. I padded through the bedroom toward the bathroom, where I vowed never to drink again.

At breakfast that morning at a local coffee shop, Adam left Olivia and me at the table in search of a *Washington Post*. I stirred my coffee, pushed up my glasses, and never made eye contact with Olivia. My head was killing me. I felt almost too nauseous to drink coffee, which has never since happened, thank God. Olivia smirked across the table and busted me about my "rough morning." I smiled. It hurt. She showed no signs of our previous night. Thinking back, I was the only one ordering the blue drinkies. That would explain this morning. I apologized for bothering their sleep, even though they had not awakened. I thought she might offer some explanation for their bizarre sleeping arrangement if she knew I'd seen them. I could hear my spoon hitting the sides of the coffee mug as we sat in silence.

"He needs his sleep, you know," Olivia said, cutting her muffin into eighths.

"Oh. Is that what the . . ."

"The beds? Yeah. He can't waste one night's sleep, you

know. It's so rare that he gets a full night, he just needs to make the most of it."

"Oh, that sounds . . . practical." I couldn't imagine anything more sterile and haunting.

"It must have looked weird when you walked in, you know . . . us in different beds?"

"No, I . . . uh, was a little preoccupied. I didn't even think twice about it."

Lie.

We never spoke about it again. I sensed Olivia was having a hard time with the arrangement as well. It was the ultimate in Adam not making room for her in his life. She wasn't even allowed to share his bed.

The phone rings, snapping me out of my reverie.

"Hey there, Bobo," Kate says. My sister has instinctively saved me once again.

"Hey there, Fatty," I say, clutching another stack of fun party photos I will feverishly flip through cursing, crying, and regretting. We have this lifelong family game where one of us is fat, Fatty, and the other Bobo, which means "stupid." The point is to decide which one you are. So if you get called Bobo, then you must respond by referring to the other as Fatty. I have never minded being called Bobo, but full-fledged fistfights have broken out when I was called Fatty.

"Whatcha doin'?" She senses something is wrong in the universe.

"Nothin' much," I say as I relive every blue-neon mushroom moment.

"Then are you free to take Emily and Bella down to Buster's for ice cream while I go drop some papers off with the scout leader?"

"Where's Vincent?"

"Vincent had to finish up some work today, but he'll probably be home before me. We could really use the help."

I can feel Kate on the edge. She is teetering. The next words out of her mouth are going to be *forget it . . . never mind . . .* , then dial tone; or *forget it, I'll ask Mom.* Then the race is on to call Mom and tell her your side of the story first.

It's never about watching my nieces or, as I call them, the girlies. I just can't imagine making myself presentable right now. I promised myself I would not get out of my favorite outfit all day. If I could just walk around in this gray men's tank top and these black terry-cloth pants, I would be the luckiest woman alive. I have been planning around this outfit for days now. With this phone call, I will have to put on a bra and panties.

"Just let me get washed up." I start putting the lids on the shoe boxes.

"Don't say it like that . . . I'll even buy the ice cream." Kate's voice is smooth.

"Damn right you will, and double scoops, little missy," I huff.

I stuff the shoe boxes back into the cabinet and the contents back into my subconscious. I climb into the shower and look forward to seeing my nieces. Kate lives minutes away from Mom in a house she and Vincent bought almost a year ago.

Sitting in front of Kate's house, all washed and wearing pants with a button, I curse my sister. Emily and Bella, who have the hearing of bats, run out to greet me.

Emily wears her hair short this month. At eight years old, she has the kind of courage about her appearance that most women never attain. She's blessed with flawless olive skin, feathery green eyes, and perfect, thick brown hair; it's getting harder and harder for me to remember the day Kate first brought her home from the hospital.

Bella looks like she's right out of Central Casting for the

Little Rascals. Her alabaster skin is dotted with dirt, snot, and whatever else she's been rolling around in that day. Her wavy brown hair is cut in a short bob while her newly self-cut bangs show off her huge sky-blue eyes. Her knees have permanent Band-Aids, and she always wears her favorite red cowboy boots I gave her for Christmas.

"Hey, crazies," I say.

"No, you're crazy," Emily says.

"What you do?" Bella's voice somehow never evolved past that of a raspy seventy-year-old smoker. I always feel I should make it a double when I talk to her.

"Well, I was going to go to Buster's and thought that maybe your mom wanted to come with me. Can you guys hang here for a while?" I say, beeping my car's alarm on.

"You came to get us, crazy, let me get my backpack." Emily skips inside with my cleverness floating behind her.

Kate comes from the house with her wallet, a sheet of paper, and Bella's kid car seat. Kate and I look exactly opposite from each other. Where I am pushing six feet, she is barely five feet tall. Where I have dark brown hair and brown eyes, Kate has white-blond hair and ice-blue eyes. I tend to have issues about my weight, yet Kate stays at a perfect size 2 no matter what the world throws at her. Pregnancy? She takes yoga and prenatal classes. Second pregnancy? Now she's teaching the yoga class and is at the top of the phone tree in her prenatal class.

There is something about our appearance that ties us together enough so people can tell we're sisters, but it's nothing you can put your finger on. Kate and I have taken this physical oppositeness and run with it in our personal choices. Kate is a wife and mother, while I have been forcibly single for what looks like it might be a good fifty more years. Kate revels in being a wife and mother and is confident and forward; I have a bachelor's in art history and a master's in museum studies but I work at a coffeehouse making minimum wage. I allow myself to daydream about a career, but haven't mustered the guts to start applying again. I just find myself gazing at my unframed diplomas like they should go out and wrangle us a job.

"I knew you came for us, too, Maggie," Bella concedes.

"We all knew," Kate whispers.

Bella climbs into the back, sticking her little pink panties in my face as I fasten her into her kid car seat. We wait for Emily, who needs many accessories to join us this afternoon. I see she now has a new necklace and a fabulous charm bracelet dangling from her tiny wrist as she exits the house. Bella looks on enviously, but she's cradling her Molly American Girl doll and looks somewhat pacified.

"Here." Kate passes me a sheet of paper downloaded off the Internet as Emily settles in her seat.

"What's this?" I flip the paper so it's right-side up.

"Just read it." Kate squeezes past me and helps Emily into her seat belt. I fix my eyes on the paper.

The Getty Conservation Institute works internationally to advance conservation and to enhance and encourage the preservation and understanding of the visual arts in all of their dimensions—objects, collections, architecture, and sites.

The Getty Museum has an active internship program. Twelve-month internships are offered in several of the Museum's conservation departments. The internship program is organized and administered by the Museum's education department.

"What do you think?" Kate raises herself out of the backseat. It's those damn diplomas' fault.

"What do you mean? What am I supposed to think?" I feel ambushed. This whole ice cream trip is just a con to hand me this piece of paper.

"I just thought . . . you know . . . it sounds amazing and it's been a while since you last sent out résumés, right?" Kate says.

"Yeah, I guess." I feel like crying.

I don't know where the emotions are coming from. I secretly know I'm living half a life at Joe's. But I get to stare at Domenic two or three times a week and I get to have this dream. The dream is: I'm in the basement of the Louvre. There I am in the center of the room, Walkman on, wearing a basic white T-shirt, a charcoal cashmere sweater, and worn-in jeans—barefoot of course—restoring the *David*. It apparently fell over in some freak disaster and they have called me in because of my "international reputation." The curator nervously questions how the sculpture is as I answer him in fluent French. He breathes easy and says he is forever indebted. The door is left open, and I faintly hear someone else enter. It is Domenic. He is dressed in pajama bottoms and an aged Cal sweatshirt. He is holding a steaming mug of Earl Grey tea (my favorite) and his novel that was once at our bedside. He sets the tea at my feet and gently kisses me before settling in with his novel for the night. But the only reason the dream lives is because I haven't sent my résumé out. If I send my résumé out or make a call on any job openings, the dream will die and be replaced with the reality that I'm not good enough.

"I called," Kate says. I am quiet.

"They've got this Marcus Aurelius sculpture. AD ninety-five." Kate looks away. I breathe in and try to control my emotions in front of the girlies. I stare at her.

"And what else? Are they paying people? Are they accepting applications? Or do they just want you to apply so they can reject you? Huh?" I try to watch my sailor mouth in front of the girlies.

"Oh, sweetie. Yes, they're paying—pretty nicely if I do say so myself. And yes, they're accepting applications this summer." Kate is calm.

"Oh." Shit. I feel a tear roll down my face. Kate wipes it away. It's as if the numbness subsides and all the emotion and hope I've tried so hard to push down and ignore just erupt.

"Just take it. I wrote the lady's name on the back. She's waiting for your call. The sculpture is being disassembled now, but they'll need a gap filler and an in-painter by fall." I flip the paper over. In Kate's perfect Catholic Nun writing is the name Beverly Urban and a phone number. Kate has written in parentheses that this is her direct line.

I fold the paper and shove it in my pocket. The pants are tight, and the inner workings of the pocket are revolting against any new contents. Frustrated, I pull the now balled-up paper out of my "pocket." Kate sighs. I walk around the car as indignantly as I can and throw the paper on the passenger seat as I pull out of Kate's driveway.

"Who's Marc's Face and Tell Us?" Bella asks. I throw the car into drive and head down Kate's perfect suburban street explaining to a six- and eight-year-old about the life of a Roman emperor.

Once at Buster's in South Pasadena, Emily orders Daiquiri Ice, pronouncing it *Da-kweeri Ice,* while Bella orders Pink. I order my usual Cappuccino and Chocolate in a dish with a cone as a hat. That way you can crumble. It's an art.

"I'm moving," I say across the ice cream parlor table.

"Where?" Bella asks.

"I'm not sure. I need to find a new home. For me and Solo," I say.

I hear myself saying it. I don't think I really believed it until right now.

"You don't know where you're going to go?" Emily asks.

"No," I say.

"Will you live with Grammy and Papa Russell?" Emily asks.

"Will I what?" I stutter, almost choking on crumbled bits of cone.

"Grammy and Papa Russell have a house," Bella says, with Pink ice cream now on her forehead.

"Yes, but Grammy and Papa Russell don't want their twenty-seven-year-old daughter living with them," I say, stabbing at my ice cream.

"Why not? It would be like a sleepover. Bella and I slept over one night when Mommy and Daddy went to Fran San Sisco, and Grammy made up two beds for us with pillowcases she got special for us," Emily says, lifting her napkin to her mouth.

"She could do that for you," Bella adds, Pink ice cream now everywhere.

I try to find some reason that would make sense to Emily and Bella why a grown woman shouldn't live with her parents. Besides the obvious rant that I'm repeating in my mind about not being a loser, being independent, having a life, and being too old for this . . . I have big plans.

Don't I?

CHAPTER FIVE

Channeling Mae West

I begin the process of looking for a new place by circling FOR RENT ads I might have a shot at. It's only six days until the bulldozer crumples my life and belongings in one afternoon. The balled-up paper Kate gave me about the Getty internship now rests on my kitchen counter. I find myself staring at it. I fold it and unfold it but never open it to reveal Ms. Beverly Urban and her fancy direct line.

"Hi, I'm calling about the ad?" I say.

"Yeah?" the voice responds.

"The one-bedroom on Michigan Avenue?"

"Yeah."

"Could . . . could . . . do you think you could maybe tell me a little something about it?"

"It's one bedroom. Seven fifty a month. Utilities included."

"I have a dog."

"Oh, God, no . . . no dogs." And then dial tone.

It's as if I had said, *Well, I've been known to spray in the corners of my dwellings as a sort of territorial thing—do you mind?*

Looking into the half-packed kitchen, I rub my forehead

until it feels good. I have to pack this entire house. Alone. One object at a time. This is going to take a while. Maybe I'll grab some dinner and then take Solo for a walk.

It is common practice during my dog walks that I openly talk to myself. I figure no one really cares or notices, and if they do I can act like I'm talking to the dog, because that would somehow make me *less* crazy. Usually on my walks with Solo, I think about relationships. I know—a dog named Solo. I thought it would be so cool. Now she's just this little self-fulfilling prophecy who I pick up after twice a day. But I digress.

For Peregrine's birthday one year, she threw one of those sex-toy parties. As I sat there among the lotions, lubes, and various other marital aids, I felt nothing except embarrassment. My few brushes with sex have been these uneventful fumblings where there was never any time to reach for edible glitter or a feather tickler, let alone try any other position besides "fully clothed and humiliated." The notion that there would be time and even the proper lighting to utilize such tools is completely mind boggling.

During my first year at Cal I lived on the same floor as Mason Phelps, a math major who studied nonstop. Whether in the library, the student lounge, or the cafeteria, Mason was rarely without a textbook, graph paper, and his calculator. His brownish hair was cut poorly and seemed to only play up his massive cowlick, which stuck straight up in back. His eyes were this beautiful yellow-brown color, which is what I finally decided made me like him. Well, that and he seemed to like me. Even during his twenty-four-hour study sessions, he would find time to knock on my dorm room door and sit on my bed, talking about class and the campus. I found myself laughing at jokes that were wholly unfunny while working harder than ever to just keep the conversation going. Why did he come over if he didn't want to talk? And why did I keep talking to him if he bordered on mind-numbingly boring?

I eventually discovered the purpose of Mason's visits. While the dorm erupted in Saint Patrick's Day festivities, Mason knocked once again at my dorm room door. We immediately got into a heated conversation about the choice of cereals in the cafeteria. As I extolled the virtues of Cap'n Crunch, Mason leaned over and kissed me. I remember very little after that, as everything seemed to move in fast forward. The lights were off, his pants were down, and before I had time to ask myself if I even liked this person, I had pulled him on top of me. I could hear bursts of laughter from other students just outside my door. The pure adrenaline of what was happening pushed me through the fears of that first time. But as Mason got up after a magical ten seconds had elapsed, he leaned down and pinched my thigh, commenting that I wasn't wearing green. He didn't close the door all the way as he left, and a small shaft of light from the hallway allowed me to see what he had seen: me naked. I vowed I would never feel that vulnerable again.

I was steadfast in my promise to myself, giving in only once—at a Halloween party in San Francisco, where I slept with a guy in an alien outfit. I learned later his name was Bobby Bol and he was an electrician in Daly City. I was drunk at the time, and I've never forgiven myself for that.

During my first months at Joe's, I met Steven MacKenzie, a slow, drawling Texan who could never commit to anything stable, not even friendship. I spent night after night in his apartment with my head on his lap, lazily watching art-house movies in the dark. Unlike Mason, Steven never leaned down and kissed me.

Steven and I went so far as to take trips with each other. My earliest definition of lust was the feeling I got when Texas Steven got out of his kayak with his wet suit unzipped about halfway down his chest during one particularly frustrating jaunt to Catalina Island. A beam of light from the heavens illuminated his golden skin, and the blond hairs covering his chest . . . wait, a moment of silence for the chest. Okay . . . the blond hairs, which covered his chest. He had hooded hazel eyes that made him look boyishly ravishing. His golden hair was always cut short. Of course, if you swing the camera around you'll find me: sitting in the water while hurling myself out of my kayak, which is now hermetically sealed to my ass.

◆

I spend the rest of the day packing, being rejected by prospective landlords and avoiding The Paper, which now rests on the top of the television. I have to be at work early, so I decide to turn in. I check my messages for a call from Olivia letting me know she is in town, but there are only messages from Mom and Kate about leads they have on possible apartments. I get caught up in not hearing from Olivia. I can't get past why she hasn't called. We're best friends. Her wedding is in a matter of weeks. I'm her maid of honor. How do you not call your maid of honor when you're in town? Lately, I'm beginning to think Olivia is just a figment of my imagination and that I've dreamed up the whole friendship. You'd think I'd develop a more reliable Dream Friend.

Mom says she has a lead on a house for rent and I write down the phone number of the management company. I will have to tell her about the internship sooner or later. As if she doesn't already know. I bring the phone into my bedroom and sleep fitfully, thinking I hear the phone every two hours. I awake watery-eyed the next morning and dress quickly for work. I refuse to be late again.

"Hey there, latey, there's something clipped to the bulletin board for you," Cole says.

"I'm not late. What is it?" I ask, noting that I am, in fact, eight minutes late. How can that be?

"You *are* late, but I'll humor you. And I don't know what's clipped to the bulletin board because I didn't open it up. I'm in a good mood, so I will give you two minutes to find out what it is, and then you may come to work officially unlate."

Is it a note from the owner of Joe's? That fucking Cole has tattled on my chronic lateness. I fucking know it. I don't know why I'm late. I just look at the clock and keep pushing it. Five more minutes. What an asshole. I've done this to myself. Stupid. Here I am, moving and all the moving costs and I lose my . . . wait a minute.

"Is this mine?" I point to the package.

"Huh? Yeah—what?" One of the backup staff, Christina Dahl, an aspiring model-actress, is washing dishes in the back room.

"Who left it?" I am flipping the package around, trying to not disturb the mechanics.

"I'm not sure. I just got here about an hour ago, and it was already, like, up there. I don't even know what it is . . . it's like wrapped up, huh?" Christina is still washing dishes.

I'm not paying any attention to her, which is a foreign concept for Christina. And yet, I'm female, so maybe not, unless she's trying to steal my man. I'm sure she gets plenty of female attention in that arena. Christina walks out with her plastic bin for dirty dishes and leaves me alone with the package.

I pull the pushpin and make sure it goes right back where it was. It's wrapped in today's Calendar section of the newspaper. I unfold the newspaper to find a blank CD case. There are four

words scrawled in black marker on the gold surface of the
burned disc:

To Maggie
From Domenic

"Oh . . . my . . . God . . ." I hear myself say the three words
out loud.

To Maggie
From Domenic

My first thought is, He wrote my name. That's what my
name would look like on a scribbled note he left on my pillow-
case the morning he had to leave early for work: *Maggie: Thank
you for last night. YOU WERE AMAZING!—Domenico.*
I go back to the CD case for some answers as to what could
have possibly motivated Domenic to do this, as he isn't at work
today. On the inside flap of the CD cover is a note. Once again, I
stare at the writing. This is to me from him. He was thinking
about me. *Domenic Brown was thinking about me.* Wait. Domenico.
Brown. Was. Thinking. About. Me.
"Maggie—Here's a few hidden tracks I think you'll like.—
Domenic." I can't feel my legs.
The back room door swings open, and I instinctively try to
hide the CD.
"It's been two minutes. So . . . what is it?" Cole has a taster
spoon from the ice cream case in his mouth.
"What's what?" I obviously missed my calling as an interna-
tional spy.
"I can't even pretend I'm not annoyed with you right now."

Cole has now bitten the taster spoon in half and is flossing his teeth with the jagged edges.

"It's just a CD." I show it to him, flipping it around like it doesn't mean a thing to me, even though I secretly know this CD is going to be treasured by our firstborn daughter as the first gift her daddy ever gave me.

"Who gave it to you?" he asks.

I am in physical pain. What if he makes fun of me? What if he makes fun of Domenic? I know he doesn't see me as a woman in any shape or form. So what is he going to think about Domenic giving me a gift? Am I overthinking this? Am I breathing right now? Am I talking out loud?

"Well, uh . . . remember when you guys were talking about some hidden tracks on that album and I said, 'Hey, what's a hidden track?' you know . . . and so, Domenic was there, and he tried to explain it to me, you know, you were there, too. But you know me . . . I . . . I didn't understand."

At this point in my retard monologue, I am inspired to non-chalantly toss Domenic's CD on the metal rack next to the sink as proof it means nothing to me. As it sails through the air I fight every urge to dive after it. But I continue my explanation.

"So Domenic made me this . . . I mean that CD, and I guess it's got some hidden tracks on it, or something. I really don't know," I breathe. By now, Christina is peeking her head behind Cole and waiting for him to move from the doorway.

"Excuse me, Manager." Christina holds the plastic bin at her hip, causing her pants to go even farther down her ass.

"Oh, Christina. Sorry." Cole looks over his shoulder and right down Christina's shirt. Then he moves in closer, letting Christina into the back room so she can wash the newly bused dishes. He is silent for a good five seconds.

I am standing there in joy, fear, and excitement, waiting for

Cole to check out Christina's model-actress ass. I am hopeful this ass will aid me in my plan to get the CD once more. Cole reaches for the CD on the counter; I can't believe I let it out of my hands for one second.

"Oh. Oh yeah. It's burned. That's cool. Domenic makes some good mixes. Does he say what's on here?" Cole is now investigating the inner workings of our firstborn daughter's sixteenth-birthday present.

"Nope." I am now in full cardiac arrest. Must. Get. CD. Back.

I snatch the CD from Cole and hide it in the folds of my long black sweater, which I put on a shelf in the staff bathroom. Peregrine comes back from the smoking section, putting her cigarette out on her boot. This time, however, she is coming on shift.

"Hey, what's up?" I preemptively blurt as Cole heads back out front, tossing the broken taster spoon in the trash as he walks past. Peregrine waits.

"It's nothing. It's just a CD," I continue as Peregrine passes. I am oddly embarrassed. I've never seen myself as someone who has boyfriends or gets gifts—and to be standing here with a gift from a man is so foreign. My face is hot and I feel like I just got caught making out on the couch by my mom.

"Just a CD? Honey, it's never just a CD. Who's it from?" Peregrine hides the soul of an eighty-year-old truck-stop waitress within her thirty-three-year-old tattooed body.

"Domenic." I hear myself say his name. Inside my head, I am saying *Domenico*.

"He totally likes you, doll," Peregrine exclaims.

"I don't think it means anything. We were just talking about hidden tracks. So what?" I say.

"So you've got a little admirer, button. Cute, don't you

think? If that doesn't work out, I've got a line on another guy for you. A real looker, too. Okay, so he's the guy who picks up our recycling, but he did ask after you the other day—said you had a 'nice rack.' A little crude, but you don't have to marry the guy. Remember Movie Night—don't bring anything. I've got popcorn, beer, and I rented *A Star Is Born*—both versions—Garland and Streisand!" Peregrine whirls into the front of the coffeehouse to start her shift, leaving me alone in the back room with my CD.

I'm afraid this gift will be like all of the others. Texas Steven's *Blade Runner* DVD I got for my birthday. Bobby Bol's single rose wrapped in copper wire. Mason Phelps even gave me his meal card with an unlimited amount one month. Is this CD yet another token of friendship or fleeting desire? What if for once this is the real thing? What then? Domenic isn't working today, so I have no idea.

We close early on weekday nights, so I get home before 8 PM. I clutch the CD in my hand and walk into my packed-up house. I check my machine. I have two new messages. Both are from people I called about an apartment. Olivia has been in town for a whole day and hasn't called. Maybe she was just a voice in my head—a very tangible well-dressed psychotic episode. I call her cell phone and leave another message. In the back of my mind, I am excited to tell someone about Domenic. But I stop myself. Here she is getting married to a cardiologist from Washington, DC. While I roll up with my "cute crush": a twenty-eight-year-old busboy who lives in a loft with four roommates. I begin to hyperventilate. I will be undone by my own second-guessing. I call the two prospective landlords back. Once again, I am practically drawn and quartered for owning such a wild beast as a seventy-pound dog.

I try not to analyze the CD like the other gifts. No listening to each lyric as if it were a declaration of love. I can't do that with this one. I have to remind myself that this CD is probably what all the other gifts have turned out to be: an affirmation of friendship. Nothing more.

As I listen to the CD, I smile when I know the song. A couple are new to me. Most aren't that meaningful, and some are so underground punk rock they're barely enjoyable. I am packing up the bathroom when I hear it, the hidden track of the hidden-track compilation. It's a whispery ballad. I stop, my face in the depths of the cabinet. I know this band. I don't know this song. Should I read into this? Is this just another friendly misunderstanding? Or is this Domenic metaphorically leaning over and kissing me?

I walk toward the CD player; the number on the digital face is 99. I don't want to touch anything, afraid I will never be able to hear this beautiful song again.

> if I were to one time
> ask for what I want
> maybe I would receive it
>
> as the days go
> by and by and by
> I learn not to ask
>
> So I will never get
> Shown anything
> . . . or at least anything
> that will hurt me . . .

I stare at the CD player, toilet brush in one hand, my heart in the other.

CHAPTER SIX

Oh, Dr. Farrell, You Are Too Much

When I was a junior in high school, I missed having a boyfriend by five minutes.

Olivia and I made our usual daily stop at the local ice cream store. Olivia went in without me, because I couldn't find my wallet. While I searched the depths of my 1984 Chevy Chevette, Olivia went inside to begin the detailed process of ordering. Unbeknownst to me, Owen Lynch, my new high school crush after The John Sheridan had been unmasked that fateful night, was talking to Shannon Shimasaki, our perpetual nemesis. She worked behind the counter at the ice cream store. When Olivia walked in, Shannon began, for some unknown reason, grilling her about who I liked. Olivia, always the weak one, gave up that I had a crush on the one and only Owen Lynch. Shannon howled with laughter and turned to ask Owen if he would ever consider dating me. Owen Lynch said, "Maybe." That's the closest I've ever come to having a real boyfriend.

◆

As I stand with the toilet brush in one hand and Domenic's lyrics echoing in my head, the phone rings. "Hello?" I'm breathless as I answer. I can't believe the lyrics I just heard.

"Hey, girl. Where have you been?" It's Olivia. I can hear clinks and laughter behind her.

"At work," I say.

"Come meet us for a late dinner." Olivia takes an audible, but genteel sip of her drink.

"Sure." I look down at myself. I am wearing my "favorite outfit," still holding the brush. Cleaning up to go for drinks seems an impossible feat.

"Okay then, hurry up, and can you bring over that list we made when I was out there about a year ago. Remember? We wrote locations for my wedding on the back of that napkin from El Coyote. I put little hearts and stars around city hall. I want to show Adam how it came true." She puts her hand over the receiver while she retells the story to Adam as I hold . . . panicking. I haven't seen that napkin in months.

After we hang up, I pull out the shoe boxes of pictures from the day before. Thank God, there is the crumpled napkin among our old school photos. Olivia and I went out to dinner at El Coyote in Los Angeles the night she told me Adam proposed. That was the night she asked me to be her maid of honor. I must have kept the napkin as a token of the occasion.

I take a shower and put on a pair of black pants and pull a white V-neck T-shirt from my hamper. I find myself bringing the shirt cautiously up to my nose to gauge the odor. It passes. I put it on. I pull on my long black sweater and convince myself it will be air-conditioned in the restaurant because I'm already hot from wearing too many clothes in the summertime heat.

Olivia and Adam are at a table for two in the corner of the restaurant. I tell the hostess I am meeting friends and walk over to the intimate table. Olivia is wearing an off-white peasant top with linen pants. She has on large gold hoop earrings, and her hair is in its usual mussed state of perfection. She has added a jeweled barrette (pink), which pulls a tiny portion back from her face. She has gotten even smaller since I've last seen her, putting her somewhere near a weight even Hollywood would consider thin. I smile more widely than I have in weeks. Just seeing her calms me and makes me feel at home. I feel the hostess's eyes on me as she looks around to see why no one has brought a chair for me. Olivia jumps up as I approach. I see Adam dabbing his chin and rising behind her. I imagine there is a golden glow around him this evening. She calls the hostess back and asks for a chair.

Adam is wearing a pressed oxford-cloth shirt and khaki dress pants. He is wearing woven leather loafers. The hostess brings me a tiny, brittle-looking wooden chair and sits it at the table. Olivia hugs me and asks if I found parking, did I bring the napkin, and how work was all in a span of three seconds. Adam reaches across the table and shakes my hand. His hands are baby soft and small-ish. The busboy brings flatware and a plate for my dinner, moving aside the centerpiece and a finished appetizer of some kind of grilled asparagus. I am tempted to introduce the busboy as my boyfriend just to see how it flies. I decide against it.

"How long have you guys been in town?" I ask, settling in and shuddering at the deafening creaks emanating from my gingerbread prop chair. I am starving and eye the remnants of the asparagus.

"We flew in yesterday morning. Olivia and I are staying at the Ritz." Adam is pulling his cell phone from its holster and examining the numbers.

"Have you spoken to the event planner?" I ask.

"She's meeting us there tomorrow morning. Will you come?

You always know exactly what I'm talking about and I just don't think that bitch understands me sometimes. This whole Italian café light thing has been a disaster. I just can't imagine . . ." Olivia trails off, taking a slow sip of her martini. I think that is the most she'll be "eating" tonight.

"Sure. I work tomorrow night, so that'll work." The waitress approaches as Olivia and Adam order their dinners. I haven't even looked at a menu. I pick up one of the two menus and study it as everyone, in turn, studies me—except the waitress, who can't take her eyes off Adam. I order the chicken with a diet soda. Adam sips his red wine and looks around the restaurant while I try to situate myself so there will be no more chair creaking. I have positioned myself so all my weight sits toward the front of the chair and a little to the left. The rest of my weight is distributed on the table, where I am pressing my elbows furtively. One wrong move and the whole thing could topple over. I am so globally uncomfortable, I hear nothing but the creaks of the chair and the teetering of martini and wineglasses.

"So how do you like Pasadena?" I ask Adam.

"Charming. I always enjoy visiting Olivia's mother and seeing the place my girl grew up. She really is a treasure."

"Oh, Dr. Farrell, you are too too much." Olivia turns bright red, giggles quietly, and lifts her hand to cover her mouth. Are they making fun of someone right now? Is there a couple behind me who actually act like this—and are we going to take turns mocking their Victorian courtship traditions? I scan the restaurant for a man in a top hat or perhaps a woman's parasol leaning against a booth. Confused, and a little disappointed at not finding such specimens, I turn back to Olivia and Adam as the reality hits me. This is how *they* act together.

"What? What is it, honey?" Olivia continues as Adam is now patting his napkin on his chin in disgust.

"Just . . . will you . . . just look?" Adam is staring at a booth at the far end of the restaurant. I am horrified as I turn. Olivia gasps.

A slight man is looking on as his wife slides out of their booth. Her stomach is sitting on top of and below the table for a sliding-glass-door effect. Her napkin is still perched on her large bosom, and she is nervously laughing for she has—horror of horrors—become stuck in the booth. She is trying to push the table forward, but it is bolted to the floor. As she pushes, the booth behind her is being rocked back and forth. The young man in the booth gets out and asks if he can help her in any way. Acting oblivious, the woman's husband, now on his cell phone, moves out of the restaurant. The woman's laughs are becoming more and more hysterical as she sees her husband leaving. The young man waves down the waitress, who tells him if they just push the booth back, the woman will be freed. The woman yanks the napkin off her breasts and looks down on herself. I can't watch anymore. I know that look. I know that moment. She is promising herself she will never eat again, and this is the day she will begin her new exercise regimen.

"Ridiculous," Adam whispers.

"What?" Olivia leans in, smoothing her shirt down over her flat stomach.

"How does a woman allow herself to get like that? That is the manifestation of what has gone wrong in this country. I shudder at what her heart looks like right now." He sips his wine. If Dr. Farrell wants to call me fat, he should just come right out and fucking say it.

"Yeah." Olivia's voice is breathy as she lifts her martini glass and swirls the olive around.

The restaurant is abuzz with the goings on of the past fifteen minutes. I look over once again at Olivia. In a moment of pure fear, she catches my eye and I understand. I knew Adam didn't know to what extent Olivia had battled her weight. I thought he knew about the surgery and the complete metamorphosis of the past five years. Now I realize he has no idea how big Olivia was. That woman could have been Olivia without the bypass surgery.

The evening ends, and Olivia and I make plans to meet at the city hall gardens at ten thirty the next morning. Adam is meeting a colleague early for some "time on the links." I wave good-bye to him and hug Olivia one last time. She is tiny. I feel her bones as I hug her and cringe. My best friend is wasting away and loving every minute of it.

CHAPTER SEVEN

Domenic's Underpants

I have always dreamed of getting married in a mountain cabin with the snow falling outside. It would be a small family affair, close and warm, lit by firelight and candles. We would invite everyone for a holiday party and surprise them all with our nuptials. He would cry as he vowed his love to me, thinking secretly that he never thought life could be this beautiful. I would look at him and know this is the person I'm going to be with forever. That I never have to be alone again. Should it worry me that even in my fantasy, the man is getting married for love but I just don't want to be alone anymore?

I stop for coffee and meet Olivia on the steps of city hall at 10:30 a.m. She is wearing 1940s-style pants that button on the side. Her white-and-pink polka-dot top is fluttering in the wind of the morning; her tanned, flat stomach is visible with every other whispery breeze.

Pasadena City Hall, built in 1927, was fashioned in the style of sixteenth-century Italian architect Andrea Palladio. Using building materials such as Alaskan marble, vertical-grained white oak, Cordova clay tile for the roof, and fish-scale tile for the massive dome, the city hall serves as a focal point for the entire city. The gardens have a Spanish Colonial feel to them, but the eye is drawn to the huge cast-stone baroque fountain in the exact center. Around the garden, paths of crushed granite set apart flower beds bursting with hydrangeas, azaleas, and hundreds upon thousands of annuals that are rotated throughout the year. Needless to say, it's not your average suburban city hall.

"She's late," Olivia greets me.

"It's just now ten thirty. I'm sure she's just finding parking somewhere." I sip my coffee and look around at the empty parking lot. We smile at each other as my ridiculous statement hangs in the air. Olivia laughs and shoves me aside, regaining her composure.

"Are you meeting us at Martine's on Tuesday for the wedding dress? Badgley Mischka, can you believe it? This is my final fitting and I can't believe I've left it to the last minute. But I just couldn't, you know. I couldn't even think about walking down the aisle in anything but a size two. Just this weekend I bought this pair of jeans and the four was too big. I thought maybe . . . maybe. I asked the girl to run get me a two. She did and it fit. You can't imagine how incredible it feels to look at the tag of a piece of clothing *you're* wearing and see SIZE TWO just staring right back at you. Girl, it's amazing. So I knew this week was it. I called Mommy right from the store and told her we were going to that last fitting as soon as I could catch a flight out." I try to picture a size 2 tag staring up at me. That *would* be incredible, because I would probably have a tiny person stuck in the back of my pants, struggling to free herself.

Olivia looks at me, as I am obviously a little speechless. I never, not once, thought about getting gastric bypass. I know it has worked for her, but I can't fathom such a last resort. Not that I'm doing any better. Doing nothing is certainly not something I'm comfortable with, either.

"I have Tuesday off work. We can do it then," I say, sipping my coffee. A flash of recognition of her faux pas passes over Olivia.

"I'm sorry, Maggie. I know you're struggling, and I'm just over here rambling on about size twos and shit like that. Whatta bitch, huh? I'm sorry. Just please give me a little leeway right now, I think I'm going a little nuts, you know? All this wedding stuff. I just never thought it would be this big of a hassle. All of my clients are completely pissed at me, and I haven't worked out in days. I just feel everything slipping away, you know? Just please, don't pay attention to any crazy shit I say, okay? And there'll be plenty, I promise you that. You've got to be the one that holds me steady. Just please keep me grounded through all of this. Please? Plus, I don't even know what you're worrying about anyway—I've always told you you're fine the way you are." Olivia is flipping her cell phone open and closed.

"I know. But a size two would be nice," I say.

"Don't try to be all pity-pot, girl. Let me just run get my Rolodex of stories that prove when it comes to being pitied for getting called fat, you need not apply. Don't make me reenact the *Thar She Blows* night. I will. I'll bend my ass over right now and make you play the parts of those fucking dickheads in that car." Olivia grows angrier and angrier as she remembers that night.

"I know. I just want to look nice at your wedding. I'm not trying to take away your crown, Moby." Olivia smiles, but it quickly fades. It's as if she wants to joke about the good ol' days, but when she actually commits to it, she regrets it immediately.

"So will you come? To Martine's? You're the only one who is

ever honest with me about what looks right on me. Need I bring up the velvet pants?" Olivia quickly changes the subject again. She snaps her phone shut.

I remember those velvet pants. They were a deep navy blue and had a huge embroidered butterfly right across the ass. Olivia wore them constantly throughout the summer before our freshman year in college. As she packed for orientation, I finally broke it to her that the butterfly made her ass look twelve times bigger than it actually was. You couldn't even make out that the embroidery was a butterfly at all. It looked more like an homage to our nation's purple mountains majesty.

Olivia and I stand in silence for the next ten minutes. Her anger is escalating. She paces up and down the steps of the city hall. I sit on the top step and drink my coffee. The morning is crisp, a wonderful reprieve from one of the hottest summers I can remember. Olivia is pacing at the bottom of the steps when a high-end sport utility vehicle pulls up and parks next to her rental car. The woman behind the wheel pulls down her mirror and reapplies her lipstick. Olivia taps her foot and puts her arm at her hip. I push myself into a standing position.

"Olivia! You look amazing!" The woman is just shy of her third face-lift.

"Patrona? You are fifteen minutes late and I have a two-page list of problems with this site. You're not charging me for a full hour, are you?" Olivia asks.

"Of course not. Let's get right to that list." Patrona is a professional. She offers Olivia a Pellegrino from her purse and takes her hand as they enter the city hall gardens.

I trail into the gardens behind them, Pellegrino-less, and behold the setup for an event that evening. Bustling caterers and jumpsuit-clad workmen wind their way around the gardens with various tables and bunches of flowers. The fountain is lit with white pillar candles on silver plates with gardenias floating in bunches on the water. The tables are done in all-white, with large glass bowls of cabbage roses in the center of each. Olivia gasps. She walks through the setup in a daze. There are twinkling white lights winding around every pillar, while bell jars, with a single candle in each, hang from every tree. Patrona and Olivia discuss lighting, flowers, the cake placement, the DJ stand, the dance floor, and the head table. Patrona uses the already setup event as a guide for Olivia, and it works perfectly.

"Mags!" Olivia calls. I snake my way through the tables to find Patrona and her at an obvious focal point.

"This is where the head table is going to be. Can't you just imagine? You and me sitting here—everyone will have a clear view of me, right, Patrona?" Patrona nods excitedly.

"And Adam?" I add.

"Oh my God, of course, Adam." Olivia's voice catches as she tears up. "This is really happening, huh?" I put my hand on her shoulder. Patrona takes a few steps back, sensing our need for privacy.

"Sweetie, are you okay?" I whisper.

"I just never thought it would happen, you know? Remember when I used to walk my fat ass here all by myself every Sunday—hoping there would be a wedding going on? I never thought . . ." Olivia trails off. She pulls a perfect handkerchief from her purse and dabs at her eyes, careful not to let her mascara run.

"Everything is going to be beautiful." I wipe an errant tear away from her face. Olivia smiles and turns once again to where the head table will be.

"You and me at the head table for the whole world to see." Olivia spreads her arms wide and beams at me.

Patrona slinks back over and begins the business of planning the wedding once more. Olivia is checking off items on various lists and passing Patrona color-coordinated card after color-coordinated card. But then suddenly at one point in their tour, Olivia holds up one finger, shushes Patrona, and tells her she is "dismissed." Patrona skulks away as I stand there, mouth open. Who is this person?

That night, Olivia and Adam fly back to Washington, DC. Olivia will then catch a return flight to LA for her final dress fitting. It seems Dr. Farrell didn't want to fly home alone. As I walk Solo, I think about who Olivia is becoming: the night at the restaurant, that whole bit about the size 2s, and how she acted with that event planner. I am confused. I wonder what happened to the fourteen-year-old Olivia who brought a cricket into our homeroom one morning and named him Elmer. Does Olivia think she has to be someone else to marry Adam? She's not fat anymore. How could she think Adam wouldn't love her if he knew about these things? These are the things I love about Olivia. Her humor. Her uniqueness. Her confidence. It's like it's all but disappeared. Her new confidence is somehow forced and disingenuous. How can she not be proud of her own life?

I walk into work a good five minutes early. Cole feigns a heart attack.

"Whatever." I sound like a thirteen-year-old girl when her dad asks her what is the deal with that homework and the little attitude, missy.

I walk into the back room. I am met with the object of my suppressed desires.

"Hey," Domenic says as he stands over the sink.

"I didn't know you were working today," I say. I manage to act calm and cool, pretending not to notice he is wearing a new light blue T-shirt I have never seen before. I have carefully documented his entire wardrobe. I use these observations for the random fantasy when I am not doing so well at the repressed-desire thing. He looks up. I am in physical pain.

"I switched with Dre. I guess there's a big wrestling match on TV tonight and some people are getting together to watch it." Domenic dips each glass in soapy water. His hands are strong and wet. I look away.

"Wrestling, huh? And Cole isn't there?" I say.

"Oh. Well, maybe he doesn't know about it." Domenic is mumbling.

"Cole not know about professional wrestling? You've got to be kidding. Let's make fun of him for having to work tonight and missing out on all of the fun." I turn around and make for the front of the coffeehouse and a bigger rock to throw at my Goliath.

"Did you get the CD I left for you?" Domenic blurts out, not looking at me.

"Oh, yeah. It was amazing," I say, turning back. I wonder if *amazing* is a bit over the top. Now *I'm* mumbling.

"Thanks. Which song did you like the best? I mean, were there any songs you especially . . . um . . . you skipped? I always like to know the songs people skip past." He smiles, but keeps his focus on the dishes and not me.

"I love song four. I put that on an old mix I had way back in the day. I remembered it was a hidden track, but that was definitely a nice surprise. I skipped seven and eight because they're a little too punk rock for my tastes. And where did you get that one song—*that*." I can't help myself.

"The Reverend Horton Heat song?" he says quickly.

I wasn't talking about that song. Who would *ever* talk about that song? I was talking about the other song, *the* song, the one that stopped me dead in my tracks as I packed that night. The song that plays in the background of my every fantasy: Domenic slowly walks toward me, he's a little shy, maybe thinking I don't have the same feelings for him, but he cradles my face in his hands and kisses me gently to *that* song. And this time maybe there is time for edible glitter and feather ticklers. In reality, I realize I am standing in front of Domenic, who is now staring at me. I chicken out. I agree with him that the song I want to pull out of the chorus for its solo is the Reverend Horton Heat song, rather than the sweet ballad.

"Maggie?" I hear Cole from the front of the coffeehouse. Domenic picks up his plastic bin and opens the door for me. Another time, my sweet Romeo. Another time . . . another balcony.

CHAPTER EIGHT

Cottage. Hardwood Floors. Fireplace.

M om provided what she could when we were growing up. She quit her nowhere job and decided to become a lawyer when I was around ten years old. She worked in the law library when she could, but we made ends meet by being on welfare and cutting any corner we could find. Olivia, on the other hand, was from one of the wealthiest families in Pasadena, so I was able to experience things our family could never afford. Mrs. Morten signed me up for camp and paid for it; she took me and Kate to dinner when she knew Mom was studying late. We were members of the Morten family. We never felt like we were too poor to be in their beautiful home.

Mom was my only parent until Russell came into the picture ten years ago. I was young when my father left. Mom got us through while my father went to "find himself." Apparently he never quite tracked himself down because we have yet to hear from him. My mom is, and always was, my own manifestation of God. But even from her, I still feel uncomfortable with too much scrutiny. Attention, like most things, feels tight on me.

"Phone's for you." Cole points to the perched receiver.

Domenic moves past me and heads to the outside tables. I watch him as he stops short and bends to pick up a loose Equal packet.

"Hello?" I ask, but wait, drumroll . . . the suspense is killing me. Ah, the boxers—are those martini glasses? Martini glasses?

"It's Mom."

"Is everything okay?" I try to focus. What would those boxers look like in my house? In my washer and dryer. There I am folding those boxers as he approaches with a small, velvet box.

"You got it. The house on Wilson," Mom blurts out. I am snapped back into reality.

The house: a tiny cottage with picture windows and hardwood floors and creeping vines that make it look right out of the English countryside.

"Holy shit! When did you hear? When did you hear?" I scream.

Cole walks toward the phone and gives me a nonverbal warning for my sailor mouth even though there are no customers in the coffeehouse. *Nonverbal* meaning he zips his mouth and then gives me the finger.

"Marian from the management company called me last night to tell me. She said your credit reports looked great and you can move in Fourth of July weekend."

"Oh my God! Oh my God! Can you believe this?" Another look from Cole shoots my way. I recoil. "Thank you so much . . . oh my God!" I whisper.

It is one of those Vaseline-lens moments. I am a 1950s ten-year-old tomboy with a red baseball cap, striped shirt, and dungarees. I hold my dog after being saved from the rapids and say, through the tears, "We did it, girl . . . we did it." Cole throws me a washrag and grunts at me to clean the counters. Nothing could bring me down off this high. I am free from Faye's indentured servitude.

After work, Mom picks me up and we head over to the new house. Mom and I pull down the street and count down the numbers. We park in front of an aged green archway leading into a courtyard of twelve identical Green and Green Craftsman cottages. The scents of night-blooming jasmine and honeysuckle float through the air as we look for the individual numbers on the homes. The doors are open, and I can hear voices and music playing. We walk past cat after cat after cat. Black and white. Orange and white. Calico. There must be thousands. There it is. Mom and I scamper around the house, looking in windows, measuring the side yard, and trying to figure out wall space to ascertain possible art placement. We are giddy.

"Gh-ello? Can I help you vis somesing?" A small German lady wearing a frilled white skirt and a tight black belt is cautiously approaching us.

"Hi. I . . . uh . . ." I don't know if it is common knowledge that number 12 is being vacated, and I don't want to give out confidential information. More importantly, I don't want to say something that might stand in the way of me getting that cottage. Maybe this German lady has a niece or something. A homeless niece. A homeless, German, cottage-thieving niece.

"We . . . we heard that maybe one of the cottages might be for rent, so we thought we'd take a look at it. I just got off work." I cross my arms and look at Mom, who is writing down measurements.

"Oh, yes. Number twelve, right? How did you find out about zis? Haf zey advertised?"

"Oh, my mom's law firm is in the same office building as the management company. She gave me a heads-up about this place." The minute I say it I know I have made a mistake. Mom smiles absently as her name is mentioned.

"Oh, so dis is how it verks." She tangles her fingers together in this odd mafiosa kind of way. We'll be sleeping with the fishes for sure.

"What? No . . . I just need a place to live, and my mom . . . I mean we heard about this place, so . . ." I grow nervous and once again look to Mom. The German lady is not even a blip on her radar. At least she'll look better in a bathing suit than Faye.

"Can we help you with anything else?" Mom says in her stern attorney voice.

"Vell, good luck vis da house. I vill see you later." Off the little German lady goes. We are left in the courtyard alone again.

"I don't know what Der Führer's problem is, but you'd better watch out for her," Mom says as she walks back over to the porch of the house.

The cottage is stunning. The porch is covered with red bougainvillea and purple clematis. French doors lead inside the living room; windows line every wall of the small house. And I do mean small. The house is a mere 462 square feet, which means it quite possibly could have less space than my current home. The size is the only "flaw" that makes the rent affordable. The tenants are still in the house, but they aren't home this evening. I peer in the living room window, taking it all in. There is a full working fireplace. On the other side of the front room is a built-in buffet. All the woodwork is done in old Craftsman style. There are hardwood floors throughout. A galley kitchen completes my visual tour.

Later, Mom drops me off at home, and I knock on Faye's door. She answers with a sort of grumble. I'm sure this is her version of a greeting to those lesser beings who live in little rented houses that can be packed into thirty-six boxes.

"I want to confirm with you that I will be moving out Fourth of July weekend." I don't breathe the entire time I speak.

"You have to sign a letter that Stan is writing saying you

offered to move out in such a short time." She speaks through her metal screen. I feel the constant urges to snatch her through the metal pinholes.

"I'm not signing anything, Faye." My mom's a lawyer; I barely sign greeting cards anymore. I begin to turn away. I'm not going to fight with her. As a matter of fact, I have already taken pictures of the damn bulldozer and documented every crazy-ass thing Faye has done over the years.

"Well, Stan'll bring it back when he's done and you can take a look at it." She is now emerging from behind her black security door. I feel honored until I see her tiny pink terry-cloth robe. It doesn't quite fit and seems to separate at the only portion of her anatomy that hasn't been exposed to years of California sun. I shudder.

"Faye, I have not, nor will I ever, sign anything you put in front of me. I didn't sign a rental agreement and I'm not signing a forty-eight-hour eviction agreement. I'm moving out and that's that." I approach her straight on, my breath quickening. My fists tighten and my shoulders rise. Faye perches herself on one leg as she itches the back of the other with the disfigured yellowing toenails I always refer to as "The Kraken." I continue.

"Furthermore, since you're tearing the house down, I won't be cleaning it before I leave." Faye nonchalantly closes her robe, cutting off my view of the gates of hell. I continue, "And I'll sign a letter confirming that."

I stand there just long enough. Faye leans against the doorjamb in all her glory, highball in one hand and *TV Guide* in the other. What could she possibly be thinking? Why am I standing here waiting? I am paralyzed.

"Well, Stan'll bring it back anyway."

CHAPTER NINE

Who's That Big Fat Girl, Mummy?

Following Olivia's directions to some elite bridal salon in the thick of Los Angeles, I feel like a traitor. This is the biggest event of my best friend's life and I can't seem to get invested in it.

In the beginning, Olivia used to carry her "before" picture around in her wallet, proudly showing off her incredible weight loss. But, she confided to me one night, she had gotten rid of the picture after noticing that the people who'd seen it looked at her differently—as if she were somehow flawed. She felt she was no longer perfect in their eyes. So she set about building a history of the Olivia Morten who stood before them now. The Olivia Morten her co-workers came to know played competitive tennis, was homecoming queen twice running, and did some catalog modeling on the side during college. It served no purpose, she argued, to tell them the true stories of our adolescence, because they all had to do with our isolation and humiliation or take place in a drive-through. But those stories show our determination to survive and how we leaned on each other during those times. Our history *is* that woman getting stuck in the booth at the restaurant. Still, it's all being taken down frame by frame. Apparently, Olivia told her mom to get rid of all the pictures of when she was fat before Adam came for his first visit. Mrs. Morten has rid her shelves of all our pictures, whether Olivia's fat is in them or not. Sometimes I don't feel up to being in this new life of hers.

I remember the first time I met Dr. Adam Farrell. Olivia had dropped his name a few times, and I had a good feeling about him. I had a crush on a boy named Adam in college. My Adam wore a red suit to graduation. Whether this was Olivia's Adam or the memories I had of my red-suited Adam, I liked him the moment I heard Olivia mention him in passing.

Olivia was invited to his parents' house for their annual Halloween get-together where the invited guests ooh and ahh at the sons and daughters of some of Washington, DC's, best-heeled citizens. Adam is the child of two university professors. His mother teaches Byzantine architecture; his father teaches philosophy. Adam reads the *Washington Post* in the morning while he holds court at some of the most erudite DC tables.

I flew in to DC on that Halloween weekend despite my fear of flying. I arrived just after the big holiday get-together was over. I called her, a little drunk and slightly hysterical from my flight. We planned to meet in Georgetown. I stood on the corner by one of her favorite bars and watched as Olivia frantically pointed to Dr. Adam Farrell in the car behind her.

"He wanted to come," Olivia gushed.

"Is this *the* Adam?" I asked.

"What do you think of him? Isn't he gorgeous! How is this even a guy I'm dating, you know? He's even more beautiful than Ben Dunn and Shane Presky combined!" Shane Presky was the guy Olivia lusted after in college. He was a world-champion swimmer who went on to medal in the Olympics. Needless to say, Shane Presky didn't know Olivia existed. She continued.

"How do I look? Oh my God, the party, I have to tell you . . . isn't he amazing? I am so glad you're here. What if this is the beginning? I just want to fly him back to Pasadena right now and show him off, you know. I can't believe a guy who looks like that is . . . you know . . . willing to be seen with me. Go out with *me*?" Olivia was talking so fast. Where was this coming from?

She would have gone on and on, but Adam had left his car unattended and was inching his way up to us to see what the holdup was.

"What's going on?" Adam was unreal. Looking at him was like seeing a celebrity in real life—you just can't believe how beautiful they are. Oddly, he looked nothing like my red-suited Adam from college.

"Oh, we were plotting out our night . . ." Olivia was speaking so fast it sounded more like, *O, we'replodnight.* But we all got the gist.

"You must be Maggie. I can't tell you how much I've heard about you," he said, extending his hand. I felt faint at the prospect of touching him.

Adam's handshake was weak. Still, I thought, You're the one. He was the man in our fantasies. Gorgeous. Successful. Intelligent. You're the one who's going to take my best friend away.

I finally pull into the parking lot of Martine's Bridal Salon. Olivia and her mom are waiting by their car in front of a corner coffee shop because Martine's is not open yet. Paulette Morten is the absolute embodiment of the Pasadena ideal. Her Barbara Walters blond hair is perfectly coiffed. Her face is pulled a little tight, yet the crow's-feet around her eyes remain pronounced. She hates it, but it's my favorite thing about her. She wears only St. John suits with matching Ferragamo handbags and shoes. Paulette Morten never leaves the house without her organizer, a lunch date at the Valley Hunt Club, and her ex-husband's credit cards.

Mr. Hobbs Morten, not present today, is a businessman based in Los Angeles. I've met him twice: once at Olivia's high school graduation and once at her college graduation. I don't think anyone really knows what Mr. Hobbs Morten does for a living except that he makes lots and lots of money. I've never really thought much of him at all. I'd like to say that he was this imposing character with a reddened face and cigar dangling— but he's not. Mr. Hobbs Morten looks like our accountant. He's now shorter than I am and is slightly balding. His face is pale, and he always looks worried. I remember when Olivia told me he was going to be at the high school graduation. I imagined a cartoonish Boss Hogg character rolling across our football field in a white Cadillac with bullhorns mounted on the front grille. Instead, he drove a Japanese import, wore a red bow tie, and was all around quite pleasant. Mr. and Mrs. Morten were divorced when Olivia was eleven years old. Ever since then, Olivia doesn't talk about him or his new family. I do know he is invited to Olivia's wedding, but nothing untoward will take place because Paulette Morten surely would have none of that.

We decide to have a small breakfast before the big day. Upon entering the coffee shop, I catch a glance of myself in one of the mirrors. They have many. I now hate this coffee shop. I lean into Olivia as we wait in line.

"I'm not eating today." I say. "I had this vision of the wedding pictures." Years from now, Olivia sits with her towheaded children-of-the-corn kids reminiscing about her wedding day. She pulls out the wedding album and the room falls silent. "Who's that big fat girl, Mummy?" one of her children says in a Dickensian British accent, pointing at me in the photograph. "She frightens me, I shall have bad dreams if we have to keep looking at her." Olivia closes the wedding album forever, tousling her child's hair. At that, they all scamper out to their rose garden to have high tea.

"I know, huh? Just be glad you're not the one who has to try on your wedding dress in less than an hour. I haven't eaten in days," Olivia says, waving off the muffin her mom is offering.

The bridal shop is an emporium of white dresses. Dresses saddled with so many hopes and fears, perfect bodies, perfect weddings, and even more perfect marriages. Olivia has made an appointment, or rather Mrs. Morten has made this final fitting appointment. We are led over to our space.

This space is my own personal hell. There are mirrors everywhere: to the side of you, to the back of you, to the front of you. Every possible angle. The bride stands on a small platform in front of everyone and presents herself for inspection. I catch glimpses of my body from the side, from the back, and from the front. Every possible angle. I dry-heave. All I can see is my Area. I have completely forgotten Olivia is trying on her wedding dress. I have completely forgotten there is anyone else in the room.

"Maggie?" Mrs. Morten asks. "Love, can you run and get a disposable camera? Adam has got to see this." She stands in front of me. Where did she come from? Why isn't there yet another mirror directly in front of me?

"Sure." I gather my purse and take a twenty-dollar bill from her.

Olivia is in the fitting room being pinned and sewn into a size 2. She will be a size 2 for her wedding. Where will I be? Olivia has not spoken to me since we entered the bridal salon. Part of me knows she still fears this mirrored, platformed performance space as much as I do.

I return with the disposable camera to find my best friend

standing on a platform looking like a fairy princess. She is stunning. There is a crowd forming around her. Olivia is magnetic. She is the envy of everyone around her: the maids of honor who are here for support, the brides who will try on their dresses for their big day, and the teary-eyed moms who stand back gazing at their grown-up girls. Olivia is the perfect bride. I snap a picture.

I watch Olivia stand and twirl. She's staring at herself in the mirror. Is she blown away, too? She's probably used to looking at her perfect body by now, but all dressed up in a wedding gown has got to be something of a mind fuck even for her. Still, somewhere in this process the magnetic Olivia becomes the barking-orders, condescending Olivia, shooing people away with a royal flick of her hand. There is a collective sigh of relief from the entire bridal salon. At least that pretty girl in the size 2 is a bitch. They wouldn't know how to deal with Olivia if she were friendly and self-effacing. Instead, she gives everyone in the store exactly what they want: a common enemy.

Mrs. Morten has taken over the role of photographer. It didn't hold my attention. I have spent the first hour running around grabbing pins and telling Olivia how the dress looks from every angle. At one point she asked me at what angle it looked the most like a size 2. I had to bite my tongue to keep from saying *The one staring down at the tag.* I'm no longer in on conferences regarding the dress. I'm reduced to giving thumbs-up or thumbs-down. But no one really minds one way or the other what my thumb is doing. I could shove it up my ass for all anyone cares.

Mrs. Morten is snapping pictures from every angle. My new game is avoiding being in the background of any of the snapshots. After that gets old, I start watching the girl by Olivia. I noticed her when I came back with the disposable camera. She is

quite heavy and holds it all in her middle. I know Olivia spotted
her as well. It's the reason she's positioned herself four platforms
away. Once again, it's the Fat Entity Theory. As in any subculture, there is a pecking order among the overweight ranks.
Those afflicted with the disease of obesity constantly compare
themselves with other overweight people, the perennial question being whether they are as fat as that woman or this other
unfortunate girl. And being in close proximity with another of
your overweight brethren doesn't bring you comfort. Quite the
contrary. It brings shame and backbiting. No one wants to shop
in the second-floor Plus Size department—the proverbial Fat
Girl HQ. And once you no longer have to shop there—like the
welfare line or traffic school—you want to forget you were ever
there. This is the club that Olivia has distanced herself from.
She doesn't want to be among the alumni. She doesn't want the
monthly flyer. She wants nothing to do with the culture of being
fat anymore. And really, who can blame her? I wear my mem-
bership with shame—covered up with coffeehouse aprons and
untouched by human hands.

Today, Olivia must do the unthinkable: try on her wedding
dress next to a woman of size without imagining people are
comparing her with the girl on the next platform. The overweight bride's maid of honor is snapping pictures of her day as
well. The maid of honor is dressed in funky fashions that look
thrift store vintage but actually cost more than new clothes. She
and the mother of the bride, who weighs about a hundred
pounds wringing wet and who's ravishing in a white-and-black
Chanel suit, look on and commiserate about the outcome of this
session. They fret about the outcome of this session. What are
they to do? The dress they ordered came in the wrong size and
there's only six weeks until the big day, I overhear. They can't
order another dress like this in her size and guarantee it will

arrive on time. The girl stands on the viewing platform and is silent.

I watch her. She is me. Bridal shop workers run to find bigger sizes. When she emerges from the fitting room, there is no celebration, no thumbs-up. Just someone to quickly throw a shawl over her shoulders, an accessory they feel is a must. Sometimes she emerges with her girdle fully visible in the back because some dresses can't be buttoned at all. Then the call comes.

"Go get the next size up!" Martine herself cries, with chiffon wrap in one hand and a tape measure in the other.

What young girl imagines her wedding day as a fat bride? How many months passed during which she told herself she would lose weight? I identify with the look of horror on her face as she tries not to act like she's dying a little each time a dress doesn't fit. I identify while at the same time distancing myself from her in every way. You smile for your mom and best friend and suck it up. They assure you the dress looks great. But there's always a beautiful girl next to you who has the salon helpers ogling her. The beautiful girl they never once hand a wrap.

CHAPTER TEN

Most Like a Supermodel

Once in an English class at Cal, the assignment of the day was to write about your favorite place. I sat there, unable to think of anything. I looked around at all the smug faces of the other students who couldn't wait to tell everyone about sitting on a porch in some chair their grandfather whittled or standing under the great oak where they received their first kiss. Then it came to me. I was most happy while driving in my car. What does it say about me that my favorite place is en route to somewhere else?

"Hey there, Christina, how's everything going?" I walk into work early and find myself in a good mood because of it.

I don't know what it is about Christina. I want so badly to get along with her to prove to myself that I'm not a skinny-woman hater. Just because someone has a great body doesn't mean I have to insult her or think her inferior. Christina Dahl is turning out to be a tough one, however.

"I applied for this acting school, like, to help my career." Christina's "career" consists of some morally questionable fashion shoots on an assortment of chrome-plated vintage cars where her only direction was to "look hot."

"Oh, that's great. When will you find out if you got in?" My voice is high and forced.

"Yeah, I got in . . . I said I applied." Christina stops and puts her hands on the rim of the sink. "I don't know why people have to be such bitches sometimes."

"Are you having problems with someone?" You stereotypical tart.

"My best friend started all these, like, rumors about me. I know it's just because she thinks I'm jealous of her and her boyfriend."

"And you're not?" I ask.

"Fuck, no. Her boyfriend is like this hairy guy with clothes, you know . . ."

"Yes, people with clothes can be very disconcerting."

"It's, like, not even about that, you know. I mean if she really had something, like, going on that was good, I would be jealous." I finish tying my apron around my waist and pull out my T-shirt.

"But that's hard to find," she continues in a quiet voice, whisking her bangs out of her face.

I stop. Has Christina Dahl said something mildly insightful and touching? Can she be one of us underneath?

"You'd be jealous of a man like that, of a relationship like that?" I ask.

"Who wouldn't? I mean, like, most guys I go out with are much older, you know? Sometimes I think *they* think all I'm about is being sexy. I *was* voted Most Like a Supermodel at my last acting school." Christina has told me that nugget of information ten times since the big election. I have already drafted my letter to the Better Business Bureau regarding an acting school that has elections with categories such as this priceless example.

I only have seconds before Cole notices I am gone and about thirty minutes before Domenic comes in for his shift. To be seen back here chatting up Christina Dahl would definitely be something. Maybe I can learn from The John Sheridan. I am doing charity work. I will look at my relationship with Christina as a bit of mentoring volunteer work. Wouldn't it be great if she turned out to be a girl who isn't all caught up in her looks, who believed herself to be intelligent and good at other things rather than showing off her midriff and ass crack at the drop of a hat . . . a hat, a spoon, a leaf from an autumn tree . . . hell, at the drop of a mention from some frat boy wanting to see some ass. Enough. I am not jealous. I will find the good in Christina Dahl. Underneath that tiny, barely clothed figure there is a girl who just wants to be accepted and loved, to have somebody hold her hand as she lies dying. I will find our common ground.

"I'd better get on out there. You know Cole." Maybe later. That common ground will still be common tomorrow.

Christina begins to get the mop bucket out of the bathroom. She has to make the back room look perfect before Domenic arrives. Once again, she has fallen behind. She looks hesitant. I get a sudden wave of energy to start my mentoring right now, so I stop a second before I walk out.

"Your best friend sounds like she may be a little jealous of you," I say. "She knows you disapprove of her relationship and thinks it's the one thing she's got that you don't. Just try to understand where she's coming from. Women can be especially cruel to each other, you know, and jealousy is usually at the root."

"Well, I know she's jealous of me. I mean . . ." Christina trails off and traces the outline of her figure as proof. "But that doesn't mean she has to be a complete bitch about it."

Fucking conceited ass . . . this is going to be harder than I thought.

I shake my head, push open the door into the coffeehouse, and wonder how it is that a brainless twit like Christina has such confidence and I, a worthy candidate for it, have nary a speck. I never think anyone is jealous of me, except maybe bulimics and anorexics for eating anything I want and keeping it down. But this girl just walks around knowing people want to be her.

I remember Kate telling me a story about when she enrolled Emily in ballet class at the Pasadena Athletic Club. Kate was told to bring Emily to class in full ballet togs so she could hop around for an hour with a former ballerina named Miss Janie. Upon their arrival, Kate was horrified to see that all the other little girls were wearing little black leotards and pink tights. Emily, on the other hand, was in pink from head to toe, including her tutu and sparkling wand. Kate turned to Emily thinking her daughter would be humiliated.

"Sweetie, are you okay?" Kate asked gently.

"Yes, Mommy, I'm fine," she said. "I hope all the other girls are okay with what *they're* wearing." And into class she walked, sparkling wand in the air, to greet Miss Janie.

I want to be like that. I want to be seven years old again. I want to go back to the day my confidence left me and was replaced by an apology.

"I found a place," I say to Cole.

"Where?" Cole is going through the pastry shelves in search of the perfect victim.

"Pasadena. A house. A tiny house, but it's got a great vintage look to it. You know, woodwork, a fireplace, and hardwood floors. The whole shot."

"Oh yeah? Sounds nice." Cole is pulling out a piece of mocha chocolate cake and a piece of cheesecake.

"Sounds nice? What it sounds like is a goddamn miracle."

"Hey, sailor. Watch the mouth, okay? I said it sounds nice." Cole is now putting two pieces of cake, two scoops of Fossel-man's chocolate ice cream, and whole milk into a blender.

"I'm moving Fourth of July weekend," I announce as I pour my nightly cup of decaf coffee into my favorite porcelain mug.

"You're moving?" Domenic asks, walking in fifteen minutes early.

"Oh, yeah . . . I got thrown out of my old place and found a great new one. I'm moving in Fourth of July weekend." Wanting to act suave, I keep the porcelain mug at my lips. Somehow, in my mind, this seems European.

"Independence Day, huh?" Domenic strides past me into the backroom.

"Yeah, Independence Day!" I shriek, as Domenic walks out of earshot.

I decide to clean the toppings area by the ice cream case before Cole tells me to. I will begin refilling the sprinkles, nuts, and cookie bits, which are all coincidentally stored in the back room. Where Domenic is. Heh.

I stack four jelly jars of ice cream toppings on top of each other and push through the back room door butt-first. Butt-first? I have obviously gone temporarily insane. The door swings shut behind me. I set the jars on the metal rack that holds the dish dryer, extra ice cream cones, and all of the delectable topping refillables.

"Hey, there." Domenic is sitting outside with the back room door open. Domenic is comfortable sitting with his latest novel and a soda in one of those 1950s brown plastic cups.

"Hey there, whatcha reading?" I glance at Christina, who is now bending over, dustpan in hand, sweeping up the last bits of trash on the ground. I glare at her ass. I sneak a look at Domenic. Is he looking? Is this the ass of his dreams? Does it matter that this perfect ass is connected to an insipid, arrogant tart?

"*Darkness Visible*? William Styron?" Domenic flips the book to reveal the cover.

"Oh." I've never heard of it and have no idea who he's talking about. I am silent.

"So are you excited about moving?" Domenic continues.

"Absolutely. It's kind of magical. The house is beautiful. Just beautiful." I am now the type of person who uses words like *magical*. This is new.

"What makes it so good?" Domenic sets his book down.

"Nothing. Well, not nothing. I mean, it's pretty boring stuff, you know. Like girl stuff." I look to Christina. She blankly stares back at me with the eyes of a circling shark. I once asked her how she decorated her bedroom at her parents' house. She said she loved matching black, white, and red. "Kinda like those pictures at hair salons."

"Makes sense." Domenic takes a sip of his soda as punctuation and picks his book back up.

"Boring stuff like hardwood floors and a fireplace," I almost yell.

"It has a fireplace?" Domenic turns the page.

"Yeah. The house is tiny. It's four hundred sixty-two square feet. But it's big enough for one person. You know, and my dog. The rent's okay, a little more than I was paying, but definitely worth it, considering." I have finished refilling the toppings. Now I find myself wiping down the metal rack itself.

Peregrine walks through the door right on time for her shift.

She gives me a big thumbs-up as I talk to Domenic. My face turns bright red and I feel like I have feathers sticking out of my mouth—like I've been caught. At what—I still don't know. Flirting? Behaving like a woman? Blocking Christina's perfect ass from Domenic's view?

CHAPTER ELEVEN

Sam

M adonna's "Crazy for You" was playing in the background at Bellis Music Camp's farewell dance. I played a mean viola. He was first-chair upright bass. The only problem with my fantasy evening was we were wearing the same charming outfit—plaid shirt and khaki pants. If we'd danced together that evening, we would have looked like an old couple celebrating their fiftieth anniversary at a hoedown somewhere in the Midwest. But we didn't dance. As I lurked on the fringes, he sat on a piano bench oblivious to my affections, sipping his yellow-colored drink from a Dixie cup. That was the last time I spent my birthday with a guy. Technically, he didn't even know it.

"Christina? Cole says you can go home. Domenic will finish anything you didn't get to," Peregrine says.

Christina unties her apron and meets her waiting flock of model-actress friends in the coffeehouse as Cole beckons Domenic. I am alone in the back room with Peregrine. Her face is drawn, and I am uncomfortable with having to ask her what's the matter. You don't do that with Peregrine. Well, I don't do that with Peregrine.

"So Movie Night, huh? What made you choose Garland and Streisand? Remember when they sang together that one time and Judy was all hopped up and grabbing on Barbra? Funny, huh? Hey, is Inez going to be there?" As I babble, Peregrine is rummaging through the medicine cabinet in the employee bathroom. She pulls the dental floss from behind the mouthwash.

Peregrine and Inez met at a Gay Pride parade. Inez was at a booth gathering signatures in support of gay marriage. Peregrine was "dressed" as Lady Godiva on the back of a white horse completely naked, save the long blond wig.

"I went to my grandparents' last night and brought Inez," Peregrine says. I can barely understand her through the act of flossing and for one second think she's said that she fucked her girlfriend in front of her grandparents.

"Oh?" I hesitate.

"I was finally going to introduce her as my girlfriend. I e-mailed my mom and told her, but she couldn't care less. But my grandparents, that's a different story." Peregrine never talks about her mother—though everyone knows that this little move out west was not about running to something. It was more about running from someone.

"So what happened?" This is my stock conversation filler. Peregrine may love to talk about herself, but she demands active listening. If I don't make some attempt at a proper reaction, Peregrine will assume the story is dull and either add more hyperbole or pepper the narrative with juicier details. This could add hours to an already lengthy tale.

"They're the only family I really give a shit about . . . so." Peregrine walks outside and lights a cigarette.

"What happened?" I ask.

"I totally backed out and introduced her as my friend, 'like sisters.'" Peregrine takes a drag. She looks off into the distance.

"So what happened?"

"I'm all right. Inez is a little . . . unhappy. She's been out to her family for years, and she thinks I'm embarrassed about us. That couldn't be farther from the truth. I just don't know how my grandparents are going to take it, and I can't risk it. What if . . . I can't imagine not having them in my life. Something about that made me think of you and Domenic."

She said *you and Domenic* like we're a couple. I think I'm missing the point here. Peregrine continues.

"That moment where I lied to my grandparents. That one moment—maybe two seconds—that's how you've lived your whole life so far." As a closeted lesbian?

"What?" I ask.

"You have feelings for Domenic."

"Maybe." I think about the sheet of paper next to my telephone that harbors my elaborate doodles. Mrs. Maggie Brown. Mrs. Margaret Thompson-Brown. Mrs. Margaret Brown. Mr. and Mrs. Domenic Brown. Domenic. Domenic. Domenic. Domenic and Maggie. Maggie and Domenic.

"So go after him. What are you so afraid of?"

"Nothing." Everything.

"Is this the whole sex thing?"

"Hey, I've been with someone, you know." I start biting my nails.

"Ten seconds with the great mathematician doesn't count." My face goes bright red. Peregrine continues, "Would you do me a favor?"

"Sure." I think she's going to ask me to stock the straws.

"You get your eyebrows done over at that spa on Green, right?" Peregrine is digging through her pockets as her cigarette dangles from her mouth.

"And pedicures," I brag.

"Look, if you refuse to get yourself laid, will you at least go over there and get a massage? Maybe that'll stir something up." Peregrine pulls the pencil from behind her ear and writes down a name and direct line on a piece of paper she pulls from her pocket. Another direct line. Great.

I take the paper.

"Sam? Do I have to get naked in front of her?" I stutter.

"Just go. Tell me when you've made the appointment." Peregrine puts the pencil back behind her ear and gets up from the table.

I follow Peregrine as she opens the door to go back into the coffeehouse. Christina is there introducing Domenic to all her model-actress friends. He looks uncomfortable but steady. He is shaking hands and smiling. The girls are happy to meet him. One especially aggressive Jezebel has her hand on his elbow as she talks to him. He looks down at her fingers. He is charming in that unavailable quiet way that makes you think he doesn't give a shit about anything. What could be more attractive? I walk behind the counter and help the next customer. Cole is sipping espresso, staring at the girls. Peregrine walks behind me and pours herself a cup of coffee.

At closing time, Cole opens the front door long enough to let the three of us out while he sets the alarm for the night. Peregrine, Domenic, and I sit on the benches in front of Joe's. There is so much subtext that no one says anything. We are all having conversations with ourselves when Peregrine interrupts.

"So are you guys going to be able to make it to my birthday party on Thursday? I booked the roof of the Pasadena Museum of California Art—pretty amazing, huh? You did get your invitations, right?" The theme of the party is the 1980s. All of Peregrine's parties must be themed. The invitation was amazing. It was a hand-painted wooden box that had been decoupaged with magazine articles from the decade. Once you opened the wooden box, you were met with a puff of white powder and a rolled-up dollar bill. Peregrine, being the current-events maven that she is, never once thought that in today's political climate sending a wooden box filled with white powder might not be the best idea. Nonetheless, after several false alarms to the FBI, guests could find all the party information printed on the dollar bills. Even with that buildup, I had forgotten about the party until right now. I never put it together that our birthdays are within weeks of each other.

Aaargh—I had completely forgotten about my impending birthday. Twenty-eight. The march of time isn't quite so daunting as the day itself. I can handle New Year's Eve. I've convinced myself I don't mind spending that holiday alone. I tell people it's "spiritual" for me to ring in the New Year alone. And in a way, it's actually true. But birthdays? Everyone asks what you're doing. You can't use the old spiritual, alone thing for some reason. Luckily, my family throws a huge birthday celebration for me, my sister, and my stepdad, Russell, because all our birthdays are within days of each other. I'll go to the party alone. But then I'll go home by myself—again. Another year.

"Yeah, that sounds fun," I say.

"Yep." Domenic is sitting straight-legged with his backpack on, arms behind his head.

"So you guys will be there?" Peregrine asks.

"I move that weekend, but it may be a nice last fling on that side of town," I say.

"Do you need help moving?" Domenic asks.

Did he just say what I think he said? Did he just fucking say what I think he said?

"W-w-what?" I stutter.

"Moving? Do you need any extra help? I have that weekend off," Domenic says.

Peregrine blows out a shaft of smoke.

"That sounds great. I don't have that much stuff. I asked my family, but I could absolutely use more help. So, gosh, thank you . . . that's super . . . supercool of you." I have never used the word *super* in any conversation, let alone *supercool*. How the word *gosh* made its way into my vocabulary is a whole other conversation.

"Well, we'll talk about it on Thursday night at Peregrine's party, okay?" He looks me dead in the eye and smiles. Then he wraps his hands around his backpack straps and walks to his car parked in back of the coffeehouse.

"Wow," I say.

"So gosh . . . thank you . . . that's supercool of you," Peregrine mocks.

"I've been here before. This is just about being a friend."

"How?"

"I've known Domenic for almost a year now and he's never made any kind of move," I reason.

"You mean like asking if you need help moving? Like something as overt as that? Unthinkable!"

"It's not as easy for some of us. I'm not saying this in some kind of sad-sack way, either. Sometimes people just don't like you that way. Mason was a complete aberration." Peregrine looks confused. "The ten-second mathematician has a name, you know." I continue, "It's not all flowers and boyfriends for some people. I'm not being shitty about myself, it's just . . . it's just how things are for me."

"You make it that way. You and I are not so different."

"I know I'm a good person, but I think if you put me and

Christina in front of Domenic, his instinct would be to choose Christina."

"Have you ever asked yourself the same question?"

"What are you talking about?"

"If you had the chance, would you choose to be Christina?"

To be Fatty or Bobo.

"If you can't even choose yourself, how can anyone else?"

With that, Peregrine takes the knife out of my back, gives me a kiss on the cheek, and walks out into the dark of the night.

CHAPTER TWELVE

Golden

I don't know if I'll ever be ready for Domenic. I don't know what I'll do if he leans across the bed like Mason Phelps, the ten-second mathematician, did. There was an innocence to Mason that I understood. A newness that I knew he was feeling as strongly as I was. His pale chest and textbooks helped me see him as somehow harmless. Domenic is not harmless. While he appears vulnerable, there is a definite feeling that lets you know he knows what he's doing. And unlike poor Mason, ten seconds would hardly describe anything Domenic would be capable of.

It's eight thirty at night and I'm alone. Peregrine is right. *I* would choose Christina over me. What I wouldn't give to throw on a pair of jeans, look at myself in the mirror, and *not* roll my eyes.

The phone rings. I wipe away my tears and gently push a worried Solo away.

"Hello?" I ask.

"Hey there, girl." It's Olivia.

"Hey, how's the wedding?"

"Great, great. Patrona took Mommy through a big tasting

dinner and she could not stop talking about it. I got a proof of the centerpieces from Patrona, they're gorgeous, by the by, and I got the last of the measurements from Martine. Say hello to a size two, girl. The photographer we met with is sending over proofs of her work and I just couldn't be happier." She finally takes a breath and asks, "What's going on down there?"

I need my best friend. The only thing I feel is frustration. Frustration at dooming this crush before it even gets off the ground. Here it is the most important time of her life. I feel embarrassed at how I am behaving. For one second, could this conversation just be about Olivia's wedding?

"Boy trouble," I say. Obviously not.

"Who is it? I'm not breathing, by the way." Olivia doesn't miss a beat.

"His name is Domenic." She now knows.

"Domenic. Damn, that just sounds fine. Either tell me more about him or get me a brown paper bag to breathe into."

"Yeah, well. He's twenty-eight, lives with like four hundred people in a tiny loft in downtown LA, and is a sculptor of some kind. Makes tiny hands and heads, or something," I reveal.

"What? Tiny heads?" she asks.

"A dollmaker. His grandmother and mother are dollmakers . . . it's a family business. He's really a sculptor, but he does the doll thing, too. Dolls?" I say.

"Are you . . . I mean, do you feel weird about this? Did you not want to tell me about him? He sounds perfect for you. If one of his little sculpty heads breaks, you can get right in there and fix it. What's going on here?"

"I just . . . I don't know . . . he's beautiful. Tall. But I just look at him and get terrified . . . I mean he still buses tables. Just watching him walk around with that plastic bin . . . I don't know . . . it freaks me out. He's basically running the doll business with his grandmother. I guess he does the hands and feet. He says no one can do faces like his grandmother. I don't know. For all of Mason Phelps or even Texas Steven's shit, they were able to . . . I don't know . . . do man things. I don't know if Domenic can do that stuff."

"Was Texas Steven a fucking lumberjack or something?" Olivia asks.

"He was golden."

"Maggie?"

"His hair, remember that? It wasn't brown or blond—it was naturally golden. And the body . . ."

"Maggie?"

I am silent. Golden.

"Mags . . . come back to me." Olivia laughs.

"Not the same with Mason Phelps . . . more Steven—you know, more . . . I don't know how to explain it." I am caught once more in the goldenness of Texas Steven.

"You know why Mason doesn't affect you like Texas Steven?"

"He wasn't golden?"

"No—remember the concert?" Olivia is silent. Waiting.

"Yes." I don't want to talk about it. It was traumatizing.

"And?"

"I saw . . . I saw . . ." I can't say it.

"You saw Mason Phelps air-humping the stage."

"Yes. Yes. I think he thought it was dancing. But it wasn't. It wasn't, Olivia. It was so far from dancing. And then I pictured Saint Patrick's Day and . . . well, you know." We both fail to control the giggles that ensue.

"You do this all the time. When someone stops being this perfect man, you pick something completely random and decide it's a deal breaker. Remember John Sheridan?"

"John Sheridan was plain stupid and only parroted back whatever Caroline Pond said earlier that day."

"But it's the same deal. He was always that stupid, you just turned him into this huge fantasy. When you found out who he really was, you weren't interested anymore. See what I'm saying? And he wasn't half as good looking as you made him out to be, by the way."

"Well, he's no Ben Dunn, I guess."

"Who is? Oh right—my Adam!" Olivia shrieks with delight. I am silent.

"Do you see what I'm saying?" Olivia continues.

"A little."

"What about Owen Lynch?"

"What about him?"

"Why did you stop liking him?"

"He had that booger hanging out that one time." Come on. A booger. Who wouldn't be repulsed by that?

"That alien you slept with?"

"His name was fucking Bobby Bol, for the love of God."

"And Adam—your red-suited Adam from college?"

"You remember when he wore those black basketball shorts—and he had those white-white legs, and his leg hair was really black. You *must* remember that."

"See where I'm going with this?"

"What does this have to do with Domenic?"

"I think you're doing it again. You're holding him up to a standard no one can live up to, except men who never, I guess, become ungolden—or something."

"I don't know."

"Is he nice?"

"Yes."

"Is he cute?"

"Yes."

"Well, then?"

"I don't know," I say.

And I don't. Apparently, I don't know anything.

CHAPTER THIRTEEN

We Wouldn't Want Any Skyrocketing Going On

I've always imagined Olivia's wedding as the high point of our friendship—two fat girls finally making good. I have visions of toasting with champagne and dancing until all hours to old Salt-n-Pepa jams. I've been a bridesmaid twice. When Mom married Russell, I cried like a baby. At Kate and Vincent's wedding I wore white Converse All Stars and made funny faces in all the wedding pictures. I have played the roles of daughter and little sister well. Olivia's wedding will be the first wedding where I finally get to play the role of a grown-up.

During a pause in our phone conversation, I have flashbacks comparing Mason with new visions of Domenic. Not bad. Then Olivia wastes no time in getting down to the business of the wedding. Once again she breaks out the checklists, color-coordinated card files, and three-ring binders. Maybe I missed the boat on what our fat-girl zenith would be like. In my fantasy, Mary Benicci is catering the affair while she shouts at poor Shannon Shimasaki for eating all the puff pastries. Now I see that the reality is all this organization and planning. It's just plain drudgery. My fantasy world has succumbed to the harsh realities of best friend bridezillas who want to put a spotlight on my Area.

Olivia's begging me to fly out to DC for another engagement party where we'll plan her bridal shower. "Can't you just fly out on Friday and get back early Sunday? You can move Sunday afternoon. I planned a cocktail party on Saturday night for all the girls. Friday you can have to yourself. Adam has a dinner with the head of his department, so you would only have to come out for the cocktail party. Please? I just really need you right now." Am I supposed to spend hundreds of dollars on plane tickets, anti-anxiety pills, bottles and bottles of vodka and Valium, just to come out for one cocktail party?

"I can't do it. I'm moving. It's not like I can do that another weekend. Why don't you give me these girls' e-mail addresses or phone numbers and I'll call them and set up your shower that way?" I am wondering how our cute little chat about my Domenic suddenly turned into me flying to Washington, DC?

"No, that's fine. I'll just tell them you're busy. Maybe I'll ask another one of the girls to help plan the shower. *Gwen* is flying out. She asked after you." Olivia throws what she knows to be the final blow.

Olivia met Gwen Charles when Olivia interviewed for an internship at one of the top talent agencies in Los Angeles after she graduated from Cal. Gwen is the personification of perfect. She is about five foot one and weighs about—and I'm guessing here—five, okay maybe six pounds. Her hair is almost black and cut in the height of style by someone with one name. Olivia didn't get the job (the CEO's daughter did, what can you do?), but she did find a lifelong fan in Gwen—her first "real" friend after the bypass surgery and after Olivia rid herself of her wallet-size "before" picture. Gwen got Olivia interested in public relations and still lives in Los Angeles as a talent agent. Throughout our early twenties, I was not included more times than I'd like to remember in Olivia's impromptu meetings with Gwen. Something about Gwen makes me competitive.

"Gwen?" I ask. I can hear the opening chords of "Do Not Forsake Me" in the background. It's High Noon. Gwen and I are standing on opposite sides of the ghost town, fingers tickling the ivory handles of our six-shooters, dueling for Olivia and her friendship.

"Yeah. *She's* flying out for the cocktail party. Maybe she can help me plan the shower. No one is going to do it as well as you, but maybe she can get us a little farther along," Olivia says.

"Sure, she can help, but we've been talking about your bridal shower for fifteen years. I'm sorry I can't make it, but I would still like to be a part of this whole thing." I'm becoming upset.

"Well, we'll see. Have fun moving. I'll say hi to Gwen for you. And we'll keep you updated on the shower. I'm going to miss you. Are you sure about this?"

"There's nothing I can do." I have images of Gwen, Olivia, and all their perfect Washington, DC, friends all sitting around drinking Cosmopolitans and talking about the Big O—which is how all women's films and fiction invariably end up.

"Well, I guess that's okay then. Give me a call when you get to the new house. I'd better call Gwen. Talk to you later." Olivia hangs up. I hang up and feel like someone was holding a hand over my mouth forbidding me from speaking.

My hand pulsates. Domenic. I have to set up the move, and now is as good a time as any. What's one more rejection? I pick up the phone and dial quickly, reminding myself that he offered. Why would he offer if he didn't want to help? Wouldn't he expect me to call? Any friend would call. I'm just following the normal friend protocol. I dial Domenic's number and hang up quickly before it rings. I repeat this three times.

I decide instead to make my appointment with Sam the Massage Therapist first. I call the spa and make my appointment for later that week. She apparently had a cancellation. The receptionist confides that Sam is the most popular massage therapist and that I'm "lucky" I got in so quickly. I thank her profusely. I dial Domenic before I have a chance to stop myself. I can't feel my extremities.

"Hello?" I'm not completely sure it's not Domenic.

"Hello, uh . . . is Domenic there?" I have somehow spoken without breathing.

"Sure, may I ask who's calling?" the man says.

"It's Maggie . . . from work," I say.

"Just a minute." I hear the phone placed on a surface and muffled voices. Then I hear the lower tenor of Domenic's voice. He's being told there is a girl on the phone named Maggie. He's either smiling or looking confused. He's walking toward the phone right now with thoughts of us. Thoughts of what he thinks of me.

"Hello?" he says.

"Hey, there." I can say no more. I am hyperventilating, and my voice catches. Why am I so incredibly socially retarded?

"So what's going on?" He's doing his best to move this dying conversation along.

"Not much, I just wanted to see if you were still interested in helping me move this weekend?"

"Just let me know what time."

"I think we should start early, that way we can finish before the temperature skyrockets." Skyrockets? Yeah, that's verbiage I use every day. Supercool of you, gosh. Magical.

"Yeah, we wouldn't want any skyrocketing going on."

Is he making fun of me? Did he just use the Christina Dahl tone of voice?

"Well, it is Fourth of July weekend." I try to convince myself that I'm getting more comfortable.

"That it is. What do you have planned for today?" I hear Domenic tapping a pencil on a table.

"I've got some packing to do. You know, the onesies. I plan to put together an entire box of nonrelated items in a haphazard fashion and label it with an unintelligible title." Am I trying too hard?

"Well, make sure it's off balance and the box isn't taped well. Then we'll really have ourselves a party."

"I'll be sure to do that." My voice is rising in tone. I resolve to calm down.

"Well, I don't want to keep you. I'll see you at Peregrine's party tomorrow, right?"

"Absolutely!" Once again with the shrieking. Domenic and I sign off.

I can't remember a time when I just did something without unremittingly second-guessing myself and finally opting for the road more traveled. I let every opportunity walk right by instead of grabbing it by the collar and bringing it in for a long, sweet kiss. Once again, Peregrine is right—what *am* I so afraid of? What's worse than sitting here now—alone and tormented by my own safe and comfortable life? If I am forever cast as the fat, jolly sidekick, it's my own damn fault.

CHAPTER FOURTEEN

No Kids, Kay?

I wake up the next morning with a start. All of my clothes are packed and I have nothing to wear to Peregrine's birthday party tonight. I put in a call to Mom. She has left for work, Russell says. I'll call Kate.

"Hello, who is it?" It is Bella.

"It's Maggie," I say, in my craziest voice.

"Hi, Maggie," Bella says.

"Is your mommy there?" I ask.

"Yes." Bella is holding the phone so close to her small cheek I can hear every exhalation.

"Can I speak with her?" I ask.

"Yes." Bella holds the phone even closer to her mouth.

"Do you think I can speak with her now?" I am smiling. I want to be in the warmth of the home Kate has created.

"Yes." Bella still holds the receiver.

"Thank you, baby," I say.

"Wait." Bella pauses.

"What is it, sweetie?" I ask.

"I like you." Bella drops the phone on the table and yells for Kate to come to the phone.

"What's going on, Bobo?" Kate asks.

"Nothing much," I lie.

"You sound a little . . ." Kate trails off.

"I need an outfit for this stupid party tonight. A party this twenty-eight-year-old busboy is going to be at—so I can let him walk right by me and never ever grab anyone by the collar. Not once, Kate!" I can barely get a breath out.

"Sweetie, why do you think you need to grab twenty-eight-year-old busboys by the collar?" Kate asks.

"He made a CD for me. I didn't want to like it, but I did. There was this one song . . . but he's a busboy at Joe's. How do you do that? Twenty-eight years old?"

"Okay, you're a little vulnerable right now so I won't remind you that you, too, work at that very same coffeehouse. No, you're not twenty-eight, but you will be in a matter of weeks. How come I haven't heard about this guy?" Kate is much more distracted about not being in the loop than by Domenic's career choices.

"Yes, but I have a master's," I say.

"Sweetie, I know you're going to find your way back to the museum of your dreams. So for now, why don't we talk more about why you haven't told any of us about him."

"Because . . . I've just been . . . I don't know, kind of embarrassed."

"About what?"

"That he's this guy who still buses tables at a coffeehouse and Adam Farrell is Dr. Adam Farrell. Soon to be Mrs. Dr. Olivia Farrell."

"Mrs. Dr. Olivia Farrell is about to make one of the biggest mistakes of her life. That guy doesn't know who she really is and couldn't care less."

"I know, I know. I just . . . I think I'm having a hard time looking at this realistically, if that makes any sense."

"It does. Maybe this is a good thing, you looking at all of these factors you never thought about before. You know, Texas Steven was a complete loser, but you never even gave that a second thought."

"You thought Texas Steven was a loser?"

"Honey, he was a loser."

"He was golden."

"Well, then he was a golden loser."

We are silent as I mourn Texas Steven. Kate sniffs.

"So what's going on with you?" I change the subject after crossing myself.

"I got Olivia's wedding invitation in the mail today."

"Yeah?"

"There's this classless handwritten note on the bottom that says, 'No kids, kay?' Is she kidding me?"

"At least you got an invitation." I haven't received mine yet. I have a sinking feeling I might not get one at all.

Kate and I go on to cattily discuss those quiet, intimate moments before Dr. and Mrs. Adam Farrell initiate some kind of sexual intercourse. We picture them in two huge, queen-size beds. They yell sweet nothings across their respective beds as Olivia romantically plucks the bright orange earplugs from Adam's ears. He stops. Drops. And rolls over to his beloved. Some nights he keeps the black sleeping mask on; other nights he pulls it off in a fit of passion, only to catch a glimpse of himself in the full-length mirror behind the door. I am officially cheered up after several minutes of imagining these scenarios and dissolving into fits of laughter about what Dr. Adam Farrell's tiny hands *really* mean.

"We'll go shopping with you. What about Mom?" she asks.

"She's at work."

"Well, we'll just have to go it alone."

I close my door and leave Solo in the House of Emptiness. She has become more and more ornery since we have decided to move/been evicted. The lack of a routine and the fact that all our belongings are in boxes have been just the recipe to turn my dog into a raving lunatic. So I called around and found this huge dog emporium that grooms dogs and has obedience classes as well. I thought I would take her to get groomed the day of the move and, if things go well, sign her up for obedience classes. I rub Solo's ears as she leans into me.

I drive over to Kate's house lost in thought. I find myself somewhere on Colorado Boulevard and can't remember how I got there. I've been driving for a full five minutes and can't remember one turn or one red light.

Because I've never had an actual relationship, my family treasures these little crushes as the crumbs they can feed on until the real thing comes along. So naturally I worry what Mom will think of this newest crush. Does she ever look at the man Olivia snared and wonder why I can't reel in one like that?

I pull up to Kate's house and once again the Bat Daughters run out to greet me. Kate saunters out behind them.

"You ready?" I say.

"Mom is on her way," she says.

"Oh." Bella and Emily stare at me and wonder why their Aunt Maggie isn't excited to see their precious Grammy.

"What's going on?" Kate asks. She continues, "Emily. Bella. Can you go inside and get whatever you want to take to the mall with you?" This is the battle cry of moms everywhere. Sending the children away. Not only that, but sending them inside to search for unspecified items to take with them to a mall. This is a precedent-setting offer.

As soon as the girlies leave, I begin. "I don't think Mom is going to be as gung-ho about Domenic as you are. Her little grandchild light is flickering as it is." I'm speaking quickly. I shouldn't really put so much stock in what Mom thinks of the men I like, but I just can't lie or keep anything from her.

"Honey, we just want you to be happy. For pete's sake, you don't have to marry the boy." In a moment of horror about what she has let the girlies do, Kate turns to the house. Then she turns back to me. "His name is Domenic?"

"Domenico," I breathe.

"How could she not like that? Look, at some point you just have to bring someone home and not worry so much." Kate becomes distracted again by the time that has elapsed since the girls ventured into the house in search of the ill-gotten booty. We hear a crash from inside and quiet shushes.

"She just wants what's best for you. That's all we've ever wanted." Kate starts walking inside, calling the names of her lovely daughters. I follow her and decide to try one last point of debate.

"Did Mom approve of Vincent when you first brought him home?" I ask.

"Of course she didn't and he's not a stray I found on the side of the freeway, you know." Kate is walking into the girls' room.

"I know. So what did you do?" I ask quietly, now in the presence of the girlies.

"What Mom saw was a work in progress: the long hair, the loud music. He wasn't husband material . . . at that time. But he had a good heart, and we adored each other. It stops being about the loud music and it starts being about wanting not to let go of what you now know is the best thing that's ever going to happen to you. It has to start with you." Kate calls to Emily and lets her choose just one doll and one Matchbox car. She is satisfied and proudly slings her backpack over her tiny, wise shoulders.

"I wish I could bring Domenic anywhere, Jesus."

Bella begins to emerge for her turn to choose. "Are you guys talking about the Baby Jebus?" she asks.

"She calls Jesus, the Baby Jebus. Vincent and those Simpsons—*he* thinks it's cute." Kate shakes her head and opens Bella's backpack. Bella chooses a diamond tiara and a hot pink feather boa.

"It's the Baby Jesus, Bella. Mom, are we about ready to go?" Emily floats back into the room. She has added a strand of carnival beads to the journey. Mom honks out in front of Kate's house. The girlies rush out to greet her. Kate and I follow behind. We all climb into Kate's minivan.

The doors slam behind us. The silence is deafening.

"I like a guy who buses tables at Joe's and wants to be a sculptor," I whisper.

"You like someone?" Mom is fiddling with her seat belt again and can't make out one word I'm saying. My plan is working. Emily and Bella are quieter than they've been in years. Kate adjusts the rearview mirror. I hear Bella whisper, "What's a sculperr?" Emily shushes her, knowing that the grown-ups will stop talking if they notice the little ones are on to them.

"His name is Domenic and he works at Joe's."

"Well, what's this Domenic's story?" Mom asks.

"He works at the coffeehouse and wants to be a sculptor."

Once again, Bella whispers in the back to Emily, "What's a sculperr?" Emily flounces in her chair in complete indignation. Bella whispers "Gosh" and begins combing her Molly doll's rat's nest of a head of hair. Emily rolls her eyes. Kate lets out a laugh.

"What kind of sculptor?" Kate flips on her turn signal.

"It's the family business. They're actually dollmakers. He works with his grandmother making the feet and hands in porcelain. His mom sews the clothing. They're pretty famous . . . in the doll world."

"Well, it sounds like a good beginning," Mom nudges.

"That sounds fair." I secretly fear that *a good beginning* is all any of my relationships are.

Bella whispers to Emily knowingly, "Sculperrs make dollies." She leans proudly back in her kid seat, pointing at her Molly doll. Emily sighs and flips open her diary.

I splurge a little and buy a long brown leather skirt and a crisp white shirt. I also purchase what I refer to as a "tightener." This is a magic undergarment that shoves your entire body into a spandex casing and smooths out where there were once rolls. I get a small. My thought process: If I buy a small, I will become a small. When I finally writhe my way into the tightener, my middle is now a "small." Even if in the end, I look like a slug caught in a straw.

CHAPTER FIFTEEN

There's Always an Erin

I've been on so many diets, I've forgotten what eating without a calculator and judge and jury in my head feels like. Whether for comfort or out of boredom, I reach for food rather than a brisk walk or a long hot bath. When I am not overeating, I ruthlessly deprive myself of food. I've never looked at food as nourishment or fuel. Instead, I look at it as a savior or a taboo. Maybe I'm feeding some other hunger.

Getting ready for Peregrine's party, I brush out my hair. I keep it down, instead of going for my usual ponytail. I stand back and look. Nice hair. Nice "exotic" eyes. Must close the mouth so as not to unleash the Chiclet teeth. The V-neck of the crisp white shirt draws the eye to the cleavage. The leather skirt is oddly slimming.

It is around ten o'clock as I park outside the Pasadena Museum of California Art. Looking in the rearview mirror, I try to pull myself together. I want to go home already. Every second I'm here is just one second I'm not at home with my dog in my black terry-cloth pants and gray men's tank top. As I'm getting out of my car, I notice Cole walking toward the museum, too.

There is a large sign announcing that Peregrine's birthday party is on the roof. Cole and I climb the stairs together.

"You two together?" the bouncer growls, stamping the back of Cole's hand to ensure there will be alcohol consumption tonight.

"Hell no, brother." Cole physically moves away from me and huffs off. The bouncer stamps the back of my hand and waves me through. Great start.

The Pasadena Museum of California Art is situated one block east of the Pasadena City Hall. As I walk into the event, the number of people here strikes me. There must be close to five hundred partiers on this roof—all in costume and all waiting for the birthday girl to spend a little time with them. There is a DJ over in the corner playing all-retro hits as people crowd the dance floor. There are hot pink and black lanterns dotting the entire roof along with an open bar complete with bartenders in Ronald Reagan masks. I make a beeline for the bar.

"What will you have, young lady?" ex–President Reagan yells. I'm not that big a drinker, but I am a genetically thirsty person.

"Can I have an Amaretto Sour?" I try to make my voice sound high and feminine. The bartender waddles off. I stare at the back of the bar. I don't want to see Domenic yet.

"There you go, young lady." I leave him a two-dollar tip and begin to scan the room for a familiar face.

"Maggie!" I whip around to see Peregrine in a kid's party hat and an early-1980s pale blue sateen prom dress, complete with tacky wrist corsage. Her blue-black hair is up in a snazzy chignon updo with pale blue carnations dotting her hair. Her makeup is all hot pinks and blue eye shadow.

"Happy birthday!" I kiss her on the cheek and hand her the card I made earlier in the day.

"Your boy is here. Brought some bitch named Erin or Errol. Should have been named Acne. She's got issues with the complexee-own, if you catch my drift. Inez is here. She's been dying to meet you!" Peregrine hugs and air-kisses a group of people who have just arrived.

I can't breathe. He brought someone? Why would he bring someone? And her name is frigging Errol? For once I want Peregrine to be right.

She is still excitedly talking. "Your party bag is in the back room, there's a raffle later on for a day shopping with me. Presents are being opened at midnight—oh, and I got a male stripper to pop out of the cake, don't tell, okay. Oh! Here's your hat!" Domenic brought someone? That's it. I'm officially in the pits of hell.

The group of well-wishers is still huddled around Peregrine. They tell her she looks fabulous, and she twirls for them. I'm now feeling claustrophobic. This hat is trying to suffocate me. Peregrine directs them to the bar and gives them a rundown of the evening's activities. We then noisily begin chatting about the stripper when Peregrine's girlfriend walks up.

"Inez, this is my Maggie." Peregrine downs her drink, smearing her hot pink lipstick.

Inez Dawson is a smallish woman with long, wavy black hair. She is dressed in an exact replica of the dress Molly Ringwald wore to her prom in *Pretty in Pink*. I know Peregrine made it for her to wear tonight—that's all she's been talking about for the last three weeks. Well, that and humming the theme song nonstop. Inez looks stunning. I notice only then that Inez has a bit of a potbelly. And it's not a little belly, either. But it's sexy. Peregrine can't stop staring at her. Shit, *I* can't stop staring at her. What does Inez have that I don't? She got a belly. I got a belly. She got a lover. I got a belly. I take her hand and shake it, but I get thrown off when Peregrine bunches us all up in a group hug. I begin to panic realizing how liquored up Peregrine is. Where is Domenic and how can I get out of this hell? This is not what I meant by having fun with people.

"There, there, sport. Enough of that, you crazy birthday girl." Cole is the only one big enough to break up Peregrine's ruckus. After being mistaken for his girlfriend, I'm surprised Cole allows himself to touch me, let alone be seen in the same room with me.

"Aw, Coley, but this is *my* Maggie!" Peregrine wraps her arm around me and snuggles tightly. She is greeted once more by a pack of admirers. They say she looks fabulous. She twirls for them as well. Cole continues.

"I know. I know. She just needs to put her purse down and maybe get herself another drink so she can catch up." Cole whisks me away to a table in the corner of the museum's roof.

Cole and I walk silently over to the table. And then I see her.

I now suspect Peregrine's antics were a distraction technique. This is classic Peregrine: the ultimate hostess. She must have wanted me to be in a great mood when I saw the man I love and the girl he brought with him. I turn back around and see Peregrine. She is fighting every urge to throw herself between this girl and me. I make some kind of face that conveys I will be fine, or at least that's what I hope I'm conveying. Peregrine smiles and mouths that she's sorry. Birthday guests engulf her once more. I turn back around.

The girl is pale and thin with thick brown hair. She does have bad skin. Even drunk, Peregrine can nail down a flaw. Domenic is speaking with Dre, the distractingly tall busboy, and doesn't even look up as we approach.

"Maggie, these are Christina's friends. This is Erin," Cole says. She looks up at me. Her eyes are flat. Nothing about me registers with her. It's as though one look at my Area calms every woman down. I am no threat to her man. Erin doesn't bother to smile or even extend a hand. I loathe her even more now. Cole continues, "And this is . . ." He stops at the next girl. She is alarmingly beautiful in a Los Angeles Exotic Dancer kind of way.

"Cheyenne," she says, sipping her beer. Well, then . . . she was destined to be a stripper from birth. Poor dear.

"Oh, yes. Cheyenne," Cole slurs. I can't stop myself from looking down at his crotch to see if he is becoming aroused. Unfortunately, during my covert operations I am caught by the entire table checking out Cole's package. Domenic is staring right at me.

"Hey, there, partner, see anything you like?" Cole has his hand on my shoulder. He jokes with me like a couple of guys about to smack a high five in celebration of Cheyenne's ample breasts. I'd like to remind him that according to the bouncer, I am his fat, possessive girlfriend.

"You know I can't see anything." I swing my purse off my shoulder and decide to head back to the bar. The large table is alive with drunken conversations and explosions of laughter. I leave the gaiety and march back to the bar for another drink. Domenic has yet to say word one to me. This, Peregrine, this is what I'm fucking afraid of.

I return and sit at the end of the table closest to Cole and farthest from Domenic. Peregrine and Inez have their purses there. I figure I'll just wait until they come sit down, and then I'll be able to look enticingly fun. I pull the maraschino cherry from my drink and drop it into my mouth.

"You clean up good," Cole says.

"Don't try to be nice." I drink my second Amaretto Sour of the night.

"I'm not. I feel a little bad about before." I can smell Cole's breath.

"Good, you should."

"That rhymes," Cole says, trying to smile.

"So does Fuck off." I am beginning to slur.

"No, it doesn't," Cole says.

"Really? How about you do it anyway," I say.

"Fine. Fine. Just let me apologize." Cole slams his beer on the table. The whole table turns toward Cole and me.

"Maggie?" Domenic says, leaning over Cole.

"Hey," I mumble. I can barely look at him.

"I'm glad you made it." Why? So you could make sure I know you see me as just a friend? Yeah, I got it.

"Do you get the one with the big ones?" Cole asks Domenic in a forced stage whisper.

"What?" Domenic looks over to see if any of Christina's friends heard what Cole said. They didn't. But they might notice Cole miming a girl with huge breasts.

"She's a Stone Cold Fox, D. Brown!" Cole high-fives me.

"I'm all aglow with pride, Cole," Domenic says and leans back, rejoining the conversation with Dre, the distractingly tall busboy. I begin to hatch a plan to maim Christina and all who walk with her. I'm sure at some point I will remember this little vignette, but right now all I want is another drink.

"I'm heading up for another one. What are you drinking?" I ask Cole.

"Seven and Seven. I'll go with you." Cole stands up, straightening his shirt.

Maybe Cole *is* sorry for what he said. Maybe the reason I'm here tonight is to make something happen with Cole? Domenic? Screw Domenic. He couldn't care less. Cole might secretly like me, too. He did call me *little* one time.

"Fuck these bitches." Cole waves his arms over the table and turns to follow me. He's burbling something about "big-ass titties" when I snap out of my trance. I grab my wallet from my purse and sneak a peek at Domenic. My "peek" becomes a slow-motion stare. He is sitting back with his arm around Cole's now vacant chair.

He looks good. He did something to his hair. I don't know what it is but he looks amazing. He is wearing a light blue dress shirt under a dark blue V-neck sweater. The shirt is not tucked in and falls below the sweater. It complements the khaki pants that actually fit his lean body. He dressed up for this girl. I walk to the bar with Cole and catch a final glimpse of him saying something to Christina in confidence while Erin does her best to act like she doesn't notice.

"Can I have a Kamikaze shot, another Amaretto Sour, and a Seven and Seven, please?" I ask Ronald Reagan behind the bar.

"Kamikaze, huh?" Cole finds a few bar stools and plops himself down, pulling a bowl of pretzels over.

"I'm a little thirsty," I lie.

What I am is a little fucking fed up with being the other girl. Erin is over there having a normal night, being set up on a date by her girlfriend and on her way to having a wonderful time. The guy likes her because she is cute and small, however pock-marked she is. They'll get married and have little zit-faced kids together. I down my shot and breathe in quickly.

"Can I have a sip of yours?" I ask Cole, who's genuinely thrown by my uncharacteristic behavior.

"You can have it." He slides the 7 and 7 over and asks the bartender for another. I down his drink. I pull mine over and bring it to my lips.

"Are you okay?" It's Peregrine. Thank God. I might have shared my feelings with Cole if she hadn't shown up. That would have been frightening and awkward for both of us.

"I'm fine," I slur. I have never had so much to drink in such a short time before.

I feel drunker than I've been in a long time and even more hopeless—a magical combination. It's taken exactly thirty minutes. Why did I even come? There's always an Erin.

"What do you need?" Peregrine strokes my hair while trying to block Cole's view of us. It gives me a false sense of privacy. Partygoers are beckoning Peregrine to the dance floor. She waves them off.

"I need you not to tell me I'm better off without him. I need you not to tell me that she's a silly little whore." I stare at her.

"She needs some coffee." Domenic is suddenly standing over me and even in my drunken stupor I panic that he's heard too much.

"Puddin', go on back to your little date." Peregrine tries to shoo Domenic. Her first instinct is to protect. I am her cub tonight and she perceives Domenic as the orange-vested hunter who has me in his sights. He steps forward.

"She needs to go home." His face is distorted like he's behind a fishbowl.

"Your little date is wonderin' where ya are, why don'tcha head on back," I slur.

"She's fuckin' smokin' hot, man." Cole wipes his mouth with the back of his hand and raises it so Domenic can give him a high five in celebration of his "smokin' hot" find. Domenic doesn't even look at Cole.

"Maggie? Come on." Domenic grabs my arm.

"Leggo. Pickie Pock Mark wants a drinkie," I manage, pointing back at Erin.

Peregrine stands back, and I can see her mind working. Or maybe that's what's happening. Let's face it, how credible am I at this point? Inez pulls closer into Peregrine as the thought finally cements. I look to the back table and Erin is staring over at us. It seems Pickie Pock Mark is getting jealous.

"D. Brown hittin' it with the hotties," Cole says to no one in particular.

"I'm the only sober one here. Let me handle this. I'm sure you'll let Erin know why I've left, and there are so many people no one will even notice we're gone." Domenic moves close to me.

"Maybe you should take her home?" Peregrine toys. Inez smiles.

"I wanna go home." I lean back into Domenic. He puts his arm around my shoulder. I "secretly" smell him.

Domenic steadies me with his arm and grabs my purse. I can see Inez lean back into Peregrine. Peregrine is whispering wildly into her ear. Another pack of partygoers drags her and Inez onto the dance floor as we're leaving. The last thing I see as I'm walking toward the stairwell is Peregrine standing on top of the bar, reaching down for Inez as Modern English's *I Melt With You* pounds in the background. I wobble into the stairwell of the museum in the arms of Domenic Brown. I can smell his shampoo from where I am leaning on his shoulder. And I am *leaning,* which is freeing in one way and completely horrifying in another.

The world is spinning. I wonder if I'm really leaving the party with Domenic. I'm not so sure. I look up and stare right at him—every inch of him. The black stubble on the bottom of his chin. His long black eyelashes. He has a cut on his neck, probably from shaving. His skin is blotchy in patches, but on the whole it's definitely clear, unlike *some* people. *Echem.* His lips are chapped right at the top, but puffy and full in general. Pink. Very pink.

"You've got good skin. Pink lips," I burble.

"Thanks. Are your keys in your purse?" Domenic stands me up and rummages through my purse, looking for my keys.

"My keys are in my purse. Are you driving my car?" I am swaying back and forth. I am screaming inside my head, trying to stabilize.

"I'm going to take you home. Is that okay?" Domenic retrieves the keys and comes over to me. I stare at him again. Is that chest hair? Interesting. I'm noticing now that he's wearing a buttondown shirt as opposed to a T-shirt. He is angling his body to lead me across the street to where my car is parked. But, always on the alert, I cunningly deduce that he's leaning in for a kiss, so I pucker up and wait. I'm now on some corner in Pasadena kissing the air in front of Domenic Brown.

CHAPTER SEVENTEEN

No, in *Your* Eyes, Lloyd Dobler

The first crush I can remember was in fourth grade. His name was Josh and he had strawberry-blond hair in a classic bowl cut. In the days before Olivia, when I wasn't on the edges of popularity, I found solace on the monkey bars. Not the act of going across the monkey bars, but sitting atop observing the landscape of the playground. One fateful day, Josh came up below me and stole my shoe—a slip-on Van (blue and yellow). Even then I remember thinking—This is it. He's now my boyfriend. The whole shoe thing? Elementary school foreplay. After swooning for far too long, Josh returned the shoe—okay, threw the shoe up at me as he yelped "Weirdo." My knight in shining armor. I climbed atop those monkey bars for the remaining seven months of fourth grade. I never changed shoes—thinking somehow it was the intoxicating blue-and-yellow slip-on Van that drew him to me like Circe's call. You'd think after over fifteen years, I would have come down off those monkey bars.

Domenic is soooo gentle. Wow, those lips *are* soft, I can't believe this is happening to me.

"Babe, we've got to get you in the car." Did he just call me babe? Was I kissed? His hands are on my shoulders and he is softly shaking me. I believe I have fallen asleep. I put my hand out to balance myself, and the coldness of the street sign shocks me.

"Babe? I'm not your babe. Pickie Pock Mark is your babe. You're all fancied up for her, forfuckssakes . . ." I believe there is, in fact, my own drool on my chin. Yes . . . yes it is.

"I'm here with you. Can you make it to the car?"

What? Without throwing myself at you? "Yeah, I think I can conshrol mesself," I slur.

Domenic and I walk across the street together like we're in a three-legged race. He opens the car door for me and I climb in. My car looks different from this angle. Domenic opens the driver's-side door and eases himself behind the wheel.

"You're taller than I thought you were." Domenic adjusts the mirror and puts the key in the ignition. I pull my seat belt around and come to the realization that I'm far too drunk to be witty. I'll just sit here and be quiet. I won't say another word and maybe I won't humiliate myself any further. I search my memory for evidence that Domenic and I kissed. I am deep in thought, feeling my own lips, as Domenic signals and pulls out onto the street.

Surprisingly, I am able to direct him to my back house with little difficulty while keeping my witty banter to a bare minimum. Domenic Brown is coming over to my house. I don't care what the circumstances are. He's coming over. I am starting to get unbelievably thirsty, and my eyes can no longer stay open. I roll down my window and allow the fresh air to revitalize me. I look like someone's dog. Domenic finds parking on the street in front of my house.

"Just take the car." I heave myself out.

"One step at a time. First, let's get you inside." Domenic takes my hand as we cross the busy street. It feels so natural and right. His fingers curl around my hand, and I can feel the heat of his body soaring up through my arm. I have never touched Domenic before. Sure, we've bumped into each other "accidentally." I have stood next to him and quietly smelled him. Maybe there has been some fantasizing that could be considered virtual touching. But this is the first time we've actually touched on purpose for a prolonged period of time. I feel places tingling in me that I didn't know existed. I can't think straight. I hold his hand back.

"Which key opens the front door?" Domenic opens the screen door and holds up my key chain. I try to stabilize myself on the bulldozer and concentrate on the keys. I'm completely distracted by the hand-holding. I can't seem to focus on anything but Domenic's amber eyes.

"You can ask for it if you want, you know . . . as the days go by and by and byyyy." I can't fathom why I choose these words in response to his key query.

"What? Maggie, I *am* asking you." Domenic is trying each key in the slot, figuring this method will take less time.

"Oh, not that. In the song. The song on your CD. I'm not gonna hurt ya." I lean in; he tilts his head into me. I proceed to stage-whisper: "I heard the hidden track on the hidden-track CD." I am tapping my head on the side and winking elaborately to let him know he's a genius for thinking up such a concept.

"Yeah, well." Domenic finally gets my front door open and Solo begins her barking, growling, and running-away routine. He seems a little startled but continues into the house.

"G'grrrrl . . . g'grrrrl." I approach Solo and try to calm her down.

"Nice place." Domenic puts my keys on the counter and sets my purse on the floor. The entire house is packed up in thirty-six boxes.

"Thanks." I go into the bathroom to take out my contact lenses with the exacting hands of a surgeon. I have taken my lenses out in darkened movie theaters and on amusement park rides. Now I can add drunk to this impressive list. I am putting on my glasses as I come out of the bathroom. Domenic is standing in the living room, letting Solo smell him. I start uncontrollably jabbering.

"I get it, you know. I'm the girl in the window and you're Lloyd Dobler . . . and that song is just a good song . . . but then I think you're trying to tell me something. You know? That *thing*. That . . . it's so hard to tell someone right to their face . . . and I get it. I talk that way, too." My arms are raised above my head as an homage to Lloyd Dobler and Peter Gabriel's "In Your Eyes," one of those climactic movie moments where the wall-flower hero finally leaps past his comfort zone to profess his love for the impossibly popular, yet astonishly available, love interest. Domenic approaches me slowly, pulling my arms down into a normal position.

"I'm not Lloyd Dobler and I think Peter Gabriel's 'In Your Eyes' is highly overrated. But you are the girl in the window, so let's just get you in bed so you can sleep this off." Domenic leads me through my bedroom door. I don't know whether to be terrified or excited. I am a little of both. I take my boots off. Thank God, my socks are respectable. This whole thing could have gone really bad really fast.

We are standing by my bed. I can't help but look up at him for some kind of answer to what the hell is going on here. My thoughts are jumping all over the place, starting and stopping. I feel weightless. Then I start thinking about the heat of his hand and I can't think of anything at all. The world begins spinning again. I wish I could really appreciate this. Instead I find myself swaying uncontrollably in front of Domenic Brown and my own queen-size bed, saying things I wish I had the balls to say to him sober.

I reach my hands up and set them gently on his shoulders. Domenic is holding my arms and unconsciously rubbing my elbows. As we stand there, the sound of his hands on my crisp white shirt is the only sound in the room. I stare right at him and let him see the truth of what I want. If I'm correct, this same lack of inhibition is allowing me to finally see clearly that he wants the same from me. He looks away and clears his throat.

"Okay. Let's get you to bed." Domenic leans over me and pulls the sheet back on my bed. His hand rests on my arm as he gestures for me to climb in.

"I'm not gonna hurt ya, you know . . . I'm not gonna hurt ya. Please, I heard the song. I didn't read into it. I didn't. I just . . . okay . . . wait . . . wait . . . I guess I did. I guess I did read into it. I didn't want to . . ." I have my hand over his heart. I let my thumb swipe over the part of his chest exposed by the V-neck of his dress shirt. His skin is warm. Domenic closes his eyes and breathes in. The world begins spinning.

"I know. I know. We just need to have this conversation later when we're all a little less drunk. Just get to bed, Maggie, please?" Domenic sits me down on the bed and gently takes off my glasses. He puts my legs under the sheet and pulls the sheet over my clothes. He tucks in bits of the sheet underneath my body. He smooths the fabric over me. I can feel every fiber of my being stand on end as his hand passes over every inch of me. I get this wave of emotion. I love the feeling of him touching me. I close my eyes.

"G'night, Maggie. I'll see you Saturday." Domenic's hand is lingering on my waist. I don't remember falling asleep. But I remember what it felt like to not be alone as I drifted off that night. It was the most beautiful thing I've ever felt.

◆

I wake up the next morning exhausted. It's nine thirty; I'm hung over and more than a little confused about what went on last night. I have one day to get ready for the big move. I get to the kitchen, find my one mug, and set up the lone coffeemaker. I have just enough coffee left in the freezer for my last pot in this house. I grab a filter from an open moving box.

I'm petting Solo when I see it. A little bed made up on the couch. A couch pillow was pulled down, and the blanket that usually hangs over the armrest is also pulled down as if someone has just climbed from beneath it. I look to Solo for answers.

The phone rings.

"Hello?" I'm suffering a tad from vertigo as I answer.

"Hey, Maggie? Were you sleeping?" It's Domenic. For the love of God, it's Domenic. Is this like the urban legend where the phone call is actually coming from inside the babysitter's house? Is he still here?

"No," I say.

"Tomorrow is the big day and I was just checking in about the time. And . . . and I wanted to know how you were feeling after last night . . . just minor details." Domenic laughs.

"Oh, are you still up for the move?" I ask. My face is flush with embarrassment.

"Why wouldn't I be up for it?"

"I don't know, I just figured . . . I don't know." I don't have a reason that wouldn't sound completely insecure and childish. So, best to act like I'm put out and horrified that he doesn't know why I'm asking. If he doesn't bring up last night, then I won't, either.

"How are you feeling? You had quite a night." Shit.

"I just got really drunk. I never drink, so I just didn't hold it that well, I guess. But I can't remember anything." A flash of Domenic sitting on my bed hits me like a ton of bricks; he's looking down at me lovingly. The warmth of his chest. I bite back the memory.

"Oh, well. You just said some things. I didn't know if . . . you . . . um . . . meant them . . . but I guess . . . you . . . Anyway, see you tomorrow?"

"You want to stop by around eight, we can get everything over to the new house by nine or ten and then you can be on your way by eleven, if all goes well." I speak quickly. I get that Domenic wants clarity about last night. So do I. Why bring a date to a party if you like another girl? It's simple, really. You don't.

"I've set aside the whole day, so don't worry about me."

"Okay, then," I choke.

We are silent. The shock of Domenic holding my hand floods my brain. I can't believe how stupid I am. Did I call him Lloyd Dobler? Here's where I have to prove to myself that he loves me, that last night was all about me and Erin is now completely out of the picture.

This is where I become my worst enemy.

"So who was that girl you were with?"

"Erin is actually pretty nice. For being a friend of Christina's, she's pretty intelligent."

"That's an achievement."

Domenic is silent.

"Erin seems like a nice girl, if you like that sort of thing," I blurt out.

"Yeah, well. At least I remember *my* night." I hear a pencil tapping in the background.

"Oh, I remember my night. Yeah, I may have said some stupid stuff, but at least I . . . you know . . . I was there with people I could talk to." What does that even mean?

"You were completely drunk. You weren't talking to anyone. You slurred and spit through conversation after conversation, and they slurred and spit back . . . I don't think you *do* remember your night."

"Oh, is that right? Well, then it looks like we have ourselves a difference of opinion."

"Yeah, that's exactly what we have."

"Well, then," I stammer.

"Well, then." The pencil is now almost deafening.

"See you tomorrow?" I yell. I can't think of any other way for me to come out on top of this conversation. I'm so humiliated. I feel like the stupidest person in the world.

"Yeah, see you tomorrow." Domenic hangs up the phone slowly. I call Peregrine before I can think better of it.

"Hey, there," I say.

"Hi," Peregrine says.

"I made the appointment with Sam." I am openly sobbing.

"Aw, button, what happened?" I can hear Inez in the background asking after me. Peregrine is shushing her.

"It was this perfect night and now it's all gone. Wherever we were last night—it's awkward history. I just think I've messed it up. But I didn't, you know? Why can't *he* make a move, huh? Why is this all on me?" I ask.

"Men are idiots, lamb. He probably convinced himself that you were so drunk, you didn't know what you were doing." I can hear Inez again. Peregrine puts her hand over the phone and I can hear her retelling the uneventful story.

"So what do I do?" I sniffle.

"Target practice, love. Until you find a man who can really step up, just think of all these other men as practice," Peregrine says.

"Okay. Target practice," I repeat. Target practice.

I hang up once again and put my head in my hands. My whole life is packed up in thirty-six boxes. I feel like I'm right back in fourth grade—sitting atop the monkey bars. Waiting. Waiting. I can't face this day right now. I am having flashbacks of last night. I've never felt so embarrassed and frustrated. I've been up for approximately eight minutes and already I've had enough. I decide to sleep off last night. I fall back into bed and try to erase any memory of last night.

I pull the sheet over my shoulder and press my head deep into my down pillow. I will my brain to turn off. The last thing I feel is my hand twitch with exhaustion. The last thing I hear is Solo growl at my movements.

CHAPTER EIGHTEEN

Pink Pastry Box o'Magic

My first kiss took place on a stage at my high school during my senior year. His name was Brody Schroeder and he had psoriasis—but just on his hands. Olivia had talked me into trying out for the Christmas play that year. I got the part of Ma Joad in *The Grapes of Wrath*. The drama teacher told me Ma Joad was a major part and I should be honored to get cast for it my first time auditioning for any type of play. All I saw was that I was playing an elderly lady who didn't have to be young or vibrant at all. Who better than a fat girl to play someone ageless and sexless? The director wanted Ma and Pa Joad to kiss good-bye at some point during the play. It was supposed to be a peck on the lips to show the bond between the parents during their trials and tribulations. I remember Brody and I sitting in the rehearsal hall while the director mapped out the scene. We both stared straight ahead, not comprehending what was about to happen. We got up to start blocking and the crowd fell silent. Line. Blocking. Line. Blocking. Then it was time. Brody slumped his shoulders, took a step forward, and kissed me softly on the lips. Later that year, he told me it was his first kiss, too.

I wake up from a restless sleep. I kept waking up over and over again thinking that I wasn't going to be up early enough. I decide to go pick up doughnuts and take Solo to the huge dog emporium for her grooming/test drive.

I hand Solo off to one of the emporium employees. She is barking and chewing her own leash. I wish I had the balls to act like Solo sometimes. No second-guessing, no fears—she is who she is. The employee gingerly walks her behind the counter and gives me a nervous wave as he is tugged uncontrollably off balance. Then I pick up a dozen doughnuts. I laughingly tell myself the doughnuts are for Domenic and my "moving team," even though my "moving team" (read: *my family*) isn't meeting me until lunchtime at the new house, thereby negating the need for doughnuts. I ask for a maple bar and a twist on the side. That way I can eat the two extras on the way home and it will look like I haven't opened the pink pastry box o'magic.

I have a theory about pink pastry boxes. So much joy comes from those boxes. When someone walks into a room with a pink pastry box, joy immediately fills the room. World peace? Three words. *Pink pastry box.* I get a big cup of coffee and finalize my plans for world domination.

I pull up to my house and Domenic is waiting for me. I wave and push my shoulders back. This move is in the same category as the coy head tilt—makes you look thinner. Now, exiting from your car with a dozen doughnuts while angling out to make the departure look smooth: That makes you look fat.

"Hey." Domenic looks tentative.

"I'm sorry. I drank a lot and then I acted like a complete idiot. I'm sorry. It's really nice that you still want to help." I am almost crushing the box with my fists.

"It's okay. Do you want me to carry any of that?" Domenic is trying to commandeer the pink pastry box o'magic. It's intoxicating, isn't it? You like that?

"Sure. Let me just grab my coffee." How do I reach back into the car without shoving my ass in the face of my beloved? "Check out the doughnuts. Do you see anything you like?" I ask. He peers into the box; I dive into the car and grab my coffee.

"Did you get any of the little cake ones with the sprinkles on top?" I am taken aback. He is picking past legendary bear claws and humongous jelly-filled bundles of joy to look for the reject cake doughnuts, which I, of course, didn't bother purchasing. Leave those secondhand doughnuts for the suckers who don't have a say in the dozen they buy.

"No, I . . . uh. There's a twist in there? Did you see that one? There's a bear claw?" I beg. We are awkward and uncomfortable. I don't know if it's because we're trying to remember or forget last night.

"Yeah, I don't like those. I'll just take glazed." Glazed. Fucking amateur.

We squeeze past the bulldozer. He goes first. I make sure of that. I open my front door and set the pink pastry box o'magic on the counter and watch as Domenic enters my house.

"Here we are again," Domenic forces.

"Yep." Target practice. Target practice.

"Nice."

"Thanks. I tend to decorate in modern, forty-eight-hour Eviction Notice style. Saw it in this month's *Architectural Digest*." I let out a nervous laugh, and my coffee spills on the rug. I make no attempt to wipe it up.

"So what does your new place look like?" Domenic mills throughout the house.

"Cute as hell."

I realize I've never seen the new house from the inside. The man who repainted the living room is leaving the key under the mat. Today will mark the first time I enter the house in which I will live.

"Well, then. Who can argue with that?" Domenic picks at his doughnut. The two secret doughnuts are sitting in the pit of my stomach.

As we drive to pick up the rented moving truck, I sneak side glances at his arms and his knees. I back the moving truck into The Sacred Driveway right behind the bulldozer as Domenic guides me with hand signals (backing vehicles into tight spaces is a hidden talent I have). I believe this might finally make him like me. I mean, a girl who can back a moving truck into a tiny residential driveway? Mother of your children? I think so.

"Nice shooting, Tex," Domenic says.

Well, that's a nice masculine comment. Maybe he'd like to arm wrestle?

The next forty-five minutes are spent carrying various boxes from my house, past the bulldozer, and into the rented moving truck. I watch as my entire life is carried out and loaded into the back of a moving truck. This is what it would look like if we moved into our own place.

I see Faye poke her two-week-old hairdo around the corner. The curl in front looks exactly the same as it did that blessed day at the salon. Everything else is a mangled, blown-out rat's nest. Oh no, not now. Not in front of Domenic.

"What the hell is that?" Domenic whispers. He's standing close. Is he wearing cologne? Those tingles are back.

"That's my ex-landlord. Please don't judge me by the following interchange." I skulk toward Faye, who has now come out to the driveway.

"You killed my roses," Faye dribbles.

"Of course I didn't."

"When is this going to be out of my driveway?" Faye asks, pointing to nothing in particular.

"The truck? The moving truck?" I ask.

Faye is staring back at Domenic. "Where'd you find him? Is he a cousin or something?" She untucks a rogue bit of bathing-suit ruffle that has lodged itself in her abdominal rolls of flesh.

I hear Domenic pulling down the door to the back of the truck. Then I hear him closing the front door to my house. He squeezes past the truck and opens the door to the front cab, flipping the keys in his hand.

"No, he's not my cousin, but thanks for the back house and . . ." I look back at Domenic, who is fiddling with the truck's AM radio. "Why don't you cover your shit up, for chrissakes." I'm waving my hand indiscriminately around her exposed nether regions.

I climb into the cab with Domenic, give Faye the middle finger, and tell him to drive. He puts the truck in gear. Then, and only then, do I exhale.

◆

My relationship with my body is like that of an egomaniac with a self-esteem problem. Mostly I think about myself and how much I suck. But there are rare moments when I walk around for hours and think I look amazing. Either I feel great about myself or I've decided some guy is checking me out. Then I catch a side view of myself in a store window or a department store mirror and I'm plunged into despair. If I could always live in a place with no mirrors or disapproving glances, I would think I was the prettiest girl around.

I find the key under the threadbare mat of my tiny English

cottage. I stand on the little porch and see mornings with coffee and the *LA Times*.

"Is this it?" Domenic stands behind me.

"Yeah, isn't it beautiful?" I hold the door open for him as I step inside. The curtains on the many windows are a drab smoky yellow color. Those will have to be dyed. This is a job for Stubborn Workshop—a Thompson family phrase, meaning everything *will* fit and anything can be improved with a fresh coat of paint, new drawer pulls, and some brute force.

Domenic walks in and begins milling around. He fits so perfectly it hurts. My little Craftsman cottage and Domenic. His black flips of hair fit so right.

"They left it pretty nice," I hear Domenic say from the other room.

"I guess," I slip.

"You guess?" His eyes are narrowed as he comes back into view.

"Well, I haven't actually seen the inside until now."

"You rented a house you've never been inside?"

"It's not like I never saw anything. I looked through windows. And did you not see the outside of this house?"

"Do you know if the plumbing works? The electricity? Um, little things like hot water? Heater? None of this is ringing any bells, right?" Domenic is resting his arms on the top of the door-jamb into the bedroom. I know his mouth is moving, but I can't quite make out the words over the roaring fantasies of him standing like that.

"Okay, um. Once again, did you not see the front of the house? This is a cottage. The porch is dripping bougainvillea and little purple clematis? Did you see that? Can you not envision for one minute a cup of coffee on that porch?" I say.

"Clematis? Can't you get that from a dirty toilet seat?"

"It's a type of flower. And no, I believe it's sexually transmitted."

"The flower?" He is breezily smirking. How do you learn that?

"No, chlamydia. That's what you're thinking, right?"

"Yeah, that's right. Well, let's hope the water works, so you can make your coffee. Let's hope all those clap vines haven't choked some mechanical system like, I don't know, the electrical service?"

"You like it."

"I like it for you. Your dog is going to love this place. Are they okay with the dog?" Domenic turns around and opens the windows in the bedroom. I almost fall over from my imaginings. I can see the muscles in his back shifting in and out. Who's golden now?

"Well, we kinda had to fib a little on her size."

"By how much—and *fib*? What's that? Are we using words like *fib* now?"

"The management company doesn't have a problem with Solo. It's the landlord who thinks dogs are the downfall of land barons everywhere. So Mom did some research and we settled on a weight that seemed to be okay in most rental situations. I put that number down. And *fib* makes it sound a little less harmless, don't you think?"

"And how does that weight relate to your dog's actual weight?"

"Well, we put down twenty-five pounds/one small dog." I let that hang there for a while. In our heads we are both envisioning the Hound of the Baskervilles.

"Certainly, no one will be the wiser. I'm sure you'll have nothing to worry about. Shall we?" he says, leaving the bedroom.

I explain that we should put the contents of the moving truck toward the middle of the house. I plan to paint the "Anchor

Pieces" and dye the curtains, so we need to be able to get to them easily. Sometime during the morning's activities, I have taken to calling the fireplace and the built-in buffet my "Anchor Pieces."

"Are you allowed to just paint stuff?" Domenic asks as he undoes the latch on the truck.

"As long as you have it back the way it was when you move out. I figure I'm never moving out, so . . ."

"You'll never put it back to normal," he says, pulling out a small blue rocking chair from the back of the moving van.

"*Normal* is such a relative word." I smile.

It's eleven o'clock in the morning and I have officially moved.

CHAPTER NINETEEN

He Never Threw Scissors

Watching Domenic help my mom serve lunch to the exhausted moving team ripped out every thread I'd stitched over the pain of the other night. The normalcy of that one simple act and how deeply it spoke to me makes me realize how hungry I am for someone to be in my life. Outgrowing the fantasy of white horses and long, slow gazes across impossibly formal occasions brings me here—to the simple beauty of watching someone I have feelings for become real. Seeing the simplicity of what it would be like in my day-to-day life and never taking one thing for granted—not even passing out paper plates and plastic cutlery.

My worldly belongings are bunched in the middle of my new house so they don't impinge on my "Anchor Pieces" and their upcoming transformations. It is now past two in the afternoon. Domenic stands on the porch talking with Vincent about a novel they are both reading. Mom and Russell made their appearance, brought lunch for everyone, then drove off up the coast for an afternoon in Santa Barbara. Kate and Vincent have been a great help. They are now getting ready to go home.

"So?" Kate comes up behind me with a diet cola in her hand.

"So, what?"

"Jesus, Maggie." Kate stomps her foot.

"Did you just stomp your foot?" I ask.

"He's a little pale. Tall. Supernice, though. Pretty eyes. The girlies love him. They won't leave him alone," Kate says.

We look to the porch where Domenic is now playing Rock, Paper, Scissors with Bella. Bella only throws Paper. Domenic switches back and forth between Paper and Rock. He never throws Scissors. He's squatting in front of Bella so they can have an equal playing field. I can see his boxers. Hula girls.

Kate calls to the girlies and tells them they are leaving. They throw the expected tantrums and Kate tells them after choir practice they can go to a special dinner because they were such big helps today. The girlies gather their toys, and the exodus begins.

"Bye, crazies."

"Butterfly kiss?" Bella asks.

I buzz as close to Bella's face as possible and "land" on her smooth face with a kiss. Her giggles and laughter are what make me know what true love could be like. Bella doesn't care about my stupid Area. Bella just wants her aunt to give her a butterfly kiss.

"Octopus kiss?" Emily asks.

I sneak up on Emily and pucker her face over and over. She is writhing with delight and that open, Emily belly laugh. Kate and Vincent wave from the minivan. I walk back to the house. Domenic is on the porch leaning over the banister. My breath catches, and I trip over some stupid plant I will later sacrifice to the gods of social retardation.

"I'd better be heading out." He puts his pizza plate in the sink and drains his soda.

"Thank you so much for everything. You were absolutely amazing. Thank you." I feel myself blushing. Damn involuntary bodily responses. "Do you need a ride back to my house?" I still have to take this moving truck back, and the company would be nice.

"No, my grandmother is on her way. We've got a load of dolls in the kiln, but thanks, though." Domenic looks down and is, I believe, snapping his fingers.

"I'd love to meet her."

Domenic and I wait the next fifteen minutes in one of our worst attempts at idle chatter. We talk about everything except what we're both dying to talk about—what happened the other night. I can't believe some of the comments that come out of my mouth. I'm apparently now a big fan of reality television and nature hikes. I don't watch television and I hate hiking. I don't mention the Getty internship or the Marcus Aurelius. Domenic, more than anyone else, would think this internship is exciting. I just can't. I packed that paper in with the Pandora's box of pictures. He continues snapping his fingers and rarely makes eye contact with me. I feel so muted and embarrassed. He's probably as embarrassed as I am and grateful I don't remember or think that night meant anything. Just then, Domenic's grandmother pulls in front of the green Craftsman archway, saving me from any more humiliating lies. He waves her over.

She is the most beautiful woman I've ever seen. Her white alabaster skin is made even more stunning by a shock of black wavy hair dotted with flecks of porcelain. She wears an oversize flannel shirt with grubby jeans, also flecked with porcelain.

"Gram, this is Maggie." I know by now the thrill really should be gone, but Domenic just said my name.

"My actual name is Genevieve, but I go by Gram most of the time." Her hands are strong and rough, and her voice is rumbly.

"We'd better get going, Domenico, we have a batch in the kiln. It was wonderful meeting you, Maggie." Genevieve looks to Domenic. Now I know the one person who calls him Domenico.

"Thanks again." I wave.

"No problem. See you later?" Domenic follows his grand-mother to the car.

"Absolutely!" I yell, just that much louder than I should.

He did everything right today. And for once I didn't seem to mess it up.

I watch them drive away, lock up the house, return the moving truck, and head over to the dog emporium. Solo is incensed. I have left her there the entire day. She wants me to pay for it. I look at Solo and decide to go ahead and sign her up for obedience classes even though it's money I can ill afford. I nervously babble on about her genetics and how she's always been nervous. The woman behind the counter winces as I fill out the necessary papers and pay the tuition. She then nods and tells me we need to come in for an evaluation first. I schedule a time and walk to the car feeling like a proud and responsible pet owner.

◆

I drive home and don't know what to feel first. Peregrine is right. I drop the key on my filing cabinet that sits right next to the door. Solo is wandering around among the boxes smelling the old scents. I wish I could just talk to Domenic about that night. Ask him what the hidden track means. Ask him what he was thinking bringing another girl to Peregrine's party. Ask him to be honest. I feel like so much of my life is spent hiding what I really feel. That's an exact quote from Peregrine. I hate that she's right. I hate that even as she stared in a bathroom mirror thinking up trivia questions about herself—she hit the nail on the head about my entire life.

Why can't I just thank Domenic and, in a breezy tone, ask him if he'd like to see a movie. Or ask if I could take him to dinner as a thank-you. Maybe I can make that a goal for this week.

I need my best friend. I want to tell her all about Domenic, the guy who just sounded fine to her. I put in a call to Washington, DC. The machine picks up.

"Hey, Olivia . . . it's meeee . . ." No one answers. I keep talking into the answering machine.

"Well, I am officially moved. I thought I would give you my new number . . ."

"Hello? Hello?" It's not Olivia.

"Hello?" I question.

"It's Gwen! Where are you? This *is* Maggie, right?" There's that tumbleweed again. I can hear the saloon door swinging behind me as I reach for my six-shooter.

"Yeah, where's Olivia?"

"Oh, she's here. We're all here. Girl, you are missing out. Olivia? Olivia? You want to talk to Maggie?" Does she want to talk to me? Who the hell is she? Gwen puts her hand over the receiver and I hear talking and laughing. I should just hang up.

"Is this Maggie?" It's still not Olivia.

"Who's this?" How many people are going to get on this phone before the actual person I called is able to speak to me?

"This is Shawna. Shawna Moss. Olivia works in the office next to me. Oh my God, she does sounds exactly like Olivia. Olivia? Olivia? She sounds just like you!" Shawna Moss drops the phone in a fit of laughter. I wait with my head in my hands.

"What did I tell you, girl! You are missing out. We have champagne and it is flowwwing!" Gwen toasts the receiver.

"Hey, Gwen?"

"Yeah? What is it, girl?"

"Hey, can you put Olivia on the phone, please?" *Girl?*

"Oh. Sure. But you *are* missing out. Oh, and by the by, we chose the Bellagio in Las Vegas for the bridal shower. We're planning on tons of shopping." There are gales of laughter in the background. Gwen continues, "Can you make the reservations? Olivia and I in one room. Shawna, Hannah, and Panchali will share another. I hear you're bringing your sister?"

"Kate?"

"Whatever. You can stay with her. Can you make the reservations?"

"Yeah. Can I talk to Olivia now?" She sets the phone down, and once again there is distant laughing and talking.

"What up, girl?" It's finally Olivia.

"Hey." I relax.

"Is everything okay? Everyone can't wait to meet you. I can't believe you couldn't make it."

"I just want to give you my new number."

"Oh, just call back and leave it on the machine." There is an explosion of laughter in the background. "Hannah? Hannah? What the fuck are you doing? Gwen! You get that girl under control. Shit, Maggie, I've got to go." I hear Olivia swigging her champagne.

"Oh, okay." Should I have gone out to DC?

"Call back and leave your new number, kay, and can you make those reservations? Congratulations on the move. Talk to you later." Olivia hangs up. She might as well have said, *Dismissed.* I sit there among my thirty-six boxes, wringing my hands. Paralyzed by confusion.

I stop staring off into space and find my sheets in a box marked KITCHEN UTENSILS. I make my bed and set out all of my sundries in the bathroom, the brush and the toothbrush trying to create some kind of homey feeling. I look in the mirror of the medicine cabinet and smooth on my moisturizer. I stare some more. I shut the light off and hear Solo jumping on the bed. She's ready for bed and is finally calming down. I'll make the reservations for the bridal shower tomorrow.

CHAPTER TWENTY

Texas Steven

The alarm has been going off for twenty-two minutes.* It's amazing the math you can do on such depleted brain capacity. It is now 9:47 a.m. I have to be at work by 10 a.m. I should have left two minutes ago. I brush my teeth and throw my hair, once again, into a ponytail. I'll stick with the glasses today and forgo the extra mile with my contact lenses. Some days you're Superman and some days you're Clark Kent.

"Hey there, Maggie." Cole's voice is soft.

"Hey." I rush past him and scoot to the back room for an apron and a peek at the schedule so I can plan my invitation to dinner with Domenic. Christina is bending over the sink washing her newest batch of dirty dishes.

"What happened to you the other night? At Peregrine's party, you know? On Thursday?" Christina asks.

"Yeah, I know which night and which event. I went home."

"You were taken home . . . what's, like, up with you?" Christina inches up her pants.

"Nothing. What's up with you?" A little reverse psychology and she'll be talking about herself in 5 . . . 4 . . . 3 . . .

"I met this guy over at this frozen yogurt place in Old Town the other night, well, it was like Thursday night. Funny, huh? We left the party pretty much right after you did. It was pretty fun, but then it wasn't, so we decided to leave, you know?"

"You guys left right after me?" I ask.

"Erin stayed, but me and Cheyenne left. That's where we met up with these guys at the yogurt place. It was perfect because there were like two of them and like two of us. It totally worked out."

"Erin stayed?"

"Her and Domenic totally hit it off. Which is cool, but I think Cheyenne might have liked him first. I'm not sure Erin really should have gone for him, you know? Anyways, she, like, waited around for him, and . . . well, you know, he never came back."

"Cheyenne liked him first?" I ask.

"Oh, yeah. She met him the other day out in front. You know, of the coffeehouse?" Christina points toward the front of the coffeehouse. She waits for me to acknowledge. I nod. She continues, "She thought he was cool. He's not all that hot, so I don't know." Christina still uses the word *hot*. She tends to drag the *o* out like a Canadian adolescent.

"Yeah, he's not that . . . hot."

"I guess Domenic and Erin went out again last night."

"Last night?"

"Yeah, Erin called me first thing. She couldn't call Cheyenne, could she?"

"No. No, she sure couldn't. I'd better get out there, you know Cole." My stomach lurches.

The rest of the day is a blur of downward spiraling and knocking my head against any hard surface. How could I have thought for one instant that Domenic would actually be interested in me? This is classic Maggie—falling so hard and falling so fast and never asking any serious questions. It's me on the monkey bars again. I jump from an offhand glance in my direction to marriage and babies. I had convinced myself that Domenic had a "nervous energy" around me. Then I ran with the "nervous energy" idea and concocted whole scenarios about him liking me and the fantasy was born. In reality, he's dating this Erin girl and we're just friends . . . again.

I should be spending my time finding someone more suitable for me. Someone more mature and ready to be in an adult relationship. Someone who is not already dating shredded-wheat-haired girls named Erin.

Texas Steven.

I could be spontaneous and call him right now, out of the blue. I'll show Olivia and her fantasy theory and Domenic and his misleading nervous energy. It's been months since we spoke, and Steven called me last. Why didn't I think of this before? I don't care what Kate says about Steven being a loser; I just don't want to be waiting around when Domenic and Erin send out their wedding invitations.

On the way home from work, I dig my cell phone out of the bottom of my purse. The battery is dead as usual. Why do I even have one of these things? I find the charger, plug the lifeless phone into the power outlet, and scroll through the saved phone numbers to find Texas Steven's. Ahh, that's why. A cell phone really is just an expensive address book.

What's the worst that can happen? I'll have a harmless dinner or a meaningless drink with an old friend. No, the worst that can happen is I call this number and leave a funny, heartwarming message and never, ever get a call back. He would just never get around to it. Okay, back to the best that can happen. Sparks. Fireworks. Exploration. Slow dancing with my head on his chest in the city hall gardens under strands and strands of Italian café lights.

"Hello?" Steven answers quickly.

"Steven? It's Maggie." I hold the cell phone to my ear with my shoulder as I park in my assigned space.

"Heeeeeeyyyyy." His voice is warm and happy. That twang makes my knees weak every time.

"What have you been doing with yourself these days?" Just being breezy.

"I started another internship. This one is at a production office over in LA. Nothing big. What about you?"

"I just moved into a fabulous little cottage," I say, fumbling with the key to the front door.

"What are you doing right now?" Besides being in my fabulous little cottage?

"Nothing." I need to stop saying the things that come naturally to me. I need to rethink every single word that comes out of my mouth. *Nothing?* You can't say *nothing*. You're burning CDs with hidden tracks and calling them albums. You're in the middle of your book club and it's your turn to discuss theme and symbolism. You've hired a stripper for the evening on a whim and he's standing naked and aroused before you.

"I was about to head out to a late movie. You up for something like that?"

"What time?"

"The movie starts at ten fifty. Can you get there in time?"

"I'll meet you out front."

We work out the details and as usual he signs off by saying, "Late."

"Okay, bye!" I beep my cell phone off and look at the shambles of my house, dishes and everything still in boxes. The only art I've hung up are my three favorite pieces over the fireplace. Everything else is blank. I think of Domenic moving all my furniture into this tiny space. He looked so right in this house. He played Rock, Paper, Scissors with Bella and never threw Scissors. What am I doing here? Why am I not calling Domenic and asking *him* to go to a movie? Why aren't I lying to Domenic about strippers and book clubs? Because, I remind myself, he's probably out with Erin again.

I try to put together some kind of outfit. Have I gained or lost weight since I've last seen Steven? Who can really tell anymore? Have I gotten to the point where I'm so far from my Goal Weight that I'm now making deals with myself that I just won't get any bigger? I put on a pair of linen pants and a white T-shirt. I grab a wine-colored cardigan as camouflage. I plan on feigning cold spells like I'm a fifty-year-old woman embarking on The Change throughout the night.

I pull up to the theater parking lot and check the rearview mirror. I apply a little pink lip gloss, suck in my gut, and crawl out of my Fancy New Car. Steven is standing in front of the theater waiting. He stands out from the crowd. His golden hair has grown a bit shaggy since the last time I saw him. His eyes are squinty, and his smile makes them almost disappear. He is wearing cargo shorts, flip-flops, and a navy-blue, pocket T-shirt. Steven is the kind of guy every woman wants to have waiting for her outside a movie theater. He is naturally good-looking and has every bit of that Southern Charm. He smiles at passersby and holds doors open for women of all ages, whom he later addresses as "ma'am."

"Hey," I say.

"Hey, yourself," Steven says.

We hug, and I feel his arm nestle into my Area. At the midpoint of the hug, Steven's arm has officially nestled. I can't bear one more second and break the hug, smiling and checking my

Area to get some kind of idea what Steven has just felt. Steven holds the back of my arm and leads me over to the theater line.

"I bought your ticket. You ready to go on in?" Steven asks.

His twang is barely there. If he could hold his vowels a little longer, deepen those R's a little more like good Texas Boys love to do. I think I might not be able to breathe while watching such regional mouth contortions. Texas Steven motions for me to go through the turnstile first while he gives our tickets to the waiting theater worker. I panic. Walking in front of anyone is against my code. I walk quickly while maniacally making small talk to throw him off looking at my ass. Steven barely touches the small of my back as I pass through. Tingles?

I buy a large diet soda. Steven passes on the concession stand. We walk to the theater and I already feel different. Texas Steven is exactly equivalent to Dr. Adam Farrell. He even has grown-up man hands. I think he mentioned he reads some kind of newspaper every morning. I think it's the *New York Times*—which trumps the *Washington Post,* I'm sure. Proof enough. We're early for the movie, so we have time to talk in the dimly lit theater.

"Sooooo, what's this internship about?" I set my Diet Coke in the cup holder of the movie chair.

"Screenwriting." Steven crosses one leg over the other—the manly way, not the effeminate European way. I can kind of see up his shorts.

"An internship is how you get started in any business. It's money in the bank," I say, not seeing the obvious irony in this statement at all.

"I don't really see myself pursuing it. What it's supposed to be . . . I mean, whatever I'm supposed to be gettin' out of it, I'm not. There are some cool people there, though."

Steven has this habit where he licks his bottom lip during speaking. Just a quick dab, but I wait for that shit like Old Faithful.

"Try something else." My voice is getting louder, and I'm sitting on the edge of my chair. The tongue thing is driving me crazy. I believe I am now panting.

"I guess." Dab.

"Well, this is what this time in your life is about, searching for something that you will get something out of." I will myself to calm down. Act cool. Why am I being so tolerant of Steven's explorations and not my own?

"Don't you worry about me, Maggie May." Dab. Dab.

"Have you really—"

"Are those seats taken?" a woman asks as she stands at the beginning of our row of seats.

"No, ma'am, go ahead," Steven answers. They think we are a couple right now. Technically, everyone in this theater does. I want to throw my arms up in the air touchdown style and yell, *He's with me!* But I control myself.

"Thank you," the woman's husband says as he squeezes past me. The lights dim further, and the movie begins.

Steven is someone who's fun to be around. Why ask more of him than that? Why ask him to be committed and consistent? He will never be those things. But I cling to the idea that I'll be the one who tames him—who makes him committed and consistent. He's the ultimate Big Game—lions, elephants, and unavailable Texans. If Olivia and Domenic are not being who I want them to be, is it their fault? Or is it mine?

The lights finally come up and I'm pretty sure I have given myself some form of palsy from the contortions I have put my body through during the past two hours of trying to "look breezy." The couple to our right says, "Excuse me," and Steven and I stand. Steven unfolds himself from his chair and quickly exits the theater. I follow.

"So, what did you think?" he says over his shoulder as he walks out.

"Great. Great locations," I yell, as I'm tossed and turned in the thrusting exodus of hopped-up foreign-film viewers.

"You up for a coffee or something?" Steven asks, calmly waiting by the door to the theater.

"Sure."

I have to be at work by seven thirty the next morning. I can barely keep my eyes open. Coffee at 1 a.m. is the last thing I want, but Steven is close to the top of the list of things I do want.

We decide to meet at a hole-in-the-wall coffee shop in Old Town Pasadena. He waves good-bye and says something about meeting me there. Steven is already halfway to his car. Couldn't he have walked me to my car? It's one o'clock in the morning and I parked in a lot that is not that well lit.

I suddenly realize I'm tired of taking care of myself all the time. If something breaks in my house, I fix it. If the dog needs washing, I do it. If my car is in a poorly lit parking lot, I'd better buy pepper spray or learn kung fu. I always thought I'd be married by now and have kids. Instead I'm someone's fat maid of honor walking alone to her car in the dark of the night. I'm clutching my keys between my fingers just like they say you should, so you can poke out the eye of an intruder. You know what would really work? A six-foot-two Texan. That could poke out any eye.

Texas Steven is exactly on a par with Dr. Adam Farrell. He's a fantasy. He remains golden because I've never demanded that he be real. He gets to saunter in every six months, call everyone "ma'am," dab his beautiful lips, and then leave. I feel like I'm in junior high school again always playing those boyfriend games with fictional characters and never real people. I truly believed if I played my cards right I could marry, live in a mansion, and have five kids with Ponyboy from *The Outsiders*.

How could Texas Steven know what I need? Why didn't *I* ask him to walk me to my car? Why didn't I just say no to his invitation? Is it that I don't want to be seen as the needy girl? If I want Olivia to be the kind of best friend that I need, why don't I just talk to her about it? If I want that internship at the Getty, why don't I just call and set up an interview? If I want to go on a date with Domenic, why don't I just ask him? I have to stop waiting for people to come to me. It's time I started putting myself out there. Tonight is where it starts. I pull up to the coffee shop and find Steven's car. He is just getting out of his car as I pull up next to him.

"Hey," I say.

"There's a parking space back behind the building next to that dark alley. I'll get us a table." Steven walks past my car and is halfway to the door of the coffee shop.

"Steven?" I call to him through my car window. He turns around in the light of the awning.

"I'm going to head on home. I'm tired and I have to get to work early in the morning." My heart is racing. I can see him mentally erasing me from every phone book he has.

"Oh, okay. Well. . . ," Steven says, shuffling in place. "Okay, well. Get a good night's sleep, then. Talk to you soon?" I take my foot off the brake and coast a bit forward.

"I have two tickets to Steve Earle at Royce Hall at the end of summer, if you want to go?" Steven is approaching the car. The Royce Hall in never land? I think not, cowboy.

"Maybe, let me check my calendar." I sail away from the parking lot. Steven goes into the coffee shop anyway. I knew he would.

I get home around 1:30 a.m. and drop my keys on one of

the many packing boxes that fill the room. Solo follows me around the house while I shut off lights and close windows. I pull back the covers on my bed and crawl in. I'm proud of myself. Solo hops up on the end of the bed, circles, and finally lies down. I say good night to her as I turn over and set my alarm for 7 a.m. I toss and turn as my mind races. I went tonight thinking Steven would be the answer to all of my problems. Now all I've got is more questions. If Steven is this ultimate male, do all males have clay feet? Why can't anyone remain golden?

CHAPTER TWENTY-ONE

Blue Buckets

When Olivia left for Washington, DC, to move in with Adam, I walked to the humane society in San Francisco and asked to adopt the dog next in line to be euthanized. Without hesitating, the dreadlocked girl behind the counter called for Cage Ten. A shiver went through the entire building as the occupant of Cage Ten was readied for its imminent release on the public. The door opened and a big-pawed, auburn puppy with the biggest, brownest eyes I had ever seen stepped out. She barked, whimpered, and yelped at the slightest noises or movements. I connected with her instantly. I filled out the necessary papers as Cage Ten pulled and tugged at the makeshift leash. She was strong for her size and skittered away from anyone who approached. Except me. She hid behind my legs even on that first day. That was close to four years ago, and she's been the first member of my own family ever since.

Lately, I've become concerned about Solo. Throughout our four years together, I've tried socializing her to no avail. There is a small part of me that likes to watch how the world deals with a force like her. She's unable to budge outside of her comfort zone, and when she's threatened, the pure unaffectedness of her reaction makes me envious. But now I see that this comfort zone she's set up has become stultifying for her and me. Parades of dog-sitters would rather starve than watch Solo. People are afraid to come to my house for fear their jugulars will be ripped out any second. So after work today we're going to be "evaluated" for obedience classes. I buckle Solo into her doggy seat belt and we set off. I'm nervous. We don't do well in "evaluations."

As we walk into the huge dog emporium, I talk Solo down. Her tail is between her legs, and she continually tries to bolt for the front door. The constant barking and whimpering coming from the Doggy Day Care catacombs agitates us both. The shelves of the dog emporium are lined with different dog foods, doggy bowls, doggy beds—you name it, there are five different kinds somewhere in this lobby. Solo is now in full retreat. I wind her leash around my hand and pull her close. She is terrified.

The trainer comes out to meet us. Her name is Tori. She's far too tiny to control Solo. I'll tell her I've changed my mind. Let's face it: We'll fail this evaluation, and Tori will send us on our way in no time. She's already clutching her jugular in fear. She sits down and goes over the questionnaire I've filled out. I hold Solo's leash tight to calm us both down.

"What commands have you taught her?" Tori asks as she reviews my answers.

"Oh, um . . . just the one," I say, pointing at the form as Solo's low growl builds in volume.

"*Move your body?*" Tori looks over her clipboard at me and my socially inept dog.

"Yeah, well, I use it when she's in the way. You know, *move your body*. Funny story, I said that once when my niece, Bella, was at my house, and she thought it meant to dance." I demonstrate Bella dancing to everyone's horror. It's so quiet, I believe I hear crickets, but I continue. "So there's Bella dancing and Solo is just trying to, you know . . . move out of the way." Tori is silent. Well, it was fucking funny when it happened.

"So you've never really challenged her?" Tori makes some notes on the back page. I hang my head in shame.

"Okay, why don't we go to the training room and take her off the leash," Tori continues as she flips the clipboard closed and stands.

I feel like the worst mother in the world.

Tori, Solo, and I walk back into the catacombs of the obedience school. The sound of barking gets louder and louder. Tori opens a chain-link gate and motions for us to go inside. It's a big warehouse-style space with old couches lining the walls and commercial drains in the middle of the dark cement floor. I feel like a prisoner of war. As I unleash Solo, Tori takes a link of plastic-covered meat out of her pocket. It looks like some type of sausage casing, but with beef or some dark-colored alternative inside. Solo paces the cement floor sniffing at the new smells. She completely ignores both Tori and me.

"So I'd like to start with the language you use to communicate with her. Besides *move your body,* how else do you get her to do the things you want her to do?" Tori is watching Solo as she moves away from me and closer to her.

"Well, I just talk to her. Like a normal person, I guess. I don't really ask her to sit, because really, how often is that necessary? So it's mostly, you know, *come here by me* or *dinnertime . . .* that kind of thing." I might as well just spell out how lonely I am. Oh wait, I already have.

"Well, why don't we just start with *sit.*" Tori stands back.

I stare at my dog. She's smelling her own ass over in a corner that couldn't be farther away from me.

"Come here, girl. Solo?" Solo comes running over to me. Tears spring to my eyes.

"Okay, now tell her to sit." Does Tori want us to fail?

"Go ahead and sit, Solo."

She does. She sits. A tear rolls down my face.

Tori approaches Solo with the liquid meat sausage and kneels down. Solo skitters away but slowly comes back. Tori tells her to sit and she does. She offers some of the meat to Solo, who takes it from her hand. Tori moves a couple of feet over and repeats the same maneuver. Solo follows her and once again sits. Tori offers her the meat standing, but Solo toddles off distractedly.

"She can be pretty willful," I say, a little more confident since we're obviously doing better than little Tori thought we'd be doing.

"She's not willful. She's racked with fear." Tori walks over to a corner of the room and kneels. Solo follows. Fear?

"Fear?" I ask. I put my hands in my pockets and walk toward Tori. She stops me.

"Just stay there. She's obviously smart and understands everything we're saying. But she won't trust anyone new. She's ruled by her fear of the unknown." So are you a fucking psychologist now? Huh?

"And you know that because . . ."

"I'm a dog trainer." Tori should go into stand-up.

"Yeah, I get that you're the dog trainer and I'm the client here. But I'm just curious, how can you break down someone like that in less than ten seconds based on a couple of tricks and a weird sausage in a roll thing?"

Tori looks like she's fighting the impulse to throw a choke chain around my neck. Instead, she ignores me and walks into another corner of the training room. There are blue buckets on either side of the wall. Tori kneels between the buckets. Solo walks over to the wall, looks back and forth at the blue buckets, and walks away.

"Hm." Tori stands and walks to another corner.

"Hm, what?" I ask.

"It's just interesting. The buckets. She checked them out and then walked away. It's just interesting." Tori kneels. Solo follows and sits. Tori gives her some meat.

"Interesting, how? Like she may have been beaten with blue buckets?"

"No, Ms. Thompson, because she won't trust me enough to walk by an unfamiliar object. The bucket. She's not sure what it is and she doesn't trust me not to betray her." Maybe Solo's afraid the bucket doesn't like her "like that" and if she grabs the blue bucket by the collar it'll just laugh and tell all of his dollmaker friends that some fat girl has a crush on him. Huh? Ever think of that, Dr. Freud? I stand back watching my dog pace nervously around the cement floor. What happens if Solo fails? What happens if we're untrainable?

Solo's so smart, she knows what Tori is going to do before she does it. She comes when Tori calls. She leaves the treat when Tori asks her to. She even lies down when Tori says, "Down."

That's when it happens.

Tori sits next to Solo. Solo doesn't move. Tori slowly moves her hand toward the crown of Solo's head. Solo watches every move Tori makes. Tori places her hand on Solo and begins scratching her ears. Her favorite thing. She knew exactly how to make Solo calm. Solo leans into Tori and flips over on her back. Tori rubs her belly as Solo's tail wags with joy.

I finally see myself in the harsh light of that training room. I've convinced myself that I'm unlovable, untouchable, and invisible. But is the reality that there is someone out there for me who will know exactly what it takes to comfort me? That all I need to do is allow it?

Kate and I used to play the *Xanadu* soundtrack and dance until Mom came home from the law library. I specialized in all the ELO songs, while Kate preferred all things Olivia Newton-John. When Kate had homework or was playing with another friend, I retreated into my room, where I had built a make-believe time machine. I played for hours—pushing buttons, giving orders, and feeling safe and comforted in my imagination. I want that feeling of safety and freedom that came with those memories back. I don't want the new feelings of momentary happiness followed by insurmountable guilt that comes from reaching for food for comfort. I need to go back to the person I was at eight years old. She had it all figured out. Maybe I'll build another time machine.

CHAPTER TWENTY-TWO

Urban Life

I do not fear the unknown. I do not even fear death—in the event that I've lived a good life. What I fear is a life of mediocrity.

We're sold this script for life with lovers like Romeo and heroes like Jack London, but we've got an hourlong commute to a job we hate and a utility bill to pay every month. I crave a life of freedom and passion—but I've sentenced myself to a life of quiet desperation and prime-time sitcoms. I've numbed myself and it's going to hurt like a motherfucker when I wake up.

I crawl into bed and sleep fitfully. I have to work the night shift tomorrow, so I can sleep in. I have my massage with Sam in the morning, so I'll be all relaxed when I see Domenic. How am I going to do this? No more. I'm just going to walk past that fucking blue bucket and ask him out. It's all fun and games until he figures out I want to be more than just his friend.

I sleep until eight thirty and wake up staring at the clothes I have laid out on the chair. I swing my feet out of the bed and get up. My body aches. I should have recovered from the move by now. I'm a young woman, why do I ache so much? Should I be worried about this? I start brewing my morning coffee and get ready for my shower.

While toweling off my hair, I think about the past couple of days. I'm tired of being the girl who waits. I pad over to the mantel and pick up the creased piece of paper. I am rejuvenated and excited as I unfold the paper. I pick up the phone and dial the number. The phone is wet and slippery.

"This is Beverly Urban." Her voice is affected in a Bette Davis kind of way—not quite British, but not really American, either.

"Hello, Ms. Urban, this is Maggie Thompson. My sister, Kate di Matteo, spoke with you regarding an internship restoring the Marcus Aurelius." Surprisingly, I am calm and speak with confidence.

"Yes . . . yes. I was wondering what happened to you." She stops. Is it my turn? Do I need to make an excuse? Should I explain my thought process? Should I tell her about the blue buckets?

"I apologize, Ms. Urban. I have finally finished moving and I'm ready to give you and the Getty my full attention." Good. Professional. Honest.

"The position is still open and I am still interviewing. You are a lucky woman, Ms. Thompson. How does this Monday look for you?"

"Monday is perfect. Thank you for this opportunity, Ms. Urban." Solo starts licking my wet legs.

"We'll see you then, Ms. Thompson." We finalize the details and hang up.

I call Mom to give her the news. While I'm on a roll, I make the necessary arrangements with the Bellagio for Olivia's wedding shower: three suites for the last weekend in July. I put one suite in Kate's name, one in Hannah's, and the third in Olivia's. Then I call Prime, Bellagio's steak house, and make reservations for seven. I let the hostess know this is a bridal shower, and she assures me they will make the night special. I also arrange for a high tea at the Petrossian Bar. Callie, the hostess, will have a tiara waiting for Olivia at the table. She asks me about the bride's colors, which of course, I know by heart. She assures me she will set up the entire tea. I needn't worry. I hang up and get ready for the spa.

Unwind is the hippest salon to open in Pasadena in years. The staff wear all-black and offer you everything from cappuccinos to mojitos as you enter. Peregrine turned me on to this place as sort of a backhanded compliment. She gave me an eyebrow wax and a pedicure for my birthday last year. The pedicure was the compliment part; the eyebrow wax was her way of telling me I was starting to look like Frida Kahlo. I still don't feel like I belong in such an atmosphere, but I keep going. Hoping. One day.

The girl behind the counter welcomes me with a grunt. This is the hipster method of greeting. Her piercings are distracting. I'm trying to connect the chains as I tell her I'm here to see Sam for my massage. She clicks the mouse a few times and announces that I can follow her. She walks away, never looking back.

I go through the beaded curtain past the Indian god Ganesha and enter the inner sanctum of the spa. Bustling, black-clad employees walk back and forth from closed door to closed door. My pierced guide leads me into the bathroom and points to a shelf of terry-cloth robes. She tells me to pick one out, then wait in the seating area with the fountain. Sam will pick me up from there. She adds this last bit as the door closes behind her. I say thank you to the closing door as I stand in the bathroom completely alone.

I sort through the robes and finally settle on an oversize, hot pink number with UNWIND in thug-style writing across the back. I look like I'm entering the ring in a battle to defend my heavyweight boxing title. I decide to keep my bra and panties on until I reach the massage room, just in case. Just in case there's a tornado or some other natural disaster where I suddenly have to run from the building without being able to re-dress. I cinch the belt tight and find a seat by the fountain. I pick up a random magazine and wait.

"Maggie? Are you Maggie Thompson?" I look up from the magazine and my mouth falls open.

"Hi, I'm Sam." He is over six feet tall. His curly blond hair falls in perfect ringlets around his impossibly beautiful face. He has the bluest eyes I've ever seen. He extends his hand, and I can see that his arms are sleeved in tattoos. He wears his khaki work pants low-slung and a white Unwind polo shirt.

I cannot speak. I cannot move. I certainly cannot take this robe off in front of this perfect cherub. I can, however, throttle Peregrine and proceed to kill her with my bare hands.

"Hi, you're Sam?" I manage, shaking hands with him. His hands are so strong. I'm not going to make it. I'm not going to live through this day.

"Yeah, why don't you come on back?" Sam pulls me up as I anxiously tug my robe closed.

"So what are we working on this morning? Where are you feeling tight?" Sam walks with his hands linked behind his back. I cannot look at him.

"Mostly, my neck. You know, around my shoulders—that kind of thing. Really nothing lower—I'm fine . . . you know, down there." Somehow I've managed, with just one sentence, to insinuate that my privates are in no need of massage. Well played.

"Well, we'll just play it by ear then, I guess." Sam opens the door to the massage room. The only light comes from several votives on a side table. The ambient music is set low. There is a massive massage table in the middle of the room with a white sheet pulled back.

"Go ahead and get undressed, lie on the table facedown, and I'll be right back." Sam closes the door. I panic. Has Peregrine sent me to a gigolo? Is there such a thing anymore? Are they even called that nowadays?

I slip the robe off my shoulders, finally accepting the fact that I'm trapped like a rat. I am standing there paralyzed with my fingers under my bra straps. A quick slide show of Sam fleeing, piercing laughter, black-clad employees brought in to point and laugh flashes in my head. Fuck it. Fuck it. Fuck it. I pull my bra off and then slide my panties all the way down. I hide them both under the robe on a chair in the corner of the room. I am completely naked. I sprint to the table and pull the sheet up to the back of my neck. I tuck my arms underneath my body, hoping this move will take some of my Area with it. I hear a faint knock on the door. I can't see a thing as my face is now embedded in the massage table.

"Maggie? You ready for me?" I am sick to my stomach.

"Yep!" I bark, my face deep in the massage table. I hear him open and close the door.

Sam walks around the table, one hand tracing the outline of my body. I feel like a horse that might kick her trainer because she can't see past her own hindquarters.

"So we're going to go ahead and start, okay?" I hear Sam squirt lotion in his hands. He works his hands back and forth, back and forth. He pauses—then more back and forth. I concentrate on the music. Is that "Danny Boy" on a sitar?

Sam takes hold of my head, massaging my hair and elongating my neck. It feels amazing. I realize how much I miss touch. I read once about a research study of Romanian babies where they discovered that people who go without touch for extended periods have a stunted outlook on life.

Okay, maybe he will just work up . . . What the fuck? Sam takes hold of the sheet and folds it down all the way to my ass. I hear myself gasp. My entire body goes tight. This massage has just become a complete waste of time and money. I'll need a massage just to recuperate from the massage. Sam works the lotion into his hands once more. I can feel his body as he stands by my head. He reaches over me and, using both his hands, rubs all the way down my back—from my shoulders to my ass. He repeats this over and over again. To my horror, every time he gets to the base of my back, the sheet is pushed even farther down my ass. By the end of this little rubdown the sheet will be somewhere around my knees.

I have never been touched like this in my entire life. I analyze how Mason Phelps consummated anything that day while touching me so little. Sam's hands are everywhere. And not just accidental brushes. He kneads my Area at one point. I can't really remember that exact moment because I think I momentarily blacked out from sheer terror. He starts massaging my right leg. He's getting alarmingly close to parts of my body I had set aside for that fateful day when Ponyboy came a-knocking. It's when he's on my left leg that I finally talk myself into calming down. He's seen it all, I tell myself. He's a professional. He looks at naked people for a living. You're just another naked woman he's massaging today. I will myself to enjoy what's left of the massage. I fantasize about the ways I will maim Peregrine. There are a lot of weapons in a coffeehouse. Hot steaming water? Shove her tiny body into the ice cream case and scoop around her? Suffocate her with rainbow sprinkles? Why would she do this to me? What would make Peregrine send me to Sam, of all people?

"Okay, Maggie. Go ahead and turn over onto your back." Sam holds the sheet up, giving me privacy as I turn over onto my back. I let out a long sigh.

"That was my mouth, by the way," I say, panicked. Sam smiles as he fixes the sheet right at the top of my breasts. Once again, I tuck my arms underneath my body. Sam takes hold of my arm before I finish tucking. I keep my eyes closed. He takes my hand and begins massaging each finger individually. I can feel the hair on his arm as my hand curls around his. I am jolted by what this simple thing does to me. It is that same feeling I had that night with Domenic. The tingles are everywhere. My face goes bright red, and I tense up once again.

"Now, don't do that, Maggie, you were finally loosening up." I keep my eyes closed as Sam shakes out my hand. I smile as he makes me give him a high five with my own hand.

"Good." He continues. I can feel my shoulders lowering a good four inches.

The hour fades as I make myself comfortable with Sam working on my body. We never speak again until he tells me that we are done and he'll meet me in the hall once I'm dressed. I hear the door close behind him, and for the first time I open my eyes. I look down at my body. In that moment, there is a lifting, an erasing of sorts. Mason Phelps and his pinch are gone forever.

I arrive at Joe's a good ten minutes before my shift that night.

I walk past Peregrine and Christina behind the counter. Peregrine gives me an eyebrow raise while she looks at herself in the mirror.

"I met Sam," I say to Peregrine over the counter.

"What did you think?" Peregrine turns around excitedly.

"Funny, you didn't mention Sam had a penis," I say. I hear the creak of a chair in the distance of the coffeehouse. The word *penis* has piqued someone's interest.

"Didn't I?" Peregrine beams.

"Must have slipped your mind, huh?" I open the door to the back room.

"Hey," Domenic says, his hands elbow deep in suds.

"Hey there, stranger." My body is so completely relaxed.

"Where have you been? I haven't seen you since the move."

"Well, I worked yesterday and I, you know, I've been around," I say.

"Well, I've missed you," Domenic says. Even in this altered state, I grow angry. How dare you. How dare you play with me like this. You're dating someone else, Domenic. You've been on as many as two dates during our little flirtation yet you insist on keeping whatever investment you have in me going. But once again—where am I in all of this? Let's face it, I need to be more honest about how I see him, too.

"Really?" I begin to calm down.

"Well, yeah. What have you been doing with yourself? Unpacking?" He is wiping his hands on his apron, which stretches the fabric along the front of his pants. It is like a strobe light. I feel a seizure coming on.

"I wanted to know if you wanted to maybe grab some dinner. I'd love to buy you dinner . . . as a thank-you. You know, thanks for helping with the move, maybe we can grab some dinner."

"Sure," he says and moves forward. I almost stumble backward head over feet.

Blue bucket. Blue bucket.

"What are you doing Saturday?" I pant.

"Nothing. I work that day, but I have Saturday night off. What are you proposing?"

"I just thought we could just grab something to eat." Have I said that about a hundred times now?

"Sounds good. Do I have your new number?"

"I don't think so," I say. Domenic grabs a pad of paper and pencil by the schedule and hands them to me.

I write down my new phone number. I'm handing it to Domenic as Christina walks through the door to the back room. I probably should feel like I am caught trying to steal her friend's man. For a millisecond, I do feel like that. My stomach drops, again . . . but I compose myself. This will not even register on Christina's radar. It's like John Sheridan taking me to the homecoming dance or lying on Texas Steven's lap watching art-house movies. I know what the agenda is. I will befriend Domenic and he will thank me for being there for him. He will reassure me that the other night meant nothing. That the kiss was a drunken delusion. He was just being chivalrous holding my hand. Then he'll thank me for all of the absolutely insightful advice I give him on his real relationship with Erin.

Christina introduces herself again, as if we've never met. Domenic and I wave hi. He grabs his plastic bin and heads out into the coffeehouse.

"You guys are cute together." Christina is putting her bused dishes into the soapy water.

"What?"

"You guys look cute together. You know, like the way you are when you're together." I stare at Christina. She looks up at me and continues.

"Erin was, like, a total bitch that night. Cheyenne totally had dibsies on Domenic and Erin, like, snaked him as usual. I mean, at least you're all friends and everything. It's cute." Now we're puppies in a cardboard box in front of a grocery store.

Friends. Right. Don't I get some kind of medal for walking past the blue bucket? No. All I get is this minefield of more blue buckets. Blue buckets filled with bitches named Erin who apparently men never think of as just a friend.

CHAPTER TWENTY-THREE

El Grande es Para la Gordita

For a while I used to keep a photo album where I would put cutout pictures from magazines. I would cut out teensy celebrities with their custom-made Barbie clothes and fantasize about the day I would be able to buy those very same outfits. I even cut out pictures of my own head and pasted them on various famous bodies as I tried to visualize what I would look like as an anorexic fashion maven. But overnight, it was like I lost all hope that I would ever be able to look like those people. So I started cutting out shoes and hats I liked. After that, I started cutting out just furniture and home decorating tips. Now I look for the random destination hot spot I'd love to visit on vacation, and I'll cut that out. I thought that this was an exercise in reality setting in. But looking at it now, it's not all bad. I really don't want to look like those women—the price is too high. I want to look and feel beautiful in my own way. Maybe cutting out beautiful furniture, home decorations, and amazing vacation spots made me focus less on what *perfect* is.

Come Saturday night, I panic about what I am going to wear for Domenic. I sift through my closet and start noticing a pattern. No color. No style. Just coverings. What happened to my style? After twenty minutes of tossing, trying on, cursing, and crying, I choose my tan linen pants, a black tank top, and a light corduroy coat. I am hot already. This outfit would be just fine for fall or winter, but in summer it's already stifling.

Domenic arrives a little bit before 6 p.m. He is wearing the same outfit he wore at Peregrine's party. Are these his Date Clothes? He has a tiny red box of chocolates in one hand. He awkwardly hands them to me.

"Helloo," Domenic says in a faux British accent.

Interesting. Not the most attractive habit. Accents? Keep him golden, Maggie. Keep him golden. That was not a deal breaker. Talk yourself down, girl.

"Hey, there. Come on in." I open the door, set the chocolates down as if I'm completely disinterested in them. I do notice that they are a charming milk chocolate sampler I will investigate at a later time. I push Solo back with my leg. She is growling and barking.

Domenic tries to put his hand out to Solo, but he looks more like Frankenstein. He reaches out stiffly. Solo and I both stare at him as he circles the steamer trunk I've been using as a coffee table. Now Solo has her tail between her legs. She is sure The Creature is going to maul her after they pick daisies together.

"What are you doing?" I finally ask. First we have faux British accents, and now this nasty Frankenstein impersonation. Maybe busing tables is the least of his problems. I did, however, score a box of chocolates.

"I'm trying to reach out to her."

"Are you Frankenstein?"

"No. I'm approachable."

"Everyone in this room thinks you're Frankenstein."

"You and the dog?"

"Yes. Me and the dog."

"Well, that's believable."

We both stare at Solo. She's now barking at nothing and biting at the wall.

"I've enrolled her in obedience classes," I announce.

"Good luck with that. You ready?" Domenic asks.

"Sure, what did you have in mind? What are you in the mood for?"

"Anything," Domenic says, moving toward Solo again.

"Sitdown or order at the counter?" I start to spiral. I can't control it. I want this night to be perfect. I want us to be perfect. I can't get Erin out of my head. I can't stop thinking that Erin didn't have to have a plan. Erin didn't have to ask Domenic out on a date. Domenic was delivered on a silver platter to Erin while I have to work just to get last night's leftovers.

"Well, let's get in the car and start driving," I suggest. I try to calm down. I try to find myself somewhere in this tangled mess of insecurity, doubt, and jealousy.

"Do you want to drive?" Domenic asks.

"Sure." Might as well, I'm obviously the man tonight. We'll talk about the Dodgers and maybe throw in some dish about supermodels being hot. What fun.

We drive aimlessly. Masa? I ask. He doesn't like Japanese food. What about going into Old Town? I ask. They've got several eateries down there. Like what, he asks. I name three or four places. None sound good to him. He asks if I know of a place that has tacos.

"So is this whole night my responsibility?" I joke, but not really.

"I thought you'd have a better idea of where we could go."

"I do have ideas. But you don't like any of them." I'm right in the middle of a temper tantrum.

"Maybe Solo's not the only one who needs obedience classes."

"What? What did you just say?" I am livid.

"We're just trying to find a place to eat." Is he smiling?

"Can you at least admit that you are being a bit maddening right now? Y'all knows of a place that's got them tay-cos?" I put on my best white-trash accent. I continue, "I mean, why did you dress up for tonight?"

"You noticed," he says.

"What?"

"You didn't notice the first time I wore this for you." Domenic smirks. For me? For me? Was Erin just an elaborate accessory?

"Wait, you brought another girl to a party where you knew I would be and you're trying to sell to me that the outfit you wore that night was for me?" I can't take this anymore—if this is fun for Domenic, I won't be a part of it.

Domenic is silent.

"Well?" I honk at someone. Okay, no one. I honk at no one.

"Why don't we just go to that Taco Truck off Colorado?" Domenic's voice is soft.

"The one by the auto parts store?"

"Yeah."

"Sounds perfect." Domenic leans back in his seat and pats my hand on the gearshift. His hand lingers. I can't look at him. Tingles everywhere. He never raised his voice during the whole scene. Not once. He didn't explain anything, either. At least, I finally told the truth about how I feel for once.

Domenic and I pull into the Nishikawa Auto Service parking lot near Fair Oaks Boulevard. The legendary Taco Truck is parked parallel with the street. The smell of the carne asada wafts into the car as we inch into the tiny parking space. The Taco Truck is famous for having the best chicken and steak tacos this side of the 101 freeway. There's no sign to mark this truck; it's simply a magically reappearing carriage of happiness for all who seek it. A small woman takes orders at the window. She's fast and efficient. Domenic and I quickly get to the front of the line and order.

"Two chicken tacos and a large diet cola, please," I say, and move aside for Domenic to order. I'm proud I didn't order chips.

"Three carne asada tacos, please, and a regular cola," Domenic orders.

"Okay, two chicken tacos, three carne asada tacos, a large diet cola, and a small regular cola?"

"Right," he says.

"That'll be five seventy-nine." Domenic puts his body in front of mine and hands the girl a ten-dollar bill.

"Allow me," he says. I giggle uncontrollably. I start choking on my own spit. Domenic pats me on my back and asks if I'm okay. I nod and try to get myself together.

"Let's just get our food," I finally wheeze.

The girl calls our number and sets my basket of two chicken tacos next to Domenic's three carne asada. The cook walks out and asks, "Which one gets the large drink and which one gets the small?"

"El grande es para la gordita," she says.

I stand there frozen. The man looks right at me and hands me the large diet soda.

Most of the Spanish I know is purely for survival. The word *gordita* is at the top of my list. Loosely translated, it means "little fat girl." People have tried to convince me that it is actually a term of endearment—like describing someone as "cuddly" or "chubby"—but I don't buy it.

I take the soda and stare at the man. How dare you pick me out of this crowd? How dare you look right at me and hand me this soda: the *gordita's* soda. So I have this amazing epiphany about blue buckets. What if I didn't act quickly enough, and this is the universe's way of teaching me the hard way? What if I finally decide I'm not going to be invisible anymore, and right out of the gate someone starts shoving me back in? Fucking blue buckets. Solo was right. Stay away.

Maybe I'm not working as hard as I should to lose weight. For the love of God, I'm not actually doing anything at all except obsessing about how shitty it is to be fat. How many epiphanies is it going to take to finally get me to *do* something? I get why I eat. I get why I stay this way. Now I have to decide if I want to continue to live like this. Not because of this bitch calling me out tonight, but because of the way I'm living my life. Or rather, *not* living it.

Domenic and I find a seat on a nearby wall and balance our dinners on our laps. Sitting there on a tiny wall with a basket of unhealthy chicken tacos and my goddamn large soda mocking me from the ground, I finally get it. Peregrine and her huge, monster-size ego were right again. Those two seconds where she betrayed herself and lied to her grandparents is exactly how I live my life all the time. I constantly hide the person I really am under this disguise I've been wearing for far too long. Enough. Blue bucket my ass. This stops now.

"I forgot a straw," I say. Domenic asks me to get him one, too. I stand and walk toward the window. I cut to the front of the line. It's something I should have done fifteen years ago.

"Do you need napkins?" she asks.

"Napkins? No. I understand Spanish. I know what you said,

la gordita?" I am pointing at her. My finger is so rigid it is arching upward.

"So?" she says.

"That's fucked. You're fucked. It's fucked up to say that," I say.

I grab two straws from the cup on the counter, give her the middle finger, and turn on my heel to walk past the line of people waiting for their food. My back straightens a little. Domenic is waiting at the wall completely oblivious to the entire goings-on. I approach him with a wide smile. The line continues to move as the girl takes orders. I have never stood up for myself. I've never made myself visible. My enemy has always had the ultimate weapon: They might call me fat. Or so I thought. I thought if I fought back the insults would multiply, and so would the insulters. But no one is laughing at me. No one gives the girl at the window high fives for calling a spade a spade. Instead, I said what I had to say. If I'd known this earlier, maybe I would have lived by another code.

But I know it now.

CHAPTER TWENTY-FOUR

An Engraved Invitation

I have a picture of me when I was about four years old. I was standing on the top of a jungle gym on some playground smiling down at my mom as she snapped the picture. I'm wearing this teensy light blue dress with red knee-high socks and the ever-present navy-blue Vans. The older I get, the more I realize that this little girl knew more about me than I do now. So here it begins. I will find that jungle gym and start climbing. I have to believe that no one is going to point and laugh at me as I stand on top of it.

Back at home, I put on a random CD that's not random at all and toss the chocolates Domenic gave me in the trash when he's not looking. I feel like a filter has been peeled back on how I view life. The clarity I have tonight is unprecedented. Domenic plunks down on the couch, moving various pillows and decorative throws out of the way. Solo is sniffing and jittery, but she's not barking. I think she's taking to him. I ask if he wants something to drink. I even have a leftover bottle of white wine in the refrigerator from when Russell tried to teach me how to cook some kind of fancy chicken. I still can't cook the chicken, but at least I've got this here wine. Domenic says the wine would be wonderful. I pour him a glass and one for me as well. I sit next to him on the couch.

It's the reality of Domenic that gets me. The way our bodies and minds fit together in the simplest of ways. Long sentences twirling around a shared perspective. Complete ease with each other mixed with the awkward flutters of unknown goings-on. It's nights like this that make those illogical jumps that much easier. I can see us curled up on the couch night after night in front of a crackling fire. His body makes my fantasy more real. There's an odd familiarity about him. Like he's the embodiment of someone I've been looking for even longer than I knew it was Domenic.

The hours roll by, and soon the clock reads a.m. We finished the bottle of wine hours ago. His arm is now resting on the back of the couch. His hand is inches from my shoulder. I keep itching my ankle because then I bend forward just enough to brush his fingers. In my mind, I'm throwing myself at him.

Even with all the epiphanies and blue-bucket moments of the night, I find myself uncomfortable and terrified. I'm good at being the fat, jolly sidekick. I've perfected that role. I have no idea how to be the ingenue and I certainly don't think I could fit into any of her clothes.

"Can we talk about what you said earlier?" Domenic says as he puts our wineglasses in my kitchen sink. I panic and think he's talking about my little run-in with the girl at the Taco Truck.

"What did I say earlier?" Domenic makes a face like I'm being coy. Trust me, I'm really just trying to clarify here.

"About Erin. You know, the party. The outfit. You know?" Oh.

"Yeah, what about it?"

"I felt bad that I left her at the party, you know? So . . . but you don't even know why I was at the party with her in the first place. Right. I don't know. She is a cool girl, but . . . I just . . ." But? But? Solo puts her head on Domenic's lap, and he begins to pet her.

"But what?" I calmly ask. Once again, I relegate myself to prying friend. I am oddly comforted.

"Christina set us up that night at Peregrine's birthday party. She seemed like a nice girl. Her friends were idiots, but she seemed like she had her head on straight."

We're silent once again. Solo is nudging Domenic to pet her. I wonder what he'd do if I crawled over and put my head in his crotch, too.

"Sometimes . . . it's just easier, you know, when you know for sure how someone feels. Does that make sense?" Domenic looks up.

"Don't you think bringing another girl to a party would send a pretty clear message?" I want him to rise above the ranks of Target Practice. If he really wants to be with me, I have to believe I'm worth getting outside his comfort zone. Lord knows, I'm way the fuck out of mine.

"Do you still have the CD I gave you?" Domenic asks.

"Yes."

"Did you listen to the whole thing?"

"Yes."

If I don't pass out in the next couple seconds, I'll be shocked. Domenic stays silent. Should I mention the hidden track? Should I mention that night? No.

"I'd better get going." Domenic quickly stands and pats his pockets for his keys. My heart chokes.

"There's this internship," I blurt.

"What?" Domenic pulls his keys from his pocket.

"The Getty is restoring this sculpture of Marcus Aurelius

from AD ninety-five, and they need a gap filler and an in-painter. Do you know what that is?" I ask.

"Yeah . . . yeah. You do that?" Domenic puts his hands and his keys in his pockets.

"I have a master's in museum studies with a focus on the conservation end. It just clicked. My sister discovered this internship at the Getty. I'm going on an interview this Monday." I can't look at him. If you lean over and kiss me right now, Domenic Brown, I swear I would kiss you back.

"You'll do great." Domenic smiles and walks toward the door. I walk behind him.

"I had fun tonight." Domenic looks over at me. I feel tingles all over my body. It's frightening and new but I could definitely get used to it. Shit, if I can handle Sam . . .

"Me, too. See you later?" I can feel the sadness already crawling up my throat. He's leaving.

"Well . . ." Domenic leans in and gives me a full two-armed hug. I breathe in. I don't think about anything, I just hug back. I can feel every inch of our bodies together—not one of those LA hugs where you look like a couple of conjoined twins who are connected at the shoulders. I nestle my head in the crook of his neck. He's warm yet there's something so . . . hot about him. It's that thing. The carnal connection you have with someone that can't be explained. There it is. He squeezes me tighter . . . tighter. I reach up and feel the hair on the back of his head. It's so soft. The flips of black hair. Can I reach up and bite them? Time is lost. But I pull away first. I can't bring myself to be pulled away from.

The next day I call the local gym and ask to speak with the next available trainer.

CHAPTER TWENTY-FIVE

Could Eric Gagne Save Me, Too?

I have forgotten who I am. It's that simple. I have forgotten what it feels like to be me. I just tasted the real me—the girl who stood on that climbing structure in the teensy, light blue dress with red socks and blue Vans tennis shoes. This apologetic, mediocre substitute is growing increasingly tiresome.

"If Olivia doesn't want to register anywhere, give me that consideration, then I won't show her any, either," Kate announces at EuroPane before my big Getty outing.

I've confirmed my meeting with Ms. Beverly Urban and already faxed her my résumé. I've put another copy of it in a classy navy-blue folder along with recommendations from my professors and the museum curators I worked for in the last year of my master's. I put pictures of all my restorations, awards, and commendations in a photo album. I also included photos of my final project for my master's—a sculpture of a woman with a pitcher. When it first got to my corner of the studio, it was a woman, an arm, and a pitcher. My adhesions were so perfect that she is now the centerpiece of a private gallery in Pacific Heights. I'm nervous, but excited. I feel like I just got strapped into a roller coaster and we're climbing that first big hill. I hear the clicks beneath my chair, but I can't keep myself from looking down.

"You could think about what Olivia and Adam would want, not what some little radar gun picks for them," I say, sipping my coffee and playing tic-tac-toe with Emily. Bella is peeling the outside of her cinnamon roll off and licking just the cream. If only all of us could do that . . .

"Registering is not just about being greedy with the radar gun," Kate says.

"Guns are bad," Emily says.

"I know, sweetie. This gun isn't really a gun, it's like a little laser that remembers what presents you would like people to give you when you get married," I say as my stomach flutters around.

"Oh." Emily has managed to squeeze in an extra turn during my *guns-are-bad* discourse. I have been bested. She writes a big E over our game and draws another tic-tac-toe grid. I sip my coffee and pick at a strawberry. The days are closing in fast until Mom and I have to walk into the gym and let some strange man named Gabriel "train" us. Mom has decided to join me on my path to freedom. She says she doesn't like how weak she feels now that she's a woman of a "certain age." I picture some medieval torture device that pulls your shirt up over your Area while this Gabriel clown makes you do it ten times for three sets. Of course, there are mirrors everywhere and the entire gym is staring at you. One blue bucket at a time.

"It's not about being greedy. What about your grandmother and great-aunt way back in Margate, New Jersey? They haven't seen you since you were ten years old, but they want to get you something nice. Something they know you'll not only like, but also need. That's where the consideration thing comes in," Mom explains.

"And maybe thinking about someone besides themselves," Kate adds.

Kate hasn't been a big fan of Olivia's for a while. Always the protective older sister, she has been around for too many months without calls or visits and too many hurt feelings. In Kate's mind, Olivia has not stood the test of time. She thinks Olivia has become snobby, arrogant, and ever more neglectful of her devoted childhood friend. I wonder where she would get that idea?

When I heard that Olivia was marrying her first boyfriend and having the fairy-tale wedding we had always dreamed of, I was ecstatic. I told and retold the romantic proposal story to all who would listen and shared in the happiness of Olivia's family and friends. But a part of me felt I knew a secret. Adam and Olivia weren't this perfect couple. On the contrary, Olivia was marrying a man who could never give her enough and never make room for her properly. Dr. Adam Farrell is the third man Olivia loved but the only man to know Olivia existed. Since she never had an actual conversation with Ben Dunn or Shane Presky, Dr. Adam Farrell is the sole manifestation of her lifelong fantasy.

Olivia asked me to be her maid of honor at El Coyote on that infamous "Napkin Night." Maybe I felt it was finally my turn to cash in all those neglected friendship chips. When I felt myself growing apart from Olivia, I selfishly wanted to stick around because I hadn't had my trophy moment yet. Olivia's wedding would be just as much my moment as hers. Our friendship had turned into a souvenir book filled with history and cool childhood-friend stories that we trotted out at parties.

It was the envy of all our new acquaintances. It was like an old set of company china—carefully set out to be viewed and shown off, but no one actually eats off it. The friendship hadn't been functional for some time.

I knew this truth in the dark of the night. I tried to think around it or rationalize it. Surely this lack of communication could be explained away as a horrible side effect of our busy lives. We were the perfect friends. We sound like each other. Our mannerisms, our inflection—we finish each other's sentences. I see it in the faces of people around us. They need us to stay friends because it makes them believe in friendships that last a lifetime. Am I fighting the good fight to remain Olivia's best friend or am I just, once again, afraid of being alone?

I went to Washington, DC, the summer after Adam proposed to Olivia at the Washington Monument. I purposely chose a weekend Adam was going to be at a cardiology symposium in Flagstaff, Arizona. While I understand that the significant other comes first when you're in a relationship, I always felt I was intruding on Adam and Olivia's time together. So I made the trip when I thought Olivia and I could have some time alone.

I called Olivia from Dulles Airport, a little drunk and a lot hysterical from the bumpy flight. She wasn't at the gate as we had arranged, and I became concerned. I had forgotten my cell phone, so I called Olivia from a pay phone by baggage claim. When she finally answered, she announced excitedly that Adam hadn't gone to the symposium after all and, wasn't it great, we could all hang out for the weekend together. There went my plans for some time alone with Olivia.

Worse yet, she had apparently forgotten that she had promised to meet me at the airport and drive me into DC. Instead, she asked me to meet them later at a bar near their apartment for drinks and dinner. She made a pathetic effort to make this right by offering to pay for the airport shuttle.

As I hung up the sticky, greasy pay phone at Dulles, I knew the elephant in the living room could no longer be ignored: Our friendship was in trouble. I stopped and browsed in the tiny airport bookstore, picking up several magazines for my weekend with the happy couple. I then bought myself a draft beer and watched the tail end of a Dodger game on one of the million televisions in the bar—holding the cheers back as Eric Gagne saved another one. Looking back, I should've gotten right back on the plane and flown home.

The airport shuttle took a detour through Virginia, and after approximately three hours cramped in a tiny van, I finally arrived at the bar. Olivia and Adam had long since finished dinner and were now nursing their glasses of red wine. Adam was still in his scrubs from the hospital and looked exhausted. Olivia looked upset and stressed. I sat down across from them as a waiter handed me a menu.

"Sorry I'm late." And I'm sorry you're a horrible friend. And I'm sorry you're a complete pompous ass.

"It's okay," Olivia said as she massaged the back of Adam's neck.

"So what's the plan, Stan?" I say.

"Would you mind if we just went home? Adam has had a really long day. We can go out tomorrow. I already have it all planned out," Olivia said.

"Sure. Sure. Sleep sounds good." Lie.

I never asked myself why I stuck around that weekend. The only thing I worried about was what I'd done to turn Olivia against me. Why didn't she like me anymore? Why didn't Adam like me? Why wasn't this working? I think the reason behind Olivia's attraction to Adam—besides his being the ultimate male—was that everyone except her annoyed him. She could feel like she was in on the joke, and no longer the butt.

When we finally got back to Olivia and Adam's apartment, Olivia had already set up Adam's camping mattress for me to sleep on.

"Liv, this is that show I was telling you about." Adam was sitting on the camping mattress (aka my bed), watching the only television in the house. The one in the living room. The one you had to sit on my bed to watch. It was now past midnight, and I was becoming exhausted.

"Oh, yeah. I remember you talking about this. Wow, is it on right now?" Olivia said.

"Yeah, they must be replaying it." Adam pulled his keys and wallet out of his back pocket and set them down on the camping mattress next to him.

His wallet and keys sat next to him. I realized that Olivia couldn't sit down as she watched the show, either. There wasn't enough room on the camping mattress, and Adam never moved over. Neither did Olivia. I decided to take a shower and wash myself up a bit. I grabbed my bag, found my toiletries, and told them I was going to take a shower. I was hoping this would give Olivia the opportunity to let Adam know that it was time to go to bed. Maybe he could watch his show another time, tiny-handed bitch.

I came out of the shower feeling even more tired. I was relaxed and clean and cuddly in my pajamas. Adam was still sitting on the camping mattress . . . alone. Olivia was standing exactly where she had been before I took my long shower.

I loaded my toiletry bag back in my suitcase and loitered around my waiting bed. Adam was absolutely focused on the television. Olivia was standing stock-still with her hand on her hip, staring blankly at the television screen. I don't know if she was pissed off at Adam, or if she was as riveted as he was to this seemingly vapid show. I tried to make eye contact with her but got nothing.

I sat at the kitchen table and waited it out. I was beginning to get cold, so I put an afghan over my shoulders as I sat on the hard wooden kitchen chair. My head began to bob, and my eyes could no longer voluntarily stay open. I ended up sitting in that chair for almost an hour as Adam finished watching his show, grabbed his keys and wallet, and silently walked into the bedroom. Not one *thank you* or one *good night;* nothing. Grabbed keys and wallet—went to bedroom. Olivia made a silly face and fussed with my bed. She wished me good night, tucked me in, and said she couldn't wait until tomorrow. Yeah, me, either. Whoopee.

She also told me Adam would be working all day tomorrow. I thought that this was payback for that evening's antics. Honestly, I couldn't tell you for sure. That night was a peek into what Olivia and Olivia's life had become. The two queen-size beds were a mere trailer to the full-length film that unfolded here tonight. I didn't like what I saw. I didn't like that Olivia never considered advocating for me. Hell, she didn't even feel the need to advocate for herself. Her best friend of fifteen years was sleeping with an afghan over her shoulders at the kitchen table and she never once thought that this was anything but business as usual. I wonder how many times she's sat in that exact same chair waiting. This is what happens when you don't think the fantasy through. Adam decorates with black leather couches, and I hear he goes to black-tie affairs a lot. The part you don't hear about is the two queen-size beds and nights spent with an afghan over your shoulders waiting for the king to go to bed.

Back at EuroPane, I ready myself for a day at the Getty. Kate and Mom are taking the girlies to the Huntington Library to see the famous paintings *Pinkie* and *The Blue Boy*. Emily shows me the pamphlet she saved from last time they went. Kate rolls her eyes as she loads the girlies into her minivan. Bella can't stop chattering about sculperrs and how there's no dollies at Huntington, just "nakeds with their ding-dongs showing." Emily fans herself with her beloved pamphlet and buckles herself tightly into her seat. Mom gets into the front seat and begins fiddling with the seat belt. I almost lunge at the van and beg them to take me with them.

CHAPTER TWENTY-SIX

Hemming a Degas

After parking in the lower lot, I board the pristine white tram that will climb the hills overlooking Brentwood and Santa Monica up to the Getty Museum. I am nervous and at the same time calm. I've made this trek hundreds of times. I often come to the Getty to get some peace of mind. This tram ride means I'm safe. I am not thinking about Olivia or Domenic. I can't even begin to go to the place in my mind where I would deny myself this place, this tram ride and Marcus Aurelius. The tram jostles forward. I catch myself and smile at a pregnant lady who is sitting two seats to my left. If this is about trust, let's see if I can trust in myself.

I check in with the guard and let him know that I am here for an interview. He taps a few buttons on the computer and presents me with a name badge. It has my name on it in all-capital letters, MARGARET THOMPSON. I can picture it on my bulletin board now. He tells me to have a seat and Ms. Urban will be right out.

I wait for only a few seconds before I notice a woman approaching who has got to be Ms. Beverly Urban. Her stark white hair is perfectly straight and hangs below her shoulders. She has milky white skin and wears no makeup. She wears black matching separates and accessorizes with what look like African beads around her neck. Her chandelier earrings hang low and only accentuate her beauty.

"Ms. Thompson?" Ms. Urban extends her hand. I stand.

"Yes, wonderful to finally meet you." I pull at my shirt as I stand, almost dropping my interview materials. I am trembling, yet I shake her hand firmly.

"Follow me, please." Ms. Urban walks in front of me past the security officer. I continue to follow her down into the basement.

The office is filled with all kinds of art—all original. Sculpture. Tapestry. Paintings. Some photography. She sits behind her desk, flips open a file, and asks me to sit.

"So, Ms. Thompson?" Ms. Urban is looking through a file on her desk. "I received the résumé you faxed over and suffice it to say, I am thoroughly impressed." Just listen. Let the résumé do the talking until I have the balls to jump in.

"Thank you," I manage.

"Magna cum laude from the University of California at Berkeley and then on to San Francisco State. From there it appears that you did restorations for some of the top museums in San Francisco." Ms. Urban looks at me. Not quite ready. Am horrified. No balls.

"You've got recommendations here from some of the most respected curators in the business, Ms. Thompson." Ms. Urban is flipping through the photo album I apparently pushed at her sometime in the last five minutes. I am breathing so hard I can't make out the words Ms. Urban is saying. I want this internship so badly, I can't bring myself to come down to earth and be present. On top of all this, I believe I'm being complimented.

Enough. No more. If I can't believe in my own talent, how can anyone else? If I fear mediocrity, why am I struggling so fiercely to hang on to it? It's staring me right in the face and I'm having a nervous breakdown at the thought of someone complimenting me on my own talent. I am qualified. Enough—enough of this half life of numbness and the daily grind.

"Mr. Frankel was a big fan of my in-painting. I won him over with the cherub on page nine—if you look at the 'before' and 'after' pictures, you'll see the subtlety of my work. I worked for him several times. He was very generous in his recommendation." I have forgotten to breathe. I look at Ms. Urban so clearly. I deserve to be here.

"He wasn't generous at all. Your work speaks for itself, Ms. Thompson. Is this a Degas?" Ms. Urban's voice catches as she holds my photo album as close to her face as she can get it.

"Yes, ma'am. They brought her in from a rough international flight. It was due at the Norton Simon Museum for their spring installation. They brought me in to hem the skirt and reconnect her third finger—you have to look close." I scoot my chair up and lean over the table to point out the restoration to Ms. Urban. She nods in agreement as she flips between the "before" and "after" shots of the sculpture.

There are blue buckets passing me at the speed of sound. I am on. I am funny. Even Ms. Urban laughs at a joke about the *Venus of Willendorf* and myself. All hips. It's a fertility-goddess joke. In the end, she shakes my hand and tells me she will call within a couple of weeks. I tell her it was a pleasure and I actually mean it.

I drive home and can't keep one thought in my head. I am a mixture of joy, fear, excitement, and a little sadness. I haven't seen Domenic since our "date." Was that night some kind of beginning or was it just another night with a friend? Of course, I'm feeling anxious about it. I know he's not with Erin anymore. Maybe . . . maybe he's not with her anymore because he secretly loves me? I find myself thinking about Beverly Urban. I finally have someone who gets my jokes about ancient fertility goddesses. It's a small demographic, sure, but when you find them they're loyal as hell. I get home and turn on my computer. My mind is reeling. I decide to check my e-mail.

There's a note from Olivia that includes the addresses of bridal-shower invitees. She recommends I send everyone a bulk "Save the Date" e-mail. It's ironic that the three women who celebrated her shower a couple of weeks ago know more about the actual event than I do. I read on. She thanks me for her birthday gift, which arrived two days early. I sprang for a spa package for her in Las Vegas so she could have some time to herself during the big bridal-shower weekend. I got her a hot bath in rose-scented water with a scalp massage, followed by a Vichy shower where she will be rubbed down with coconut and other tropical oils. Our birthdays are only days apart. Over the years, Olivia has showered me with embarrassing gifts like dancing Candy Grams, Ferraris rented for the day, and a weekend at the famous San Ysidro Ranch outside Santa Barbara. When it comes to my birthday, Olivia goes all out. Even as our friendship waned over the last few years, Olivia has never dropped the ball when it came to my birthday.

I scroll back up to her list of shower invitees. Gwen is at the top of the list, of course. I hate that we are communicating via e-mail. I would love for her invitation to get lost in the mail. Now it would just be me lying about getting her e-mail address wrong. Where's the drama in that?

Olivia gives me a full bio on each of the remaining three girls. Panchali Nagra runs an art gallery in Georgetown. She mentions that Panchali lives with her husband and their dog,

Luciano, in an apartment they've renovated over the gallery. She also mentions offhandedly that she competes in triathlons around the world. Yeah, there's someone I can relate to. Hannah Ratner is a corporate lawyer for one of the top firms in the nation. She is single. That's all on Hannah Ratner. She is single. I guess that's enough said. Then there's Shawna Moss, a girl who's famous for having bowls of M&M's in her office, which is dangerously close to Olivia's office at the PR firm. Of course, Olivia goes on a three-paragraph tirade about how Shawna just wants to get her fat. Or anyone to get fat—for Shawna is, and I'll quote Olivia here, "an anorexic bitch who won't let her narrow ass get past a size 0." There's a true friend. I can just see the toast now at the rehearsal dinner: "Hi, I'm Shawna Moss and I'm trying to get everyone fat because I'm an anorexic bitch who won't let anyone get skinnier than my narrow ass." And . . . cue applause.

I reply to Olivia confirming the "Save the Date" e-mail. I go over some of the details I've arranged for her shower in Las Vegas. Olivia and I will meet for a martini before the festivities begin. I e-mail her that we should meet at the Caramel Bar in the Bellagio, where they have a whole menu of specialty martinis. I am looking forward to spending an afternoon with just Olivia. Then I really think about it. What will the new Olivia and Maggie have to talk about? How many times can we fantasize about different people from high school stumbling onto her wedding and being asked to leave (rather loudly and with much fuss)? Is this it? I will try to resurrect our friendship in Las Vegas. I will set aside all of my thoughts of Adam and his teensy hands. I will set aside all of my insecurities and just focus on us.

That night, I put together and send the "Save the Date" bridal-shower e-mail to Olivia's list of friends. I try to sound as mellow and fun as possible:

Viva Las Vegas!
Join us at the Bellagio to celebrate
Olivia's impending nuptials.

That sounds too frightening. The nuptials are impending so the hospital must quarantine those already exposed. Just think breezy.

Viva Las Vegas
We're partying like it's 1999 up in Bellagio's hizz-ouse.
Woop Woop!

No.

I finally put together a basic list of the weekend's activities in a neutral format. It's sterile and could be construed by some as breezy. I can't help but look forward to the coming weeks. I know about the elephant in the living room. And I know that Olivia and I are fine china no longer fit to eat upon. But we have to have something to show for our years together. We have been like sisters through some of the hardest times in our lives—how can it all now be for naught?

CHAPTER TWENTY-SEVEN

Seabiscuit and The Corner

I'd like to think that all this introspection and digging would have prizes at the end. Find out you eat because you're lonely—get a trip to Paris. Find out your best friend is a walking leftover from a lost childhood—get a nice Crock-Pot. Realize you've run from men because the fear of rejection or commitment scares the shit out of you—take home a nice dining room set. But you don't get prizes. You get pain and an inordinately heavy feeling that you've failed in absolutely every way. Gee, I wonder why more people don't try it?

This is the day I've been dreading my whole life. The day I dress my ass up in "workout" clothes and walk myself into a gym. I imagine shrieks of horror. I imagine small children being shielded from my hideousness by their parents. Just your basic pointing and laughing.

Mom meets me out in front of the gym. She looks perfect. Her little pink sweat suit is accented with black piping, and she is carrying a matching shoulder holster with a perfectly chilled bottle of water. I, on the other hand, have on pajama bottoms and an oversize men's white V-neck T-shirt. I am wearing a pink-and-gray pair of Pumas, and my hair is up in a ponytail.

Mom and I approach the counter. She announces we are here to see Gabriel James. "We have an appointment," Mom says, tapping her diamond Rolex Lady President watch on the counter. The Rolex was an Arbor Day present from Russell. The girl behind the counter, momentarily blinded by the diamonds, regains her composure and announces over the intercom that Gabriel is wanted at the front desk.

To my horror, Gabriel James is a strapping young lad. No more than twenty-two or twenty-three years old. Internation-ally good looking, with a swagger equaled only by celluloid cowboys and the aging male movie stars who play them. He is way over six feet tall, dwarfing me. I doubt he can even see my poor, tiny mother from where he stands. His cocoa skin is flaw-less and only emphasizes his light green eyes. He wears Adidas workout pants and a T-shirt advertising some fraternity's big all-alcohol summer blowout festival jamboree. This is the man who's going to train me? This is the man to whom I'm going to tell my deepest, darkest secrets? This is the man who is going to take on my Area? I think not.

"Howdy, ladies." Gabriel extends his paw to my mother and then to me.

Mom is endearing and funny. She compliments him on his green eyes and says she knows we're now in the best of hands. I grunt something like, "Area . . . big . . . fatty . . . you . . . pretty . . ." Gabriel takes my hand and tells me it's a pleasure while looking right in my eyes. He asks us to follow him "on back" to his office. I nod. Mom bats her eyelashes.

He leads us around the gym like a couple of toddlers, show-ing us the water fountain and saying hi to virtually everyone he passes. He knows all of their names and exactly what to talk to them about. With this one, it's the Dodgers. This one, it's the stock market. This one, he talks about landscaping and car-pools. He is absolutely intoxicating. I loathe him.

He takes Mom and me into a back office filled with diplomas and framed photos. There's Gabriel in a race car. Now he's on a bike in the hills. Now he's standing next to a great white shark, which he has apparently just caught. I sit in one of the chairs and pull at my shirt. Mom settles in and takes a swig of her water.

Gabriel starts in with his spiel about health and exercise. He talks about the epidemic that's sweeping the nation—cue scary music—obesity. He says it as if it's some kind of modern-day leprosy. I sit there a full-blown victim of such a disease. I feel a tad vulnerable and even more untouchable. He goes on about metabolism and keeping the fire burning by eating six times a day. My ears perk up. He talks about almonds, avocados, and giving up dairy. It still sounds okay; I've never been a dairy fan. And eating six times a day sounds promising. He passes us two little journals across his desk.

"These are your food diaries." Gabriel flips open a file and starts jotting something down. He is left-handed.

"We have to write down what our food is feeling?" I ask.

"No . . ." Gabriel is laughing. His teeth are perfect. "This is where you write down what foods you are eating and at what times."

"Why?" I ask.

"A little accountability. So I can see what you're putting in your body during the week," Gabriel says.

"How long do we have to do that?" I ask.

"Until I tell you to stop," Gabriel says.

"Oh, okay," I say. Fucking megalomaniac.

Mom schedules Monday and Friday mornings for both of

us. We are responsible for fitting in "cardio" four or five times per week. We'll start with thirty minutes per day. I am growing excited. Gabriel never uses words that have to do with emotions or failure. It's science to him. I have this tiny glint of hope for the first time in my life. But then right after the hope, I cringe with fear. Hope is a scary thing.

Gabriel leads us out into the gym and asks us to warm up on the treadmill. He is a die-hard gentleman who always insists I go first. I am uneasy walking in front of him. I imagine he's staring at my girth in all its glory, so I walk quickly and give Mom a flat tire in the process. She whips around and tells me to "back it up." I feel trapped and hot. Gabriel puts his big paw out and steadies me.

I get on the treadmill and immediately get winded. My legs feel heavy, and they are rubbing together at such an alarming rate that I believe there will soon be a small fire between them. There is a ponytailed girl next to me running at the pace of a young colt in a Virginia pasture. Effortless and graceful. Her ponytail flips in syncopation with her perfect gait. She even smiles at me at one point—her face glowing with sweat, her eyes clear and bright. I thought girls like that in a gym were sup-posed to act snobby and point and laugh. But the only one here who looks like she might do that is me. Gabriel comes over now and again and checks our progress. Mom is just as winded as I am, so he slows her treadmill down. I feel a little better about myself. Then he slows me down, too. Seabiscuit next to me makes a disappointed face—I fight the temptation to snatch her bald-headed.

After what feels like five hours—really seven minutes and twenty-seven seconds—he leads us to our first machine. It is a bench-press setup right in front of a wall of mirrors. I am having flashbacks of my nightmare. You lie back on this bench and he helps you raise and lower a bar with weights. This is supposed to help your chest. The last glimpse I get of myself lying down reminds me of a shot that might come from a home video camera in the birthing room. All that's missing is a pair of stirrups and a crowning baby.

"Go ahead and give me seven more, Maggie. Gooood, and three, two, and ten more." I almost drop the bar. Gabriel's voice is melodic, like an X-ray technician or a doctor as he says, "Relax, this won't hurt a bit."

"Wait. You said seven more and then you went all the way back up to ten," I say, raising and lowering the bar.

"You didn't look tired," Gabriel says while he leans on the bar itself. The weight I have to lift has now doubled.

"Wait—what? Well, now you're just leaning on it!" I am horrified.

"Okay, good. Now give me three more." Now I know that Gabriel is a big, fat leaning-on-the-bar liar. As far as I know, I could be here all night. I do seven more and he finally hooks the bar back into the notch on the equipment.

Mom is next. She does approximately five total. The whole time she looks like she's in complete pain. Gabriel doesn't lean on the bar at all and even passes my mother her perfect little water bottle when she's done. As she's getting up from the bench, my mother winks at me. The bitch. It's on.

Gabriel moves us over to this other medieval torture device. On this one, he demonstrates that you're supposed to lie back down, lifting your body weight with your legs as the equipment rolls back and forth. It works your "quads," he says. All I can see is that this position is pretty near pornographic and there's no way in fucking hell I'm doing it.

"Maggie?" Gabriel asks.

"Yeah, you know what? My knee is . . . um . . . hurting, so

I'm gonna pass," I say, massaging one of my random knees. Mom shakes her head sadly.

"Oh, there's no passing, Maggie. Go ahead and hop on up there." I hate you, Gabriel James. A pox on both your houses, Gabriel James. I climb into the equipment, securing my head and then lifting my legs up into the gynecological position. Gabriel stands at the base of the machine and positions my feet so they are just so. I can't believe how uncomfortable I am—both physically and emotionally. I am waiting to bend my knees when I hear it.

"Uuuuuuuggghhhhh!" It's coming from the corner of the gym where the free weights are. In my mind, I dub it "Testosterone Corner." A corner rife with musclebound men in tiny tank tops and huge parachute pants. There is a definite Neanderthal energy wafting from The Corner. I fear the men who inhabit it will club me from behind and drag me into their cave by my ponytail. I crack a smile thinking that maybe Gabriel will join in. Mom has her hand over her mouth while she scans the gym for the grunting culprit.

"Uuuuuuuuuuuugggggghhh!" Again from The Corner. This time it's much louder.

"Do you hear that?" I ask, still perched at the top of the machine.

"Okay, Maggie, go ahead and just bend the knees all the way down," Gabriel instructs.

"*Uuu*uuuuuuuuuuuggggggghhh."

"Be sure not to lift your heels from the base, and as deep as you can get it," Gabriel continues.

"Uuuuuuuuuuggggggghhhhhhh!" I bend my knees as far down as I can go. But in this position, with that noise going on, I feel like I'm in some bad virtual porn movie.

"Is it getting hot in here?" I ask, on repetition seven, or—as Gabriel likes to call it—repetition one.

"I can turn on a fan, if you'd like. And three more, two, and six more." Gabriel is leaning on the top of the machine again.

"Uuuuuuuuggggggghhhhh! Yeah! That's the good stuff!" The man drops his weights to the ground in a fury of victory. I feel like we should all light up a cigarette.

I crawl out from the machine and grab my water bottle. Mom is next. She holds her hand out as if she's stepping into a horse-drawn carriage. Gabriel obliges. Mom lies back down on the machine and bends her knees down for one repetition. She gets back to the top and resituates her body.

"I just can't seem to get comfortable, hon," Mom says. I roll my eyes.

"Okay, well, let's just do a couple more and then we'll be on to the next exercise. And three, two, aaaand one. Great job." Gabriel extends his hand once more, and Mom hops down from the machine. There is the tiniest of smiles on Mom's face.

We follow Gabriel to several other machines. I realize that my body is hurting. But it feels good. I feel muscles in parts I had forgotten about. My shoulders feel alive. My Area is even a little sore. And not just from the telepathic messages from my head telling it that it is Evil. As the session comes to an end, I am smiling and joking with Gabriel and Mom. We say good-bye to him and promise to bring in our food diaries the next time we meet. Before I get ready for work, I make my first entry into my food diary. I decide to tell the whole truth and nothing but.

CHAPTER TWENTY-EIGHT

Then Stop Acting Like One

As human beings, we crave adrenaline rushes and roller-coaster rides as a kind of foil for the boredom of our lives. But the truth, the very essence of life, is that pure adrenaline rush of change—those terrifying moments when we find ourselves in situations that are new and unknown. Rather than redefining a relationship with a lover or asking for a raise at work, though, we go white-water rafting or buy the fastest Porsche on the rod because we're looking outside ourselves for a fire that burns hottest when ignited from within. You can control when and where that terror is felt and for just how long when you are driving a Porsche or riding a roller coaster. Looking at change and therefore life as that adrenaline rush means you hand over the keys.

I am late to work again, but Peregrine is the manager, thank God. My breath gets back to normal as I pass her with an *I'm-sorry* face and walk into the back room. I ready myself to see Domenic. He is not at the sink as he normally is. I haven't spoken to him in what seems like forever. Our work schedules have been exactly opposite, and I decided right away I was not going to call him. He didn't call me, either. I guess we were agreed on that. We so belong together. I tie my apron around my waist and head out to the counter, where Domenic is bending down filling the little refrigerator with milk.

"Hey, I didn't know you were here!" I am genuinely happy to see him—and for once I show it.

"I was hiding," Domenic says.

"Good thing I didn't do anything embarrassing." Wasn't I going to try to work on not saying the first thing that came into my mind?

"Yeah, good thing. Where have you been?" Domenic asks, standing.

"I could say the same about you," I say, noticing Peregrine watching us like a tennis match.

"We have a big deadline with some of the dolls. There were eight in the order. I also got a line on this gallery in Silverlake that is interested in my sculpture. They want me to be a part of their next installation. So I switched most of my shifts with the Dre. I meant to call."

"Solo missed you," I say.

"You met Solo?" Peregrine asks.

"Yes, I did. She loves me," Domenic says.

"That little bitch wouldn't even come near me," Peregrine says.

"Had her eating out of the palm of my hand," Domenic says.

"You don't call, you don't write," I say, turning my body so my back faces Peregrine.

"Tell her I miss her and I'll stop by soon. While I'm at it, I owe her mom a dinner," Domenic says as he heads out front to bus the outside tables. I smile as he walks out.

The hours pass with Peregrine making small talk and doing a lot of sighing. I refuse to start sputtering out an explanation to her. If she wants to know what happened, she needs to ask. So until then, she can just play her little silent-treatment game. A game that's not much fun if it's just one person playing, by the way. Not really a game at all—you're just being quiet. I know I'm being childish. But there's something oddly adult about it as well. Peregrine needs to ask and not stare at me in a motherly way or drop hints. Just ask. There's a degree of respect and equality that Peregrine can't seem to muster.

"What was that about?" Peregrine finally asks ten minutes before my shift ends.

"We had dinner the other night," I say.

"You didn't tell me that," Peregrine huffs.

"Didn't I?"

"Wait, you're not pissed about Sam—are you?"

"No, *pissed* isn't the right word. Maybe I'm insulted—kinda embarrassed?" I'm in uncharted territory with Peregrine. My face grows hot and I wish I could take back everything I've just said. Smile, Maggie. Tell her you enjoyed your little man-whore experience and if she could just change your diaper everything would be fine.

"Insulted? I don't understand." Peregrine hammers the espresso out of the coffee handles.

"I don't know, okay. Can we just drop this?" I don't think I've been this upset in years. I can't even put my finger on why. I have approximately five more minutes on shift. I pace myself and take deep breaths.

"How can you not know? Come on, button. Let's try to get to the bottom of this. You can talk to me about it." I don't know if it's the way she says *button* or how she's portraying herself as my savior-therapist, but I snap.

"I don't need to get to the bottom of anything with you. I don't need you to throw me in the water to teach me how to swim. You should have just told me Sam was a guy—that's all. I would have been ready—maybe I would have even been a little excited and turned on. I sure as shit would have shaved my fucking legs. I just felt silly, you know? Like stupid—like you didn't respect me or think I was, I don't know . . . maybe worthy of an explanation. I know you thought you were helping, I really do—and it's awesome you think of me that way—but . . . I just don't feel comfortable talking about this kind of stuff with you." I exhale.

"Then who? What—are you going to call Olivia? Are you going to leave a message on the answering machine and hope she picks up?"

What? I now know this fight is going to be that one knock-down, drag-out fight you should never have with someone other than a family member. Every one of your friends has a zinger: the one thing that you can never make fun of them about or throw in their face. It's an unwritten rule of friendships. There are some issues that are kept far beneath the surface, never to be used in anger. If you exhume these zingers, you have to be ready for an apocalypse of sorts.

"What did you just say?" I visualize the dirt cascading off the top of the coffin now, with Peregrine standing next to the hole—her red rose primed and ready.

"I was just noting that you've really got no one else to talk to about this. Olivia being a bit absent and all." Peregrine stands firm.

"Really? I'm a little curious . . ." I trail off.

"About what, lamb?" Peregrine leans in.

"How the fuck you know anything about anyone but yourself." I stare her right in the eye. She backs away.

"What?"

"I'm not your project, Peregrine. I'm not a little potato you put in a glass jar to see if roots grow. I'm also not fucking five years old—and I think, no, I *know* I'm getting sick of you seeing me like that."

"You don't want me to treat you like a child? Then why don't you stop fucking acting like one—huh? You come in here and talk and talk and talk about boys and how fat you think you are and how Olivia won't call you back . . . and I just stand here. And what? Do you think I don't remember anything? Or put two and two together? You get off on being everyone's project. You get off on other people's pity. So don't come to me and say that I'm the one treating you a certain way—it starts with you, honey."

I am speechless. I start to object. Then I slowly realize she's right. She has just wrapped my entire psyche into a neat little package and spit it right in my face. When my shift comes to an end, I storm into the back room, leaving Peregrine standing there for one second too long, mouth open, waiting for my comeback. There isn't one. My comeback is ignoring her and that neat little package. At least that feels good; no wonder Cole does it all the time.

CHAPTER TWENTY-NINE

That's One

My birthday has been the backdrop of many a fantasy: A tearful marriage proposal while strolling on the beach in Malibu. A blowout birthday party at a club where my rock-star boyfriend plays a song in honor of my birthday as I blush in the candlelight of my reserved table. A tiny cake and some company. But up until now it seems that the hours just pass and my birthday slips away without measuring up to my fantasies. This one day belongs to me and me alone. Maybe I try to make too much of it and set myself up for failure. But I want someone to bend over backward to make my day unforgettable. Period. I'm tired of doing all the orchestrating myself. I want a man who won't let my day slip away.

During my years in school, I rationalized that my birthday went unnoticed because it was during the summer. Mom, Kate, and I would go to Ernie Jr's Taco House, where I'd order my favorite bean-and-cheese burrito. Mom would tell the waiter to put a candle in an order of flan and we'd share the dessert. Kate's birthday is in late July, Russell's is one day before Kate's, and mine follows in the first week of August. Olivia fit right into the mix because her birthday landed just a few days after mine. Mom brought up the rear by celebrating her birthday in late August. As the years passed, the tradition continued, and my family began to celebrate all our birthdays at one big bash in Mom and Russell's backyard. The summer birthday season has always been like a second Christmas for our clan. But now with the big bash looming, I can feel my unfulfilled fantasies regurgitating in my throat.

"What are you up to tonight?" Christina asks, leaning over the sink. At least she didn't introduce herself to me again.

"Family dinner." Is Peregrine going to come back here and kick my ass? Why am I so angry?

"What's tonight?" Christina hitches her pants up and turns to face me.

"Our family all has their birthdays within days of each other. My stepdad's is July twenty-third, my sister's is the twenty-fourth, and I'm on the first of August. We choose a night that falls a little before all that hubbub and celebrate all three." Why is it that talking to Christina is completely calming me down after my fight with Peregrine?

"You don't celebrate *on* your birthday?" she asks.

"We do that, too. Just cake, though. Tonight is about a big dinner and presents. Russell, my stepdad, barbecues. We just really make a party out of it," I say from the bathroom, grabbing my purse and long black sweater.

Domenic comes back into the back room. He and I are both off shift at the same time. Peregrine's words are ringing in my ears: *You get off on being everyone's project. You get off on other people's pity. So don't come to me and say that I'm the one treating you a certain way—it starts with you, honey.* Am I angry with the wrong person? Am I shooting the messenger? I try to think about something else.

The birthday party. I'll think about the birthday party. *You get off on being everyone's project.* The birthday party, Maggie. Focus. I realize I have been looking forward to tonight more than I have admitted even to myself—even though I don't have someone to bring with me. Why does everything hinge on having a man?

"Sounds nice," Christina says, turning back to the sink.

Fuck it, I'll think about that hinge later.

"Domenic?" I ask. My voice is too loud. I hardly recognize it. Christina turns around.

"Maggie?" Domenic does this faux accent that's reminiscent of an inspector in some old-timey English mystery. Now that was moderately interesting—endearing.

"What are you doing tonight?"

"Nothing. The order went in yesterday, and I've finished all my sculptures for the Silverlake thing, so I'm footloose and fancy-free," Domenic says. Footloose and fancy-free? Old-timey accents? Eyes on the prize, here. Golden. Keep him golden.

"Would you like to come to my family's birthday party?" A little waver in my voice somehow feminizes me.

"Your family was all born on the same day?" Christina laughs, as if we haven't just finished talking about this. She is now the third person in this conversation.

"No. My sister, stepdad, and I have birthdays within days of each other, so we throw a big dinner to celebrate," I say, patiently, yet with building urgency. I have to prove to Peregrine and myself that I'm capable of taking the initiative.

"What time?" he asks.

"It starts at five thirty. There are little girlies involved, so we have to start early to allow for the inevitable meltdowns," I say.

"It's four o'clock now, so do you want to meet at your house around five-ish?" he asks.

"Sure. Sure. That sounds super." Once again with the *super*.

"Okay, then. I'll see you around five," he says. Domenic puts his time card in the basket and gives me a little wave as he goes through the back door to the coffeehouse. I can't help but stare at his ass.

I look past him for one second and get a shot of Peregrine. She is staring right at me. The door swings closed. I look away. Open. There's Peregrine. Closed. How do you apologize to someone for telling you the truth? Open. She is still staring at me. I've got seconds before this becomes something I'm not going to be able to fix. Closed. Seconds before Peregrine and I just stop talking and the silence becomes the norm. How can I go back in there and say *Sorry*? How can I go back in there and make her understand that I know that she was right but I still don't want to be her project? How can I convince myself of that? I fill out my time card and head home.

Once home, I hop in the shower and wash my hair. I even exfoliate my skin with some stuff Kate put in my stocking this past Christmas. It smells like pineapple, and my skin feels really soft afterward. I try on every outfit I own. Domenic has already seen me in the leather skirt and the linen pants. But do men really look at what women wear? I mean, couldn't I wear the linen pants again and a different top? I bet he wouldn't notice. I put on the linen pants and my tightening panties. A little better. I find a lightweight black sweater in the back of my closet. I try it on. It used to fit small. It doesn't look horrible. In fact, it fits me just fine now. My Area is a little exposed, but the black works its magic. Isn't it too soon for anything Gabriel is doing to be working—maybe I am just feeling better about myself?

Domenic knocks on the door at exactly 5 p.m. Solo goes crazy. I open the door while pushing Cujo back with my leg. Domenic reaches out to her, and she flinches. He Frankensteins his way across the room, and Solo skitters away from The Creature. During this display, I notice that Domenic is wearing a new pair of light brown work pants and a striped, short-sleeved collared shirt with a white T-shirt underneath. His black hair is wet, and I can smell the shampoo again. The smell brings me back to the night after Peregrine's party. I'm beginning to know these smells. The shampoo. The cologne. The aftershave. It's this combination of his smells that awakens every tingle in my body, because the combination could be nobody but Domenic.

Solo finally calms down and allows Domenic to pet her on the crown of her head. Then she backs up and stands behind me. Domenic has a present in his hand. I am stunned. "Who is that for?" I ask.

"The birthday girl, of course." Domenic hands me the gift.

"Should I open it now?" I ask.

"Whenever you want," he says, still trying to go after Solo. She is smelling and licking his hand. What a conniving little vixen.

"I want to open it now." Partly because I can't wait to see what he has gotten me and partly because I am too embarrassed to open a gift from a man in front of my family.

I sit with the gift in my lap. It is wrapped in today's Calendar section of the *LA Times*. I read about movie openings and celebrity sightings. No tape is used and it looks like origami. Why isn't the wrapping falling off?

"How was the interview? I didn't ask earlier because I figured you didn't necessarily want Peregrine to know." He is watching me fiddle with the present.

"Nice paper," I say.

"They sell it every day."

"Classy."

"The interview?" Domenic raises a single eyebrow.

"Oh, yeah. It went great. I just really . . . really want the internship. I just don't want to . . . you know . . ."

"Get your hopes up?"

"Yeah, something like that." My heart breaks as I realize my hopes are up without me even realizing.

I'm nervous and embarrassed. Anything to get the focus off me. Domenic is lying on the floor now with Solo. That's fine with me because his attention is split between the gift opening and the dog, and the dog has to be watched like a hawk or else who knows when she'll snap. I "unwrap" my gift and find a tiny doll in a box that a cell phone came in. The doll is a brown-haired girl in overalls. She is barefoot and holds a small paintbrush in her hand.

"It's an original," he says.

"How did you do this?"

"Gram did a series on artists a few years back, and this was one of the practice ones. I was just learning and she let me do the feet. They're a little big, but I thought you'd like it. She reminds me of you." Domenic is concentrating on petting Solo.

"Big-footed?" I am nervously giggling and I know my face is beet red.

"No, you know . . ." Domenic looks to the floor.

"I love it," I interrupt. He doesn't need to finish. He shouldn't have to. This is the nicest thing anyone has ever given me. I don't even freak out that he apparently thinks my feet are huge.

"I wasn't sure if you would." Solo has her paw on his arm.

"No, of course I do. Thank you so much, you really didn't have to."

"It's your birthday. You get presents on your birthday," he says, disentangling himself from Solo. He begins wiping off the thousands of auburn-gold dog hairs that are now glued to him.

"Thank you, again. It's absolutely beautiful."

I put the doll on the green table, crumple up the wrapping paper, and begin to take it to the kitchen to throw it away. Instead I turn around and approach Domenic. The whole world quiets and I just see him. I want to stare at his face until I remember every single little detail. When he's not around, I can't quite remember what he looks like. What would it be like to be able to know every inch of that face? What would it be like to see that face whenever I wanted?

There's a moment where you look at someone and it clicks that there is a real person in front of you, along with an intangible something that connects you. You get lost in him. The world goes on around you, but you don't care about anything else except this person. I want to pull him close and begin something I can't control.

Domenic stands still—or maybe time has just stopped and in that second his body is still. How long have I been walking toward him? I stand face to face with him and step that couple of inches closer than just friends do. Something in the closeness gives me courage because he's not pulling away or reaching for the door handle. I reach for the side of his face and feel his wet hair through my fingers. He eases toward me and allows himself to be pulled. I lean to the left a few inches and kiss the side of his face right at the cheekbone. My pink lip gloss swipes his skin as I pull away. Domenic reaches up at the nape of my neck and holds me there. I'm unable to pull away any farther. He is just a little taller than I am, and there is something so male about him right now. I am a woman and right now in the arms of Domenic, I finally feel like one.

"You're welcome." Domenic hesitates and then lets his hand drop from my neck as he fusses with the collar of my sweater. I stare at him trying to find a reason. Something I can pinpoint as to why he has stopped. But I can't find anything. He says we'd better get going. Where? Nowhere, fast? Check. And Check.

Domenic and I drive to Mom's house in silence. The radio is on and some inane song is playing. I am replaying those moments over and over again in my head. I begin to grow frustrated. Why doesn't he make some kind of move? Why is this a love he can control? How can he just let his hand drop from my neck and walk out of the house? What does it take for a man to finally admit that he wants me? We pull into the Gelsons' Supermarket off Green Street in Old Town Pasadena. I buy drinks and head to Mom's house. On the short drive from the store to Mom and Russell's, I try to make some kind of small talk.

"So, are you ready for this?" I say.

"Is this something I have to be ready for?" he says.

"You've basically met everyone. Same people from the move, but now you get to see them in their natural habitat."

"Is there much of a difference?"

"Russell barbecuing can be pretty scary. Don't get in the way or ask if you can help. He's killed people for less."

"Okay, got it." I question whether Domenic is even listening. He thinks I'm joking, but we've all heard the stories about Russell, an ex-marine who now specializes in security for the Hollywood elite. Domenic straightens his pants and looks out his window. The wind blows his wavy black hair around, and I swear this is some kind of porn made especially for me. It's like he's in slow motion and ripping open his renaissance-style shirt to reveal his golden muscular chest.

We pull up to Mom and Russell's and I see Kate's minivan in the driveway. I panic. What have I done? Am I honestly having this guy meet my parents? Did I bother to think this plan through? I mean, we're not dating, we're barely friends, and I decide to bring him home to meet my family? Am I crazy? How can

I just walk into my mother's house with this hastily invited guest? But wait. What's the problem here? No, this is not how it's usually done, but he said yes and even brought me a present. Maybe this is just what change feels like? Inviting Domenic to my family's birthday bash is just like going to the gym or calling Ms. Beverly Urban—I have to get used to being awake. I pop the trunk of my car and go back to retrieve the bags of sodas. Domenic is already back there, lifting them one by one out of the trunk.

"Can you shut that for me?" he asks, lifting his chin to the raised trunk.

"Sure." Sigh. I've done the right thing. Terrifying, but right. You know, it wouldn't be so terrifying if I knew where he stood in this whole thing. Why didn't he kiss me? I mean, there we were, music swelling in the background, his hand at the nape of my neck, and then screeching brakes, metal-bending crash . . . and sirens. What the hell happened?

"Hello?" I say, moving through the dining room with Domenic behind me.

"Out in back!" I hear faintly.

I walk through the staging area the kitchen has become. The three birthday-cake boxes are there on the kitchen counter. Ahh, pink pastry boxes o'magic. I am calmed. Kate has her chocolate-on-chocolate-on-chocolate cake. Russell is always a sucker for the carrot. Then I see mine: a beautiful square pink angel-food cake wrapped up like a little birthday present with a real bow and everything. It is absolutely lovely. I smile as I open the back door out onto Mom's backyard.

"Don't let the air-conditioning out," Russell says, back turned facing the barbecue.

I quickly shoo Domenic out and shut the door behind him. We approach the picnic table much the way a bomb squad would a suspicious package.

"You guys remember Domenic from the big move?"

"Sure. Grab a seat and help yourself, Domenic," Mom says.

She is holding a caffeine-free diet soda, and her makeup is perfect. Her backyard looks amazing. When Mom and Russell first moved into this house, their backyard was nothing but broken pavement and a field of blacktop. Mom has turned it into an absolute paradise through pure Stubborn Workshop and Womanly Wiles. Right off the back of the house is a pergola laced with ripening grapevines. The top of the pergola has Italian café lights strung end to end. Olivia has long been envious. I think at one point she even asked Mom if she could use hers. I believe Mom said something like, "I don't think so, dear." Olivia still asks if she thinks I can wrangle the lights from Mom. I don't think so, dear. There is a small, vintage wrought-iron patio set with upholstered benches and chairs surrounding the main table. If you go farther toward the back, you come upon a huge raised deck. There's the swing Russell gave Mom for one of their anniversaries when they didn't exchange shiny trinkets. The spa is on the very edges of the deck by the hammock. Emily and Bella are engrossed in some role-playing game by the hammock, moving terra-cotta pots of lavender to and fro. It looks like they are pretending to exchange money. Only young women would fantasize about shopping.

The table is set perfectly. Tiny silver vases hold single sprigs from Mom's cutting garden. There are plates of fruit and vegetables and assorted bowls of dips. Kate and Vincent are sitting on the other side of the table. Vincent is working on the tortilla chips and salsa. Kate has her sunglasses on, but I still feel her eyes boring into me.

"We brought sugary sodas, Vincent," I say.

"*Ooo*hhhh, it's like high school vending machines all over again," Vincent says.

Domenic puts the bags on the ground next to the cooler and begins to set the sodas inside. He hasn't said two words since we got here. He brings over some pineapple-orange concoction and presents it to Vincent.

"This is still pretty cold from the store," Domenic says.

"Why, yes it is," Vincent says, cracking it open and taking a giant swig.

"We have about ten minutes until the meat is ready," Russell says.

"Which means ten additional minutes for everyone who doesn't like their meat blood-raw," I say.

"That's one," Russell says, back turned facing the barbecue.

"I've got one," I say to Domenic.

"One?" he says as he cracks open his own pineapple-orange concoction.

"Russell likes people to think that they've only got three chances. After that, he's not responsible for his actions," I say, smiling.

"That's two," Russell says, back turned facing the barbecue.

I hold up two fingers and smile.

"That's three," Russell says, back turned still facing the barbecue.

"Emily! Bella! Dinner's ready," Kate says to the fully enthralled little girls.

They run over and crumple into my arms. They are obviously dressed in outfits they put together themselves. Emily is wearing a blue jumper with a necklace ending in some type of green perfume in a vial. She is wearing pants underneath her dress and tops all of this off with a pair of lavender socks and pink sandals. Bella is wearing a tiny floral dress that shows off her cartoon panties. She also has on a diamond tiara and the ever-present red cowboy boots.

"Hey, crazies," I say.

"You're crazy," Bella says in that smoker's voice of hers.

"Why did you bring him?" Emily asks, her finger one inch from Domenic's face.

A hush falls over the crowd.

"I brought the sodas," Domenic says with a wide smile. I find myself dopily smiling right back at him. It's so freeing not to second-guess every single emotion I have. I just wish I could look just a tad more intelligent.

"Oh," Emily says, slowly checking him out head to toe.

"Where did you put 'em?" Bella asks, picking her nose.

"In the cooler. With the ice so they can get cold." Domenic is trying not to notice Bella's social faux pas.

Russell begins to plate the meat from the barbecue, and the family settle into their seats. Bella picks at everything and eats only one dinner roll. Emily is a more adventurous eater. She tries the seared ahi tuna, as well as the grilled vegetables. Domenic helps himself to the meat but steers clear of the vegetables. He also ends up mostly eating a dinner roll.

"You and Bella seem to have the same palate, son," Russell says.

"She's got good taste," Domenic says.

"For a six-year-old," Russell says. Domenic sneaks a small wink at Bella. She giggles and points at Domenic, crumbs of bread flying out of her mouth. "Donemic . . . Donemic has my same palace!"

We begin to clear the dishes and get ready for cake and presents. Domenic and Vincent have begun talking about some new show coming to one of the networks in the fall. It's all the rage, I guess. Emily and Bella have gone back to their role-playing as Russell begins to clean his beloved grill. I am left alone in the kitchen with Kate and Mom. Trapped like a rat.

"How was the interview?" Mom starts in.

"Amazing. Fabulous. Everything I could ever want." I am whipping up the cream for strawberry dipping. Do I have to write down the whipping cream in my food journal if I swipe some from the bowl?

"How do you think it went?" Kate slams the utensil drawer.

"I think it went great. I just feel so . . . weird." I can't describe it any better.

"Weird? Weird, 'cause you're finally putting yourself out there, or weird because of little Mr. Maggie's New Boyfriend out there?" Kate is pleased with herself as she leans back on the counter.

"Kate, get the candles and start putting them on the cakes and give your sister a break." Mom is pointing to the grocery bag with one eyebrow raised. Kate jumps.

"Weird, because it just seems like all of this stuff is happening at the same time—the internship, going to the gym, Domenic, and all this stuff with Olivia. Even work is getting so boring . . . I feel like I don't belong anywhere." I lop a spoonful of the whipped cream in a Depression-glass bowl Mom pulls from the cabinet.

"You're finally caring about what's going on in your life. It's not all totally random, here, honey." Mom adds fresh mint leaves to the sun tea.

"Yeah . . . I guess." I lick the whipped cream and set the empty bowl in the sink. What am I going to write down, "Lick of whipped cream"?

"Can I talk now?" Kate has put close to a thousand candles on the cakes during her silent tantrum.

"Oh, for chrissakes, Kate." Mom laughs.

"I got your 'Save the Date' e-mail," Kate says, turning to me.

"Oh, Olivia wanted to invite you even though she thought

you probably couldn't make it. She already feels bad that you guys have to find a babysitter for the wedding," I say.

"I think I'm going to go to the shower," she says.

"Really?" I say.

"What about the girls?" Mom asks.

"They *do* have a father," Kate says.

"Is he okay with that?" Mom asks.

"Why wouldn't he be okay with watching his own children?" Kate asks.

"He's been working long hours lately," Mom says as she looks through her drawers for a cake knife.

"I'll set up some playdates. Emily has a sleepover that weekend anyway. I'll set one up for Bella as well, so he can have a whole weekend to himself," Kate says, hands on her hips.

"That sounds great. I've already reserved a suite, and we can drive together," I say.

"Drive?" Kate asks.

"We are not flying, I can't. I planned on driving. If you want to go with me, you're going to drive, too." My heart rate accelerates as I imagine flying.

"Have you ever thought your fear of flying is just a ruse so you don't have to travel?"

"That doesn't even make sense," I say.

"Sure it does." Kate licks the icing off her cake.

"I went to Washington, DC."

"Yes, you're right, then. You've been everywhere," Kate says, lifting each cake out of its respective box.

"Can we get these cakes outside?" Mom asks.

"We have to shop for clothes for the wedding and shower soon," Kate says on her way out the back door, her cake in her hands.

"We'll plan for that sometime this week. I hear there are amazing shops at the Beverly Center," Mom says.

"So we'll plan to go there on your next day off," Kate says.

"Sounds good," I say, already dreading that day.

"And don't think we've let you off about your little friend out there. You might even get a breakfast invitation for that little stunt," Kate says.

Kate is known for breaking earth-shattering news after inviting us to breakfast. Mom and I found out that she and Vincent were getting married over bagels at Noah's Bagels in Hastings Ranch. We found out about Emily's impending arrival over scones and coffee at EuroPane. We found out about Bella over Charlie's Breakfast at Green Street. Now we've learned: We never go to breakfast with Kate anymore unless she answers a battery of questions about her personal life first.

The rest of the night goes off seemingly without a hitch. I catch glimpses of Domenic and try to make myself remember his face. I want to know it so in case he leaves, I'll remember what he looked like. Those details that matter. The curve of his lips. The hooded eyes. The flips of that black hair. That leaning-back laugh. As the night darkens and the Girlie Meltdown Watch begins, we close the party.

CHAPTER THIRTY

Reading Stories in Feety Pajamas

D omenic and I say good-bye to everyone and climb into my waiting car. I feel so relieved that I don't have to go home alone again after one of these functions. I look at Domenic as he eases way back in his chair and leans his head on the headrest.

"So? What did you think?" I ask.

"Your family is great. They really are," he says.

"Thank you," I say.

"No, really. I mean, I like my family just fine. I wouldn't change it for anything. But yours is nice. Real, I guess."

"A little too real sometimes."

"Yeah, that's true. I thought I saw a red laser dot on my forehead when I didn't eat all the meat on my plate."

"Russell is an ex-marine. Special Forces, no less."

"There are no ex-marines."

We drive in near silence all the way back to my house. Except for the embarrassing sign-reading thing I do every once in a while when I'm nervous or when I don't like the deafening silence of perceived rejection. Every three minutes the silence is broken with,

"Pottery Barn," I announce.

"Crate and Barrel," I say.

And on and on. Domenic politely nods or smiles, but never does the sign reading start another conversation. We pull onto my street and I see his car in front of my courtyard. A subtle reminder: He's going home soon.

"I'm going to head on home," he says as we walk from my now parked car. I am oddly relieved. The whole idea of having someone close to me is so new that it's absolutely exhausting.

"Oh, okay," I say.

"What are you doing for the rest of the night?"

"Cleaning. Unpacking the last bits."

"Sounds like fun."

"Thanks again for coming. It really meant a lot to me. And the gift—that was really great."

"Not a problem."

"Okay, well, have a safe drive."

"I will," he says and begins to walk to his car.

"Can I ask you another favor?" I yell after him. I don't know if I'm yelling after him because I need something or if I just don't want him to go.

"Sure," Domenic says, not missing a beat.

"I'm going to Las Vegas for my best friend's shower and I was wondering if you could stay here and watch the pup? She likes you, and she doesn't like anyone. I'd stock the refrigerator with sugary sodas. I'd pay you." Just having him here—standing in front of me is such a luxury. I want this new life—I want to drive this Porsche as fast as it can go.

"You don't need to pay me, but sugary sodas, yes. That's a quality-of-life issue."

"Okay, then. I'll give you a call and we'll go through all of her routines and that kind of thing," I say. Domenic gives me a small smile, hesitates for one second longer than he should, and then turns to leave. No hug. No hand on the nape of my neck. Nothing. What did I do at some point tonight to not even get a hug?

Domenic drives off, and I get that feeling again. Right now, Mom is cuddling up with Russell in their den. Russell is futzing with the surround sound and Mom is reading a mystery. Kate and Vincent are putting the girlies to bed. They are reading stories in their feety pajamas. Emily is chewing and twirling her hair and Bella is sucking her thumb. Their hair is wet from their big-girl showers, but they still smell like babies. Vincent is wearing his glasses and Kate has her fluffy slippers on. Vincent is seeing if there is anything sports-related on television so he can catch a glimpse before Kate turns the channel to whatever sitcom she can find that features a large ensemble cast.

As I open my front door, an empty house and an untrainable dog meet me. I have my bag of presents and the Tupperware filled with cake in my hands. Solo bounds out of my bedroom. I set my cake on the table and rest the bag of presents on the floor. I pet Solo but I just can't stop feeling lonely. So I'm alone now? It doesn't make me alone. I was just around an entire family of people who adore me. Mom gave me a series of facials with this amazing facialist in Sierra Madre. Kate bought me an outfit I will never wear—a time-honored tradition. Bella got me a purple felt hat and Emily got me a singing plastic watch. I have this little doll with huge porcelain feet made by Domenic, a doll that reminds him of me. This is not the booty of a lonely person. I tuck myself into bed and wish Solo a good night, as usual.

I wake up the next morning to Solo itching herself at the foot of my bed. I unwind from my bedsheets. I've added turning on my laptop to my morning sequence. I will focus on getting my office organized today. I've got the computer and Internet hooked up. Now I just have to get the papers where they should be. My house is perfect. Everything looks amazing. Everything feels amazing. This house is everything I would have dreamed. There's something so wonderful about seeing it all put together like this. I pad over to my laptop and check my e-mail. The first one is from the M&M maven herself, Shawna Moss. It reads:

Dear Maggie:

It is v. great to finally hear from the one and only Maggie Taylor! Am I being repetitive? Sorry! Anyway, it is great to finally hear from you! I can't wait to meet you because Olivia talks about you all the time. I feel like I already know you. I'm sure this shower is going to be so v. fun and if I can help in anyway please let me know. I hear I'm an amazing party planner! :o) By the by, us gals are trying to get in touch with the bride herself. She said she would call me with her mom's phone number in Pasadena, but you know that bitch hasn't! JK (just kidding—hee hee). She is probably so busy she forgot and she refuses to come into my office for some stupid reason, that girl! Do you have her mother's number, by any chance? We are trying to find a hotel for the wedding where Olivia said there might be some extra rooms. Again, it's great to finally talk to you. See you in Vegas, baby! Maybe we can all go grab drinks, I'd love to hear your side of all of Olivia's crazy escapades.

Can't wait to meet you,
Shawna Moss

Taylor, huh? Ms. Shawna Moss can't even get my last name right. I feel my IQ drop ten points and have this urgent need to end all of my sentences in exclamation marks! More importantly, though—no one gets calls back from Olivia? Even her new friends who are trying to book a hotel for her wedding aren't a priority with Olivia these days. I am also confused that Olivia is talking about our "crazy escapades." Olivia will have to debrief me so we can be on the same page about what exactly she's said to these women. The "crazy escapades" I remember certainly aren't the ones Olivia is talking about to her new friends. I remember one in particular. It featured Olivia and me in my little red piece-of-shit Chevy Chevette sitting under a street lamp eating Nachos BellGrande together on prom night. I know for a fact that Olivia hasn't told that story to any of her new friends. Olivia hasn't told any of these women she ever had a problem with anything. As long as they've known her, she's had Adam. The perfect little couple who summer in Nantucket and know what kind of wine to order with fish. My curiosity is definitely piqued about what escapades this Shawna girl may have been hearing. V. Piqued! V. Piqued, indeed!

I want the shower weekend to be about rediscovering my friendship with Olivia. I want to put aside all the chores and other distractions of the wedding. Read: *Gwen.* I imagine we'll drive around Las Vegas and laugh and talk like we used to. Recalling those memories and making new ones are what I want this weekend to be about.

I realize I haven't spoken to Peregrine since our little run-in. How can I apologize now? How can I make her understand I already have a mother and what I need from her is to be a friend? I can't think about it now. I just don't feel strong enough. Not to mention I haven't heard a peep from Ms. Beverly Urban since our interview. Is that good or bad?

I am at work when Mom calls around ten thirty to confirm our shopping day from hell tomorrow. I hang up and dread it immediately. Once again, I will be in the Mother of the Bride section yelling out to anyone in earshot that my boobs don't fit.

CHAPTER THIRTY-ONE

Let the Games Begin

When I was in college, I started hanging out with a girl from one of my art classes named Karen Thomas. It seemed like Karen was a lot like me: studious, funny, and not internationally beautiful. Nothing set her apart, yet she was unnervingly confident. She always had a boyfriend and a line of men clamoring to go out with her. What was her recipe for success? Karen had this crooked, pigeon-toed walk, and she told me early on that she could only hear out of one ear. I believed these things were the key to her success, so I devised an elaborate scheme in which I tried to convince people that I, too, could hear out of only one ear. The pigeon-toed walk was easy, but it was hard on the knees. To this day, some people still speak only into my right ear out of respect.

"Who was that?" Cole asks.

"My mom," I say.

"What'd she want?"

"Why do you care?"

"I care because it took her ten minutes to tell you about it."

"Were you able to handle all one of the customers who shoved their way in?"

"Cut the shit, Maggie." Cole almost spits, he's so pissed off.

Cole has gotten worse over the past few weeks. Ever since our incident with the bouncer at Peregrine's party, our conversations have been strained. I know he and Peregrine have talked about our big blowout. They've worked together for longer than we have. He's mentioned it a few times and tried to engage me before this. I haven't taken the bait. I don't know why I do today.

"Dial it back, partner," I say.

"Partner?" Cole asks.

"Yeah, you've been after me for weeks now. Is there a problem?"

"Problem? Me? Let's see, you ask for too much time off, you're pretty much always late, you fucking went off on Peregrine, who actually works for a living." Cole moves closer to me.

"You're right," I say. Thwack.

Finally, the rock hits right between Goliath's beady, little eyes. What comes after this job has always been the ultimate blue bucket. Conceding that Cole is right is just the first step toward passing it.

Why *am* I here? I have a master's in museum studies. I hemmed the skirt of a fucking Degas and I'm letting a playground bully who makes me constantly walk on eggshells take over my days. I had an interview at the Getty—an interview I nailed, by the way. I just don't need this anymore. First Peregrine—now Cole. I'm sick of fighting. I'm sick of being bullied. But I'm also sick of being controlled by the *what-if* game. What if he doesn't accept me? What if I get left behind? What if I'm not his favorite? It's never worked for me. Not fighting back has never worked. No one has ever loved me more because I allowed them to abandon or mistreat me. I can't put up with this fear anymore.

"What?" Cole says. Even *he* is thrown.

"You're right." I am calm.

Cole is silent. He doesn't know what to do with himself. Life is like a football field to him. He doesn't know how to deal with it any other way. I just moved out of the way and cleared his path to the goalpost. He thinks it's some kind of trick.

"I quit. I've had it." I untie my apron and burst through the back door. Cole is right behind me. My breathing is steady, but the flutters are starting. I can't believe what I've just done, but I can't deny how amazing and free I feel.

"You can't fucking quit." He is so close to me that, for the first time, I actually feel like he may belt me one.

"I just did." I am so scared. This doesn't even seem like my life anymore. I think of Marcus Aurelius. What would Marcus do? Right now he's in a million tiny pieces somewhere in the Getty Museum. Marcus needs me, goddammit.

"Just because I bust your balls sometimes?" Cole backs away and looks out into the coffeehouse.

"You bust my balls *all* the time, Cole."

"I know, I know. I mean . . . you're not quitting because of me, are you?"

"No."

"Good."

"But you're still an asshole." I grab my long black sweater from the bathroom and fill out my time sheet one last time. Cole is watching my every move. I take my keys out of my purse and step right up to Cole, who is standing in front of the door. I refuse to sneak out the back door.

"Excuse me." I look up into his eyes unblinking. I cock my head to the right and sigh as he takes a full minute to "think about it." Cole steps aside. I thank him. I walk out into the coffeehouse. I wave to Christina, who is refilling the sugars. She waves back. Now if I can just round up all the other Coles in my life, I may be able to quiet these demons.

CHAPTER THIRTY-TWO

The More the Merrier

My first real job was at the Gourmet Donuts in Pasadena. It was a match made in heaven. I worked nights after school to make a little extra walking-around money. Some people believe that if you work around a food long enough, it will become unappetizing. That theory is incorrect. Doughnuts became my life. I smelled like doughnuts. I constantly found wondrous flecks of glaze in my hair at the end of a long day. But as is always the case with greed, I was corrupted by the abundance of the doughnuts. I started to hatch a plan in which I could have all the doughnuts I wanted without being caught. I knew each employee was allotted a certain number of doughnuts per day. I also knew that certain employees never ate their share—amateurs. So I would sneak back to the magical tray loaded with all the doughnut rejects and swipe twice and sometimes three times my daily doughnut allotment. Three days later, Jennie, the morning manager, noticed that her allotment of doughnuts was missing. It didn't take the owners long to follow the flecks of glaze in my direction. We parted amicably—me and the doughnuts.

After a night of the deepest sleep I've had in months, I meet

Mom at the gym for our thirty minutes on the StairMaster. After our big gym outing, Mom makes me her special kind of coffee and serves fruit and oatmeal for both of us at her house. I am glowing. That StairMaster couldn't have been any harder, and I had it on the lowest setting. I used drinks of water as a ruse to catch my breath. But I just can't deny how good I feel right now. I had forgotten what it's like to be in touch with my body. When Kate and I were little we would roller-skate for hours on our street after school. I feel that young again. I forgot what playing feels like. As I sit eating Mom's Irish oatmeal, I am bursting with the news of Joe's, but I just can't quite tell her yet. My speech isn't perfected, and my courage is waning. My mom is my hero and I don't know if I can deal with her disappointment right now. I didn't have a chance to call Domenic, either, to tell him that I quit. I'll tell him when he comes by to learn about taking care of Solo. He probably won't hear it from me, anyway. Chances are he's already heard every word.

The dreaded day of shopping is here.

Kate honks in the driveway about fifteen minutes later. Mom and I go out to meet her. I pull open the big, sliding mini-van door. Emily and Bella are sitting in the way back to make room for me. They greet me with loud laughter and nonstop questions. Everyone knows I get carsick, so they try to make me as comfortable as possible in cars to avoid the possible risk of getting vomited on.

"You sit in front of us, Maggie," Emily says, always the hostess.

Mom buckles herself in and says hello to the girlies. They give a rousing hello back and ask Kate to turn the music back up. Kate has mastered the balance control on her car stereo so the music is louder in the back than it is in the front. This makes the girlies happy, along with everyone over the age of six who doesn't want to listen to the latest animated movie anthem.

"I quit Joe's," I blurt.

"What?" Mom says. The girlies are suddenly as still as statues.

"Good for you," Kate says.

"Sweetie, you didn't belong in that place," Mom says.

"Aren't you worried about how my bills are going to get paid?" I say.

"Should I be?" Mom asks.

"I have a plan," I say.

"Would this involve a certain Roman emperor?" Kate asks.

"Marc's Face and Tell Us!" Bella screams. Emily nearly explodes with frustration.

"I figure I'll hear from Beverly Urban any day now, and if I don't, I'll find a job with one of those temp agencies until I find a job at another museum."

"Sounds good," Mom says.

"So you're okay with this?" I say.

"Of course. You'll make more as a temp than you ever did at Joe's, and I don't think you're going to be waiting long for Beverly Urban to get back to you," Mom says.

"So what do you need to get today?" Kate asks. I am breathing easier. According to this family, quitting Joe's is the best thing I could have done. Apparently, they've been waiting for this for two years.

I try to hold back the tears. It doesn't matter how much you tell the girlies you're crying because you're happy. They still think it's because you're sad. I try to take deep breaths. But I *am* crying because I'm happy. Who else has a family that would celebrate quitting a job? I was bred to succeed. I was bred to stand atop jungle gyms.

Kate, Mom, and I discuss possible color combinations for

me and talk about what they might wear. I've been saving money ever since I found out Olivia was getting married. I wanted to be able to buy some new clothes for the festivities.

"Who is watching Solo while we go to Las Vegas for Olivia's shower?" Kate asks.

"I asked Domenic."

"Domenic from the party?" Emily asks.

"Yes. Domenic from the party," I say.

"Donemic is crazy," Bella says.

"I think somebody has a crush on Domenic," Kate says, pointing at Emily.

"He's nice." Emily laughs.

"He brings sodas and has my same palace," Bella adds.

"Yes, he's pretty nice," I say.

"Does he know about Solo's . . . tendencies?" Kate hesitates.

"She's been to obedience classes," I say.

The entire minivan is quiet.

"Yes, he knows about her tendencies," I admit.

We pull into the mall parking lot and unload. I am feeling a little carsick from constantly looking back at the girls and their demands. We take the outside escalators into the Beverly Center and begin the search.

As I walk through the stores, I fear I've already let myself down as I drift to the back of the racks where they hide the bigger sizes. I should have lost X amount of weight before this day came. But there's a small part of me that is oddly okay with it. I feel strangely hopeful that working with Gabriel and writing my food down will finally work for me. The rest of me, the scared part of me, believes I will probably fail again. No matter what I buy here today, will I still be seen as Olivia's fat friend? My cell phone chirps as we are going up yet another escalator.

"Hello?" I ask.

"Hey, girl." It's Olivia. I mouth this information to Kate. She rolls her eyes.

"Hey, there. What's going on?" I ask.

"Wedding mayhem," she says.

"I would suspect," I say.

"So Vegas, huh? Did you make all the reservations?" Olivia asks.

"Yep. Martinis at the Caramel Bar first thing, just you and me. Then high tea at Petrossian, dinner at Prime . . . shall I go on?" Mom and Kate are staring at me. I think Kate is asking me to hand her the phone. I stumble off the escalator. Bella tells me to be careful.

"No, no. That all sounds great. So I'm going to fly in with Gwen. Did you reserve a room for us? Did you get her e-mail about upgrading us to a better suite—one of those villas if they have one—my Adam said he'd pay for it." I did get that e-mail. I made the call, and now this phone conversation is reminding me of one you might have with a travel agent—not a maid of honor.

"Yep, got the e-mail. Everything's taken care of," I say calmly. Kate and Mom are now walking in front of me talking shit about Olivia in very loud voices. The girlies skip and dance about ten feet in front of them, oblivious to everything.

"Okay, just making sure. Is there any way you can have the Bellagio just send me a confirmation e-mail about the villa?" Olivia asks.

"I don't know if the Bellagio does confirmation e-mails, but I'll check." Who the hell am I talking to? Or more importantly, who the fuck does Olivia think she's talking to? "Okay, well, see you in Vegas, I guess," I continue.

"I can't wait! I wouldn't be surprised if the Birthday Girl

had an extra-special weekend . . . I'm just saying . . . you might want to look out for a little something from your best friend, that's all. Do you want to know what it is?" She is giggling and excited.

"No, I want it to be a surprise," I say, a smile spreading across my face. I have forgotten, for the moment, about Gwen and her confirmation e-mail.

"Okay, fine . . . but can I give you a hint? Please, please, pretty please?" Olivia begs.

"No! Nothing. Not one hint, you do this every year, and every year I guess! Try to control yourself, woman!" I am now laughing. Mom and Kate have stopped, mouths open, watching what must look like a reenactment of *Sybil.*

"Oh, okay, fine. But it's small and you can wear it. Bye!" she quickly blurts. I beep my cell phone off and look toward Mom and Kate.

"She is unbelievable," Kate says.

"What was she talking about?" Mom asks.

"She was talking about my birthday present—you know how she goes all out every year," I equivocate.

"No, the other thing." Mom is stone-faced.

"Oh, yeah." I deflate.

"Yeah, that," Kate says.

"She and Gwen want one of those villas at the Bellagio. She wanted to make sure everything was set up." I figured it was because I was bringing Kate that Olivia didn't want to room with me in Las Vegas. Now I'm not so sure.

"That's just tacky. You don't call your best friend up right before the wedding and tell her you're sharing a villa with another bridesmaid. This has nothing to do with you," Kate hisses. Mom looks softly at me. I concentrate on taking deep breaths.

"I just think . . . I got the impression . . . it just sounded like . . . she didn't even invite me. Like I wasn't . . . or I didn't want or couldn't fit into . . ." I lose control quickly and start to cry. This is new; I usually don't start crying until *after* I've tried the clothes on.

Kate and Mom rally around and hug me. The girlies run back. I hide my tears from them as we walk into the first shop and begin searching for perfect outfits for a wedding I am barely invited to.

I knock on the door to the dressing room Mom has set aside for me. I am let in by a naked Bella. She's not trying anything on, mind you, she's just decided to take off all her clothes. Emily is sitting on the floor putting clothes that have been rejected back on the hangers. Bella continues to check herself out in the mirror. I hang up my clothes and take off my pants.

"Cute panties," Emily says.

"Thank you, they're pink," I say.

"I know. That's why they're cute," Emily says.

"I'm an outie," Bella proclaims as she spins around pointing at her navel. Emily and I share a moment of awkward validations for Bella's outie belly button.

I have not worn a tightener today for some bizarre reason. Everyone knows that you never try on clothes without a tightener. Here I am trying on the mother of all apparel without one. I won't panic; I'll just visualize how these clothes would look with a tightener. I get the vapors. The black skirt fits. Kate pops her head in and assesses the progress.

"That skirt is a size smaller," Kate says, perfectly comfortable with the spectacle of the Exhibitionist Bella.

"What?" I am sliding the skirt around after zipping it up.

"You've gone down a size." Kate smirks.

I stare at myself in the mirror. I didn't starve myself. I didn't drink lemonade laced with cayenne pepper and maple syrup. I didn't eat boxed lunches from the frozen section. I didn't drink a shake instead of a meal. I am learning how to feed myself. I am learning how to play again. Oddly, it seems to be working.

"Try this one," Mom says, handing me a white wraparound shirt.

"She's gone down a size," Kate yelps. Mom smiles at me and gives me a thumbs-up.

"I'm a six-X," Bella adds. Emily rolls her eyes.

The white shirt is a little short, but I imagine the magic a tightener will work. Olivia has specifically outlined that I am to wear black and white to the rehearsal dinner. I am unsure of the outfit. I'll have to wear this outfit all day and in pictures that will last forever. I feel light and strong at the same time. I feel proud of myself.

◆

"You looked amazing in that skirt," Kate says as we stand at the cashier with all my purchases. I've got enough clothes for the entire wedding affair—and all one size smaller.

"Really?" I say.

"Absolutely. Really statuesque and classy," she says.

"Thank you," I say. Instead of Fatty and Bobo, it should be Statuesque and Classy. I think I'll start today.

Bella eventually puts her clothes back on and Emily reads me the book she has started writing as we move to another shop to find outfits for Mom and Kate. Kate finds a beautiful pale pink linen sheath she'll wear with a simple strand of pearls. Mom finds an amazing pale blue Richard Tyler pantsuit she'll wear with an abundance of gold accessories, I'm sure. She finds a pair of Marc Jacobs shoes and splurges on them. We all applaud her and use this as a teaching tool for the girlies in how to pamper yourself.

We stop for lunch at the Quality Cafe on Third Street right

by the Beverly Center. Kate, Mom, and I dish about Olivia and Adam. Olivia's phone call seems like a distant memory.

A feeling of pride in myself overwhelms me. As we make our way back through the winding freeways of Los Angeles, I think about Olivia's phone call. How long has she been like this? This shower has got to be about redefining our friendship and proving to myself that Olivia and I can be friends on equal terms.

I am driving home from Mom's house, switching radio stations around, as usual. There's more traffic on the streets than normal and I keep getting caught at red lights. I switch the radio station again. I know this drumbeat. I'm immediately transported back to university housing with Kate and me and our beloved Electric Light Orchestra. I played this track over and over again. Kate sang the harmony.

Don't bring me down, grroosss
Don't bring me down, grroosss!

Another red light. My window is halfway down. I start keeping the beat on my steering wheel. I turn the volume up a little bit. A little bit more. I whisper the lyrics to myself, looking to the left to make sure no one sees. I look at a bus stop full of people. No one is looking.

I look to the left. A mom in a Volvo station wagon is disciplining a little boy in a kid seat. The light turns green. I screech forward, singing a little louder. The clapping part! I take both my hands off the steering wheel and clap along. The little Volvo boy is laughing and pointing at me. I smile back. He giggles and waves.

I roll my window all the way down. I am singing so loud, I can barely hear the radio. I haven't felt so free in a long time or so purely me. I have a good feeling about the shower. This is going to work.

CHAPTER THIRTY-THREE

This Is My Area

I am meeting Gabriel alone this morning to go over my food diary and to have my one-hour training session. After warming up on the StairMaster for ten minutes, I meet Gabriel at the counter. He tells me to follow him out back. For one second I think he's going to put me out of my misery. I follow him to a small patio out in back of the gym. He's set up a small obstacle course of sorts. My breath quickens. Yes, I'm more confident—but I'm not ready to be clocked running, or clocked doing anything really. My eyes dart from medicine balls to small blue mats and then to a large green exercise ball. I am silent. Scared shitless and silent.

"Okay, Maggie we're going to start over here on the wall. Go ahead and grab that medicine ball for me." Gabriel moves to the wall. I follow and try to understand how this course is going to work if we start from this point. Apparently I'm now a marine.

"Great, thanks. Okay, go ahead and put your glutes up against the wall." Glutes? Does he mean my ass? I'm standing here with this blue medicine ball, which weighs a good ten pounds, and I have no idea what he wants me to do. Is this some sick form of dodgeball?

"Glutes?" I finally ask.

"Oh, yes, I'm sorry. Your pelvis. Go ahead and put your pelvis on the wall." Is there some trainer handbook that dictates you're not allowed to utter the word *ass*? I stand against the wall, holding the blue medicine ball—which now weighs close to a thousand pounds.

"Okay, great job. Now what I want you to do is go ahead and raise the ball over your head and then bring it down in front of you and tap the ground." Gabriel demonstrates this action. It looks like he's bowing down in front of me. Worshiping his new goddess. This momentarily distracts me from the absolute horror at what he's asking me to do.

I grab the ball and raise it over my head. My arms are bent—not because the ball is heavy, but because if I straighten them my entire stomach will be completely exposed. I bend forward and tap the ball to the ground. I can feel the fresh air right around my "glutes." So not only is my shirt rising up in the front, but it's also slipping down in the back to reveal my white granny panties. Great. This is sure worth the physical benefit. This whole emotional suicide thing is just a silly side effect.

"Okay, great. Now, straighten those arms fully, and give me three, two, and ten more." Gabriel is standing directly in front of me watching every move I make. I start to panic. My own shit-talking is getting so bad on the fifth go-round that I am actively holding the tears back. Raise the ball—there's my Area. Lower the ball—there's my ass. I don't think my own mother has seen this much of me in years.

"Okay, um . . . I'm feeling a little uncomfortable," I snap.

"Okay, go ahead and tell me where it feels tight, Maggie." Gabriel looks concerned. Poor fool.

"Nothing feels tight. I just . . ." I'm holding on to the medicine ball for dear life. I take a deep breath.

"This is my Area," I say, motioning to my belly with the medicine ball. Gabriel listens intently. I continue.

"I'm just not comfortable raising and lowering the medicine ball and all that because I am superweird about, you know . . . my Area," I stutter.

"It's just us back here, Maggie," Gabriel reasons. Yes, and you're gorgeous. It's not like I'm back here with Solo, for crissakes.

"I know . . ." I trail off.

"I understand what you're saying," Gabriel says.

"And?" I hold the medicine ball.

"Go ahead and give me ten more," Gabriel says.

"But . . ." I'm shocked. He doesn't want to talk about my Area? He doesn't want to sit by a campfire and sing "Kumbaya" while we talk about why I think I'm fat?

"No buts. I'm not checking out your Area or even noticing what you're talking about. You'll just have to trust me on that. Is this some sophisticated plan to get out of this exercise, Maggie? NASA would be envious. Can we continue?" Gabriel smiles.

I raise and lower the ball fifteen more times—because, of course, Gabriel still doesn't know how to fucking count. But the weird thing is there is a freedom in just showing my Area. Lifting my arms as high as they could go, challenging myself to lift higher. This could be the start of something. First Gabriel, then maybe someone else. I have visions of flashing my belly to the checker at the grocery store, then at the gas station . . . and then standing in front of Domenic Brown. Well, maybe.

CHAPTER THIRTY-FOUR

Marcus and Russell Sitting in a Tree

I call Kate to tell her about the idea I have for the shower invitations. Refrigerator magnets! I will print out the invitations and secure them to magnets so the recipients can keep them on their refrigerator as a reminder. No risk of losing them. Genius.

"Isn't it a little late?" Kate asks.

"Well, there are only seven people going. Olivia wanted something for her scrapbook."

"So?" Kate asks.

After I hang up with Kate, I head out to Vroman's Bookstore to buy envelopes and ten business-card-size magnets. These invitations are going to be tiny. I design an invitation that will fit on the head of a pin and start addressing the envelopes. Shawna Moss. Panchali Nagra. Gwen Charles. Olivia Morten. I know all the names now. Soon the faces will come into focus. What will the weekend bring? A grown-up friendship or the realization that we're not kids anymore.

I drive down Fair Oaks and make a right on Mission. The post office is on the north side of the street. I park my car and run inside with my six tiny invitations. I stand in line and as I am doing so, something unnerving happens: The invitations start sticking to one another. I now have one large invitation. I have three people in front of me and one giant invitation. These fucking things took me forever and now I find out that they are unmailable? I begin maniacally separating each invitation from the others. I approach the post office window with a six-invitation Spanish fan. I look ridiculous. The woman behind the bulletproof window stiffens.

"Can I help you?" she asks.

"I'd like to mail these," I say shoving the full fan of invitations through the window's door. Not one separates from the group. The woman awkwardly holds up the fan. Not one invitation falls.

"We can't mail these," she says.

"Sure you can. Just pop them in the mail slot one at a time," I say.

The woman peels the first invitation off the top of the fan and inserts it into the mail chute. It magnetizes to the chute and stays right where she dropped it.

"We can't mail these," she says as she's peeling the invitation from the metal postal chute.

I take back the invitation and stick it back to the top of the fan where it was before the Chute Incident. I dejectedly walk back to my car and go home. Since I'm newly unemployed, I have plenty of time to obsess on the invitations. I decide to put the tiny envelope in a larger envelope. Maybe that way the second sheet of paper will reduce the strength of the magnetization. I go back to Vroman's and pick up another box of envelopes. I readdress the new envelopes and drive to the post office praying I don't get the same lady. I find parking right outside and run inside with the stack of less magnetized invitations.

I get in line. The lady who helped me before is still there. I hold my newly enveloped invitations with courage and moxie. Oh, you'll mail these now.

"Can I help you?" It's the same lady.

"I'd like to mail these," I say.

"We can't mail these." Her tone is a little more annoyed.

"Sure you can," I say, shoving the same pile of invitations through her bulletproof window gate. A few of them separate from the pack.

The woman peels the first invitation off the top of the fan and inserts it into the mail chute. It slips down the chute slowly but makes it all the way down. I feel victorious.

"That'll be fifty-five cents each," she says.

"That's fine," I say, pulling out my wallet.

I imagine the invitations sticking to the sides of mailboxes across the country as my cell phone chirps. I forgot I even had the damn thing with me. I sift through my purse and find the culprit.

"Hello?" I am annoyed.

It's Ms. Beverly Urban. "Ms. Thompson?"

"Ms. Urban, yes."

"Ms. Thompson I'd like to offer you a paid internship where you'll be working on the Marcus Aurelius." I can't believe what I've just heard.

"Oh my gosh! I am honored . . . thank you, Ms. Urban. What a . . . this is just such good news." I'm hyperventilating. I want to hang up so I can call Mom and Kate and screech the good news.

"The internship starts in the fall, so you have one month to settle your affairs." Settle my affairs? Are they going to kill me?

"Yes. I am honored. Thank you so much." I am stuttering.

"It is our pleasure. I will be mailing you the contracts.

Please have them looked over and mail them back to me as soon as you can."

"Yes, yes . . . I will."

I hang up with Ms. Urban and begin dialing Mom's phone number. We scream and screech to each other for a full five minutes. We plan to meet for a congratulatory dinner at six thirty that evening. I call Kate and we go through the same screaming screeching routine. I am tempted to call Domenic, but don't.

The wagons are circled around Mom's house at six thirty. We will celebrate my internship in style. Russell has a prime rib he'll cook too rare, and the girlies have made cards. The crowd is buzzing with excitement. I am smiling from ear to ear and can't help but be proud of myself. This isn't just some gift shop job in a museum. I am the official in-painter and gap filler for this project. That means that when Marcus—we're on a first-name basis now—is finally assembled, I will come in and put the finishing touches on him. At the Getty. I will report for work every day to the fucking Getty Museum in the hills overlooking Los Angeles.

I will ride that tram every day and check in with the security guard, who will begin to know me and eventually just wave me in. I have to get through this last month without a job. I might be able to find some kind of waitressing gig just to make ends meet. I can do anything for one month. But after that, it's Marcus Aurelius and me. And my first real job. I've never felt more proud of myself. Russell lowers the barbecue lid and motions for me to come over. Either that or I've done something wrong and he's going to kill me. I approach slowly.

"I want you to know how proud I am of you," Russell says.

"Thank you." I am being taken out. That's it. There is some

member of Russell's recon squad hiding in the bushes, and this is my last supper.

"Your finances for the next month are being taken care of," Russell says stoically. I am silent. I can't choke the tears back. My lip begins quivering. I can't help feeling so lucky and blessed. Mom walks up beside me and rubs my back. My family has always known I have talent and potential. All they've wanted for me is great things. I'm the only one who has ever doubted it.

"Please don't cry, Maggie. I just wanted you to know that you will be taken care of until the internship kicks in," Mom says. Russell is angling to free himself and get back in front of the barbecue, where he feels safe.

"Oh, for chrissakes, Russell." Mom sidles up next to Russell and is beaming at me.

"I just feel so lucky, you know," I whimper.

"I told you she was going to cry. That's why I wanted you to tell her about the money." Russell takes a swig of Mom's caffeine-free Diet Coke and makes a face.

"We're just so proud of you, sweetheart." Mom holds Russell's hand, more as a way to keep him in the conversation than as an affectionate gesture.

I lean up and give Russell a kiss and say thank you over and over again. I hug Mom and can't control the tears. I feel so amazing—like this life isn't even believable anymore. Those fantasies where I'm in the basement of some museum in my charcoal cashmere sweater and Levi 501s are becoming a reality. It's a bizarre phenomenon—real life is so much better than any fantasy.

On the way home from dinner, I decide to put a call in to Domenic. I have a lot to tell him. Throughout this whole ordeal all I've wanted to do is call him and tell him about quitting Joe's and getting the internship. This is where I get scared. Do these milestones need Domenic's approval now to mean anything? Am I unable to feel happy or proud of myself for just the act of doing these things? No, I have to retrain myself. This is not a loss of independence. This is not a loss of self. This is one simple phone call where I get to tell a friend that I've done something good.

"Hello?" It's Domenic.

"Hey there, it's Maggie." I can't wait until I can just say, *It's me.*

"I knew it was you. So anything new going on in your life, stranger?"

"Nah, nothing much." I am smiling from ear to ear.

"You haven't, oh, I don't know, quit your job? Told off your boss? Stopped talking to a friend? Nothing?" Well, when you say it like that.

"But the best part is I got the internship!" I yell.

"Are you serious?" Domenic asks.

"Yeah! Can you believe it? She called this morning while I was at the post office. Amazing, huh?"

"I knew you could do it," Domenic says.

"Thanks!" We are silent. "So when did you want to meet up to talk about Solo?" I stutter.

"Oh, um, we could do it Friday at around ten?" My mind is racing. Isn't this where he invites me to go out for congratulatory drinks? Am I completely off base on everything relationship-related—I mean, is this how the beginning of dating usually is? Maybe I just don't know. But I sure as hell liked my fantasy better.

"That sounds good. I'll see you then." And he hangs up.

What did I do? What the hell is going on? First the nape-of-the-neck thing, then I don't get a hug after the party, and now this? If this is what love and trust feel like—they're sorely overrated.

CHAPTER THIRTY-FIVE

Telepathy School

Once you taste a little of the sweetness that life can be, there really is no going back. I think that's why I fought it for so long. I knew once I started, I wasn't going to be able to stop. Now I find myself with my fingers curled around the bottom of my shirt, getting ready to raise it as high as I can, exposing every flaw I've ever imagined.

"Hey there," I say, as Domenic arrives the following Friday. Solo bounds to him and is jumping and whimpering as he bends to greet her. The back of my neck is wet with sweat from my morning training session with Gabriel. I got a gold star in my food diary this time. I can't begin to express how much that little stupid star meant to me.

"Hey," he says, mouth full of Solo.

"Okay," I say, trying to act perfectly normal, "I've made a chart of everything. Hopefully this will answer some of your questions." I hand him my color-coded spreadsheet.

"I'm sure it will." Domenic stands to look at the spreadsheet.

I have listed phone numbers of vets, emergency vets, and next of kin. I have explained Solo's feeding regimen and sleeping behaviors. I made photocopies of her rabies vaccinations and attached the most recent picture I have of her. Just in case she gets away and he has to go door to door. I have given him the approximate times she usually needs to be put out and/or walked.

The whole time I imagine what he will look like sleeping in my bed. He'll be sleeping here for two nights. He'll be in my shower . . . naked. He will be living in my house and taking care of my girlie. Here I am explaining the ins and outs of my life to him. I feel conflicted because on the one hand I'm happy and I know he'll do a good job. On the other hand, I can't figure out what's going on with us. In the end, I know this is not about Domenic taking care of Solo. This is about Domenic taking care of me.

"I'm picking up my sister at around six in the morning tomorrow. Come over anytime after that," I say.

"And when will you be getting back?" he asks.

"I hope to be back early evening on Sunday," I say.

"Your birthday?"

"Yeah, I'll probably do some cake thing with my family that night," I stutter. How had I forgotten about my birthday again?

"So you're flying to Vegas?"

"Driving," I say.

"You're driving? For a weekend?"

"I don't fly unless absolutely necessary."

"Okay, but you're going to be damn tired of driving come Monday."

"I'd rather be tired than hanging upside down in a tree bare-ass naked."

"Excuse me?"

"I saw this news program once about a search party that went in the jungle to find dead bodies after an airplane had gone down in Colombia. There was this dead guy in a tree. He was completely stark naked, hanging upside down."

"Should we mention at any point that this poor man was dead?" he asks. I am silent. Horrified. Domenic continues. "So I'll be here tomorrow and see you when you get back on Sunday," he says.

"That sounds perfect," I say.

Domenic takes the key I made for him and pets Solo one more time. Am I next in line? I step a little closer and the tips of my fingers are tingling. I miss him. I miss what it feels like to be touched by him. I want to end those stopgap measures I've had to come up with in the meantime, like imagining it's Domenic as Gabriel leads me to a machine with his hand on the small of my back. But Gabriel's touch is not Domenic's. I want my turn at the real thing. Domenic waves and closes the door behind him, saying he'll see me Sunday night. I want to scream at the top of my lungs for him to stay. I want him here with me. I don't want to be alone anymore. But I'll see him on my birthday, and those few minutes will give me some solace. I am standing at the door as Solo starts barking again. Domenic is coming back. Finally, all those years of telepathy school have come in handy. I open the door.

"I have something special planned for your birthday," Domenic blurts.

"What?" He couldn't have said anything more ludicrous.

"I just wanted you to know. I know I've been acting weird, but I . . . I just wanted you to know. So can you set aside some time for me?" Domenic is flipping his keys.

"Yeah, sure," I say robotically. Is this really happening?

"Okay. So you're not just using me because I'm the only one your dog likes, are you?" Domenic breaks a smile.

"No, you're the only one *I* like." Gasp. What did I say? I literally have my mouth open—horrified.

"Okay, good. See you Sunday then?" Domenic leans into the screen door. I am still completely dumbfounded.

"Yeah . . . Sunday," I mutter. Domenic turns around and walks down the courtyard, looking back once and waving. I feel like crying.

I go to the store and pick out foods to stock the refrigerator for Domenic and for the road trip as well. Kate says she'll bring old Girl Scout Thin Mint cookies she found in the freezer while she was defrosting. I throw every snack food I can find in the cart. Then I take inventory of what's there.

I have to write down all that shit and show it to Gabriel on Monday. I start putting stuff back on the shelves. I keep about a fourth of what I had and grab a thing of celery, a big bag of almonds, and some grapes. I am packed and ready to go by ten thirty that night. I give the house a final once-over and decide it's time to turn in. Tomorrow will be a long day of driving, and I definitely need my sleep. I set the alarm for five o'clock in the morning, turn over, and go to sleep.

CHAPTER THIRTY-SIX

The Salem Witch Trials, 1692

I was Kate's maid of honor at her wedding. I stood at her side as she married Vincent di Matteo on a Saturday in a backyard in Altadena, California. They were so opposite that you could only see the overwhelming love they had for each other. Kate had swaths of chiffon over every piece of greenery in the backyard. Vincent had all of his groomsmen wear black Converse All Stars. Kate wanted their wedding song to be "Can't Help Falling in Love," so Vincent compromised by picking the version by Irish rocker Luka Bloom. It was a true marriage of acceptance and inclusion. I wonder what I will be thinking standing by Olivia's side in the gardens of city hall. Is hers going to be the marriage of two people like Kate and Vincent, or will it be the final gasp of the old Olivia as she loses herself in her thin fantasy life?

I awake slowly as the alarm blares the next morning. My body is still aching from yesterday's workout with Gabriel. I am still smiling about Domenic. The automatic timer on the coffeemaker goes off and the machine begins to percolate. I put Solo in her side yard and start my shower. I'm excited about the trip. I'm trying to treat at it as a mini-vacation, rather than Olivia's shower. Otherwise the excitement will be replaced by dread and anxiety. I pad to the kitchen in my towel and pour a cup of coffee, adding plenty of nondairy creamer. I grab the pair of Adidas sweats and white T-shirt I laid out last night. I don't mind getting dressed anymore. It's not that my clothes are falling off me. They're just more comfortable. I'm not packed into them like I once was.

Once I'm dressed, I let Solo in from the side yard and set the house up for Domenic. I leave a note thanking him again, letting him know there are surprises in the fridge. I sign off by saying I'm looking forward to his "surprise," knowing I will be three hundred miles away when he reads it. The terror of an actual acceptance is far enough away that I may only feel the aftershock. I leave my cell phone number, the hotel number, Kate's cell phone number, the vet's number, and Mom and Russell's home number. I pet Solo, grab my suitcase, and head out into the early morning.

I pull up to Kate's house a little past 6 a.m. All the lights are on, and the girlies run out in their pajamas to meet me. I walk into Kate's warm home and see two thermoses full of coffee and a pink pastry box o'magic.

"Mommy took us to the doughnut shop in our pajamas," Emily says.

"I picked out your favorites," Bella says.

"Thank you," I say, still bleary-eyed from the early hour. Will I have the strength to turn these little drops of heaven away? But then I remember what Gabriel says. "Go ahead and have one, but you eat the normal meal as well." Don't substitute the sweet for the meal. I've already eaten my breakfast; maybe one doughnut would be all right? Will I be able to stop at just one?

"It's past six o'clock," Kate says, going through her bag.

"You're turning into Mom," I say as Kate tells the girls to go in and brush their teeth.

"No, if I was Mom I'd tell you that it's past six o'clock, asshole."

"Your children are still within earshot."

"I thought we could take these with us," Kate continues as she opens the pink pastry box o'magic to unveil two doughnuts: one maple bar and one chocolate bar.

"The rest are in the fridge for Vincent and the girlies' breakfast." Kate winks. I sigh with relief.

Kate grabs her bag. I take it to my car and head back inside as she is saying good-bye to the girlies and Vincent. Bella has her thumb in her mouth, and Vincent is gently trying to dislodge it. Emily is making her way through the comics, and Kate has to bend down to her for her morning kiss.

Kate sips from her commuter mug as we merge from the 210 freeway to the 15. We are officially on our way. Every fiber of Kate's being yearns to jump in the driver's seat and take charge of the vehicle. She has grown accustomed to driving little people around and being in absolute control. Her arm is propped against the window, and whenever she feels I am getting too close to the car in front of me she pumps her imaginary brake pedal to make sure we stop in time.

Kate and I go over the invite list, dishing on what we think each woman will look like. Based on the women's innocent e-mails and our growing intolerance for Olivia, we have made the lot out to resemble a coven, right out of the Salem Witch Trials, 1692. I've received eight e-mails from Gwen letting me know she has gotten us on the VIP list to the Ghostbar at The Palms and confirms the weekend itinerary at the end of each e-mail.

I have planned high tea and dinner that night. Later, we'll go to Gwen's *must-be-on-the-VIP-list* bar. But I'm the maid of honor. This weekend is my show. It says so in black and white in all of the etiquette books Olivia has purchased over the past year . . . whether Gwen likes it or not.

Kate and I stop at Bun Boy for an early lunch of good all-American fare. Everyone who drives from Los Angeles to Las Vegas stops at Bun Boy. It's either that or a candy bar at some odorous rest stop. I order an amazing turkey sandwich and wash it down with some fruit from the car. Kate picks at her burger and still only finishes half. Damn that girl and her ability to turn away from the siren song of fried foods. We fill up the tank, and I make a trip to the restroom. Upon my return, I see that Kate can no longer control herself: She's sitting in the driver's seat. I concede and buckle myself in for the rest of the drive. We continue chattering about whatever is going on in our lives as the flat scenery passes outside the windows.

We are avoiding talking about Olivia. I am excited to find out what she got me for my birthday. But I haven't unveiled my plan to resurrect our friendship this weekend to Kate. I know what Kate's response will be. Shit, I know what anyone's response would be at this point. I feel like I'm on *Sesame Street* and Big Bird has all of my life's achievements out in front of him while he tries to coax the audience to choose "which one of these things is not like the other." Olivia's friendship has been a cornerstone of my life. Moving on without it seems like a titanic task I don't think I have the strength for. But another part of me continues to rear her ugly head. I want to rub my title *maid of honor* in all these women's faces this weekend. I see Gwen's envy. But it's a fact of life now. I'm Number One. I have the bouquet. I hold the rings. I have the history.

It's just past noon as we pass over the Nevada state line marked with seedy casinos and murky hotels. We're in the home stretch. I call Olivia from my cell and leave a message saying we should be at the Bellagio soon. I give her my cell phone number again. I feel good about myself as I sit in the passenger seat of my own vehicle. I am in control. This is my show.

I can see the lights of Las Vegas even in the superheated daylight of early afternoon. We see castles, golden buildings, pyramids, the New York skyline, and the Eiffel Tower. The streets are packed, even in the 116-degree heat. Tourists in sun hats, beer bellies, and gas station visors bob from one casino to the next. Kate lowers her sunglasses and looks high at the skyline of Vegas—taking it all in.

The Bellagio is right on the Strip, and Kate navigates us to the check-in line as we pull into valet parking. I open the trunk. The bellman retrieves Kate's bag and then mine. Kate hands the valet my keys and we enter our hotel. Kate checks us in, and we go up to the room. I don't care how old you are, staying in a hotel still feels like a treat. I am having so much fun. Kate is feeling the same way—I can see it on her face. We are looking at the mirror on the ceiling of the elevator and making funny faces, commenting on how thin we look from that angle.

We get out on our floor and walk down the hall in search of our room number. I'm feeling tired from the road and the early wake-up call. The happiness from the elevator-ceiling mirror only lasts so long. Kate opens the door to our hotel room and we immediately plop down on the beds and turn on the television. I check my cell phone. No one has called. I put in another call to Olivia telling her we've arrived at the hotel and that I'll wait for her call so we can meet for martinis before the high tea at three.

As Kate showers, I ball up on my bed and watch television. I am getting that sinking feeling with Olivia. Of course, she's doing this. This is why I'm questioning my trust in her after a lifetime of being best friends. I can see Big Bird now flapping his seven-foot wingspan at the photo of Olivia. "This one," he chirps. "This one," the squeaking audience mimics. I know I have made the right decision being here. I remind myself, I'm not alone this time. I have Kate. Fuck the whole martini idea. Kate and I can go to lunch and still meet everyone for high tea at the Petrossian Bar.

Kate gets out of the shower and I look forward to my turn so I can wash some of these feelings away. I give Kate an update as I strip and she looks lazily at the television. Everyone knows about Olivia but me. No one is surprised by her negligence. Kate says something like "fuck her" and turns the station to some sitcom.

The shower feels good, and I am beginning to get back some of that feeling of joy I had in the elevator. I can't expect Olivia to be there for me. It doesn't make me too intense or needy. It means that she and I have grown apart, and it's time to face that fact. I rinse my hair and soap my body. I am starting to feel some changes in my body, mostly from the inside out. I feel more secure when I'm walking up stairs. I'm not so off balance. I have this sneaking feeling that my belly button may be visible. I feel as proud as Bella about her outie. I return to the main room of the hotel room in a towel and wet hair.

"You got a call," Kate says.

"Olivia?" I say.

"No, Hannah."

"She's part of the coven. Is Olivia with her?" I say, toweling my hair off.

"It doesn't sound like it."

I have now left four messages for Olivia, each one more frustrated. I have to keep my eyes on the prize. I am sitting on the edge of my bed watching the hotel's promotional channel touting what a beautiful hotel the Bellagio is for lovers.

"And nothing from Gwen?" Kate throws the remote control to me as she walks to the bathroom and plugs in her curling iron. The acoustics of the bathroom make these words reverberate.

"No." The couple on the television are walking arm in arm around the fountains.

"What do you think about that?" Kate says, emerging once more from the bathroom with a chunk of white-blond hair in the warming curling iron.

Yes, I know they're together. I have some lady named Callie waiting for Olivia to arrive downstairs at Petrossian so she can present her with a tiara that says WORLD'S BEST BRIDE. I know this has nothing to do with me, but all I can think about is this will be like every other party I've thrown where no one comes.

"What's to think about?" I say. The couple on the television are now feeding each other gelato.

"We can just leave right now and forget this whole thing," Kate says as her curls settle.

"Hannah's head would explode for sure." Why can't I just walk away?

"Okay, maybe we don't have to leave, but we don't have to show up, either." Kate approaches me, and I can feel myself beginning to cry.

"I just don't know what I did." I have visions of having to tell some new, faceless friend all about Owen Lynch, Mason Phelps, and The John Sheridan. You never realize how much history you share with a friend until you have to tell story after story to someone new just so you can get on the same page.

"You didn't do anything. You know you didn't do anything. This is Olivia's problem, not yours. Let's just go down there and make the best of it. If Olivia doesn't show, then you get out of going to the wedding. That's fair." Kate pats my leg and makes her way back to the bathroom.

I wipe my tears away and click the television off just as the loving couple sit down to twin slot machines.

CHAPTER THIRTY-SEVEN

World's Best Bride

Once, in high school, Olivia and I were invited to a party. The popular kids were getting together up in the hills at one of their huge houses, and they asked us to come. I imagined, even then, being stripped of my clothes, tarred, and then feathered. Olivia convinced me we were finally being accepted and that this was a great opportunity for us. Obliged to my best friend, I drove us up into those hills and right into certain death. As we let ourselves in through the large Craftsman door, we found all of them sitting in Owen Lynch's hot tub drinking beer and barking inappropriate propositions at each other. Was this what high school dating was like? "Yer purty, Mary Benicci," I imagined him saying as the teenaged ogler eyed her newly formed breasts. But Olivia walked in confidently, cracked open a beer, and sat at the side of the hot tub. She flipped her blond hair as she talked to her half-naked audience. I walked over to the refrigerator, pulled out a diet soda, and flipped on the television. Olivia left that evening feeling like she had finally made it. The next day Mary Benicci spread a rumor that Olivia had almost drowned poor Shannon Shimasaki when Olivia tried to squeeze her way into the hot tub.

◆

The Petrossian Bar, set in the corner of the Bellagio lobby, is mostly known for its caviar and vodka tasting. But they also offer a high tea, which is what brought us here today. I approach the hostess and identify her as Callie by her name tag.

"Hi there, I'm Maggie Thompson." I already feel like a five-year-old arriving at a birthday party without a present.

"Oh," the hostess squeals. "Where's the lucky bride?"

"She is still en route," I say.

"But we'd like to sit if that's okay," Kate interrupts.

"You're Maggie Thompson?" I sense a tiny wisp of a peasant bounding toward me.

"Yes," I say, raising my arms over my face in defense.

"I'm Hannah? Hannah Ratner? From the phone?" Her eyes bulge with desperation.

Ah, the first to arrive, Goodie Ratner: It's a title I'm sure she's held since she was Hall Monitor in elementary school. Her wispy brown hair has the effect of male pattern baldness or a bad dye job. Hannah is alarmingly thin. Her designer clothes hang on her like a third-world child who can be fed for just five cents a day. She follows the hostess to our table and begins asking what the specials are as she is a vegan and wants to make sure she won't be ingesting anything "inappropriate" this fine afternoon.

The table is beautiful. Dainty teacups are set out for seven, and the WORLD'S BEST BRIDE tiara sits at the head of the table. A glaring reminder of Olivia's absence. Champagne is chilling at the end of the table, and Callie is waiting to put our napkins in our laps. I make a note to come back here with someone I am actually happy for.

I see two women coming our way through the tables, passing Callie as she exits. Panchali is on the right. She is stunning. Her black wavy hair is parted in the middle just enough to show off beautiful almond eyes. She is wearing a wine-colored blouse with gray Capri pants and moves gracefully through the restaurant. I can see her calf muscles from here. She made eye contact with us when she entered the restaurant, but has yet to smile or wave hello. Shawna Moss, on the other hand, is frantically waving and smiling from ear to ear. She is dark-skinned with straight hair that is newly done and perfect. She, too, is painfully thin and accentuates this by dressing in clothes that hug her adolescent figure. I stand to greet the women. If it is humanly possible, these three women make Olivia look overweight. Callie has returned. She is being hailed by Kate.

"You must be Maggie." Shawna is approaching rapidly.

"Yes, nice to meet you. This is my sister, Kate," I say, pulling Kate up by her arm.

"It's so great to finally meet you. Olivia talks about you all the time," Shawna says.

"Good to meet you, Shawna," I say, backing away slowly.

Kate and Shawna shake hands. Shawna has this tendency to purse her lips before she talks. It's somewhat unsettling.

"You are just like her," Shawna whispers.

"I'm sorry?" I ask as Kate settles herself back in her seat, spinning the champagne around to read the label.

"You are just like Olivia. Your mannerisms, your voice. I mean, it's uncanny," she says.

"Maybe I am Olivia," I say.

Shawna stops and stares at me. I can hear Kate let out a huge sigh behind me.

"And you're funny. Just like Olivia," Shawna says, laughing out her nose.

"Do you have anything to drink?" Kate asks, as Callie finally approaches our table.

Shawna sits next to Kate at the end of the table. Panchali squeezes around the back and sits next to Hannah. Hannah has calmed down nicely, and Panchali approaches her carefully so as not to rile her up again.

Shawna quickly engages Kate about her life. Kate gives her usual spiel about the girlies and Vincent. Pictures are presented, and Shawna is a rather active listener. Kate's stories are dotted with oohs, aahs, and gales of inappropriate laughter. Peregrine would definitely approve. Then Kate must pay the ultimate price. She must now obligingly ask Shawna about herself. We learn that Shawna is single. No surprise there. Shawna begins her canned rundown of the "single life." I imagine her late at night practicing her pauses and facial expressions as she breathlessly makes her way through her monologue. She has worked at the same PR firm since she got out of school, again no surprise. And she loves the Thursday-night television lineup. I ask her how she knows Olivia. She thinks this is funny.

"The PR firm. I introduced her to Adam."

"Did you?" Kate asks. She's getting a tad tipsy.

"Not like Olivia would ever have trouble getting a boyfriend. She's always been so popular." Kate and I exchange a look. I was not properly debriefed about Olivia's new "history," so I decide to just keep quiet.

"So how did you introduce the two lovebirds?" Kate lifts her glass.

"I booked Adam for this conference and then told Olivia to go pick him up. I guess you could say the rest is history, you know. But I knew. I knew," Shawna confides.

"Knew?" Kate asks, popping a petit four in her mouth. I almost can't hold back my laughter.

"They belonged together," Shawna whispers.

"So you're to blame," Kate insinuates.

"I guess you could say that." Shawna beams.

I can tell this is Shawna's favorite part. She gets to tell secrets to perfect strangers and let the entire table know they are not privy to this knowledge. I look across the table as Panchali takes apart a finger sandwich while she and Hannah discuss what they believe the meat to be. Shawna is peering over to them and then back at us. She leans in. "Adam was the one," she whispers. You're telling me. The *only* one if memory serves. Shawna is leaning in so close to me I can smell the lox from her finger sandwiches.

"I guess she had a pretty serious boyfriend back in high school, but that didn't work out. College, you know? Of course, *you* know. This is all old hat for you. You could probably tell me a ton of things I don't know," Shawna snorts. Kate spits out her wine. Shawna knows not what she says.

Finally, Panchali reaches across the table and introduces herself. I am afraid of her in some weird celebrity kind of way.

"Panchali Nagra," she says, extending her hand.

"Wonderful to meet you," I stutter, still a little thrown by Olivia's mystery boyfriend in high school. Panchali pulls her hand back over the table. "I'm Maggie. It's great to meet you. Olivia talks about you all the time," I say.

"Yes," Panchali says as she sniffs. She flips her napkin over and resets it on her lap. I believe I have been dismissed.

Panchali orders her choice of tea. Hannah suggests Darjeeling, as it's from Panchali's "homeland." Panchali orders Earl Grey, and Hannah hands her menu over to Callie with a look of disgust.

I focus back on Kate. She is now discussing the Thursday-night television lineup as opposed to the Tuesday-night lineup.

Kate holds true to her large ensemble sitcoms, but Shawna brings some fresh insights to the table. Kate is pointing at her with a full wineglass, saying something about believability and how that many skinny people would never hang out with each other. Shawna disagrees for obvious reasons. I try to get Kate to behave, as it looks like she is trying to take a swing at Shawna, but I'm not sure. I see Hannah looking at her watch from across the table. I am beginning to understand this to be one of Goodie Ratner's compulsions. One of many.

I look at my watch, too. I can't help myself. It's three thirty. The party for Olivia started at three o'clock. No Olivia, and no Gwen. I can't help but look around the table and project every single insecurity I've ever felt onto these three strangers. These three beautiful, painfully thin strangers. I can see Big Bird again. "One of these things is not like the other," he says. I stand out like a sore thumb. A big, fat, oversize, sore thumb. Sure, I've lost some weight, but compared with these women I am still one word. *Fat.* For chrissakes, compared with these women Olivia could lose a few. What must they think of me? A maid of honor throws a bridal shower and the bride doesn't even show? This will be fodder for Shawna for sure.

CHAPTER THIRTY-EIGHT

Caught Up

At three forty-five, Hannah announces she has just spotted Olivia and Gwen in the lobby of the hotel. The crowd goes wild. It takes the pair a good twenty minutes to check in while the shower is suspended in this odd motionless quiet. Even Hannah is quiet, save a few checks of her watch. Olivia and Gwen work their way across the room. I feel like I'm in a movie theater watching the entrance of a pair of 1940s movie starlets. Olivia has a lot of makeup on. A lot of makeup. I've never seen her with this much on before. Kate notices, too.

"Are those false eyelashes?" Kate asks as Olivia and Gwen approach.

"They must be," I say.

Gwen is wearing a chiffon tank top with crisp white pants and pointy heels. She keeps her sunglasses on as she walks toward us. I have to stop myself from ripping them off her smug-ass face. I feel like a dipshit sitting next to the empty seat reserved by the WORLD'S BEST BRIDE tiara. Olivia comes over and gives me a hug. She is going in for a hug with Kate when Kate retreats from the mascara-laden eyelashes. Olivia backs away.

"Are you wearing false eyelashes?" Kate asks.

"Aren't they fabulous?" Olivia cries.

Kate and I are silent. She looks like a drag queen.

"I bought out the makeup counter this morning. I got a free tutorial, they taught me how to do everything. I wanted to use my own products when I meet with the makeup artist back in LA," Olivia says.

"This morning?" Kate asks.

"We flew in first thing," Olivia says as she removes her purse from her shoulder and begins hugging Hannah.

I don't know what to do with this information. It makes sense on the page, but in my head it gets all mucked up. Olivia has been in Las Vegas since early this morning and has not returned one phone call. Has sipped nary a martini with yours truly. And now she arrives late to my high tea bridal shower looking like a two-bit whore? How does this add up? I look to Kate, and her face is just as puzzled as mine. We are both still standing. Everyone else has seated themselves, smoothing their napkins on their laps. There is a moment of awkwardness as Kate and I slowly sit. I lock eyes with Gwen.

"You look great," I say over Kate and Shawna. Gwen has seated herself in the farthest chair from me.

"Thanks. We've just had a spa," Gwen says, rising and giving me an air kiss. Being from the Los Angeles area, I understand this odd ceremony.

"Excuse me?" I ask.

"Well, Olivia had a gift certificate and I decided I would partake of some services, too." A gift certificate? *My* gift certificate. Olivia's birthday present from me, thank you very much.

"I know how you hate the spa, Mags." Olivia fluffs her hair across the table.

Callie comes back and attempts to present Olivia with the

WORLD'S BEST BRIDE tiara. Shawna fumbles for her camera. Olivia dismisses the tiara, instead asking Callie if she has mineral water. She sets the tiara underneath her chair. Olivia turns to Kate and grills her for the next thirty minutes about basic wedding etiquette. Kate is getting more and more liquored up. At one point, she tries to convince Olivia that the bride stands at the altar from the beginning of the wedding and that the wedding march plays as the bride and groom exit the ceremony. I am lost in thoughts of Olivia and Gwen chatting on the phone. Olivia returning a call. Olivia doing a favor for someone. Olivia being on time for someone.

"Well," Olivia says. Her eyelashes brush my face as she inches her chair toward Kate. I want to rip them off and stomp on them. "It's going to be beautiful," she continues.

"What do your centerpieces look like?" Even drunk, Kate knows all the right questions to ask. The conversation at the table falls into a hushed silence. Shawna missed the WORLD'S BEST BRIDE photo op, but she can capture Olivia telling Kate about her centerpieces.

"The centerpieces are perfect. Patrona is setting up topiaries with ivy and tuberoses at every table. They're set just high enough so you can still talk to people across the table. There will be small candles at every table. I wanted the lighting in the garden to be natural yet intimate. Let's face it, we all look better in that type of lighting." Was there a study done that I wasn't aware of? Is that what these girls talk about—proper lighting?

"What about the rehearsal dinner?" Shawna asks. *Why?* I want to say. *You won't be eating any of it.*

"I am holding it in the courtyard of The Athenaeum on the Caltech campus. It has vaulted ceilings with Italian frescoes and these amazing gardens. I don't know which event is going to be more beautiful." The crowd gasps. Olivia continues. "Patrona has everything planned right down to the slide show of the history of Adam and me. You know . . . all those embarrassing little lovey-dovey shots of us." Olivia blushes as the crowd sighs in unison. Kate holds her wineglass up to Callie; tapping it with her perfectly manicured nails, she mouths, *Another.* Shawna squeals. Olivia smiles and continues, "It's going to be just perfect." The crowd oohs and ahhs. Shawna's flash goes off in her purse as she tries to put the camera away. Hannah shakes her head at Shawna's waste of a shot.

"Is it just going to be you and Adam at the head table?" Kate asks.

"It's going to be just you and me, right, Olivia?" I blurt.

"Well, Adam's brother wants to sit with his parents, and we have the other groomsmen and bridesmaids to think about. But yeah, the maid of honor does traditionally sit at the head table," Olivia says. Gwen sniffs at the end of the table.

"For everyone to see, huh?" I say. Where's the overdramatic twirling?

"It's usually a focal point—anyway, let's get some menus, huh?" Olivia snaps her fingers at Callie.

◆

High tea drags on through retellings of the marriage proposal, the engagement announcement, and how Dr. Adam Farrell told Olivia she could have any kind of wedding she wanted. Considering Mr. Hobbs Morten is footing the entire bill, I'd say Adam was being a bit generous with his offer.

Our dinner reservations at Prime, the Bellagio steak house, are for seven thirty. The high tea crowd begins to disperse. Panchali and Hannah are going to go to some of the other casinos. Shawna wants to start getting ready for dinner and the Ghostbar now, so she quickly retreats to her room.

"I've got to go to the restroom before we settle up here," I say, needing a moment to myself. Kate is counting the money left by the other girls and working out the tip that Callie will get. Olivia is checking her messages from her cell phone. She is punching in such a long series of numbers she looks like a small child with a play phone.

"I'll join you," Gwen says. I panic. How can I take back having to go to the bathroom? Can I say I'll just go in our room instead? I drop my shoulders and push my chair out from the table. Gwen knocks Kate's head with her huge Tod's bag as she comes around the table. Kate stops counting and glares up at Gwen. I assure Kate I'll hurry.

Gwen and I make our way through the babbling casino. Bells and whistles are going off and little eruptions of joy detonate from random craps tables throughout the casino. Gwen methodically walks behind me, never attempting to catch up.

I push open the bathroom door and walk through to an open stall. I quietly go to the bathroom. I come up to the sinks first and begin washing my hands. Gwen flushes and approaches the sink, straightening her waistband.

"So dinner and then this bar?" I talk to Gwen through the mirror like she's a hairstylist cutting my hair.

"Sounds great," Gwen says.

I look down at my hands and wash them as if my life depended on it.

"Thanks for planning this whole high tea thing. It was charming," Gwen says.

"You're welcome. I hope Olivia liked it," I say, wondering why Gwen is thanking me.

"I feel bad that we were so late. We just got caught up, you know?" Gwen pulls out some paper towels.

"Caught up?" I ask.

"You know, with the makeup and then with the whole spa day." Gwen is rummaging through her purse and finds a tube of lipstick.

"I'm glad you enjoyed it." You fucking bitch. I want to throttle this woman. But it's not Gwen's fault. I should be getting angry with Olivia.

"I know we missed your martini thing, but the tea really was darling," Gwen adds.

"No problem. We should be getting back," I bite out.

"Wouldn't want to be late again." Gwen pats my shoulder.

CHAPTER THIRTY-NINE

It *Is* a Big Hat, Kate

Who is the person that these women have come to know? What anecdotes does Olivia tell as she sits with friends? When she gets upset about something, does she make up a history to show that this has happened before? Or is this the same fantasy she and I used to play out driving around in that Chevy Chevette all those years ago? Except now, instead of fantasizing about our future—she looks back and creates her perfect history out of whole cloth. A history that doesn't include gastric bypass surgeries and crushes on starting quarterbacks who knew you only as Orca. When we were little girls, we'd invent scenarios where perfect men toasted us with perfect flutes of champagne. But most girls begin to see these fantasies as silly and unrealistic when they get older. Where does that leave Olivia? Is she still a little girl locked in her pink room playing with Barbies, unable to come out and play in the real world? And, if so where does that leave me?

◆

We plan to meet at Prime at seven thirty and then move to the
Ghostbar in The Palms resort hotel. Gwen has put our names on
the VIP list and assures us it will be a great time.

I have two and a half hours to think about Gwen and Olivia
shopping, giggling, sitting in baths of rose petals, waving off our
martini date and the bridal shower, while they run around trying on tiny clothing and changing in the same dressing room
showing off their equally tiny bodies. The only part that gives
me some sense of satisfaction is knowing that Olivia felt threatened enough by Shawna Moss and her Gossip Brigade to lie
about her past. Olivia has not only never had a boyfriend—she
wouldn't know "The One" if it bit her on the ass. And biting her
on the ass is certainly not something I imagine the good Dr.
Adam Farrell would be up for. I feel a sense of power and don't
even care if it's a slippery slope. Olivia lied to Shawna. Who else
has she lied to?

Dinner at Prime is amazing. The food is fresh and cooked
perfectly. I've decided to wear something a little flashy: a low-
cut chiffon tank top with a vintage brown corduroy coat paired
with black pants and a pair of 1940s-style heels. Both items fit
better than they did when I tried them on at the department
store. With my heels on, I stand a head taller than any woman
in our party. I put my long brown hair in two braids that extend
down my back. I brought a cowboy hat for later. A real Stetson.
I bought it one year as a New Year's resolution, but I've never
really worn it out in public. It seemed like too much, somehow.
And yet something about that hat makes me confident. Maybe
it's the height. I don't know. But whatever it does for me, I need
it now more than ever for the Ghostbar outing.

After dinner, we stand in the queue waiting for the next cab.
Gwen is at the front of the group with Panchali. They are com-
miserating on how many cabs we will need. They keep looking

back at Kate and me. Shawna is reapplying her lipstick as Hannah tries to put in her two cents. Olivia, Kate, and I stand at the back of the group. Olivia is getting more and more drunk as the night proceeds. I begin to question why I don't join her. It would be so much easier if I was just flat-out drunk through all of this. Gwen summons us to the cab. Olivia stumbles over to her, giggling something about "Prime Meat." This has been a constant joke of the night. Gwen puts Olivia in the cab and shoves Panchali in next to her. She waves us to the cab behind them as she shuts the door behind her. The three of them drive off. Kate, Hannah, Shawna, and I pile into the SUV cab that approaches. I feel like we've just boarded the short bus on our way to the "special school."

Olivia, Gwen, and Panchali are waiting in front of The Palms. It was a long drive, and the cab ride was not cheap. This weekend is getting more and more expensive. I'm cutting into next month's budget. I decide I won't drink tonight as much as I ache for oblivion. We walk through the hotel lobby, and the familiar bells and whistles of a Las Vegas casino ring out. Hannah finds the elevator and presses the button repeatedly as we wait for its instant arrival. I'm the last in the elevator. I am holding my cowboy hat in my hands. I'll put it on once I enter the bar. I'll need the confidence then. I look to Kate. She is drunker than she was this afternoon. I begin to envy her. She has the right idea. Survival, not temperance. The elevator doors open, and we're hit with the silver-blue haze of the Ghostbar.

Even with my experience in Los Angeles bars, the people here are unnervingly good-looking. My cowboy hat seems silly now. I hold it tighter as we ease into the crowd. Kate has her hand on my back, and we both eye the same empty table. Gwen makes a beeline to the bar. She is magnetic. Everyone watches as she passes. I see at least one man follow her to the bar and ask if he can buy her a drink. Kate and I sit and wait for the cocktail waitress to get to us. Panchali, Shawna, and Hannah follow our lead and start pulling chairs over.

"Where's Gwen?" Olivia slurs.

"At the bar," Panchali answers.

"Do you want something?" Shawna asks.

"I don't think she needs another drink," Hannah says.

"It's her party," Shawna snaps.

"I'm just saying she seems a little—" Hannah stops and mouths *drunk.*

"Let her live it up a little," Shawna whispers back.

"Where's Gwen?" Olivia is teetering but not sitting.

"She's at the bar, Olivia," I say in my strongest voice.

"At the bar? Go get her," she says.

"Go get her?" I say.

"Go get her." Olivia points.

"She's coming over here, I'm not going to go get her." I feel like I'm speaking to a toddler in a toy store.

"Where do I sit?" Olivia focuses back on the table.

"Pull up a chair," Kate yells over the music.

"What?" Olivia asks.

"Pull up a chair and sit down." Kate is the perennial troop leader.

Olivia stands, gazing around at the empty chairs. One hand is on her chest; in the other, she holds her purse like an old Victorian woman.

"Oh, for God's sake," Hannah says, dragging a chair over from an adjacent table.

"Get one for Gwen." Olivia points at Hannah.

"What?" Hannah asks.

"Get another chair for Gwen." Olivia is hooking her purse

over the arm of her chair and staring at the bar in search of her beloved Gwen.

Hannah doesn't say anything. She quietly gets up and asks a group of people a few tables over if an empty chair is taken. The crowd says it is. Hannah goes to three more tables until she finally finds an unused chair that has been vacated by a now fully enthralled couple. She drags the chair back over to our table and sits. She checks her watch and stares at the bar. I feel dirty. I should have gotten the chair. No, I should have told Olivia to fuck off about innumerable things this evening, Gwen's chair being the least of my problems. But I didn't. I just sat there.

"I need a drink," Kate says.

"Get me one," Olivia blurts.

"Get it yourself." Kate walks away.

"What's her problem?" Olivia turns to me.

I get up and walk to the bar with Kate, the cowboy hat hot in my hands.

Kate is at the bar trying to get the bartender's attention. Gwen stands next to her where two of her drinks are congregating. She seems to be waiting for more.

"You okay?" I yell over the music.

"I've had enough. Barking orders. Dragging chairs. This is ridiculous." Kate waves the bartender down.

"I know. I know," I say.

"Do you need something?" Gwen turns to me.

"No, we're fine," Kate interrupts.

"More room, maybe?" Gwen balances the new third drink with the other two, smirks at Kate and me, and walks toward the table.

"That's it. That's just . . . that's enough." Kate turns and follows Gwen.

Gwen is angling for the chair with my purse over the arm; the chair Hannah worked so hard to get is sitting vacant. She is staring at it.

"What did you just say to her?" Kate says, turning Gwen around with the anger in her voice.

"I'm sorry?" Gwen is setting drinks down for Panchali and Olivia. Olivia swirls her tongue around until she finds the little red straw and sips.

"What did you say to her? At the bar? You said something and I am asking you to repeat it," Kate demands.

"I didn't say anything to you," Gwen specifies as she sits and crosses her legs. Kate is standing over her. The table of people who refused Hannah's chair request are now staring. At her full height, Kate stands about five feet tall. Now she has her hands on her hips and looks a bit like Tinkerbell.

"What?" Kate is flustered.

"I was asking Ms. Maggie if she needed more room at the bar. You know, with that hat and all." Gwen cradles her martini glass and looks at Panchali. Panchali sniffs. Shawna is now looking so feverishly in her purse for something that she has caused most of the contents to spill on the floor. Hannah stares at the vacant chair as Olivia looks on and sips.

"The hat?" I ask.

"You know, it *is* a big hat. You'll probably need extra room for it. You need to factor that in," Gwen says, smirking. I stare at her. Kate is still in the same position: hands on her hips, face crimson red, and standing over Gwen. I quickly glance at Olivia. Is she watching? Is she seeing this? The bride is sipping her drink and looking into the ice cubes.

"I just never put it on. I shouldn't have brought it," I say, looking from face to face to face. Everyone is staring at me. They know she's not talking about the fucking hat. Is this where she passes me the *gordita's* soda? How much weight do you fucking have to lose before you're no longer considered overweight? Should I even bother with Gabriel and five cardios a week? Or has Gwen just zeroed in on every woman's Achilles' heel? How can Olivia not say something? How can I fucking not say something? *I shouldn't have brought it*—what kind of goddamn comeback is that?

"Probably not." Gwen sips.

Kate looks Olivia straight in the face. "You're going to sit there and not say anything?" Kate yells. I swear she is going to rip the straw right out of Olivia's overly made-up mouth.

"Hm?" Olivia looks up at Kate.

"Hm? Did you just say *hm*?" Kate is now openly spitting.

"Look, I think we've all kind of gotten a little tipsy and . . ." Shawna finally comes up from her purse. I am paralyzed. I am in control. I was in control. There were going to be no surprises this weekend. This weekend was about a resurrection. This weekend was about Olivia and me making things right. This was supposed to be my show. How is this happening? I'm writing my food down now. I'm working out and I'm up to forty-five minutes on the StairMaster. I'm a size smaller! I'm a fucking size smaller!

"It *is* a big hat, Kate," Olivia says into her glass.

"What the fuck did you just say? What the fuck did you just say!" Kate lunges at Olivia. I see a security man appear from behind a silvery pillar over by the bar. He is talking into a mouthpiece and coming our way.

"Kate. Please, let's just go," I plead, pulling my sister away and waving the security man down. He backs off and takes his place behind the silvery pillar. I don't make eye contact with anyone. And no one makes eye contact with me. I grab our purses, and we leave the table.

"See you at the wedding," Gwen taunts.

"Like hell! You won't see me near that fucking wedding! Fuck you, Olivia!" Kate is crawling over my shoulder now and screaming *Fuck you* at the top of her little lungs. I stand a good foot taller than her in these heels and I can barely keep her down. I am numb. Kate's curses resonate in my head just long enough to swirl once. Then the emptiness and quiet come again, broken only by Olivia's words, *It is a big hat, Kate. It is a big hat, Kate.* I'm a size smaller. I'm a size smaller.

I tuck Kate tightly in bed and escape to the bathroom where she can't hear me. I close the door behind me and sit on the edge of the bathtub with my head in my hands and cry. I haven't cried this hard in years. I keep replaying the night over and over in my head and wonder how everything got so turned around. When did Olivia become one of those people in the hot tub at Owen Lynch's house?

CHAPTER FORTY

Dirty Little Secrets

I wake to the sound of my cell phone chirping. I pat the nightstand to find my glasses. The red digital numbers of the hotel clock come into focus. It is three thirty-seven in the morning. I flip the covers back and go into the bathroom.

"Hello?" I whisper.

"Maggie?" It's Olivia doing her best impression of a stage whisper.

"Yeah?" Who else would it be?

"It's Olivia."

"Yeah, I've got that. What do you want?" I'm standing on a cold tile floor in my pajamas with my drunk sister snoring in the other room. Last I heard, Olivia was siding with Gwen.

"Are you mad?" Olivia asks.

"What are you calling for?"

"Can you meet me downstairs? Just you?" she asks.

"Why?"

"Please? I've got your birthday present, Mags. And can you . . . just let me explain." I can hear the bustling casino behind her.

"Where are you?"

"I'm downstairs. In the casino. Can you meet me in the conservatory?"

"Where's Gwen?"

"She's upstairs in the room. It's just going to be just you and me. Please?" Olivia's cell phone is cutting in and out.

"Give me five minutes." I beep my cell phone off.

I don't want our friendship to be over. I don't want to have to go out and find a new best friend. I don't want to be alone in the world without Olivia. I'm not sure I know who I am without her.

I remember once when I was waiting at an intersection for a light to change. I looked over at the couple in the car next to me. She was leaning on his shoulder. He stroked her hair. At first I reacted the way any single person would—I hated them and wanted them to stop. But then I really took them in. That moment, that little moment, is why people stay together. It could never be retold. It could never be described. But it was that deep intimacy that gave the couple the ability to share that moment together. No one would ever know about it except the two of them. And when the going got rough, it would be that moment they recalled as the reason why they were together. With friends, it's the same thing. Sitting in a movie theater unable to hold back the giggles. Driving silently listening to a CD. Already having a diet soda ordered for you as you arrive late to a lunch date. It's the little things. Those little moments that solidify caring for another person.

I head back out into the dark hotel room. What if Kate wakes up while I'm gone? She'll be worried sick. I'll just have to hurry. I scrounge around on the floor for a sweatshirt and socks. I slip on my shoes and locate my purse by the glow of the bathroom's night-light. The room key is nestled in my wallet. I close the door quietly behind me.

It's not until the elevator ride down that I realize what I'm doing. Kate fought for me tonight. Olivia didn't. It was Olivia who allowed someone she calls a friend to insult me. It was Olivia who let me leave the bar and didn't come after me. It's Olivia who is calling me two hours later after everyone's asleep like a dirty little secret that can only be walked around in the dark of the night.

I see Olivia sitting on the stairs in the conservatory. She is holding a small gold package tightly in her right hand. The conservatory is lit up like daytime. It seems unnaturally bright for such a bleak meeting.

"Hi." Olivia stands as I approach.

"Hi," I say, not sitting.

"Can you sit for a second?" Olivia asks.

I sit and cross my legs.

"I'm sorry about tonight," Olivia continues.

"So am I," I say. I'm sorry I stayed. I'm sorry I dragged my sister out here. I'm sorry I didn't yell at Gwen myself. And I'm sorry you are nowhere near the person you used to be.

"You have nothing to be sorry for. It was between Kate and Gwen." Olivia turns her body, and her knee is now touching mine.

"Kate had nothing to do with tonight and you know it." I twist my body so my knees are now facing forward.

"She had a little bit to do with it." A vision of Kate screaming *Fuck you* at the top of her lungs comes to mind.

"Why did you call? Was it to blame Kate for the way Gwen acted tonight?"

"No, I wanted to give you this." Olivia hands me the little gold package. I take it indifferently.

"Thanks."

"Can you please open it?" Olivia's eyes are beginning to well up.

"Why? So you can buy me off? Thanks for the present. It would have been a much better gift not to be run out of your wedding shower like that. So whatever is in this box is secondary," I say, dying to know what's in the fucking box.

"Okay . . . I just want you to know that I . . . I was just so drunk. I didn't stand up for you. I should have."

I stare straight ahead and bring my arms back across my chest.

"Please. Will you just . . . can you look at me? Something?" I turn my head and look at Olivia. I see a tired, overly made-up girl who in this freakish light looks haggard and overextended.

"Please just tell me you believe me? That you know I would never let anyone treat you like that? I know Gwen didn't mean anything by it," Olivia continues. I was almost there, until she brought up Gwen.

"Gwen means everything she says," I say.

"But she didn't mean what you think she meant. She adores you. All she talks about is how great you are and how amazing you've been through this whole wedding thing. She even said that she thought you had lost a little weight. Isn't that cool? We . . . we were just drunk, and the bar was crowded. Please, tell me you believe me." Olivia takes my hand. As a practice, Olivia is not touchy-feely.

"I don't know." I want to believe her.

"Just tell me everything is okay, Mags. Please . . . please . . . please tell me my best friend is still going to be my maid of honor. Please?" Olivia begins to cry.

"Don't cry. Just . . . Kate and I are going to leave first thing in the morning. I just need time to think about all of this."

"That's fine. That's fine. Just please . . . please promise me. You've got to promise me that you're going to be there for the wedding. You've got to promise me, Maggie. Tonight was so stupid. All I want is for my best friend to walk down the aisle ahead of me. Just like we always talked about, remember? And we'll be at that head table, just like we talked about. You can't walk away now. I need you." Olivia is practically sobbing. I have never seen her cry like this. I find myself just staring at her, taking it in.

"I need to think about it." I'm weakening. I can feel it.

"Did you ever want to know why that night on the bridge was the last straw? The night before I made the decision to get the surgery?" Olivia is almost kneeling in front of me.

"Yes." I *have* always wondered that.

"I just . . . I was always the fat one, you know?" Olivia begins. "That night it was just too much. Once again I was being called out and I couldn't take it anymore. And there you were smiling and . . . I guess I just wanted what you had. You know, that confidence." Olivia looks up.

"Confidence? I don't get how we could be friends for so long and you could be so wrong about who I am," I whimper.

"What?" Olivia wipes her tears away.

"I've done my absolute best to be invisible—not confident," I sob.

"You call it being invisible. Everyone else calls it confidence. Trust me." Olivia wipes her nose with the sleeve of her cashmere sweater.

"Well, either way it's no way to live." I hear myself. It *is* no way to live.

Olivia takes the gold package out of my hands and tears the paper off. She opens the small velvet box and creaks the top open. Once again, she wipes her nose as she pulls the beautiful necklace from the box. It's a gold chain with the diamond-encrusted letters M&O dangling wistfully. Olivia undoes the clasp.

"Please. Mommy let me go all out. Half birthday—half maid of honor. It was ridiculously expensive and I should really be moderately embarrassed, but I just wanted to do something extra special for you." I turn my body around as Olivia flips the chain around my neck. She smells of smoke from the casino.

"Thank you. You shouldn't have." I look down on the necklace. It is stunning.

"What are you thinking?" Olivia and I have been saying that for fifteen years. Whenever the other was silent for more than two seconds, we would bombard her with the *what are you thinking* question. The answers have included everything from needing an eyebrow wax to deciding whether or not to attend a master's program.

"I'm going back up to the room. Kate might wake up." I stand up and look down on her.

"Promise you'll still be my maid of honor?" Olivia stays seated. I am speechless. I never knew any of what she just said. I never knew Olivia saw me that way. Maybe this weekend *is* a resurrection.

"I promise," I say.

I turn and walk out of the conservatory with a lump in my throat, tears welling up in my eyes and shivers running up and down my spine. I can't tell Kate. She'll kill me. Right now I just want to get back to bed and go home first thing in the morning. My birthday. Another birthday that will go down in the books as the shittiest day ever. I take the necklace off in the bathroom and put it back in its box. I place it deep in the recesses of my suitcase.

◆

Kate rants the entire way home about what bitches Olivia and Gwen are. She replays the night a thousand times, each time from a different camera angle and every time with a new weapon. In one version, she throws a drink at Gwen. In another, she shoves my cowboy hat right in her face, yelling, "It is a big hat, it is a big hat." In the last and most memorable, she bests Gwen and Olivia in a catfight and then calls the security guard. He throws a bloodied Gwen and Olivia out of the bar as the victorious Kate is lifted up on the cheering patrons' shoulders. But in every account, Kate keeps the ending exactly the same. "Like hell! I wouldn't go near that damn wedding! Fuck you, Olivia!" And every time the story ends, Kate looks over to me and smiles like I'm not going, either. How can I tell her about my talk with Olivia in the conservatory now? How do you tell someone they fought for you for nothing?

I drop Kate at her house around dusk and finally drive home. We plan to meet later that night for cake at Mom's house. I dread it already. It is only then that I remember Domenic. He is waiting for me at home with something special planned. I don't want to be with anyone right now, let alone someone I . . . someone it just hurts to be around. I roll the window up and slowly drive home.

As I open the door, Solo bounds through the bedroom door and jumps up to greet me. No Domenic. I set my bag down on the couch and search the house. No stuff? No man things? Did he forget? I am petting Solo when I see a handmade card taped to the top of another burned CD. It's Domenic's writing.

Maggie:
You are cordially invited to spend the evening with one Domenico Brown who is anxious to celebrate your birthday. Please meet him at Surya India on Third Street in Los Angeles, where he has reserved a table for two in your honor. See you there.

> *PS: Here is a CD of Peter Gabriel songs that are much better than "In Your Eyes."*

See you tonight, D.

I set the card and the CD down on the table. I call Mom and ask if we can do the whole birthday thing tomorrow morning. I'm wiped out, I say. I can't see Domenic right now. I'm raw and I can't stop crying. I'm not ready to leave the warmth of this shithole I've lived in for so long. Numbness and invisibility are so much easier than the train wreck this whole episode has turned into. I dial Domenic's phone number. I get the answering machine, thank God. I hear the beep.

"Hey there, we're stuck in Barstow so I'm not going to be able to make it back by tonight. I hope I caught you in time. I'll call you when I get in town," I say. My voice is cracking and I can't stop crying. I turn off the lights and head straight to bed.

He'll understand when I don't show. I just can't. The only thing I can conceive of doing right now is taking a shower and curling up in bed. This Friday night is the rehearsal dinner and the wedding is this Saturday. This is the home stretch. I can finish this.

As I'm falling asleep I hear the phone ring and Domenic's voice. I catch every other word. "Barstow? . . . safe drive . . . rain check . . . missed you."

Happy birthday, Maggie.

CHAPTER FORTY-ONE

Table Nine

Why did I wake up? Why couldn't I stay in my fantasy world where Ponyboy fathered all five of my children and my best friend defended me in bar brawls?

I park the car and walk inside EuroPane for my belated birthday celebration. I see Emily and Bella propped on benches near the wall with coloring books. Mom sits with her coffee and fresh fruit plate, and Kate has a fresh orange juice and oatmeal. I order the oatmeal also and get my coffee just the way I like it. I sit down next to Bella and stir in the cream and sugar.

"Are you going to the marrying place?" Bella asks.

"Not yet," I say, sipping my much-needed coffee.

"But you're not getting married," Bella asks.

"No, I'm the maid of honor," I say.

"You're cleaning?" Bella asks. Everyone at the table laughs.

"How do you feel?" Mom asks.

"I'm okay," I say.

"Kate told me everything on the drive over." Mom spears a chunk of cantaloupe.

"We are planning how to egg the ceremony from the street." Kate is drawing fluffy blue clouds on Emily's picture.

"I'm going," I whisper.

"What?" Kate looks up, not losing all her cool, but enough so that Emily stops drawing.

"Olivia called me after the whole bar fight." I glance at Emily, not knowing how to conceal that her mommy was dragged out of a bar screaming the F word.

"Wait. When did all of this happen?" Kate asks.

"She called around three in the morning, I agreed to meet her downstairs in the conservatory. She started crying and . . . she wanted to give me my birthday present." I can't take it. Even I think I sound pathetic.

"You gave in? Again? Jesus, Maggie." Kate isn't pissed. It's worse. She's disappointed.

"Look. It's like we've said the whole time, it's just one more weekend and then that's it. You don't have to go, but Mom and I will go, and maybe we'll trip Gwen or something, you know. Come on?" I am talking fast and praying for a reprieve.

No one says anything. Mom hasn't spoken since her opening lines. I can hear Bella's crayons scurrying across her page. Kate lifts her coffee cup and sips. I can feel my temper rising. Aren't these people on my side? Why do I feel like the bad guy all of a sudden? I'm being noble, aren't I? Wasn't this the plan all along? It's not like Olivia just turned into a raving bitch overnight; she's been like this the entire time. Oh my God—has she been like this the entire time?

"You're on your own," Mom finally says.

"What?"

"I'm not going, either." Mom is staring right at me. I can feel my face getting hotter and hotter.

"Why? Why aren't you going? You don't . . . can't you just

go? Why?" I can't hide how upset I am, not even in front of the girlies.

"I just don't know what has to happen. How bad does it have to get? This has gone way beyond anything any of us thought you would put up with. And now, you went behind your sister's back and . . . no. You're on your own." Mom picks up her mug of coffee and softens her face as the girlies grow quiet.

"Can't you just go to support me? I mean I know this seems crazy, but I just have to see this thing through, you know? Olivia is my best friend and she needs me. Can't you just go with me?" Why is this new information for Mom? She has to go to support me. I'm being the good one here. I'm being a stand-up person who does what she says she'll do. What is so horrible about that?

"You don't get it. This *is* support. I couldn't sit there . . . I won't sit there and watch as more shit gets piled on you. Even you should be able to see that."

"I know that. But why am I on trial here?" I look to Kate, who has been silent as she carefully monitors the conversation.

"It's just got to stop at some point. Olivia *used* to be your best friend, Maggie. But you're just not willing to see the person she's become. No phone call should undo how she's made you feel the last few years. Don't you see who she's become?" Mom is speaking much too loudly for the small bakery. Kate and I are used to Mom's indiscretions. I am silent and crying.

"We'd better get going," Kate says, getting the girls together. Bella and Emily are quiet. It breaks my heart to see them so conflicted and frightened.

"You're leaving? Wait . . . please? How . . ." Kate leads the girlies out the door of the bakery. They all look back through the glass doors. How could this happen?

Mom approaches, and I can see she's going to hug me. But I

can't. I'll burst into hysterical fits of crying if she comes any closer. The bakery has pretty much emptied out during our show. Just the employees are watching now.

"What? What?" I sob.

"It has to stop. You're the only one who can do it. I can't watch anymore." Mom hugs me, and I lean into her. She is reaching up to my shoulders, and I bury my head in the crook of her neck. I smell her perfume and allow her arms to make their way around me.

I watch as Kate loads the girls up in the van. Mom has her sunglasses on, but I can tell she's crying now, too. I look around the bakery but I can't even muster a brave face for the employees. What have I done? How is Olivia's friendship worth all this? Maybe the question I need to answer is not who Olivia has become but who *I've* become. Or what I've not allowed myself to become. I sit and sip my coffee until new patrons come into the bakery. All-new patrons. They could infer I came here alone, not that I was just left by my entire family. The wrapped presents are still stacked on the table.

◆

Over the past few weeks, I've built everyone's hopes up, including my own, that I'm awake and ready to make some real changes. The internship. Eating healthy. Going to the gym and trusting Gabriel. Even seeing Domenic as a real man and not imposing "golden" deal breakers on him. What does he think of me now? I just want to go back to sleep. I want to turn all of this off and just go back to asking strangers whether or not that four-dollar coffee is for here or to go. I want to go back to the time when two old friends were planning a fantasy wedding. But back to reality. I've got nine messages on my cell phone from Mrs. Morten and Olivia over the past week begging for help. I finally call Mrs. Morten back the day before the rehearsal dinner and am summoned to the manor.

"Maggie!" Mrs. Morten answers the door before I even knock.

"Hi, Mrs. Morten," I say. I am introduced to aunts, uncles, and cousins who have flown in from many different parts of the world.

Through the crowd, I see Dr. Adam Farrell sitting in Mrs. Morten's kitchen with his cell phone in one hand and a slip of paper in the other. I smile my way through legions of Mortens and wave to Adam.

"Hey there," I say, approaching.

He lifts the phone to his ear and holds up one finger, the international sign for *Just a second.* I pinch back my face and hold up both my hands. The international sign for *Sorry.*

"Yes, this is Dr. Farrell. I was paged." He crumples the paper and flicks it to the end of the table. I watch as it falls to the floor.

I stand there staring at him and soak him in. He's still as good-looking as I remember. He would be the type of man you'd see in some glossy magazine touting the year's hottest bachelors. I can see why Olivia is so beside herself. Dr. Adam Farrell is the perfect man. But how can he really know Olivia? How can anyone in her new life really know her? I mean, isn't she sentencing herself to a fantasy prison, where pain and authentic memories have no place? What if she has kids—what then? What if she has a daughter who confides to her that she's having self-image problems? What then? Will she sign her up for liposuction at ten to get rid of that unsightly baby fat? If the only thing that matters to Olivia is how beautiful she is on the outside, what can her life really be about?

"So the long-lost Maggie Thompson surfaces." Adam stands.

"Mrs. Morten called me. I guess she needs some help," I say, ignoring his slight.

"Oh, yeah, that." Adam is now scrolling through his cell

phone address book. The bleeps and blips remind me of the casinos in Las Vegas.

"So how are you holding up, groomie?" I say, trying to make small talk.

"Huh? Did you say something?" And with that Adam dials another subordinate and hangs up on me. Man of the year, that one. Olivia is a lucky woman.

"Maggie? Honey?" Mrs. Morten pulls my arm into the center of the family.

"Can you still design the seating chart and place cards for the rehearsal dinner? You know, so people can see where they're seated?" she asks.

"Sure. Sure. Just give me the board and the cards," I say.

"Okay, I guess we have to buy a board and some cards for that. I also have to find a guest book." I notice she is reading from the cocktail napkin Olivia wrote on after speaking with Kate at the high tea in Las Vegas.

"We can probably find those in the same store," I say.

"Okay . . . okay . . . we can do that," Mrs. Morten says, rummaging through her wallet, giving me several hundred-dollar bills and a crumpled-up sheet of paper.

"Here's some money and the list of where everyone is sitting. Thank you, sweetie," she says.

I find tiny stationery cards and a guest book at Vroman's Bookstore. They are silver and gold just as I was told. I am sitting at a stoplight when I pull out the crumpled list of table placements for the rehearsal dinner.

TABLE ONE—THE HEAD TABLE

Adam and Olivia

Gwen and Jerry

Mark and Grace

Wait. Wait a fucking minute. That's the head table, right? Where am I? I read the list again. Adam and Olivia. I don't know this Mark or Grace, I assume Mark is Adam's groomsman. Gwen and her husband, Jerry? Where am I? Was I left off? I scan the remaining tables and find my name at Table Nine. Table Nine? What's the significance of Table Fucking Nine? Oh, Table Nine is for supposed best friends and people named Carol and Bob. I don't know who the hell Carol and Bob are, but they'd better be fucking important.

The car behind me honks, and I screech forward. I wasn't forgotten. I was put at another table. A table that couldn't be seen by the world, apparently. I just don't fit. I'm an embarrassment to Olivia. But wait. So true friendship is embarrassing to Olivia if it comes in anything over a size 2? I didn't know that. I guess her theory works because not only does friendship have to look pretty, so do prospective husbands. She wants a life carved out of cutout articles in high-fashion magazines and adolescent fantasies. I'm kicking myself. How could I have been so blind?

Olivia didn't even have the guts to tell me herself. She let her mom give me the list and figured I would see it on my own. Can I leave now? Can I crawl back to Mom and Kate with my tail between my legs and convince them that I've mended my ways? My cell phone chirps. I am maniacally searching for the phone but can't seem to let go of this crumpled piece of paper.

"Hello?" I am holding the paper in my hand.

"Hey there." It's Olivia.

"Hey." Table-Nine-putting bitch.

"I've been trying to reach you all week. Do you even turn your cell phone on?"

"It's on now." I am numb.

"Can you keep it charged up for me just this weekend?

Please? I can't take getting your voice mail all the time." Olivia sounds as if she's hyperventilating.

"I'll do my best. I just saw your whole family. Adam, too." I almost rear-end the car in front of me.

"You saw Adam?" Olivia's voice cracks.

"Yeah, he was at your mom's house."

"Ummm. Can you do me one last little favor?"

I am silent. Olivia continues.

"Can you make sure the slide show gets set up for the rehearsal dinner? Mommy has a stack of pictures Adam and I chose and she's already called a couple of places about turning them into slides on short notice," Olivia says. I suddenly remember my Pandora's box filled with pictures I found during the move.

"I'll see what I can do," I say.

"Well . . . um . . . is that a yes?" Olivia asks.

"No," I begin.

"No? No? You won't do it?"

"No, we shouldn't do a slide show. There's no time for that. I'll scan the pictures into my laptop and we'll do a slide show from there. I'm sure I can connect my laptop to whatever projection thing they have set up." I am now the audiovisual geek rolling the TV-VCR through the hallways of my high school.

"Thanks, Mags." Olivia sighs.

"Sure. Hey, did you want me to bring this board with all of the table placements for the rehearsal dinner by your mom's house before or did you want to come get it now?" I ask.

"The board? Oh . . . you know . . . um, you can hold on to that and just bring it with you." Didn't Olivia know that Mrs. Morten was going to delegate that chore to me? Did she want me to walk into the rehearsal dinner blithely thinking I would be seated at the head table only to be banished to Table Nine?

"Okay. See you tomorrow." I feel conflicted and disgusted. I have to focus and keep my eyes on the prize. I'll set up this board exactly as I've been told. Guests will find the bulletin board containing the seating arrangements for the rehearsal dinner. They will all note that the maid of honor is not seated at the head table. Then they will make their way to their table assignments and form theories as to why not.

"Hey, we're going out later for drinks and dancing. All the girls are going. Are you up for something like that?" Olivia's voice is hushed.

"That sounds fun," I say. Fun, yes. Something I would sign on for . . . no. I stop at another red light and pull my rearview mirror down. Spinning my birthday necklace around so I can see the clasp, I furiously try to undo it. I should just rip the damn thing off. Why don't I? I grab the chain and pull as hard as I can. The diamond-encrusted letters bounce around the car, both hitting the windshield. The M settles in one of the cup holders while the O is banished to the passenger-side floor mat.

I finish working on the bulletin board later that night and crawl into bed. It is around two o'clock in the morning when I hear my cell phone chirp once again. I have it plugged into the charger just as I was instructed. Doesn't Olivia have my home phone number?

"Hello?" I ask.

"Where are you?" It's a drunk Olivia.

"I'm sleeping. Where are you?"

"Everybody is here. Everybody keeps asking where you are and I don't know what to say. Are you coming?" Olivia is yelling.

"No, I'm in bed."

"Why aren't you here?"

"I'm in bed."

"You're supposed to be here."

"I know. But I'm going to stay here for the night."

"Can't you get out of bed and come here and dance with all of us?"

"No, I'm going to stay here. But I'll see you tomorrow, remember?"

"I'm getting married tomorrow."

"No, honey, the rehearsal dinner is tomorrow. You're getting married the next day."

"I told everyone you were coming."

"Well, I think they just want to spend time with the bride right now."

"I'm the bride."

"I know."

"Are you on your way?"

"No. I'm going to go back to bed."

"Okay."

"Are you going to be okay for tomorrow?"

"I'm getting married tomorrow," she slurs.

"No, honey. Who's driving you home?"

"Hannah isn't drinking."

"So she's driving you to your mommy's?"

"We're staying with Mitzi Carlson."

"At the Ritz-Carlton, honey?"

"Fancy."

"I'll see you tomorrow."

"Okay."

I hear the phone click off. I turn over and feel sad. That was the real Olivia.

CHAPTER FORTY-TWO

The Super Beetle

I framed that picture of me in the teensy light blue dress with the red socks and the navy-blue Vans on top of the jungle gym after I had finished moving. It has come to symbolize something in me that I need to be reminded of daily. One day, Mom stopped by on her way to work, picked up the framed photo, and looked at it for a long time. I told her why I framed it and why I had displayed it so prominently. She smiled to herself and set the photo down. Then she sat down next to me and told me the story behind the picture. She had just packed all of our worldly belongings in our yellow Volkswagen Super Beetle after my real father left us. I was three and Kate was five. Her own mom came to help her, and this picture was snapped at a park on the long road trip back home. Our future was uncertain; our little family was in crisis. But if you look at the pictures we took that road trip, there is no sign of that fear. There is pride. There is dignity. There is hope.

My alarm begins its morning taunt right at seven thirty-nine. I'm partial to odd numbers. I have decided to keep my scheduled Friday training session with Gabriel. I show him my food diary, and he lectures me about the evils of trans fats. He leads me through my training session. I notice we're using heavier weights. My body feels more stable. I'm not afraid my knees will give out anymore or I won't be able to get out of a low car. The core of my body is stronger. At least that's what Gabriel calls it—"Core Work." That's when he's not referring to it as "Functional Training," which makes it sound like I should be wearing a helmet to school.

I pull up to EuroPane in my workout clothes. I'm still a little sweaty. The rehearsal dinner is at six thirty tonight at The Athenaeum. I have a lot of work to do before then. Kate's minivan is parked out front, and I feel a slight twinge of pride. Now *I'm* the architect of an infamous breakfast invitation. I grab my laptop from the passenger seat and walk into EuroPane with my head held high.

◆

I am invigorated after my breakfast with Mom, Kate, and the girlies. I'm sure Patrona has the entire rehearsal dinner planned down to the last infinitesimal detail. All I'm responsible for is the bulletin board with table placements and the slide show. Once home, I sit down in front of my laptop and begin the process of scanning picture after picture using the software Kate loaned me. The day flies by as I get deeper and deeper into stacks of CDs and pictures. The slide show is turning out beautifully; the running time is about five and a half minutes. I run it one last time as I turn on my shower to wait for the hot water. I have to be at the dinner in less than an hour. I'm finally walking past my last blue bucket. No. There's one more—but I'll handle that one later.

I put on my black skirt and the wraparound white shirt. This will be my only opportunity to wear this outfit. The skirt is even looser than it was when I tried it on at the Beverly Center, and I've finally thrown that tightener in the garbage. The shirt can actually be tied as it is supposed to be—not how Mom rigged it in the dressing room. I am comfortable. I never thought I would feel comfortable today. I dry my hair and swipe on a little pink lip gloss. I stand in front of a full-length mirror and smile. This is the first time I've ever done this. I smooth my shirt down and turn to the side. I stare at my face and can't hold back the tears. Why have I denied myself this validation for so long? What good came of never looking at myself in the mirror and cursing my Area? I vow never to refer to my Area again. It's all part of me. Even my Are . . . even my belly.

I load the bulletin board and the guest book in the back of my car and set my laptop on the front seat along with all its cords and wires. I'm wearing my pink-and-gray Pumas until I have to put on the four-inch heels I bought for the occasion. Beautiful shoes, but absolutely unwalkable. Patrona is standing by the entrance to The Atheneaum. I hand her the bulletin board and the guest book. She thanks me and waves over The Athenaeum's audiovisual guy.

"You got the slide show? The one we'll be using for the rehearsal dinner before the wedding?" He is wearing a flannel shirt over a Black Sabbath concert T-shirt.

"I have it right here." I hold up my laptop.

"Come on over with me. We'll set you on up over here by the dance floor." The AV guy apparently has a habit of using too many words to convey a simple request.

I follow him, noting all Patrona's hard work. I pass under the vaulted ceilings painted with Italian frescoes. Patrona has the food and wine set up inside. The wait staff is milling around setting up wineglasses and large gold chargers under every plate. I have yet to see Olivia or Gwen.

I am led out onto the courtyard. It is a veritable fairy won-
derland. Italian café lights are strung end to end across the entire width of the garden. There are nine tables set around the
small dance floor, each seating five people. The AV guy takes my
laptop, and I get butterflies for the first time. I join the throng of
guests who are just beginning to arrive. I still have my Pumas
on. I resolve to take them off once I am seated at my table. I'll
keep them under the table until I have to leave. Or until I'm
asked to leave—whichever comes first.

As I start on the first of many glasses of wine, I see my bulletin board at the top of the stairs. It's the focal point as guests
enter the event. I see Gwen and Jerry pull their card and walk
proudly over to the head table. Gwen's wearing a lavender slip
dress with lace accents. Her black hair is in an updo, and her
makeup is perfect. Jerry, the unsung husband, is an average-
looking guy. He's the type of guy you would never be able to
pick out in a crowd twice. He's wearing a brown linen suit with
an open-collared dress shirt. He's also wearing aviator-style sunglasses. They look absolutely ridiculous on him. No doubt
Gwen picked them out.

I know which one is my table, so my lone gold-and-silver
card stays put as the board empties. Table Nine. The notorious
Table Nine. Table Nine could not be farther from the head table.
Seeing it drawn is one thing. Sitting at the actual table is a whole
other animal. The waiters continue to come around with wine.

There are four empty chairs at Table Nine, not counting the
one I will be sitting in. As I sit there, laughing guests ask me
about every five minutes if all the chairs are taken. And about
every five minutes, my heart soars until they take the chair and
head over to another crowded table far away from the now
quarantined Table Nine. Carol and Bob left their coats on the
backs of two of the chairs here at Table Nine, but they have yet

to grace me with their presence. So it's just me. Do I want someone to actually sit with me or do I just want to be alone?

Adam's brother begins the hike over to my table. It takes him about thirty-five minutes.

"You know you're introducing the slide show, right?" I assumed he needed a chair.

"Huh?" I ask.

"I'm going to make a toast. Then I'll hand the microphone over to you and you'll introduce the slide show. Everything's timed," Adam's brother says nervously. I don't actually know his name. For as long as Olivia and Adam have been together, he's only been referred to as "Adam's brother." He probably does have a name, but maybe not.

The crowd begins to settle in, and the DJ is playing the usual dining tunes: standards, badly redone pop songs, and long, winding mixes that never quite end. I am halfway through the small green salad when the people I assume to be Carol and Bob finally approach the table, laughing and having a great time. I perk up and start to greet the couple. They both say hi to me, grab their coats and bags, and walk directly over to another table. I hear Carol say this table is just too far away to really be part of anything. Now it's just me and Table Nine again. No hope of Carol and Bob. No hope of anyone. Just a tiny shred of hope that I know the waiters will be back with full bottles of wine again in about ten minutes.

I squint and can barely make out the head table, it's so far away. It is beautiful, and everyone at it looks right out of a magazine. Gwen is there with her husband, Jerry. They are grinning from ear to ear as the photographer takes "candid" pictures of them for Olivia's memory book. Mark and Grace don't really stay at the head table. They are bumping from table to table. Following the wine. They'll be at Table Nine any minute now.

"I'd like to be the first to welcome you here tonight to celebrate Mr. and Mrs. Adam Farrell's rehearsal dinner." The DJ cuts
in over the microphone to a smattering of applause and mur-
murs of disdain because the DJ didn't call Adam "Doctor." The
crowd falls silent as the happy couple make their entrance.

Olivia and Adam are radiant. Olivia is wearing a yellow
chiffon dress that dusts the ground as she walks. Her blond hair
is down and pulled back from her face. Her makeup is natural
and barely noticeable except for the false eyelashes. Adam is
wearing a gray dress shirt with a gray tie to match. Doesn't he
know the monochromatic look went out with *Super Millionaire*?
As night falls, The Athenaeum's gardens get more and more
beautiful.

"Oh, no, thank you, no trans fats," I say out loud to no one
as I push away the thousand tiramisu plates the waiters left for
all of Table Nine's occupants.

"Oh, but it is wafer-thin?" I answer myself in a French
accent.

The time passes quickly. I look at the head table every so
often and see Olivia and her chosen few laughing and having a
good time as dessert is served. I don't want what they've got. I
want what I've got. Table Nine rocks. I have busied myself by
doing impersonations of people all night. My AV guy kills.

Adam's brother awkwardly approaches the DJ and gives the
AV guy some kind of high sign. The music dies down, and
Adam's brother clears his throat. I roll my eyes. I take a deep
breath as I head to the microphone as well.

"I am Adam's big brother and I will serve as his best man
during tomorrow's festivities," he starts. Maybe he really doesn't
have a name.

Olivia and Adam stand and walk toward the dance floor.

"I remember first meeting Olivia. And I thought that she

wasn't like anyone else Adam had ever brought home. Her boobs were real!" The crowd nervously chuckles. That's about all that's real on her these days, brother.

"Aaaanyway, I want to congratulate my little brother and wish him and his bride-to-be the best of luck tomorrow," he says and raises his glass. I approach the microphone and see Gwen coming toward me. Adam's brother gives her the microphone.

He whispers, "She just wants to say a few words. Once you finish, the slide show will start automatically." Gwen and Jerry move to the front of the dance floor.

"I have known Olivia for so long, I just can't believe she's here and getting married," Gwen gushes.

Olivia is wiping away tears and clutching Adam.

Gwen hands the microphone over to Jerry, who breaks out in song about love. I look around at the audience. Oh, good, it's not just me and my bad attitude. Everyone's a little awkward with Jerry's "singing." Gwen pulls her cashmere shawl around her shoulders and stares at Olivia and Adam as Jerry finishes.

". . . it's about love," Jerry whispers as he drops his head to his chest, awaiting applause. Olivia and Adam rush the couple and hug them as they share this moment publicly. The crowd is quiet.

I walk to the microphone. Olivia and Adam settle into their poses, waiting for some kind of story. I thought I was just introducing the slide show. It becomes obvious to me that I need to say something. I clear my throat and the world goes quiet. Now it's just Olivia and me.

"I'm so happy that you've gotten everything you always wanted, Olivia. You are truly living out our teenaged fantasy." I smile to myself and I see Olivia harden. My smile fades. I look out into the audience, lick my lips, and take a deep breath. I stare directly at Olivia and Adam, lifting my champagne glass high.

"Congratulations, Olivia and Adam. Here's to the beautiful life you've always wanted." The crowd applauds. I can see Olivia sigh with relief as I finish.

The opening chords of my slide show play, but Olivia and Adam don't rush up to hug me. Instead, Olivia holds Adam and they begin to dance in front of the slide show. The DJ takes the microphone from me, and I make the long trek back to Table Nine.

I sit down and gesture to the waiter for another glass of wine.

Olivia and Adam have taken dance classes to get ready for all the dancing they'll have to do. This is a warm-up for the big day tomorrow. I hear their wedding song is "Wind Beneath My Wings." Of course it is. They glide across the floor to their song as the crowd looks on with drunken smiles and baby-shower wonder. The slide show begins on a large movie screen that has been set up at the front of the dance floor. The darkness makes every picture crisp and clear. There's Olivia on vacation in Hawaii in her yellow bikini. Isn't she cute? Ooooooh, and there's one of Adam looking up from underneath the sink with a wrench in his hand. Oh, that little stinker can't fix a thing.

Well, there's the one of Olivia and me proudly standing in front of her first car. Olivia is wearing what appears to be a small change purse on a silvery thread, or what some would call a "purse." I have my leg up on the bumper in a victorious *This is Ours!* pose. The crowd gasps in unison as Olivia's massive ass attacks all forty-seven rehearsal dinner invitees like some bad 3-D movie. I take a long sip of my wine as the whispers and shushes rise from the tables. The guests might be talking at full volume, but from Table Nine everything is pretty much whispers and hushes.

Olivia and Adam twirl even harder. They probably think they are dancing so well now that the crowd is murmuring in awe. The next picture is their engagement picture. Olivia and Adam walking hand in hand on the beach. Oh, and here are the outtakes. Aren't they cute? Adam is splashing Olivia! How could he do that? Oh, but look, she got him. She splashes him even more, and now she is jumping on his back and trying to wrestle him down. Oh, but wait, what's this? Could it be Olivia's high school yearbook picture from our junior year?

Gwen sits on the very edge of her chair as a succession of pictures follow that chronicle Adam's climb in the medical field. I squint to get a better view of Gwen. She's fingering something around her neck: a gold, diamond-encrusted necklace. Let me guess—with the initials G&O? I sit back a little more at ease and focus on the slide show. There's Adam with a stethoscope. Now he has a shiny silver chart. And now he's speaking at some seminar with a red laser pointer and half-moon glasses, from which he looks down intelligently. Mr. and Mrs. Morten are beaming. I enjoy my wine.

This next picture was one of my favorites. I remember finding it in that shoe box while I was packing. I knew I had to keep it out. Scanning it into the computer was just a natural progression. Kate's mini-tutorial at breakfast allowed me to crop and position the pictures more artfully than I could have ever dreamed.

It is of Olivia on her one trip to a homecoming dance. She's wearing a black dress with a high Victorian collar. It was the only dress her mother could find on such short notice. A young man named Franklin Bonner asked Olivia to the dance. His dishwater-blond hair stuck straight up in the back and looked a lot like Olivia's. I feared they were really long-lost siblings. He wore a black suit, white shirt, and pink-and-green tie to this particular dance. The outfit could have worked if it hadn't fit him five years prior to the dance. About four inches of his white shirt protruded from the sleeve of the jacket, and the tie barely made its way down half his chest.

At this Shawna snorts.

She has spit her wine out onto the table and is already fully engrossed in apologies and another fit of giggles.

"He's just so small!" she cries.

I look up at the pictures and can't help but smile. This was Olivia and me at our best. She actually liked Franklin Bonner and allowed him to give her a good-night kiss. Her first kiss. It just seemed right that he should be in this little slide show the night before her wedding day.

Olivia is now standing front and center and staring up at her dirty little secret.

The song plays on in the background as the buzz of my laptop whirs on. Panchali is cleaning up Shawna's spilled wine and quieting her giggles, pleading with her to calm down and get ahold of herself. But Shawna's right. Franklin Bonner is a good two hundred pounds lighter than Olivia and a full head shorter. Olivia is trying to get her hands around Franklin's in such a clawlike manner it looks like they're trying to send Red Rover Red Rover right over.

Looking down on us now are a perfect Olivia and Adam at the base of the Eiffel Tower. The laptop whirs on. There is the happy couple playing doubles tennis at a fancy tournament.

Olivia turns to Adam. He is holding her hip in a kind of distancing way. It's as if he wants to show everyone that his soon-to-be-wife's flaws don't freak him out. But at the same time, he's clearly not allowing her to come any closer to him. With this rejection, Olivia turns to her mother. The song is still playing in the background as the laptop whirs on.

"I told you not to put those pictures in!" Olivia screams as she walks over to Mrs. Morten's table.

"What, honey?" Mrs. Morten gazes fondly up at the picture of Olivia posing in front of the elephants at the LA Zoo with her arm at her nose in parody.

"These pictures! I gave you a stack of pictures to put into the slide show. Those were the only ones I wanted. Not these! Not these! I gave you a stack. Do you remember the stack I gave you?" Olivia is approaching Mrs. Morten's table in a frenzy, which is now in earshot of Table Nine.

"Honey, these pictures are darling. You chose wonderful pictures. I love every one of them. I forgot about that boy, what was his name, Maggie? What was his name—"

Olivia cuts her mother off. "I didn't choose these pictures. Why would I choose these pictures?" Olivia is pointing at the night she played Santa in our elementary school Christmas pageant.

"I chose them," I say, setting my wineglass down on my empty table.

Olivia flips around. Mrs. Morten looks at me and then back at Olivia. The laptop whirs on. The crowd is silent. This silence is different. No one wants to watch. But everyone is riveted.

"You what?" Olivia continues the long walk to Table Nine.

"You asked me to help, so I threw a few pictures of us in there." I put my hands on the table and begin to fidget with my wineglass.

"I gave my mother a stack of pictures I wanted included in *my* slide show. Putting your own pictures in there is a problem." Olivia is now standing at the other side of Table Nine. I don't even recognize her anymore. This is no longer my best friend. That little girl I stood next to against that chain-link fence is dead. Olivia is fussing with her hair. She is beginning to realize how much of a scene she is causing. Behind her, I see Gwen get up from the head table and walk out. I focus back on Olivia. She's getting ready to turn and make the long trek back to the head table—but stops and slowly turns back around.

"You just can't take that I got out," she says. Her voice is low and angry.

"Got out?" I say. How could I have defined myself by this person for the last fifteen years?

"That fantasy life—it's not a fantasy at all. I've got it. Look around you, Maggie. Everything is beautiful and perfect. There are no 'before' pictures. It kills you that I've gotten everything we've ever wanted." Olivia twirls around in victory. I can't stop shaking my head, no . . . no.

It's as if I'm really seeing her for the first time. I breathe out. And there she is. My best friend: the little girl still lost in her little pink room fantasy playing with her Barbie and Ken dolls.

I don't want what she has. I don't want to figure out why I'm not good enough for her. *She's* not even good enough for her. My shoulders slowly relax and the world comes back into focus. I wet my lips and speak.

"Well that's *all* you've got now." I smooth my hair back and walk out from behind Table Nine. I grab my Pumas from underneath the table. Olivia watches me walk across the dance floor. I begin to unplug my laptop but pause to see the final sequence of pictures. Olivia and me in front of her mom's house on Halloween. She was a flapper from the 1920s and I was in this fluffy yellow chickadee costume. Olivia's lipstick was a horrible pink shade we had stolen from Mrs. Morten's makeup case. She has her hand at her head and her hips sticking out in her best dancer pose. Her little belly is peeking out from beneath the stretched sequined shirt. I hold what looks to be like a big egg as the big orange beak lowers itself over my round, twelve-year-old face. We are smiling and in the next shot we are bent over with laughter. The final shot is of Olivia falling to the ground in laughter with me looking down at her and my hand gently placed on her back. My mouth is open in a wide laugh.

I catch a side glance of Mrs. Morten, and she quickly stands. I unplug my laptop and walk across the dance floor, cords and wires trailing. The spotlight blinds me for one second. The DJ quickly puts on some music as the guests buzz and murmur. Mrs. Morten makes her way across the dance floor.

"Maggie?" I quickly turn around. "She'll come around, sweetie. The pictures were beautiful," Mrs. Morten says as she holds my face and smiles tightly.

Olivia is still standing in front of Table Nine as Adam comes to collect his bride-to-be. Panchali rises, with Shawna on her heels, and they tentatively approach a now unmasked Olivia. I break from Mrs. Morten and feel their anger on my back as I walk toward the exit.

I don't look back and I don't slow down. The tears are subsiding and my breath is evening out. I am walking easily under the vaulted ceiling with the Italian frescoes. I look down and realize I'm wearing my heels and I'm not tripping or walking like a truck driver. I'm looking down at my shoes when the bathroom door opens.

"That was quite a show you put on out there." Gwen is straightening her cashmere shawl as she closes the bathroom door.

"What?" My eyebrows are raised. I stand a good five inches taller than Gwen. Olivia has been outed. Gwen backed the wrong horse and she knows it. Moreover, she knows I know it.

"Don't you have a rehearsal dinner to get to?" I continue. Gwen fidgets with her necklace.

"So we'll see you at the wedding tomorrow?" Gwen titters.

"Fuck you, Gwen." My voice is calm and methodical. My eyes crinkle with drying tears, and I can feel the rush of air through my lungs. Gwen stands unmoving in front of me. I don't move.

One last duel.

After what feels like hours, Gwen finally clears her throat and steps to the side. I stride down the front steps of The Athenaeum and walk gracefully to my car, never looking back once. The night is crisp as the door shuts beside me.

What did I just do?

I turn the key and drive. The car knows before I do where I'm going. I follow. Visions of the glow from the screen and the whir of my laptop play over and over in my head. I make a left.

I am stopped at the light getting my speech ready. Visions of the glow. Sounds from the laptop. Click . . . click . . . click. The light changes. I make another right.

I park out front and turn the car off. I sit in the silence of my car for what feels like hours. The diamond-encrusted M is still in the cup holder.

◆

I open the door easily and step inside. The lights are bright and the tile floor is slippery. The high-heeled shoes are solid underneath me as I walk chest-out, hips swaying, head held high. My eyes are straight ahead, staring at that back door. The door I looked through every shift to watch him. I walk quickly yet steadily.

"You're a little dressed up to come crawling back for your job, don't you think?" I stop, locking my hip into place, and take a deep breath. I slowly turn my head and see Cole leaning back on the counter with the tiny espresso mug in his mitt of a hand.

"I'd try and talk to her but then I'd be giving advice, now wouldn't I?" Peregrine is chewing gum as she retwists a blue-black bun on the side of her head. My eyes slowly move to her. I lose sight of the back door momentarily.

"I'm sorry. You were right." I walk toward her and put my hands on the counter. She finishes twisting her hair and squares me off. I will myself not to cry anymore.

"What?" I can smell her bubblegum. She begins to blow a bubble.

"You were right. Everything you said. Olivia didn't pick me. Shit, Olivia couldn't even pick herself. And I'm terrified of what is going to happen when I let Domenic—jeez, I guess when I just let Domenic do anything, huh?" Peregrine's bubble pops. She fumbles with the bits of gum on her lips. I continue, "Let me be in your life, but as your friend, not your project."

"Okay. Okay." She is picking at her lips, unable to hold my gaze. Then she lunges over the counter and pulls me in close for a hug. "Friends . . . we'll be friends." Peregrine lets me go and straightens her shirt.

I stand tall and back away from the counter. I focus once again on why I made the trip over here in the first place. I have my speech down pat. My head is high as I walk away from the silence behind me.

I push open the door.

Domenic is at the sink. I let the door close behind me and stand in front of him. The light blue shirt. Nice touch. He looks up, his hands deep in the soapy water. I stand there. I know his face, but it seems like it's in Technicolor tonight. The black hair. The curve of his lips. The amber eyes. I take a breath.

"I remember everything about that night. I just never had the . . . I didn't know if you . . ."

Domenic pulls his hands from the water. I can see the drops

of suds and water hitting the floor and the sink. I look up from his hands and look into his eyes. Closer . . . closer. I feel the hot, soapy water as he cradles my face in his hands. The water runs down my neck and past my shoulder. He brushes my temple with his thumb as he wets his lips. I close my eyes. Not because I can't watch; it just happens. He moves his hands around the back of my head and pulls me in to him. His lips are so soft. I feel the warmth of him speeding all over my body, to all my nerve endings. I pull my arms up to hold him and can feel myself being surrounded by him. Just us. I can't remember a single thing after that. Maybe nothing happened.

But I seriously doubt it.

Acknowledgments

Every night before I go to bed, I hold my breath and give thanks for the day. I wish I could say that this tiny space where I'm allowed to thank the most important people in the world means more to me than that intimate moment where it's just me and my held breath—but it's not. These people whose names mean nothing to you, the reader, are the loves of my life.

My mom, Lynne Palmer-Whalen, is my heartbeat, my hero, and my definition of love and greatness. Without her, this book would be just a glimmer of something I thought maybe I could do someday.

Don Whalen continues to be the benchmark of what a man should be.

Alex Zucco has been my partner in crime from telling each other what our Christmas presents were to giggling our way to sleep at night. Joe continues to be the best brother I could ever want. Zoë and Bonnie are turning into two of the strongest, smartest, most beautiful and confident women.

Captain Jack Kuser, Kim Resendiz, Tito, Tisha, Nico, Eli,

Rodrigo, Tasha, Diego, Nadine, Antoine, Toine, Denice, KC, David, and Michael continue to be the most amazing family.

I want to thank Brandon Dunn for dealing with a much bigger demon than I think even he knew what to do with.

Without the company of writers, I would be a narcissistic, blathering idiot—so thank you to Danette Rivera, Ibarionex Perello, Paz Kahana, Frederick Smith, David Green, and Tom Lombardi. Thank you to Henry, Norm, Corrin, Jen, Marilyn, Sharon, and Poet. Thank you to the Cake Club, who had the balls to tell me exactly how they felt about the first draft of the book—which we all know is shit.

Thanks to Christy Fletcher for being the agent everyone dreams of.

And finally, thanks to Amy Einhorn for sharing this time in my life. Without her involvement, the entire book would have been one long run-on sentence . . . joined by ellipses, dashes, and far too many *fucks*—so . . . fucking thank her.

Reading Group
Guide

Reading Group Guide

1. Discuss the dissonance between how Maggie sees herself physically as opposed to how she actually looks. Do you think that we all see ourselves through a distorted filter? Do you think this is solely an issue among women? Why do you think this filter exists and where do you think it comes from?

2. Why do you think Olivia asks Maggie to be her maid of honor? Do you think it is an act of hope, revenge, or something else?

3. Discuss Maggie's relationship with her mother. Do you think because she is the baby of the family her development has been arrested—or do you think there are other factors at work? How do you think Maggie is similar to her mother? How are they different?

4. Despite Maggie's attempts to quell her sexuality, the tension between Domenic and her is palpable—why does she not act on it? At what point did you think Domenic had feelings for her? Why does Maggie never pick up on it? Why isn't Domenic more aggressive?

5. Do you think there is one character that represents the reader more than the others? Is there one character that

you waited for to enter the scene, knowing that they would speak for you and shake some sense into Maggie when she needed it?

6. Think about your own adolescent fantasies. Do you think they are still embedded in your head today? Knowing now what you know about reality, do you still yearn to bump into the starting quarterback or head cheerleader and show them how well you turned out? How do you think Olivia twisted these fantasies and do you think her life now mirrors them? Why doesn't Maggie fit in with Olivia's new life?

7. What do you think Peregrine's role is in Maggie's life? Do you feel everyone has a Peregrine in his or her life? What do you think fuels Peregrine to be the center of attention in everyone's social calendar?

8. What do you think the head table represents to Olivia? To Maggie?

9. Kate and Maggie are opposites. Why did they turn out so differently and do you think this is commonplace among sisters? Do you think Kate is a positive force on Maggie or does she keep Maggie in that "baby-of-the-family" role? What is it about the bridal shower that sends Kate over the edge?

10. Peregrine asks Maggie if she would choose Christina over herself—if given the opportunity—to be Fatty or Bobo. What would you do? Why do you think we as a society put so much importance on physical beauty? And accordingly, those who are overweight, especially women, are ostracized as untouchables. Does society banish the overweight—or, like Maggie, is it the overweight that banish themselves?

11. There is a tragic quality to Cole Trosclair—do you think that makes him a sympathetic character, or is he so dispicable that no amount of melancholy would sway your feelings for him? Do you think as a society we spend too much time trying to save the bullies and not enough time protecting the victims? Why do you think Maggie cares so much what he thinks?

12. With years of education and obvious talent on her side, why do you think Maggie still works at Joe's after so many years? Do you think this concept of "it's just easier" could be a thematic thread throughout the entire novel? Do you see this concept in your own life?

13. What do you think of the passage in the bridal shop regarding the "subculture" that surrounds the overweight? Do you think it is accurately represented—or has your experience been different? Why do you think women compare themselves in this way? How would you react in Olivia's circumstance—would you extract yourself from that world as she did—or would you wear the weight loss as a badge of honor?

14. If you could write the next chapter what would you write? Would it be more important to focus on Maggie's happiness or Olivia's misery in your version?

About the Author

I'm a public-school kid from Pasadena, California, with just a high school diploma and elaborate fantasies of what the inside of a writing class looks like. Taking the poor man's route to higher education, I "studied" at my local bookstore. I went to author readings and sat in on their Saturday morning workshops until I felt I had learned all I could in those hallowed halls. I then gave myself an extravagant graduation ceremony and presented myself with a PhD in "Book Learnin'."

One night, newly hopped up on literary knowledge, I was driving in my car on a mission. It was like the final scene in *Indiana Jones and the Last Crusade,* the one with Sean Connery, where Harrison Ford has to pass a series of tests in order to finally get his hands on the Holy Grail. Right away in the first test, knives are coming out of the walls of the cave. "Only the penitent man shall pass . . . only the penitent man shall pass," he mumbles. Well, that was my ass at about 11:30 at night buzzing through the city in search of my own Holy Grail—a box of Lucky Charms. So I buy the box of Lucky Charms, along with nonfat milk, and as I'm walking to the cash register I grab a *Shape* magazine. This internal civil war that women and girls fight every day—Lucky Charms versus nonfat milk and *Shape* magazine—is what bore *Conversations with the Fat Girl.* Now, if you'll excuse me, I've got a soggy bowl of Lucky Charms to get to . . . oh, and a *Shape* magazine.

If you haven't had enough and want to read more, my blog is carmenandjane.blogspot.com.

5 foods and why they actually have zero calories:

———————◆———————

1. *Any birthday cake*—yours, theirs, the guy at the next table.

2. *Halloween Candy*—because, after all, they're not called fun size for nothing.

3. *Shared desserts*—how do you figure the carb count on half a crème brulee.

4. *Food from someone else's plate*—what? You mean, all I get is this freaking salad?

5. *Food taken from children*—yours, theirs, the guy at the next table's.